Salt
&
Skin

Salt & Skin

Eliza Henry-Jones

september

1 3 5 7 9 10 8 6 4 2

Published in the UK in 2023 by September Publishing

First published in Australia 2022 by Ultimo Press,
an imprint of Hardie Grant Publishing

Printed in Denmark on paper from responsibly managed,
sustainable sources by Nørhaven

ISBN: 9781914613364
Ebook ISBN: 9781914613371

For Henry. I love you in the wild.

It has been called the ghost house for as long as anyone can remember. It's set on a tidal island called Seannay, which can be reached from Big Island by crossing damp sand at low tide, or picking a careful route across the causeway when the tide is high. Once, the ghost house had had neighbours; answering glows of candlelight through door and window gaps. Answering whistles of wind on stormy nights; answering sounds of life. Its neighbours are ruins now.

The ghost house is alone.

The roof is made of old slate, and there are narrow beds pressed up against opposite walls in the small loft. There is the skin of a dead fur seal pushed into the rafters and long forgotten.

Plovers and curlews; a spirit who calls in the voice of a gull. Sometimes baleen whales sing at night, their bones stuck fast in the shallows of the bay. A trick of the light or an old curse or spell that makes the tidal island a particularly curious place. It is said that some folk, as soon as they step onto Seannay, can see the luminous traces of scars across human skin. Every injury a person has ever sustained to their flesh – every scratch and pimple and pox and burn – illuminated by the pearly light. Someone with the sight can see the scars spun brightly across the skin of their children; strangers; enemies. Their own skin, too. In this way, all skin is the same on the tidal island. And all skin on the tidal island is utterly unique.

Island witches are said to have met there on clear, still nights.

But, of course, that was years ago. Centuries.

People know more now than they did back then. They do not believe in witches.

PART ONE

Chapter One

The boat had seemed large at the dock, but now that they're rumbling away from Big Island, it seems flimsy and ludicrously small.

Luda tries to think of the last time she'd been on a boat before coming to the islands. Years ago. Someone's thirtieth birthday on the thick, marshy water of the Hopeturn River back home in Australia. Even back then, the river's level had been low and the unpleasant smell of wet things made dry had permeated the boat, making people drink more than they should have.

Ewan whistles under his breath, doing whatever a seafarer does in the cabin of their boat. Luda's two children, Darcy and Min, are out on the deck with her. Darcy, the eldest, is slouched against the gunwale, looking as though he's waiting for a late bus that's going to take him from one bland place to another. Min, two years younger, clutches at a pile of rope (Luda notices, but does not point out, that it's not fastened to anything). Min is pale and looks almost bewildered by the world viewed from the small and rumbling fishing boat. When she notices Luda's gaze, she scowls. Fierce, fractious little Min who is not so little anymore. Fourteen, Luda thinks, with the usual jolt of shock. She's *fourteen*.

Ewan cuts the engine and the boat immediately begins a slow spin in the currents. The strangely intimate sound of water against

5

the side of the boat. Ewan comes out of the cabin, his beanie low over his eyes. 'You can really see the erosion of the cliffs from here,' he says, and points.

Of course. Luda has almost forgotten why she's here. Almost. They have been here a week. Ewan is trying to help her find her feet as quickly as possible, so that she can get to work documenting the damage climate change is doing to these islands: taking photos, writing funding applications. It is, she knows, not a particularly popular topic in the local fishing circles. Through his subcontracting to the council for these sorts of climate change adjacent projects, Ewan has made himself something of a pariah. Still, he smiles at them now, smelling of coffee and brine. He looks far older than twenty-seven.

Luda studies the shoreline Ewan's pointing to. It's low tide now, the sea pulled back to reveal a short, sloped skirt of rippling sand up to the base of an overhanging, rocky cliff. Figures walk along the sand, leaving silvery footprints, their pants rolled up. Shoes in hand. Now cavorting, chasing each other. A mother and child, Luda thinks, but the shore's a bit too far away to be sure.

She cocks her digital SLR camera, focuses on the cliff face, the beach, the figures which (with her camera's zoom) she can now make out more clearly. Yes, a little girl with curling bronze-red hair. She looks six or seven or eight. She is with a muscular woman who is perhaps in her mid-thirties. Luda follows them for a moment with her lens. What she sees is the easy intimacy of a parent and child at this age – the way the child's body still touches the parent's without thought. The mindless, automatic *easiness* of it. Had Luda ever appreciated it the way she should have? She misses it now.

She feels like a voyeur. They'd have no reason to imagine a camera trained on them from the fishing boat. The idea gives her a little thrill, shivery and darting.

'Sandstone,' Ewan says. 'You can make out the bands of it, see?'

Luda has noticed that Ewan engages in quick, heavy bursts of interaction and then retreats back into himself. He continues to talk about erosion and deposition behind her, further along on the deck.

6

He will be talking to Min, but it is Darcy who will be listening closely, storing the information up in that terrifying vault of a brain he has. Min tends to let information trickle over her, off her, like water. She remembers the broad strokes and how they fit together. Darcy has always been preoccupied with the finest details of a thing.

Luda snaps a few frames. She inspects them and is impressed by the mood of the midwinter light, which she had expected to be glaring or dull. She lifts the camera back to her eye, trains it back on the cliffs. And then the world collapses.

* * *

A cracking sound. A flurry of movement as sheets of rock fall onto the narrow, sloping beach. Stillness, and then the awful keening of a woman parted from her child.

'Allie? Allie! *Allie!*'

Swearing, Ewan hurtles into the cabin, fires up the engine and begins making calls on his phone. For a moment, the three Managans are alone on the deck. Min and Darcy watch their mother, still peering through the lens of her camera.

'Jesus,' Darcy says over the throb of the engine. 'Mum, put it down!'

Luda looks up. Her face is bright, almost feverish. Her horror has twisted itself into something that makes Darcy show his teeth.

Ewan eases the boat as close as he can to the shore, and then he drops the anchor and throws himself off the side into the water. He swims until he can touch the sandy bottom, then he begins an awkward lunging.

Darcy follows, his freestyle strokes unpractised but still somehow graceful. Min, who has never swum more than a few strokes here and there, hangs over the boat's edge, white-faced. Luda, who can swim better than either of her children, stands up.

Min spins around. 'Don't! Don't go.'

Min has always been the bolder of her children – the sort who insisted on dressing herself from before she was two, who used

7

to scream until Luda unhitched the leading line from her pony's bridle. The panic in her voice is new, and so Luda sits down on the deck, holding her camera in both hands.

On the shore, Ewan helps the woman dig frantically through the rubble. Darcy stands in the shallows, staring up at the cliff face, from which stones still trickle.

'Move!' he yells, his voice carrying over the water.

Ewan looks up, but the woman, bloody-fingered from the scrape of the rocks, does not.

Ewan grunts and pulls the woman away from the rubble. She fights him. Fingernails and teeth. 'Let me go! Let me *go*! Allie!'

Darcy moves quickly to the beach where he wraps a long arm around the woman's waist. She continues to writhe, to kick. To scream. It takes both Darcy and Ewan to pull her away from the cliff face.

Min sits down, shuts her eyes and covers her ears. Luda thinks, unbidden, of red hair tangled under rocks. Blood. *No*. She can't. She cannot.

Luda has long known that the world is full of awful things and that if you let them inside you, if you let yourself linger or *think*, they'll damage you, these things, as surely as a gun or poison or the flash of a man's fist.

ISO. Shutter speed. Aperture. Luda squeezes the camera like she's holding someone's hand. She raises her camera, takes another photo, then another. Nobody sees. It's just skin. That's all she can capture of a person: skin. Luda feels like a ghost. Quicksilver. She thinks that this is her power.

* * *

'She couldn't have survived that first fall of rock,' Ewan says, later. It's dark and he clasps a glass of whisky that he's not drinking. 'Let alone the second one.'

The second rockfall, when the trickle Darcy had noticed had given way so violently that pieces of cliff had landed as far as the shoreline. The water had reared back from the land so that Min and Luda had felt the force of the cliff's collapse in the sudden agitation of the sea.

A helicopter. An ambulance.

The keening. The keening. The keening.

Min and Luda, shivering on the anchored boat. Luda found a thermos of lukewarm coffee in the cabin and some stale crisps. She and Min sat and ate them and it felt a little like watching something unfold far away. Emergency coverage on a news station, perhaps. The mother, Violet, never stopped fighting to get back to the rubble.

It was dark by the time Ewan dropped the Managans back at their house on Seannay and joined them at their kitchen table. *Home*, Luda thinks now, in the cosily lit kitchen. But the word refuses to stick. The scent is wrong; the fall of light. The accents and the call of birds. There is no Joshua here.

'I should go back and help them move the rocks …' Ewan says again.

'They'll handle it. You've done enough.' Luda pats his back, but she keeps finding herself gazing at her camera bag. Min's watching a DVD on her laptop, curled up on the couch like she's sick. Darcy sits up on the kitchen counter with his hands cupped around a mug of dark, unsweetened tea. His face, like Ewan's, is marked by the woman's fingernails.

Underneath those fresh marks, the play of luminous scars across Darcy's skin. Luda pretends not to see them. Min, she thinks, cannot see them – Min who says things as soon as they enter her head. Luda suspects that Darcy can see them. It's in the way that he sometimes studies her skin, Min's skin, like he can't help himself. It's in the furtiveness of how he looks away if Luda catches him at it.

Luda wonders how long Ewan will stay, hunched at the scrubbed kitchen table in the ghost house. They have only been on the islands a week – not long enough to learn the intricate play of expectations that binds a community together. Perhaps Ewan will stay here overnight. Perhaps she has committed some sort of faux pas by not already having offered him the couch to sleep on. She wonders how long Darcy and Min will mill down here before climbing up to the loft where they reluctantly sleep ('Mum! Seriously! How can you expect the two of us to *share a room*?').

The ghost house is the only habitable place on Seannay, which is hitched to Big Island via a causeway. Seannay has no trees, just the house and turf and gorse and piles of stone and slate where other houses and byres had once stood. The ghost house is tiny and smells of damp sand and chalk. The ground floor has a kitchen, fireplace and couch. Above the bathroom is the loft with two single beds. Luda sleeps on a pile of cushions on the ground floor. She doesn't mind – it means that she's unlikely to wake anyone when she goes out for her early-morning runs. Her late-night runs. Her during-the-day runs. With every pound of foot on earth, Luda thinks about her photography.

'Mum?' Min's voice sounds young. She's taken off her headphones.

'Hmm?'

'It's good, what you're doing, you know. Documenting all the climate change stuff. It's important.' Another pause. Her voice is unusually gentle, stilted. 'I get ... I get why we needed to come here.'

Luda blinks. 'Thanks, Min.'

In another family, in another time, Darcy might have echoed his sister's praise. Instead, he gulps down his tea and the ghost house goes quiet.

Ewan shifts. 'I should go back, help them with the rocks.'

More back-patting. Luda's gaze tracing the lines of her camera bag. 'They'll handle it, Ewan. They *will*.'

Chapter Two

FEBRUARY (THEIR FIRST YEAR)

The Managans had arrived on the islands a week ago. In the hours before their ferry docked, a storm had blown in from the north, agitating the sea into a large swell that battered the beaches and sunk smaller boats at the docks. The storm shattered a window in the ghost house; leaked water into the transept of the kirk. There were not many trees on the islands, and this storm brought down three of them.

The Managan family, still smelling faintly of their farm in Australia – of dry, loose earth and peeling paint and the wood of cracked branches – had arrived as the storm was easing. The curtains of rain had softened into a lacy drizzle, the clouds had shifted from darkly bruised to a bright and chilly grey.

Until recently, there had been four of them.

Unspeaking, the three remaining Managans lugged their bags into Ewan's waiting car. Luda and her children were not staying in the ghost house on Seannay that first night. The window broken in the storm must first be fixed. The islands are a place where broken windows and crooked doors need to be mended before the wind works its claws inside. Living on the islands means being in constant conversation with the wind; negotiating where it will and will not go.

The Managans did not know this yet. It would be a lesson they'd begin to learn a week later, watching the cliff collapse into the sea.

On the day that they arrived on the storm-bruised islands, Min hesitated near Ewan's car door.

'Min,' said Luda tiredly. 'Min, just get in. Please.'

Min took a step back. 'How long's the drive?'

'Ten minutes,' said Ewan. 'Maybe fifteen, with all the storm damage.'

'I can walk.'

'You can't walk, Min,' said Luda. 'You're exhausted and you don't know where you're going. Get in the car.'

There was a moment when it seemed that Min was not going to get into the car, and then Darcy had turned and looked at her. 'Min,' he said.

She softened a little. She climbed into the back seat.

Ewan drove them to a house at the top of Big Island, where a woman called Cassandra lived. Cassandra, who was some very aged, very distant relative of Luda's. She had orchestrated Luda's job here with the local council. And Luda had accepted because this was her purpose, her passion. She had accepted because it was right and not because she was running.

'You can see the flow from here,' Ewan said, pointing towards a huge, still bay.

'The flow?' Min asked.

'They narrowed the neck during the war,' said Ewan. 'There are thirty shipwrecks down there.'

Min shivers.

After helping the Managans carry their luggage to the door of Cassandra's house, Ewan backed away.

'What's wrong?' Min asked. 'You don't like Cassandra?'

'Oh, I like Cassandra well enough,' Ewan said. 'But I can see Father Lee's car parked just there.' He nodded at a maroon station wagon with a crucifix bumper sticker. 'And I don't go where Father Lee is, if I can help it.'

Inside, Father Lee greeted them by clasping each of their hands in both of his own and hanging on for too long. 'I'm so glad I could come and welcome you to the islands personally. The council's holding an emergency meeting but, fortuitously, it's not until this afternoon.'

Darcy extricated his hand from Father Lee's and glanced at the door behind him, as though wishing that he'd followed Ewan briskly away from this man and his maroon station wagon and too-big, too-damp hands.

'I'm still of the mind that politics and religion shouldn't mix, Marcus,' Cassandra called from the front room.

Father Lee gestured for the Managans to enter.

Cassandra was seated neatly in a floral-printed armchair. She wore a plaid skirt, beige cardigan and a large, glittering parrot brooch.

'It's lovely to meet you,' said Luda. She paused. 'Thanks again for putting me forward for the job.'

'A pleasure.'

Cassandra studied the three Managans. Luda had brown hair that was darker at the roots and heavily sun-bleached at the ends. She had large, hazel eyes, wide shoulders and a body that was narrow and wiry. Her face seemed too heavily lined for the age she must have been. Luda glanced, quickly and often, at her children. Her glances were appraising. She looked out the window, at the paintings on Cassandra's walls, in the very same way.

Wilhelmina, with short dark hair, a gap between her teeth and her mother's wide shoulders. She did not have her brother Darcy's startling beauty, but there was something magnetic about her face, something that made it hard to look away. Cassandra watched how Wilhelmina circled and circled and circled the living room. How she paused to inspect the small sea treasures that Cassandra had carried from the floor of the ocean when she was young. *Aye, it's you*, Cassandra thought. *You're here.*

Darcy hardly moved or spoke. With light brown hair and hazel eyes that were both green and gold, he was beautiful in that startling and transient way only boys of a certain age could be. The beauty would settle into handsomeness as he grew, Cassandra thought, or else it would disappear altogether. It was, by its very nature, effervescent. It was fleeting.

Cassandra marked the parts of the children that came from Luda; thought of their father, of how he'd died. She cleared her throat. 'You must have had a rough crossing on the ferry,' she said.

'I thought we were going to capsize,' said Wilhelmina, still circling. 'I threw up practically the whole way from the mainland.'

Cassandra made a sympathetic noise. 'I'm not surprised, Wilhelmina. How long did the whole trip take you?'

'It's *Min*.'

'You mean from Australia to Scotland?' Luda asked, giving Min a look. 'I don't even know. We had to drive to the airport, then a flight from Melbourne to Dubai and Dubai to Edinburgh and then the train from Edinburgh through the highlands to … to the terminal to catch the ferry here.'

'Quite a journey,' Father Lee said, as though commenting on a child's trip home from school.

'Are you familiar with the islands?' Cassandra asked, ignoring him.

Luda shook her head.

'Darcy knows plenty. He looked it all up before we came here,' Min said, and Darcy gave her a sharp look.

'Did you now?' Cassandra smiled at him. He did not smile back, but was not rude about it. Cassandra turned back to Luda, Min now pacing behind her mother's chair. 'Big Island has a population of a few thousand. This town is by far the largest one, but there are a couple of smaller places on the north and southern edges. Mostly just a pub and a general store, nothing like the town here.'

'How many islands are there?' Min asked.

'Thirty-eight,' Cassandra said. 'Not including tidal islands like your Seannay. I believe eleven are inhabited now.'

'Eleven.' Luda frowned. 'Are storms like this usual?'

Father Lee began handing out mugs of tea. He seemed very proud of himself for procuring them – holding each out to be appropriately admired before letting it go.

'They're getting worse,' said Cassandra. 'Or so I hear. It's been decades since I've been anywhere more interesting than the pub. But even watching through my window I can tell that they're more frequent. The islands further north tend to be hit the hardest.'

'I try to get out there to help as often as I can,' Father Lee added. 'Hardly anyone left on some of them now – the damage was just too much. And it's a domino effect, isn't it? Less people, less funding for infrastructure, less services, so more people leave. It's sad. A whole way of life, just gone.'

Luda nodded, trying and failing to imagine what it might be like on those other islands.

'So, it's really kind of incredible eleven still have people on them,' Darcy said quietly.

'Aye,' said Cassandra. 'It is.'

'But you'll be fine on Seannay,' Father Lee said. 'Ewan and the other council lads will be finished repairing that broken window by tomorrow.'

Cassandra generally tried to avoid agreeing with Father Lee, just as a matter of principle, but the Managans looked so worn out that she made an exception. 'Aye, the ghost house is solid.'

'It's very kind of the council to give us accommodation,' Luda said. 'We really appreciate it.'

Darcy looked up. '*Ghost* house?'

Father Lee smiled. 'Oh, it's nothing. Just a silly nickname some folk give it.'

'Why?'

'There've always been stories about Seannay,' Cassandra said, leaning in. 'Witches used to meet there.'

Father Lee snorted. 'Oh, aye. And a selkie washed up.'

Darcy frowned. 'A selkie?'

'Aye,' said Cassandra. 'Folk who look like seals but can shed their skin and become human. In the stories, men used to steal the selkie skins and then the seal women would have to stay on land with them.'

'That's awful,' Min said.

'There are all sorts of other stories about Seannay,' Cassandra continued. 'My favourite is the scars – how the light there illuminates the scars from every injury you've ever had. Only some people can see them, though.'

'It's mostly women, I've found,' Father Lee said, his voice lazy. 'Women will believe all sorts of things – particularly bored housewives.'

Cassandra's head snapped around. 'Oh, Marcus. *Really?*'

Father Lee ignored her and turned to Luda. 'Speaking of which, will your husband be joining you?'

Luda startled. 'What?'

'You put "Mrs" on your paperwork.'

Luda crossed and uncrossed her legs. Her children had both grown still. 'No. He's dead.'

Min recommenced her pacing. Darcy straightened in his chair.

Father Lee's expression flickered. 'Aye, I see. Well, I'm very sorry for your trouble. What a dreadful thing.'

'Crivvens! I told you he'd died, Marcus,' Cassandra said. 'Isn't the whole point of being a priest to remember important details about your parishioners?' She paused. 'And *potential* parishioners?'

'The purpose of a priest – which I'm sure you'd be more familiar with if you ever came to worship, Cassandra – is to be a spiritual warrior of the Scripture. It's my duty to act as mediator between humanity and God.'

'Fancy that,' said Cassandra, biting into a biscuit. 'Some would think it's not terribly godly to mock a crippled old woman for not being able to get to the kirk as frequently as she might like.'

'You seem to make it out to the pub when it suits you.'

'Aye, seeking out my own sacraments, Father,' she said. 'Just trying to make the best of things.'

Across the room, Darcy snorted.

Later, Father Lee and Min washed dishes in the sink, which was to say that Min washed dishes in the sink while Father Lee stood nearby. He clasped her shoulder in what he evidently thought was a warm, paternal gesture; it took all of Min's self-control not to shrug it off. 'I assume you'll be dropping in on Cassandra regularly now that you're here, Wilhelmina. To keep her company.'

'What?'

'Well, she's very old. She has the carers coming around, and members of the kirk council, of course, but nothing beats having your family around you.' His eyes were intent. 'Does it?'

Darcy appeared in the door, carrying a single spoon, his eyes sharp. Father Lee dropped his hand.

'Alright,' said Min.

'Excellent. I'll ask Lorraine to forward you the times that would suit.'

And then it had started to rain and both Managan children had turned towards the window, silent and almost breathless with the wonder of water on glass.

* * *

Now, watching the water stream down the window of the loft in the cottage – the ghost house – the rain already seems more normal. Min rolls onto her side in the gloom of the loft. Above her, she can make out the pattern of carvings in the wooden beams. Jagged V shapes and symmetrical flowers and loops. The sight of them soothes her. It stops her from thinking about the keening of the woman near the cliff that afternoon. The sight of her clawing at Darcy and Ewan's arms and faces and necks. The way the girl had been alive one minute and then, quite suddenly, dead.

Dead. Min swallows, tries not to think of Narra. Home. She tries not to think of the countless afternoons she will spend pouring tea for Cassandra. Min had liked her, but it would have been enough to see Cassandra for an occasional roast dinner with Darcy and her mother. Min has always craved the feeling of being close to other people and that's what she wants to focus on – making new friends her own age, not tending to an elderly relative she barely knows who already has an army of carers looking after her. Besides, what's the point in getting attached when Cassandra could clearly kick the bucket at any time? Min's not naive enough to think that she can spend the rest of her life avoiding the sort of agonising grief she's been stricken with since her father died, but she doesn't particularly want to seek it out, either.

Across the room, her brother shifts a little in his bed. Darcy breathes silently when he's awake and noisily when he's asleep. She likes that they have to share a room, although she'd never admit it.

'Tell me something,' she says to Darcy. The years of their shared childhood spun between them, as delicate and precise as a spider's web. *Tell me something.*

Darcy keeps particularly still and breathes silently.

'Darcy,' Min says. 'I know you're awake.'

The sound of their mother typing on her laptop downstairs. Min knows that she will have a wine by her elbow; that Luda – so quick to feel the cold – will be sitting close to the drowsing warmth of the Rayburn. Ewan had gone home a little after midnight.

'Darcy.' Min pauses. 'If we could see scars like how Cassandra said – if it was real, I mean – would you want to?'

'Go to sleep.'

'*Tell me something!* Then I will.'

He groans. 'Fine! Once upon a time, a motorcyclist got hit by a car on the other side of Narra.'

Min lets a breath out. 'God, Darcy.'

'And then his flight instinct kicked in.' Darcy tugs at his blankets. 'And even though his head was all crushed, his body didn't know it. So he got to his feet and ran down the road. It took the police hours to catch him.'

'That's not true.'

'Of course it is,' says Darcy. 'His sympathetic nervous system was overloaded when his head got crushed. It's basic science.'

Min wraps herself up more tightly in her blankets. 'Bodies don't get up and run around.'

'Whatever.'

'Was he alone?'

'Yeah. He was alone.'

So much between them. Delicately binding them both to things they don't have words for. The newest thread: the keening by the cliffs. The name *Allie*. The shock of so much rock and weight shifting with no warning. Min thinks that she might want to talk about it, but isn't sure *how*. Besides, Luda has always said that there's no point going over and over painful things. It is better, as far as Luda is concerned, to set your eyes firmly on the horizon and keep moving. The past will tear you apart, if you let it.

Min figures that if she was meant to talk about things, it would feel more vital and urgent, and perhaps finding the words would be easier. Maybe it *is* better to do what their mother does; to put them out of her mind and avoid getting bogged down in awful things that have already happened; things that none of them can do anything about.

'You're a dick,' she says into the gloom and hears Darcy's small, satisfied snort.

Both of them lie awake, thinking of dead bodies running across the parched landscape of Narra.

Chapter Three

It is one of those days where Luda wakes disjointed; where she wakes and smells salt and blindly reaches for Joshua. But the salt is her own. It is one of those days where she must be firm with herself, lest the sorrow and bewilderment of everything break her open.

Focus on the present. Focus on the future. As she works, Joshua still sneaks into little moments – a cup of coffee for one; a whiff of something that smells like the cologne he had worn to dinners and parties. Cutlets. Her wedding ring. The gap on her finger, when she takes it off. The smell of Imperial Leather soap. How she had managed to miss that he was so desperately unhappy.

Joshua. Joshua. *Joshua*.

This is what she knows: being haunted is not static. It is a fluid thing, a constellation of changing colours. Some days, she senses him everywhere. Other days, she barely thinks of him. On these days she will recognise his absence – her own self-absorbed carelessness – and it will be like a physical blow. She will stagger.

Her children are outside; the ghost house is entirely hers. She opens her laptop at the kitchen table and continues to go through the raw images she'd taken from the boat. They're good. Powerful. She finds that if she breaks each image down into pieces, she can face them without flinching.

This is why she is here. This work. She sits back and drums her fingers on the table.

On impulse, she opens an older file on her computer. An image of Darcy. It's one Luda had taken of him a few years ago, sprawled in the middle of their dried-up dam in Narra, his expression agonised, his limbs milky against the cracked earth. She had taken it without him realising. She had initially had it earmarked for part of an exhibition, but had sold it to the papers without telling him, instead. Luda makes herself keep looking at it. Darcy had been furious when the photo had been printed. He'd said that she'd had no right. The boys at school had plastered the photo across all the lockers and he had come home shaking and colourless. She'd felt bad immediately and yet she'd defended herself. She'd argued that the photo wasn't about Darcy. She'd argued that it was bigger than him; that it was about raising awareness of the plight of everyone living on the land and the land itself. Raising money for them, too. That if he couldn't see that, he was selfish – and she hadn't meant to raise a selfish son.

Even as she'd spoken these words, she'd been so aware of Joshua in the other room, aggravated and energetic, full of plans for bore pumps and irrigation and high-energy stock feed. In that moment, Darcy clench-fisted and furious in front of her, Luda had been so aware of how vital that image of him was – how integral it would be to tiding them all over until the rains came.

If they came.

Finances. Panic. Obligation. There are so many things that get in the way of Luda and her art. Between Luda and creating.

More privately, she is aware of just how *beautiful* it is. How it shows something primal and urgent about being human – something Luda obsessively hunts and only sometimes glimpses. How this hidden and hungry part of her is still disappointed that the image had been printed in the papers, its narrative anchored to the impact of climate change. She would have much preferred it be called *boy in drought* or *untitled* and hung in a quiet gallery space. She had wanted it to be recognised as the wordless, urgent and vital thing it showed. She had wanted it to be recognised with feelings rather than words. She had wanted people to look at it and feel seen, their skin peeled back.

She has never had anyone, not even her closest friend from back home, Leanne, understand this about her. Now, this hidden and hungry part of her acknowledges that the climate change emergency might not have been worth betraying Darcy in this way, but that her hunt for the wordless, urgent humanness was. It is. Darcy.

God, why does parenting have to be so *hard*? Why does she always lash out at them when she feels at her most guilty? She couldn't quite bring herself to *say* sorry to Darcy (Luda has never liked saying sorry), but she did her best to convey it in other ways. She had bought his favourite foods. She said that she hadn't realised how upset he'd be. She didn't want him to be upset. She had tried to explain that she hadn't done it on purpose; that she hadn't been *thinking*. That she was worried about what was going to happen to them – to everyone impacted by the drought. She had even tried to rein the image in, but it was too late. It had already spiralled far beyond her control. The magic and horror of her work.

Would Darcy have minded so much if it had been hung in a quiet gallery, instead? Probably, but maybe not. Luda has never been able to predict Darcy.

As it was, the photo of Darcy had gone viral and raised hundreds of thousands of dollars, then millions, for those impacted by the drought. The photo's international reach had meant the local council here had been persuaded by Cassandra into offering her a job right when she most needed it. She was to document the impact of climate change on the islands; to apply for grants; to liaise with the media.

Darcy had made her promise to never take photos of him ever again.

Blinking quickly, Luda finally allows herself to look away from the image. Darcy had been so damaged by living through the drought. She knows this because when she'd spied Darcy on the crusted dam bed, she had recognised his pain, his anguish, as something that existed deeply within her own body. The drought existed in all of them – an ache in the bones. A weariness. But they were away from that now. Safe, on this small, damp and salt-laced island.

She opens yesterday's images again. Like that image of Darcy, she feels that secret part of herself hum. She yearns for a gallery space, for this fleeting and powerful moment she has captured to be offered to others only as itself. But no. She drums her fingers on the table some more. And then she starts typing an email. After a moment's hesitation, she attaches the file.

And then she closes her eyes and presses send.

* * *

Darcy crosses the causeway from Seannay to Big Island, avoiding the deeper puddles, his head bent against the constant wind.

'Wait!' Min calls. She reaches him on the other side, lungs raw from rushing. 'Where are we going?'

'*I'm* going to see Cassandra.' He starts walking again.

'Okay,' she says, and follows. She expects him to say something scathing, to try to make her leave, but he walks silently, arms crossed over his body. She allows herself this indulgent thought: Darcy likes having her close, even if he won't admit it.

Getting there had seemed straightforward enough in Ewan's car, but on foot they're disoriented. Darcy asks people for directions, more than once, on these narrow, curving roads. They all mark his accent, ask him and Min about their trip over from Australia. Some make comments about where they've come from; others ask if they had pet kangaroos. They are asked about Australian politics; about refugee policies and desalination plants and the flavour of the air. Some don't talk to Darcy and Min at all, just gaze at them with a sort of weariness born from too many outsiders coming here to live and then quickly leaving.

Min only half-listens as the conversation Darcy is having with an older woman shifts to the cliff collapse. Min watches a group of girls who look about her age, clustered on the pavement a little further down the road. She will be tested on the first day of school – accepted or found wanting – and studying any young person she encounters on the street is her only way of preparing. Min feels Darcy's attention sharpen, his body tense. 'What photos?' he asks the woman.

Except he does not wait for an answer. He grabs Min by the back of the jacket and pulls her a few doors down the road to the newsagency. A couple of the clustered girls look up. Min flushes and waits for sniggers at the sight of her being dragged along, but instead the girls cluster more tightly, giggling and whispering. They probably haven't even noticed Min. It's always disconcerting to be reminded that people think her brother is handsome.

'What?' She pulls free and for a moment she wants to hit him, as she'd so often done when they were younger. Their mother does the same thing to her as Darcy does; dragging her places without any context or warning. Min is stronger than Darcy now, but some part of her always yields to him when she so rarely yields to anyone else. If she ends up being eight foot tall, Darcy and her mother will still be able to drag her places. She will (helplessly; endlessly) let them.

He jabs his finger at the cover of a newspaper. EROSION BLAMED IN FREAK DEATH OF EIGHT-YEAR-OLD ALISON REYNOLDS. But it is the photo that sends bile guttering up into the back of Min's throat. A photo of the bronze-haired girl, the rocks blurred above her. A chance photo that captured the last split second (God, Min hopes it was the last split second) of her life.

'It's a national tabloid,' Darcy says, his voice completely toneless. 'Half of Scotland will have seen it by now.'

He tosses coins onto the counter and goes to stuff the newspaper into his satchel, but Min grabs at his wrist. 'Wait.'

She can feel his pulse. Rabbit-quick with rage. The tendons and muscles in his wrist tighten beneath her fingers. Surely there had been a time when Darcy hadn't winced every time he was touched?

Darcy shakes her hand off but leaves the paper where she can see it. 'She's not credited, but everyone will know who took it. Why the *fuck* would she publish it?'

Between the two Managan children spins another wordless thread, bright and tangled in the silvery light. That long-ago photo of Darcy in the dam.

His fingers tighten on the paper. Min studies the images for a moment longer and then steps away. She wishes that there were a way to touch him without him shying away. An ache for her friends back home; for Harper and Sōta and Nico. How they'd looped arms around each other's necks and pressed their bodies tightly together. How they'd brushed hair from each other's faces and giggled into each other's hands. She misses every part of them. Back at home, she'd catalogued in advance all of the things she imagined that she'd most miss after moving here, and then she'd tried to gorge on them – food before a fast. But she had not thought of touch. She had not recognised the value of reaching across space, knowing the closest person would welcome her skin against theirs. Here, on this damp street, the certainty of such a thing seems impossible.

Darcy folds the paper crisply in half. 'Bloody Mum. Bloody *Luda.*'

'She's only thinking about raising awareness,' Min says, her voice unsteady. She is bewildered, as always, by her mother's choices. Maybe if she paid more attention to Luda, she would be better at predicting her, but it's hard to pay close attention to a mother who has never really paid close attention to you – just your skin, your expressions, the way light plays across your collarbones.

The image of Alison will haunt Min. She knows this. And if Darcy's rage were less incandescent, perhaps she would be able to meet it with her own. But there is no room for her to be angry when he is like this. She swallows her gum, regrets it. It feels like a pebble in her stomach.

'She never *thinks*.' Darcy begins walking.

'Allie's mum probably won't even notice.'

Darcy stops. 'Of course she will! Maybe not now, but she will. You can't take these sorts of images back once they're out there. And it'll tear her up. And what about everyone else, Min?' He drops his voice. 'The people here aren't going to like this.'

Min shrugs because she's not sure what else to do. For a moment, she's overcome by an urge to tackle Darcy and grind his face into the damp ground. It would be easier than standing still, swallowing back her own frustration and confusion.

Darcy gives her a look, like he knows exactly what she wants to do and also knows that she won't do it. 'You're the one who's always tied up in knots over what people think of you. How do you think this is going to go down at the school we're starting in three weeks?'

Min swallows. 'It'll be fine.'

Darcy mutters something under his breath and keeps walking. Like so many other times in the last few years, Min feels like she's missed a moment in which she and Darcy might have connected. She strides after him, keeping a careful distance between them so that he doesn't snarl at her.

She draws level with him as they begin the sharp ascent to Cassandra's house. Min has spent her spare time riding horses, tearing around on quad bikes, racing through the bush on foot. Her arms and legs are strong. Darcy has spent his spare time reading. He breathes harder than Min going up the hill, face flushed, fists clenched.

At the house, Cassandra sits in the same chair she had been in on the day they'd met her. Ewan, tearstained, sits on the couch. He wipes at his eyes. 'I'll be off, then.'

'You don't have to,' Min says.

He leaves anyway, his footsteps slow down the hallway. As he puts his shoes on, he begins to smother the sound of sobs. Cassandra studies both Managans. 'A coffee please, Wilhelmina. Black. I get so tired of tea.'

Min heads into the kitchen, flicks the kettle on and then leans against the sink, listening to Cassandra and Darcy speaking in the front room.

'You and Father Lee were talking about … seeing scars on people's skin when you're on Seannay.'

'Aye. You can see them, then?'

'No,' Darcy says quickly. Min can picture his face, that alarmed

26

look he gets when he feels he's been misunderstood. 'No, I can't. I'm just interested in the stories. That's all.'

There is a brief pause. The kettle clicks off and Min takes her time making a black coffee for Cassandra and tea for her and Darcy.

'Aye, well. If I were on Seannay and the light hit me just right, I'd see the scratches here from brambles. I'd see the cuts on this finger from opening cans of ale. I'd see the grazes I got from gorse bushes. I'd see the marks from when I got rope burn the first time I went out on a boat.'

'I still don't get it. There aren't any scars *there* for the light to show up. The skin's healed. So why can some people suddenly see them when they're on Seannay?'

Min takes the mugs into the front room and passes the coffee to Cassandra. Darcy gives her a quick glance, clearly reluctant to talk about the scars in front of her.

'Thank you, Wilhelmina,' Cassandra says. 'Perfect.' She turns back to Darcy. 'You know, witches used to meet on Seannay.'

'Yeah. You mentioned that, too.'

'Aye, so I did.'

'What … what do you mean by witches? Exactly?'

'I mean women with old knowledge of magic met on Seannay and called whales to the shore. They were accused during the witch hunts.' She pauses. 'Only one of them escaped execution.'

'How would they have called whales to the shore?' Min asks.

Cassandra shrugs. 'It was over four hundred years ago. That's just what the story says.'

Why is Min so sure that Cassandra is lying? Why does she have a sudden sense of damp sand, of cold whale skin and starlight?

Darcy frowns, threads his fingers together in his lap. 'So, what you're saying is people think that being able to see the scars is some sort of … residual witch magic from back then?'

Cassandra sips her coffee. 'Some folk might say that.'

'Do *you* think that?'

Cassandra tilts her head towards Min. 'Can you see the scars, Wilhelmina?'

'No.' Min glances at Darcy. 'I don't think so.'

'You'd know, if you could,' Cassandra says.

'Darcy, do you see them?' Min asks.

Darcy's frown deepens. 'No. Of course, I don't.' He looks away. 'They're not real.'

* * *

Luda's workspace is a tiny, cramped office above the laundromat on the main street of the largest island town. The town is grey, made of stone – should be dreary but somehow isn't. She's sharing the space with a harassed archaeologist who's employed by the council to conduct site checks before building or renovation permits are granted. He is a strange creature, all sharp angles and frustrated academic ambition. His name is Tristan, he's from the south, and he spends most of his time muttering at his keyboard, cursing his camera and reading out serial numbers to himself. The office is really too small for two people, and yet Tristan has only been affable, generous. He wears an old leather jacket, has grey-streaked hair and green eyes, and his face, like Luda's, is lined prematurely from years spent outdoors in wild and unforgiving weather.

'You shouldn't have done it, you know,' he says suddenly. His chair squeaks as he sits back in it. 'Publishing that photo.'

'We're going to do this now, are we?'

'Apparently.'

'Look, it's my job. It's what I'm here for.'

'Maybe.' He scratches his chin. 'It's also unnecessarily sensationalist.'

'Excuse me?'

He studies her, one eyebrow cocked. 'Oh dear. I get it now. You really don't see the issue, do you?'

'There is no issue. I'm a photojournalist.' She turns pointedly back to her laptop. *I'm an artist. I'm an artist. I'm an artist.* Except here, she is not. Except, even back home, she had not been an artist in a very long time. She is now something more; something less.

'I'd watch out for the kirk crowd, after this.'

She looks up, irritated. 'What?'

'The kirk crowd. The Reynoldses are big churchgoers and the parishioners here tend to close ranks like hyenas when things go awry.' He leans forward. His chair squeaks again. 'Father Lee wasn't happy about you being employed by the council. Did you know that?'

'But he's on the council.'

'Right.'

'And he came to welcome us when we arrived.'

'Yes,' says Tristan slowly. 'Because that's what's expected of him. He's very committed to keeping up appearances. But you'd still do well to watch out for him.'

'Well, thanks. I think.'

She turns once again to the document on her laptop, trying to link the dry wording of the objectives statement with the wild, magnificent, disordered places she's visited over the last few days with Ewan. Low-lying farms. Shorelines bitten viciously by erosion. She realises that she has perhaps been mistaking people's coldness for shyness on these farms. She thinks of those images. It's *easier* to think of them as images – as stills that can be viewed and filed away. No keening, no shattering of rock on flesh and sand. She breathes out. She had done the right thing, even if it was unorthodox. Even if it was *hard*. People would be talking about erosion, now. People would be talking about climate change.

The chair squeaks again and Luda grits her teeth.

'You've been out on Ewan's boat?' Tristan asks.

'Yes.'

'How is he?'

'Honestly? Wallowing.'

'Wallowing? He watched a girl die. He had to keep Violet from killing herself trying to get to her body. Being shaken by that's not *wallowing*, Luda. Christ.'

'It's self-indulgent.'

'Dear Lord.'

'Is it going to help anything? Does it make Ewan feel better? Is it going to help Violet or bring Allie back?' Her voice cracks and she winces. She frowns back down at her laptop.

Tristan watches her from across the room. 'Acknowledging that something has been hard to witness or live through isn't wallowing. It's *human*.'

'I don't want to talk about this anymore.'

'Fine. How are you liking the apotropaic markings in the ghost house?'

She sighs. 'You *know* that I don't know anything about archaeology, Tristan.'

'Hexafoil? Daisy wheel? Witch mark? *Really?*' He sighs. 'Have you noticed the graffiti carved into the walls?'

'Oh! That's what you're talking about. I haven't really paid much attention. Should I have? What are they?'

'Well, they're generally simple marks carved into stone with the intention of warding off evil. A sort of protective spell, I suppose. They're often found in places like doorways and lintels and windowsills, to stop bad spirits or witches getting in. That house you're living in is teeming with them.'

Luda is startled. 'Teeming? Really?'

'Aye. Teeming. Haven't you noticed the clusters of them?'

'No.'

'The clusters are on the ceiling and the rafters and the walls. In numbers I haven't heard of, apart from the Creswell Crags. I'd love to get funding and make a proper research project out of it, but the council goes into conniptions any time I mention it.'

'Hang on. Let me get this straight. So, you want to research the ghost house because the walls have a lot of these markings?'

'Well, there's a lot of them *and* many of them are utterly unique. They've got a classical hexafoil pattern with the addition of what looks like a scarred whale figure. Nothing like them has ever been found anywhere else in the world, as far as I'm aware.' He rubs at his chin. 'I'm not sure what the meaning of it is. I don't know whether they're meant to afford the whales some sort of protection, or whether they're meant to invoke the whales *for* protection. Maybe they viewed the whales as something benevolent and godly, or maybe as an evil spirit they wanted to trap in stone.'

Luda raises an eyebrow. 'Spooky.'

'I wrote a paper on the markings a few years back. The councillors lost their minds.'

'Why?'

'Well, I hadn't *strictly* sought permission to enter. I normally get in through the kitchen window. But that's not the point! The point is that councils are meant to be supportive of projects that highlight the cultural and historical significance of the land – but our council? Forget about it.'

'Please don't come in through the kitchen window.'

'Well, obviously I won't now that you're in there!'

'The council ... can't you go over their heads?'

He grimaces. 'No. And in the meantime, I'm up to my eyeballs with all these fun projects.' He waves a hand at the boxes and papers filling the cramped space. 'We humans have a real penchant for layering significant buildings on top of each other. It's mostly debitage, but I still have about four hundred artefacts I need to properly photograph, catalogue and store before spring.'

'What on earth's debitage?'

'You really *don't* know anything about archaeology,' he says conversationally. He has a sip of coffee and winces. 'This is truly foul.'

Luda is silent for a moment. 'Do you think the council will ever change its mind?'

'I hope so. Look, I know it's important work and some people love it, but I hate this tick-a-box, is-there-a-neolithic-chamber-under-where-I-want-to-build-my-new-family-room council work. But the alternative is relying on funding and spending all my time trying to convince people that projects are worthwhile. That they're worth embarking on and then that the sites are worth *protecting*. And even if they finally agree to fund the research, you've still got to prove that you've done everything you've said you were going to, over and over again. It's just report after report after *fucking* report.'

'Could you just keep researching it without telling them?'

'Yeah, that's the plan. But that's hardly the point, is it?'

'Would they know?'

'They keep an eye on it.' He pauses. 'And they'll keep an eye on you now, too. Don't forget that.'

'Because I'm in the house you want to research?'

'Because of that damn photo you took.' Tristan goes back to pecking at his keyboard with two fingers. The sight of him hunched over, the smell of cheap coffee. Grumpy and cynical, yes, but she thinks she glimpses an encompassing passion, a consuming hunger for his work (or what he would like his work to be). It is an arresting thing. It has been so long since she's seen this sort of passion up close. The people back home had been ground down by the impossibility of living off a dying land. Their passion had long worn thin and been transformed into grim tenacity. She and Tristan, both lit up and longing for something they could never quite reach.

'Lunch?' she says.

'Lunch.' He shrugs on a jacket.

They eat sandwiches in the local cafe and Tristan tells Luda about the south. He tells her about the town and coming here and strange things on the islands; eerie flashes and colours that were not the northern lights; voices and shadows from the deep bellies of very old crypts. He tells Luda about the foundling boy who had washed up on the shore of Seannay a decade ago. He asks her about Narra; about Joshua. She swallows and says, 'Where do you think the foundling came from?'

Tristan gives her a look and then settles back into his seat. Luda has noticed this about him; the gentle way he allows conversations to be steered away from the painful and uncomfortable (with the notable exception of his opinion on her cliff photographs). 'I think he prefers the name Theo. And no idea.'

'If you had to guess.'

He runs a finger along the edge of the table. 'You'll think it sounds stupid.'

'Well, if I do, I won't mock you.' She tries not to smile. 'Much.'

He snorts and reaches for his coffee. 'Well, in that case, I don't think he's like the rest of us.'

'What do you mean?'

Tristan clears his throat. 'He doesn't have any scars.'

What she thinks is, *You see them too.* 'So, you believe in them, then? The scars?'

'It's not a matter of believing or disbelieving. They're there. I see them on my own skin and I see them on other people's. There'll be a perfectly reasonable explanation for the whole thing.'

'Why do you think some people can see them and other people can't?'

He shrugs and looks away. 'Different eyesight, maybe? I don't know. Anyway, you were asking about Theo.'

'Yes.'

'He's … unusual. Everyone says that his hands are webbed, although he always wears gloves so how would anyone know? He can't read or write, as far as I'm aware. They've never been able to get him to kirk or to school.'

Luda sips her water. 'Bet Father Lee loves that.'

'Hmm. I'd just started working here around the time he was found; I was on someone else's dig on the other side of the island. But I remember the look of him when Iris bundled him out of her house and took him to the hospital to get checked.'

'There's a hospital here?'

'Yes. Full of oldies, mostly – you know how it is. I expect it's nice for them, though.'

'Theo.'

'Right, right. So, it would've been a couple of days after he washed up. People pushing in outside Iris's house, taking photos. Yelling questions.'

'You came out to look?'

33

'I was driving home. Curious. There was nothing human about him.' He shakes his head. 'How he's … adapted … the way he has in only ten years is staggering. I know there are anthropologists who want to study him, but Iris has always put her foot down. She's managed to keep most photographs of him off the internet, too. Anthropologists.' He sets his jaw. 'No class.'

* * *

The early dusk is settling over the islands when Min and Darcy arrive back at the ghost house (back at *home*, Min tells herself). Shortly after, Ewan turns up in his big four-wheel drive. He opens the back and pulls out two old pushbikes and discoloured helmets. Min stands barefoot on the flagstone doorstep.

'What are these for?' she asks.

'You and your brother,' he says, not quite looking at her.

Darcy comes out, nudging past Min to where the bikes are leaning on the turf. He lifts one, holds the handlebars in his fists. They are rusted and peeling and one has mismatched pedals. 'These look great,' he says, and Min thinks of him sweating up the hill to Cassandra's. Is cycling easier than walking? 'Thanks.'

Min picks up the other bike. 'Thanks!' she echoes. 'Have … have you heard anything about the mum?'

'Violet? Aye.' He grimaces. 'She's hanging on. Best you can hope for given … given everything.'

'Yeah,' says Min. She rings the bell on the bike.

'Thanks again,' says Darcy.

Ewan nods, still not looking at either of them. He is embarrassed. He had cried at their kitchen table and now he is embarrassed.

The weight of the bike feels wrong. Their complicity in keeping the rawness of his grief – the depth of him – a secret from everyone else. Min feels suddenly exhausted by it. Why, she wonders, do blokes feel the need to pretend that they don't have feelings?

* * *

Darcy watches drizzle hit the kitchen window. Min is poking and prodding her bike in the shelter of one of the ruins; a head torch strapped to her forehead. The cereal he'd made himself for dinner has become gluggy on the table in front of him. He thinks about falling rocks. It's harder to distract himself when he's tired.

Luda comes inside from talking on the phone to Leanne. She has to stand on the highest point of Seannay to get enough reception to hear her. Now, she sits down opposite Darcy, gazing at him in that very particular way she has.

'I've told you!' he snaps, crossing his arms. 'No more taking photos of me.'

'What?'

'You're looking at me … like you want to get your camera out.'

'I wasn't thinking about my camera.'

He hunches down in his chair, staring at the kitchen cupboard under the small sink.

She clears her throat. 'The cliff collapse was pretty awful, wasn't it?'

He looks at her. 'What?'

'The cliff collapse. It was awful.'

'What are you doing?'

'Just that … it's not wallowing …' She swallows. 'It's okay, you know?'

They stare at each other.

Darcy stands up from the table. 'I have no idea what you're trying to do right now, but it's weird and I'm leaving.'

He takes his time scraping cereal into the compost bin. When his mother doesn't say anything else, he feels a familiar burst of anger. He climbs up into the loft, being noisier than he needs to be.

Chapter Four

Everyone on the islands knows about Theo – the foundling child; the selkie. The stories of him are passed from person to person, sometimes with words and sometimes without. The knowing is this: Theo runs like he can't quite believe that he has legs. He roars and rages on the Wailing Cliffs, flinging rocks out into the sea. He collects old shells and rocks and sea glass from the disappearing shorelines. He stores them in his room – piles and piles of rubbish left by the ebbing tides. It makes the whole house smell like salt and rot and damp stone. Iris wrinkles her nose, but never comments.

He works on a couple of small farms, south of the town. He likes the animals and they seem to like him. Cows, mostly. A few sheep. They stay close to him if he's mending a fence or pipe in the fields, nibbling at his jumper and snuffling at his hair. The knowing is this: he has webbing between his fingers. Scales too, probably. His fingers are green. They're silver. They're brown and furred like the hide of a seal.

The knowing is this: Theo seems calmer with animals than he is with people. Soothed by the feel of their warm breath, the sound of them grazing, the cows chewing their cud. The way they drink from the trough or pick their way through the mud near the gates.

He was found ten years ago. His age, on that day, was estimated to be seven years old. It is therefore generally accepted that he is now seventeen. He lives with Iris, who is far too old to have raised a child. Who is too old, now, to be parenting a teenage foundling.

He cannot read. He pissed himself until he was thirteen years old. He creates strange artworks, all pulsing, curling greens and blues.

The knowing is this: that he hates the kirk; that he is drawn to the shore on Seannay. That he will sit there, webbed hands in his lap, looking out at the ever-encroaching sea, trying – everyone says – to find his way home.

* * *

The Managans don't notice the foundling at first. He has become very good at not being seen. He has learnt how to blend his body into the gorse and the shadows of the ruins. He can make his footfalls sound like those of a rabbit or a stoat.

Min looks up from where she is wading in the shallows of the small bay outside the ghost house, thinking of her father, thinking about starting at a new school, trying not to think about the sound of the woman's keening. The foundling's hair is a sort of silvery bronze that reminds Min of the fur seals she'd seen at the city zoo. His eyes are grey and his gloved hands are tight by his sides.

'Are you Theo?' she asks, but he's already gone.

Later, Min walks to Cassandra's place at the top of the hill. Lorraine, who seems to be in charge of managing Cassandra's rotation of carers, had left Min a dizzying timetable. She had highlighted the times when Cassandra is free.

Min knocks and the door opens a minute or two later.

'Wilhelmina,' says Cassandra, bracing herself against the doorframe.

'Min. It's *Min*.'

'Just let yourself in, next time.'

'Oh.' Min makes out the beading of sweat across Cassandra's brow. 'Sorry.'

Cassandra waves a hand. 'Come in. It's lovely to see you.'

'You too.' Min fidgets. 'Coffee?'

'Please. Black, like last time.' Cassandra settles herself back into the floral armchair and closes her eyes. 'They always make it far too milky and sweet, even if I tell them not to.'

'Who does?'

'Everyone. You get to a certain age and people start looking through you and making assumptions about you.'

Min narrows her eyes. 'How old *are* you?'

Cassandra cracks open an eye. 'Hasn't your mother ever told you that it's mortifyingly rude to ask someone their age?'

'She also told me never to go inside someone's house without knocking.'

Cassandra smiles. 'Would you think I'm losing my marbles if I tell you that I honestly can't remember?'

'No. I think if you're as old as you look, you shouldn't have to remember the exact number.'

Cassandra studies her for a moment and then smiles widely. 'Quite right.'

Min makes a black coffee for Cassandra and a weak, milky tea for herself. She carries both back into the front room.

'You know,' Cassandra says, tipping whisky from a flask into her coffee, 'I don't want you feeling compelled to visit just because of Father Lee.'

'I don't.'

'I'd quite like you to visit now and then,' Cassandra says, sounding a bit surprised by this. 'But not because you think you have to. I'm on enough chore lists as it is. I don't want to be added to yours.'

Min wants to squirm. 'You're not a chore.'

'Well, I'd like to stay that way. Come when you'd like to and not for any other reason. I may be old, but I still have my dignity. Are we clear?'

'Yes.'

'Good.' She has a sip of coffee. 'Now, tell me something.'

Min straightens, thinks of Darcy. 'What?'

Cassandra sets down her mug. 'Whatever you can't get out of your head.'

Min thinks for a while and then she tells Cassandra about swimming in Narra. Min does not mention the image of Darcy curled up in the dry dam. She does not mention the very precise sound of Allie's keening, or the way she had woken up from nightmares back home of her feet sunk into the ground like roots and her skin as parched and cracked as the earth. She does not mention the sound of metal and glass shattering against wood. Instead, she tells Cassandra about the big dam in the home paddock, and how her dad had swum with her there. There were leeches and yabbies – the sorts of things that scared young children, but Min had never been afraid. Joshua always had salt for the leeches. He could unhook a yabby. When Min turned eight, the dam shrank and shrank. As it shrank, it grew thick with mud and then with algae. Joshua began taking Min and Darcy to the Proctors' dam, instead. Lined and deep. There was a sturdy wooden platform that some of the older children dived from. When the level of the Proctors' dam also began to drop, Joshua had taken them to the river. The river smelt like ammonia and something sickly, like rotting fruit. After a couple of visits, Joshua had found discarded syringes on the banks, in among the rubbish washed from upstream.

Min tells Cassandra more, words spilling out on top of each other. She tells Cassandra about how the dams around Narra dried up and strange things emerged from their cracked, curved beds. Cars that had been reported stolen to insurance companies, rusted and corroded. Old guns and knives and animal skeletons. Bed frames and the springs from long-decayed mattresses. Pieces of old water troughs and abandoned irrigation systems. People out of work began excavating the beds – a beautiful old ring was found, tossed away in fury fifty years before. Rotted toys. A nugget of gold in a waterlogged metal box. The Managans' dam yielded nothing more interesting than an old revolver and a saucepan with its base burnt through. Still, Joshua dug – dizzy with the possibility of finding something long discarded and valuable. As more and more stock were sold. As news broke of the golden nugget stashed on the other side of town. He dug and dug and his hands came up silty and shaking.

* * *

Luda submits the funding application she's been working on over the last few days and sits back in her chair. She exhales, wishes that Tristan was at his desk, so she could tell him that the damn thing was finished. He'd say something irritating, probably, and it would make Luda smile. Instead, she researches apotropaic markings and chews on her fingernails until they feel raw. The more she reads, the more quietly outraged she becomes over the council's reticence. Why weren't they jumping at the chance to have it properly researched and documented?

The whole thing makes Luda feel restless. She's meeting with the council tonight, although she wishes she could just go home. When the workday ends, she walks from her cramped office on the main street to the council building on the waterfront. Her head aches. She gazes down at the cobblestones as she walks, wondering when they were laid, what might be under them. Back home, Indigenous connection to Country stretches back tens of thousands of years – a length of time that seems unfathomable to Luda. History is layered in a different way in Australia and she has never been able to shake the feeling of being complicit in everything that should have remained, but hadn't. It makes her feel hollow to think about it. It makes her feel – even armed with her camera, even *then* – utterly inadequate.

The drought, all that dying land. How often has she wondered how different it might all look if Australia had never been colonised? It is an unhappy thought that she often has; trying to save a land that they were responsible for wounding so badly.

At the local council offices, she shrugs off her jacket and is directed to a wood-panelled room overlooking the water where the council members are seated around a wide table. They all turn to stare at her and Luda wishes she'd thought to put on something a bit more dignified than her faded jeans and a black skivvy.

'Luda,' says Father Lee. 'Take a seat.'

Luda sits down at the far end of the table, pours herself some water and wills the pain in her head to soften.

Father Lee; a small woman with an upright posture and closely cropped greying hair called Iris; a tall, sinewy woman with a deeply lined face called Bran. There are four other older men, whose names Luda quickly forgets. And there is Doug Tiernan, the editor for the local paper. He eyes her coolly from across the table and Luda wonders how on earth the paper can maintain any impartiality with the editor on the council.

'Tell us,' says Father Lee. 'How are you getting on with everything? I trust you're finding the accommodation acceptable?'

'Yes, it's fine. Thank you.'

'And Ewan's been a suitable guide?'

'Very knowledgeable and generous with his time.'

'And how do you view your recent … publicity?'

'I was hired to undertake photojournalistic work to raise awareness and funds, and I have *engaged* in photojournalistic work that's raising awareness and funds.'

'I see.'

'And it's not *my* publicity. It's about the cause.'

'Of course.' The priest leans forward. 'The council is just concerned.'

Luda sighs. 'Of course you are.'

'The Reynolds family is completely shattered by the coverage.'

'I imagine they'd be shattered right now regardless.'

A flicker of deep dislike crosses Father Lee's face.

Luda feels a drop of sweat roll uncomfortably down her spine.

'The council's received a number of complaints, including from the Reynolds family, whom I've been supporting intensively in a pastoral role since the accident. The council expects more discretion from you in the future.'

Luda makes her voice light. 'Perhaps you'd like me to show you the images before I send them out?'

'Aye, that would be ideal.'

'And maybe you'd like to come out with me when I shoot?' Luda continues, tilting her head.

'I don't think that's –'

'Maybe you'd like to set up little scenes for me to photograph in your kirk?'

Bran snorts, struggling to repress a smile.

'I see,' Father Lee says, after a moment.

Luda straightens. Another bead of sweat dripping down skin.

'You need to remember that while you're here, you're part of the island community – God help us all. And that means you answer not only to the island council, but the community itself.'

Luda and Father Lee stare at each other until Bran intervenes. 'Aye, aye. You've made your point, Father. Some of us have bairns to be getting home to. That's everything on the agenda. Any other business?'

Luda tenses. She had been preparing to speak on Tristan's behalf. She had wanted to advocate for him and his strange fascination with the markings that crooked the skin of the ghost house. But she now realises that her advocacy would only brace the council further against his project. Right now, the only gift she can give Tristan is her silence.

The meeting is closed and she senses someone looking at her and glances up. It is not Father Lee, but the neat, upright woman to his left. Iris. She is gathering up her papers, her unreadable gaze fixed on Luda.

Chapter Five

As Darcy dreams of equations, Min dreams of her friends and Luda dreams of nothing, three young orcas strand themselves on the pebbled beach of Seannay. Wet sand, salt, salt. Like songs long sung. The Managans all stir, but none of them wake.

* * *

Luda blinks in the murky morning light. She studies her skin, but the room is dim and the flickers of scars seem to shift and buck beneath her gaze. Why can she see the scars on other people's skin so much more clearly than those on her own? The marks on the ceiling above her. She wonders what they mean. Witch marks. *Apotropaic markings.*

She thinks of the roadside memorials back in Narra. It had been one cross, at first. Painted blue against the chalky soil and cracked hide of the ironbark tree. Crosses were normal; routine. A cross on a roadside was a flick of the eye, a lurch of the stomach, maybe, and then accelerating.

The blue was striking. A sort of indigo. Like water. Like the belly of clouds full of noise and light and rain. The crosses were a yearning for things that the people of Narra did not always have the words for. The things that existed on the underside of rain.

The witch markings give her the same feeling, of something mattering deeply. She can make out the markings on the walls and eaves more easily than the pale crosshatching on her own skin. *Whales.* Spells. She had tried to explain them to Leanne, but without experiencing the islands, there is no way to understand the power of the markings carved into the walls of the ghost house.

Luda thinks that she can hear voices outside, but nobody has yet come to the door of the ghost house and so she tells herself it is just the wind.

Normally, she would be up by now – running, working, moving, moving, moving. But she feels deflated. She feels raw. The meeting last night had felt like a sort of trial that she had failed. She closes her eyes and thinks groggily of women carving whales into stone, casting spells to keep them safe. She's so sure that the spells had been an invocation on behalf of, rather than to, the whales.

The thud of a car door closing. *The wind.*

She's so sure that the casters – the carvers of the markings – had been women.

* * *

One car, then two. Mostly they come in foot. Voices, raised against wind. The people of the islands come to the pebbled beach on Seannay to save the whales, although deep down every person knows that really they have come to watch the whales die one by one.

The whales have followed each other onto sand, into air. They are each other's doom. They will die. The business of death will not be quick. The whales will linger. The island crowds will linger with them. The crowds will try to fall in love with the whales so that their passing will feel personal; the loss of something larger than themselves that they all, without realising it, will try to claim a little piece of.

The crowds come and watch and attempt to help, although there's nothing that will save the whales. They are already too far gone – burning from the inside, smothered by the weight of their own bodies. If people in the crowd can see each other's scars, they don't comment on it. Some see the bright marks and shy away from them, retreating to the shadows of the island's ruins. Others stare wonderingly at the people around them, touching the backs of their own hands, the thin skin of their own inner arms. Many in the crowd, particularly those who cannot see the sudden flare of scars, try to spot the Managans.

They look for Darcy – the son they have heard is beautiful. They look for Luda, who took those photos of the cliff collapse and, shockingly, passed them on to a tabloid. Nobody who turns up to Seannay looks particularly for Min Managan, who is neither mesmerisingly beautiful nor a capturer and seller of controversial photos. The people have all seen the photos. Some of them think it misguided; feel sorry for Luda and her outsider lack of judgement. Others are angry at her, feel like she does not belong. Others still have spent long hours talking in the Blue Fin about what it would be like to punish her; to bend her over, to press callused fingers to her throat. They wonder what it would be like to do something to her daughter, so that Luda would understand the pain she has caused in excruciating, exacting detail. This is all said over pints, said with laughter, intermingled with talk of kirk events and football scores, and so it cannot reflect poorly on the speakers. They're just chatting with the lads, after all.

* * *

Of course Tristan had come across the stretch of damp sand to the island. Orcas are not his thing; at least, not living ones – all flesh and skin and muscle. But he comes and he tries to help and he watches Luda, the strange new photographer and fundraising manager for the council. Idiot woman, so desperate to prove her worth that she'd gone ahead and published those photos of Allie. In anyone else, her actions would have alienated him, as they seem to have alienated half of the inhabitants of the islands. But there's something tentative and bruised underlying her ruthlessness, her certainty. And it's enough to keep him from turning away.

That, and the fact that she could easily deny him access to the ghost house and the markings. Creeping in through the window of an occupied house would be going a bit too far, even for Tristan. He had known, as soon as he heard that Luda and her family would be living here, that he had to be civil. He is surprised, really, to find that it is not an effort. Surprised, also, to find that he rather enjoys her company; the unexpectedly snarky sense of humour; the slow smile when he says something ridiculous.

He glances at her. Her clenched fists and intent gaze. As cars come over the causeway. As the islanders puzzle over how three orcas have managed to strand themselves on this awkward piece of shoreline.

'You should photograph this,' Tristan says.

Luda looks at him, pushing hair out of her eyes. Her skin on Seannay is unusually scarred. Her face and hands. 'What?'

He thinks that he'd quite like to touch those scars. 'The rates of beaching have been increasing astronomically. There's a paper in the office somewhere.'

She looks away. 'I know that, Tristan.'

'So? Go get your camera and' – he waves his hands – 'do your thing.'

'But ...' She looks at him almost pleadingly. The name *Allie* flitters between them. For a moment, he's surprised by the change wrought in her since he saw her at work yesterday. Christ, he'd forgotten about the council meeting. He wonders what they said to her. What Father Lee said to her. He feels a flash of anger.

'Go. Show them you can get images out there that aren't about dying children.' He nudges her towards the house, feels her flinch at the words. 'Oh! Luda. By the way, do you mind if I go inside later to look at the witch marks?'

'God, Tristan. That's what you're thinking about?' Luda shivers and he regrets asking, as though he has showed something of himself best kept private. 'Fine,' she says. 'Knock yourself out.'

Tristan watches her continue to walk away from the beach, her shoulders hunched against the wind. There are a group of teenage girls clustered near the kitchen window; even from here he can tell that they're giggling and craning their necks.

Someone claps Tristan's shoulder so hard that he feels winded.

'Ewan,' he says, his voice a bit tight. 'How are you?'

'Not so bad,' Ewan says. He looks towards the whales and sighs. 'Wish we could do more for them.'

'Me too.'

'Luda around?'

Tristan gestures at the ghost house. 'Getting her camera.'

Ewan winces at the word, then catches himself and nods. 'I just wanted to thank her.'

'Thank her?'

'She's paid for a whole lot of ales for me down the Blue Fin,' Ewan says. 'She went in last night and sorted it all. I had to nag Louise for a full ten minutes before she'd tell me who it was.'

Tristan blinks. 'Unexpected.'

'Aye.' Ewan hesitates. 'I don't think she means to be such a …'

'Probably best you don't finish that sentence.'

Ewan chuckles and they begin to walk towards the whales. 'Aye. Best not.'

* * *

Back at the house, Luda looks for her children before fetching her camera. She finds Darcy sitting at the kitchen table with a pile of library books and a dirty plate by his elbow. He is studiously ignoring the group of girls pressing their faces to the glass behind him.

Luda waves an impatient hand at the girls and they dash away towards the beach. Towards the whales. Luda swallows.

'There's nothing you can do out there,' Darcy tells her. 'They're going to die.'

'They'll be fine,' she says. 'It's all going to be okay, Darcy.'

Darcy lifts an eyebrow and says nothing.

Luda braces herself. She does not like dying animals – has seen enough animals dying back home to last her a lifetime. She also does not care much for crowds and finds the blur of voices and figures across the usually empty island unsettling and almost frightening. Still, she collects her camera, switches lenses, and makes her way down to the edge of the sea. Above her, above all of them, the sky is the colour of whipped cream.

The whales breathe deeply and slowly. At this distance, Luda can make out the crosshatching of scars across their skin – the same eerie and impossible markings that streak the skin of everyone around them. It makes her feel nauseous and horrified, and she thinks of Tristan's witch markings. Around her, people are trying to fashion slings for the orcas, Min among them, wet to the waist.

A boy squats in the shallows by the largest whale's head. It's the first time Luda has seen him properly and, for a moment, she's entranced. He rests his gloved hands on the whale's face. He murmurs things that nobody else can hear. Periodically, the whale seems to stare right at him.

He has no scars on his skin. *Theo*, she thinks. *The foundling*.

Min stands back, wipes at her face. She stares at the smallest whale. Her breath, Luda can tell, is caught in a throat thickened with tears. Luda thinks of striding into the icy, shallow water. She thinks of pulling Min to her, even if Min quickly pushes her away, red with embarrassment. But Luda does not stride into the water.

She takes a deep breath and lifts her camera.

* * *

Later, when it's clear that there are more people than useful jobs and the whole thing has started to feel like an exercise in both voyeurism and futility, Tristan lets himself into the ghost house to look at the markings carved into the walls. He knows where each one is; he walks the ghost house in his dreams.

His obsession with the whale markings had been a little like falling in love; slowly, slowly and then all at once. He has remained consumed by them, without entirely knowing why. All he knows is that these markings seem more real and urgent to him than anything else in his life. He climbs the ladder into the loft and finds Darcy sprawled on one of the narrow beds, reading. 'Shit. Sorry,' says Tristan. 'I thought everyone was outside.'

Darcy shuts his book and springs into a sitting position. 'Who are you?'

'Tristan. You're Darcy, right? Your mum said I could come in. I've done a lot of research on the witch marks on the walls here and I'm very fond of them. Bloody shame about the orcas, isn't it?'

Darcy glances up at the rafters. 'I didn't realise that's what they were.'

Tristan, still on the ladder, rests his chin on the floor. 'Markings for protection. To ward off evil. These ones are unique. See the whale shape over the daisy wheel? I wrote an article on it.'

'As in a journal article?'

Tristan nods.

'As in a *peer-reviewed, academic* journal article?'

Tristan looks baffled. He nods again.

Darcy sets aside his book. 'You're the archaeologist Mum's sharing the office with.' He pauses for a moment, deliberating. 'You can come up, if you want.'

'I'll just stay here. I'm feeling a bit creepy now, to be honest.'

Darcy shrugs. 'Suit yourself.'

'Your mum says you read a lot,' Tristan says. 'She says you're very clever.'

Darcy's expression flickers. 'Don't all parents say that stuff about their kids?'

Tristan grunts. 'You'd be surprised. Given much thought to what you want to be when you grow up?'

They both know that they are making small talk because it is easier – more pleasant – than focusing on the whales beached outside the door, or being in this small space together in silence. 'No,' Darcy says. 'I haven't decided. Maybe medicine.'

'Your mother would skin me if she knew, but she left some of your old essays out.'

'Why would she have my old essays at her office?' There's something heavy about the words, something a little beseeching that Tristan doesn't understand.

'Oh, she had to send them through to your new school for your enrolment. Anyway, I read them. You know, you could do whatever you wanted. The world is quite literally your oyster.'

'Doubt she's read them.' Darcy flushes, just a little. He stares down at his hands.

'She's proud of you.'

Darcy begins worrying at the edge of the history book he's been reading.

Tristan nods at it. 'There's no way that's on the high school curriculum.'

'It's not.'

'Right, well. Williamson's an A-grade twat. I've got some better books at the office. Ended up delving pretty heavily into that stuff when I was teaching Scottish history back in the day. I'll get your mum to bring them home for you.'

'Really?'

'What else are you interested in? I've got reference books and articles coming out of my ears.'

Darcy pauses, studies Tristan and then appears to make his mind up about something. 'Come downstairs. I'll make you a coffee.'

Tristan gives the markings in the loft one last hungry look, and then he and Darcy climb down the ladder into the kitchen. Through the window, Seannay is bustling. People drink out of thermoses and press against the flanks of the stone ruins; a brief break from the brutality of the wind.

'Who's that?' Darcy asks, handing Tristan a mug of coffee.

Tristan shifts to better see out the window. Even though the island is teeming with people, even though most of those people are too far away to identify easily, Tristan knows who Darcy's talking about.

'That's Theo. The lad who washed up here. The selkie boy.' Tristan rolls his eyes. 'You'd have heard the stories, surely?'

'Shit.' Darcy cranes his neck. 'I remember watching reports about him on the news back home.'

'Well, that's him.'

Theo is still crouched by the head of the largest whale. From the house, the eye does not easily group him with the rest of the crowd. Like the whales, the eye is drawn to him, as though he is both immense and separate.

'Oh,' says Darcy, finally. They stare out the window for a little bit longer. Tristan is quite sure that Darcy is holding his breath.

* * *

The Marine Rescue Service arrives in the form of a single, exhausted-looking vet. Blood and tissue samples are taken and rushed through testing in the back of a van. Quickly, the whales are deemed ill. Euthanasia is the only option. They are small enough to shoot in the head. Three bullets in each are judged to be sufficient. These facts pass from person to person like a ripple. The crowd disperses. Tristan shivers. Min chews her lip until it bleeds. Darcy does not watch, wondering over his own apathy.

Would he have been chewing his lip like Min if he had led a different sort of life?

Still, he stays inside the house. He gives the whales this: one less set of eyes on them in their agony.

More officials arrive. Theo stays in the water as the rest of the crowds begin to retreat across the causeway. He murmurs in a voice that the wind snatches quickly away. Darcy comes out of the ghost house, his bootlaces undone, and watches with his arms crossed tightly over his chest. Theo is guided up the hill, away from the whales, by the officials. They cannot shoot the whales with someone sitting right beside them. For a moment it seems like Theo might resist and Darcy feels his breath catch. But then Theo's distant body softens and he walks up from the shoreline, pausing where it turns to turf. People glance at him; a few nod. He is at once both one of them and completely other.

'Theo, isn't it? Go inside and have a warm drink,' Luda says, camera still in her hand. Darcy can only hear her voice because the wind blows it straight to him. 'Go on.'

'I'm ...'

'Go.'

Theo looks a bit bemused, but he doesn't argue. For all his wildness, Darcy thinks that he seems used to Luda's brand of forceful mothering (when she remembers she has children, that is). He walks slowly towards the house, pausing a couple of metres from the doorway to turn back to the bay.

Darcy studies him. The foundling. He wears a ratty shirt and a pair of gloves. He's shorter than Darcy, but most people are – Darcy is well over six foot tall.

Theo's skin is luminous. He has no scars.

'Lucky they're small enough to shoot,' Darcy says. He swallows. He doesn't know why he's saying it; he knows from hard experience that it is the sort of information that people generally aren't interested in hearing. All he knows is that he wants this wild, luminous boy to look up at him. 'It can take days for them to die without intervention.'

Theo does look at Darcy then. Slate-coloured eyes that are wide-set. His expression is wary, as though he is not quite sure what Darcy's deal is. (Darcy's not sure what it is, either.)

Darcy glances down at the turf, speaking in a torrent. 'Euthanising the bigger ones is a problem. Bullets don't work. You can inject them with pentobarbital, but then everything that eats the flesh winds up dead too. And you can't bury the flesh, either. It stays in the groundwater.'

Darcy makes himself look up and Theo raises an eyebrow.

'They blow them up with explosives, sometimes,' says Darcy. 'But the clean-up is horrendous.'

Theo begins to walk away.

'It's good, is all I'm saying!' On the pebbled beach, the gun is cocked. Darcy winces at his own words; the horror of them and their jagged shape. He feels almost panicked by the sight of the luminous boy's retreating figure. 'They're lucky to be shot!'

* * *

Cassandra had not been lying to Wilhelmina. She has forgotten quite how many years she has been in this world, this body. She is, however, completely certain that she is the oldest inhabitant on the islands by many, many years. Her house is small, warm and sunlit. She has a steady stream of visitors and carers who help clean her body and her house and who, most importantly, talk with her. Her favourite visitor is Wilhelmina, who comes by sneakily, cheeks flushed. She always closes the front door quickly, as though reluctant for people to know that she's here at all.

It makes Cassandra want to laugh. That adolescent terror of what people will think.

Wilhelmina touches all the little things Cassandra has on her shelves and asks about them, and doesn't stop moving. Wilhelmina, who sometimes mentions whatever it is that Cassandra is thinking about.

It is Iris who tells Cassandra about the whales beaching themselves. It is during one of their usual strained visits, where they either don't talk or end up sniping at each other until one of them starts yelling. Sometimes both of them do.

Iris stares out the window. 'I wish I could've gone over …' But she can't bring herself to, not anymore. Neither she nor Cassandra have been to Seannay in many years. Sometimes Cassandra will watch the easy, energetic way young people get around in their young bodies and she will try to remember how it had felt to stride across the damp sand to Seannay in her own young body. She wishes that they would not take it for granted. She wishes that *she* had not taken it for granted.

Iris and her mother, August, had once lived on the tidal island. August had believed in spells and the goddesses and faeries and selkies and marvelled at the map of scars that revealed itself on people's skin. And Iris always by her side, tiny and wide-eyed. Cassandra can still hear the softness of August's voice, still see the way her hair would catch in the wind. 'When the whales used to get beached, Mum would drag circles around them with her athame,' Iris says now. 'She used to pray for their quick release.'

'Aye. I remember.'

'It was nonsense. All of it.' Iris's voice is suddenly furious. 'All she did was make them suffer.' A pause. 'I had nightmares.'

Cassandra sighs. These tired old paths they trudge again and again. 'I didn't know that.'

'I don't like crowds on Seannay. I don't … it's not a place for crowds.' Iris gives Cassandra a brightly cross look. She reaches into her pocket to touch her prayer beads.

'Animals don't have souls,' Iris mutters, not really speaking to Cassandra. 'And yet, *They all have the same breath, and man has no advantage over the beasts, for all is vanity.*'

Cassandra says nothing, and eventually the silence deepens into something almost calm. It is the most they can expect from each other. It never lasts for long.

'I hope Theo's not there,' Iris says.

'On Seannay, you mean?'

Iris fiddles with one of her cuffs. 'I don't want him around that family.'

'That family? They're *my* family, remember.'

'Barely.'

'Crivvens! Give it a rest, Muir! I'll admit that the photos were misjudged, but they're good people.'

Iris sniffs.

'Besides, Theo's not a bairn anymore. You can't tell him where he can and can't go.'

'Oh, can't I?'

'How much luck have you had with that recently?'

Iris sniffs again.

'It'd be good if he could make some friends.'

'There are plenty of fine lads in the kirk community who'd happily spend time with him if he'd just make the effort.'

'Happen he's decided they're not *worth* the effort, Iris.'

Iris glances at her then, a flicker of something nameless in her expression, then it disappears and Iris stands up. 'I'd best be off.'

Cassandra resists the urge to say something very rude to Iris. 'Take care.'

The whales. Cassandra does not think she's ever heard of one pushed successfully back into the sea. She has always had a soft spot for whales. *I'm sorry*, she thinks. *I'm so sorry.*

She watches the trucks trundle through the town, loaded with flesh and blubber. A shame, she thinks. Time was when that blubber would have been harvested for candles and oil. When that flesh would have been charred over peat fires and eaten from stone.

Not that she has ever had much of a taste for meat.

Even then.

Chapter Six

MARCH (THEIR FIRST YEAR)

The spring equinox falls on a day when Luda realises that Tristan's collection of academic journals and primary sources far outstrips any actual experience he's had in academia. A day when Theo wakes up and notices a black car parked across the road from his house. It is a day when Iris snaps at Father Lee over his choice of hymns but then offers him a plate of island cheese on oatcakes to make it right between them. It is a day when a man pushes past Luda on the street as she walks to the office, making her stagger, and does not turn to offer an apology. It is a day when Cassandra feels particularly old and particularly tired. A day when Ewan catches some very nice crayfish and walks off the docks in the evening whistling.

* * *

Min thinks about Harper and Sōta and Nico. Thinks that it is perhaps too much to expect that their friendship, so bound up in place, would weather this move of hers to the other side of the world.

The small island school is more rigorous than the one back home. She is mystified and impatient in most of her classes. Keen for something she doesn't have words for. Something that she has always felt will start *soon*, but when is soon? What if she gets to Cassandra's age and she's still waiting for things to begin? Her new teachers look a little bit bored by her – by her poor grades and fidgeting and the grimace she knows must be on her face. She knows Darcy would not have bored them. She is aware of the other students whispering about her. Her mother's photos; her accent; the fact that there is no subject she's good at.

At lunch she stands by her locker, staring in at the roll she'd bought on the ride up to the school with Darcy that morning. He had seemed unruffled, and this had distressed her, because he always seemed unruffled and she knew that he *couldn't* be unruffled.

And now she wishes that Darcy, unruffled or otherwise, were nearby so that she'd at least have someone to sit with. He'll be in the small hall, which seemed to double as a library and a gym and just about everything else. Min knows that there will be groups of younger students clumped near him – speaking in low, excited voices about his handsome face. He is unruffled about whether or not anyone is sitting with him. Min tries not to hate him for it; her free, unruffled brother.

'Your mother's the one who took those photos of the Reynolds lass,' a boy says, leaning against the lockers next to Min. He's got a mess of dark hair, very pale skin and eyes the exact colour of the brown guttering outside. In the corridor, they're eye to eye.

'Yeah,' Min says. She shuts the locker door.

He continues to study her and then gives a small smile. 'I'm Kole. Come sit down.' He turns and begins walking, as though there is no question that she will follow. Warily, she does, to a group of older students seated on benches by the sheltered edge of the hall. They'd be in their final year of school, she thinks. Older even than Darcy.

'Min, isn't it?'

'Yeah.'

He runs through his friends' names, but Min doesn't register them.

'It's nice to get a bit of new blood,' Kole says.

Min inspects his tone, his expression, for something predatory. Finding nothing, she sits herself down and bites into her roll.

'Your brother's just started too, right?' a girl asks.

Min nods.

The girl sighs. 'He's so gorgeous.'

Min is used to the underbelly of these sorts of comments: *and you are not*. She supposes they should bother her, but she's never been that troubled about how she looks. In this way, she is her mother's daughter – preoccupied with strength and grace and stamina while her mother is preoccupied with light and texture and juxtaposition.

Kole picks up the threads of a conversation she supposes they'd been having before he'd gone over to speak to her, involving people she doesn't know and terms she doesn't understand. If she hadn't had so much riding on getting through these first few weeks without embarrassing herself, she would have wept with longing for her friends back home.

But she is fierce, stubborn Min. And she will find her place here. She tilts her chin up, straightens her back. She pays close attention to the people around her. She makes a cutting remark or two, earning her laughter. She is aware that she needs to distance herself from her mother's photographs; from the Reynoldses. She has never had to distance herself from Darcy. With his face, he gets away with everything, even studying and fastidiously ignoring the other students.

Kole is the centre of this group – the others orbit him, glancing at him to gauge his reactions before they commit to their own. He is largely quiet, apparently enjoying their company, their stories. He lounges on the seat and smiles at them indulgently. At the end of lunch, his gaze drops to Min. 'You should come hang at mine after school,' he says. 'Everyone is.'

'Alright,' she says, and Kole leaves. Min looks around, suddenly desperate for anyone familiar. She realises only then that it's true; the foundling Theo does not come to school.

* * *

Alone in the ghost house that afternoon, Darcy stands in the bathroom with the door closed and peers down at his body. Blotched and purpling, he is numb with cold. The skin, the body he is inspecting, does not feel like his. He runs his fingers gently over the scars that he hasn't seen in years. The scars that he had thought were *gone*. Healed.

He and his body.

A mess of white marks on his knees and shins from the asphalt of his childhood schoolyard. Grazes from barbed wire and blackberries. Bites from the beaks of the stressed cockatoos and galahs they'd occasionally scooped into cages, to be studied by Luda before being set free at dawn. His face is sprinkled with fine white dots – chickenpox and pimples. Stardust.

For a moment, he lets himself imagine the wild, luminous boy he'd seen on the day of the whale stranding but has not seen since. He is still unsettled by the sudden and unfamiliar yearning that has flared in him – to be noticed, to be understood. Darcy is not the sort of person, has never been the sort of person, who cares much whether he is noticed or not.

This body, prickling with cold. He shrugs his clothes back on. He stuffs his numb fingers into the nooks of his armpits and goes out into the kitchen, lit by weak sunshine. He tenses as he hears the grating noise of a low-bellied car trying to get across the causeway. The scrape of metal against rock.

Darcy opens the door of the ghost house. As though summoned, Theo stands on the flagstones, red-cheeked and damp-haired. His head is turned towards a car reversing awkwardly back off the too-rough surface of the causeway. Only four-wheel drives can make it over and, even then, many are badly damaged in the process.

'Did someone drop you off?' Darcy asks, because the silence feels electric and thick.

Theo looks at him. Those searching, wide-set eyes. 'No. They followed me here.'

'Who?'

Theo shrugs, but the motion is jerky, as though it's not a movement he's had enough practise with. Darcy lets the door open fully. The sky has become dark with heavy rain, a curtain of it over the sea in the distance. Theo doesn't move. Up close his hair is flecked with silver strands and his eyelashes are very long. That impossible, unmarked skin.

Theo suddenly steps back. 'I should go.'

Darcy takes a deep breath, determined not to talk about whales being shot, or anything else ridiculous enough to drive Theo away. 'It's about to start pouring and that car's just going to follow you if you leave now.'

Theo hesitates, his eyes sweeping over Darcy's shoulder. 'Is anyone else home?'

'No.'

Finally, he steps through the door. Rain starts to fall and the world outside contracts.

'You don't ... Do you want a drink?' Darcy asks. He had very nearly said, *You don't have any scars.*

Theo shakes his head, staying by the front door. Darcy sits down at the table with his books, giving Theo time to settle. Darcy tries to read. The tenth time he tries to read the first paragraph on the same page, he gives up and puts the book aside.

'You're not what I expected,' he says. The words, once more, have come without thinking.

A fleeting expression of weariness. 'What were you expecting?'

Darcy frowns. 'I –'

'Someone's here.' Theo twists towards the door. A few seconds later, there's a knock on the other side of it. Theo's expression flares and gutters like a struck match.

'I won't answer it,' Darcy whispers.

Theo climbs up into the loft, as though he doesn't quite believe Darcy, or thinks the door will be worked open regardless. Darcy remains at the table, staring at the cover of his book. When the man (for Darcy can see, as the figure retreats, that it's a man) has left, Darcy stands, picks up his book and climbs the ladder to the loft.

Theo is lying on the floor between the beds, staring up at the slanted ceiling. The sound of the rain is very loud.

Theo turns his head, watching Darcy.

Even with Min in the loft, it has never felt so small before. Darcy opens the book to give himself something to look at that's not Theo. 'Do you get followed a lot?'

'I did. Not so much these days.'

'That must be tiring.'

Theo breathes out, almost a laugh. 'No shit,' he says, and the words are so teenage, so ordinary, that the air thins a little and Darcy feels like he can breathe again, despite Theo's scarless skin, despite the fact that he is fascinating enough to have people follow him.

Theo points up at the sloped ceiling with a gloved hand. People said that he had webbed fingers and scales. People said that he wore the gloves to hide them. 'What are those?' he asks.

'Witch marks.'

'Witch marks?'

'Protective magic. They're meant to ward off evil.'

'How?'

'Aren't you islanders meant to know all about this stuff?' Darcy intends for his voice to sound jocular; joking. But his throat is tight and the words come out scornfully.

Theo pulls a face and sits up. Another heave of rain on the roof, the rumble of thunder from across the sound.

'Sorry,' says Darcy. 'I shouldn't have … sorry.'

Theo says nothing for a while. He is angled towards the ladder but does not rise. He tilts his head, studying the markings. 'I've never been inside this place before.'

Darcy decides that it's probably safest if he speaks as little as possible. 'Oh.'

He is aware of Theo turning to regard the book with that quick gaze of his. They are silent, listening to the rain. And then, very slowly, without looking at Theo, Darcy begins to read aloud.

* * *

Min has a headache by the time school finally ends. She goes with Kole and his friends to Kole's house along the main street, where she watches them pass a cigarette around like it's a joint, while listening to the sort of old indie rock that her mother likes. Nobody has asked her anything; nobody says anything to her directly at all. But they make space for her, glance at her when they're talking, so that she knows she's included.

'Is that Father Lee?' Min asks, noticing one of many framed photos set on top of a doily-strewn sideboard. She feels a pounding building in her temples, her legs tense as though she needs to immediately rise and sprint away.

'Aye, the island's most cherished priest,' Kole says, his voice mild. He's lying on the couch with a hand propped behind his head.

'Friend of yours, is he?' Her tone is sharp and a couple of the others turn their heads to look at her more closely.

Kole laughs. 'I hate the fucker. My parents think the sun shines out his arse.'

'Guessing they wouldn't be mad keen on my family, then.'

'No,' he says, so happily that Min feels the click of things falling into place.

Later, she walks back to Seannay. She thinks of the whales. Sees them still, othered on land, a threading of marks across their skin. She knows that this is what the scars would look like, if she were somehow able to make them out on human skin.

She pauses at the front door of the ghost house, puzzled. In the still air, she can make out the sound of Darcy reading aloud from a book. She cannot make out the words, just the pleasant rise and fall of his voice through wood and stone and glass.

She opens the front door and the reading stops; there's the snap of a book being shut.

'It's only me,' she says reproachfully.

Darcy climbs down from the loft and, a moment later, another boy follows him. The foundling.

For a moment they're all still. Then Min steps towards Theo, entranced. She has never seen him this close before. Theo takes a step backward.

'I've seen you on the rocks out near the bay.' Min frowns. 'You're shorter than I thought you'd be.'

Theo glances at the door.

'This is my sister Min,' Darcy says. 'I'd say she's not normally this weird, but I'd be lying.'

Min scowls, but the ribbing fills her with a secret joy. How many months – *years* even – has it been since Darcy said something annoyed and brotherly like this?

'You must hate how much notice everyone takes of you,' Min says, opening a pack of biscuits and offering them to Theo. 'That's how you got so good at hiding, right?'

'Why are you home so late?' Darcy asks.

Min shrugs. 'Went to a friend's place.'

'Cassandra?' Darcy asks, not very kindly.

'No. And you're a dick.'

Darcy opens his book, reading silently now. Slowly, Theo relaxes. He sits down at the table and accepts a biscuit.

'So, where on the island do you live? In the town somewhere?' Min asks, chewing her way through one biscuit and then another.

'Aye. On the south side, down near the water.' He rocks his chair onto its back two legs.

'You were adopted, right? Is your family nice?'

'God, Min. Leave him alone.'

'Nice?' Theo's mouth quirks. The front legs of the chair land with a bang. 'I don't think anyone would describe Iris Muir as nice, but she raised me and I love her.'

'Diplomatic,' Darcy observes.

'We get along. Mostly.' Theo runs a hand across the surface of the table.

'Less diplomatic.'

'Does she homeschool you? I'd kill to be homeschooled.'

Theo shakes his head. 'I work on a couple of farms.'

'Min! No more questions. He spends his whole life getting grilled by people.'

Min scowls at Darcy and then glances at Theo. 'Sorry.'

'It's alright.' Theo swallows a mouthful of biscuit. 'Most people ask me if I think I'm a selkie – trying to work out how unbalanced I am, I think – or they ask where I came from, or what my hands look like.' He counts the questions on his fingers and then flexes them.

'They're not even the most interesting questions,' Min says, disgusted.

Theo raises an eyebrow. 'No?'

'No.' She frowns. 'Although I reckon that asking where you live, if your family's nice and if you're homeschooled isn't that great either, is it?'

'No,' Darcy snaps.

Theo reaches for another biscuit.

'Okay,' Min says. 'Forget all that. What do you love?'

He goes very still. 'Love?'

'Yeah. What do you love?' She puts on a slow, deep voice. 'What makes you feel whole?'

Darcy puts his head in his hands. 'Jesus, Min.'

'I … I don't know. Farm work.'

'I have goosebumps,' Min says flatly.

Darcy groans into his hands. 'Why are you like this?'

Theo stands up, inspecting one of the rafters above them. 'I love running,' he says, eyes fixed on the rafter. 'I love the sea. I love how the colours are always changing and changing and *changing*.' He leaps up, one hand catching onto a rafter. He hangs there for a moment, grinning.

Min turns to Darcy. 'What about you?'

'What about me?'

Once, she wouldn't have had to ask him. Once, she knew him well enough not to need to ask. 'What do you love?'

'Daydreaming about being an only child.'

Theo drops back onto the floor and sits down. The strangeness of the three of them, sitting in this strange, small house on this strange, small island.

'Have you been to the Wailing Cliffs?' Theo asks finally.

Min and Darcy shake their heads.

'They're on the northern side of Big Island. I'll show you,' he says. He stands up. 'I can show you now!'

'Maybe not *right* now,' says Darcy. 'What are they?'

And though he is speaking to both of them, it is Darcy that Theo keeps glancing at. Min notices Darcy *not* noticing Theo. She has never seen Darcy *not* notice someone quite so intently before; his ears reddening at the tips. If they had a different relationship she would tease him about Theo after Theo has left. But she is Min and he is Darcy, impossible, clever, awkward, closed-down Darcy, and she cannot imagine teasing him about his ears reddening over a striking boy with eyes the colour of slate.

If she thinks too hard about people, about how they think and feel, she becomes exhausted. She feels trapped. Instead, she thinks longingly of the Wailing Cliffs; of somewhere wild and powerful enough to reset her, somehow. She had watched the whales being dismembered. She had seen the blubber and blood and flesh. And she had felt hollowed and ferocious, as though by watching, she was tearing them apart with the sharp points of her own pearly teeth.

* * *

That night, Luda brings home books that Tristan thinks Darcy will like. Min talks of the Wailing Cliffs, of making friends (she omits their ages; their family's adoration of Father Lee; the fact that Kole has only befriended her because his parents would not approve). She does not mention Theo eating biscuits in the kitchen. She does not mention Darcy reading out loud to him, and neither does Darcy.

Later, Min rolls over in bed so that she's facing Darcy, curled up in a ball across the room. 'Darcy?'

'I'm sleeping.'

65

'I've worked it out.'

'Shut up, Min. It's late.'

'Theo's like an eagle. Or a fox. Something that isn't meant to be inside.'

'God, Min.' He sighs. 'Don't be like everyone else. He's just a person.'

'And I reckon people probably pick up on that and treat him like an animal without meaning to. And it must suck, being treated like an animal when you're not. Don't you think?'

Across the room, Darcy rolls towards the wall.

Min studies the shadow-flecked ceiling above her head. 'I don't like the marks.'

Another sigh. 'They're harmless.'

'What the hell would you know about them?'

'I know that they're to ward *off* evil, Min.' The shuffle of blankets. 'Like a horseshoe or something. They're just symbols to make people feel better. That's all.'

'Yeah, but still. If that's true, why are there so many?' She draws in an uneven breath. 'What did those people think that they needed so much protection *from*?'

Chapter Seven

MARCH (THEIR FIRST YEAR)

There is a new story being passed from person to person across the islands: that an investigative journalist from London is writing a book about the origins of Theofin Muir. That he is trying to find folk to interview. 'Oh no,' everyone says. 'Not us.' Their eyes gleam with the satisfaction of being asked; of being in possession of knowledge that an important Londoner deems valuable. Their eyes gleam even more at the righteous taste of their own refusals. Theo, it is understood, is one of them. The community closes itself like an oyster against this man and his questions. Nobody admits to speaking to him, even as his book of notes gets fuller and fuller.

* * *

Luda works in the evenings, drinks wine sometimes (often). She runs loops into the town and back or sometimes just around the sea-bitten edge of Seannay shore. She watches her children. Resists the urge, always, to ask them about their scars and to trace her finger over the fine fretwork of their skin.

What about this one? And this one? And this one? And this one?

Luda and Tristan walk to the cafe at lunchtime most days, Tristan whistling softly to himself, Luda thinking of the cliff photos and the island council and all of the other things, less easy to name, that she does not understand. Neither she nor Tristan mention the dead whales. Their scarred faces. They do not mention Joshua or the girl who died under the cliffs.

Tristan nods towards the window, where outside a man in a Barbour jacket is shaking someone's hand and heading towards the hotel near the council offices.

'That notebook of his gets any more full he'll need to borrow a wheelbarrow just to haul it around with him,' Tristan mutters.

'He's the one writing the book on Theo?'

'Aye. I suspect he'll get a lot of material here, too. He's quite ... unassuming up close. You want to help him out.'

'Hmm,' says Luda.

'Although, Father Lee has apparently told his congregation not to even *look* at the man, and Father Lee's very frightening, so I suppose it could really go either way.'

'It's a wonder anyone goes to worship,' Luda says.

'Oh, he's still coasting on Father Frank's coattails. Or habit – do the clergy wear habits? Anyway, Father Frank was here before Father Lee. He was very old when I knew him, but he was great. The congregation grew a lot in his time and I think a lot of folk keep turning up out of nostalgia. Or maybe it's misplaced optimism. I don't know.' Tristan appears lost in thought, poking at his sandwich.

'How long's Lee been here?'

'Four years, or thereabouts. He's threatened by Father Frank's reputation, I think. He's very reactive to things.'

'Like what?'

'Firstly, you.'

'Thanks for that.'

Tristan chews and swallows. 'Father Frank had quite an interest in the island witch trials and the charges and all that. Father Lee hates any mention of the witches. Anything, really, that might humanise or honour the women who were charged and executed.' Tristan pauses, thinks for a moment, and then adds, 'The trials themselves are a different story. He's quite fond of them.'

'Those women were reviled, weren't they?' Luda asks.

'Aye. If not at the beginning, then by the end.'

'It seems so impossible now, doesn't it? That something like that could have happened.'

Tristan's face flickers. 'You think so? Even after the reaction you've had to those awful photographs of yours?'

She winces.

'Sorry.' He brings a hand up to the back of his neck.

'I mean it,' she says quietly.

He sighs. 'It happened because they'd pissed off the wrong men, most likely. Seventeenth-century Father Lees. A lot of them would have been scapegoated. Some of them probably worked out that witchcraft was the only way they could make ends meet. Others may have just wanted to help people – there was a lot of blurring back then between what constituted witchcraft and what was simply herbal lore. Others probably just walked past a byre at the wrong moment. Who knows.'

Luda stares out the window, her chin propped in her hand.

'On a lighter note,' Tristan says, 'there used to be a woman on one of the islands who'd sell wind to sailors.'

'Wind?'

'Wind for fair voyages.' His mouth quirks. 'She'd fart into a bottle for them and they'd take it with them out to sea.'

'Liar.'

'It's true! Anyway, it didn't take much for a woman to be accused of witchcraft back then, and then she'd be tortured – sometimes for days. Not hard to see why so many admitted to whatever they were charged with. Dead livestock, failing crops. And once the interrogators had a confession, that was it. They were dead.' Tristan has a mouthful of coffee and grimaces. Luda has come to the conclusion that he doesn't actually like coffee, but isn't ready to admit it to himself.

Luda rubs her head. 'How did it start? The witch-hunting?'

'Small things and big things.'

'You're very obtuse, did you know?'

'Political upheaval, religious upheaval, poor crops, plagues. And then something tiny. A handful of herbs, a pebble in a pocket.' He looks at her. 'A photo.'

'Can you drop it already? I'm not being hunted.'

'Surely you can sense how much … disquiet … those photos have caused here. And imagine that disquiet happening on the back of the Reformation, hideously low education rates and hideously high rates of illness and superstition. It's pretty obvious how it happens, isn't it?'

'I suppose.'

'You're quite interested, aren't you?'

'What gave me away? All the questions?'

'No, I mean – you're *really* interested.' He considers her. 'You know what? I'm going to show you my witch box when we get back to the office.'

'Bloody hell, Tristan. Your *what*?'

He leans in, lowers his voice. 'The filing cabinet where I store all the papers around witchcraft and the witch trials. I'm not technically meant to be doing that work, as far as the council and funding bodies are concerned.'

Luda presses a hand to her heart, trying not to smile. 'I won't tell a soul.'

They tug on their jackets and head back out into the clean, quick air outside. Tristan studies Luda.

She frowns. 'What?'

He steps forward, pushes a stray piece of her hair behind her ear and then clears his throat. 'Nothing. I was just thinking that you look like a street urchin. Have you been formally introduced to a hair brush?'

Luda snorts. 'I truly cannot fathom how you're single.'

'Who says I'm single?'

Luda smirks and shakes her head. They begin to walk back to the office.

'Your hair,' Tristan mumbles.

'What about my hair, Tristan? It looks like a bird's nest? It's one tangle away from being a giant dreadlock?'

'No. Just, the light was hitting it … nicely.'

'Nicely.'

'Yes. Nicely.'

Luda laughs.

'What? *What?* I just paid you a compliment!'

Luda laughs harder. 'That was you *complimenting* me?'

He huffs and stalks ahead across the cobblestones. 'Tristan, sometimes I feel like you've been dumped here by aliens purely to brighten things up for me.'

'I brighten things up for you?'

She steps forward, feeling suddenly teenaged. Young. Fizzy with silliness and games. She smiles at him. 'Only when you say such lovely things about my hair.'

Tristan ignores her. Inside, they head to Tristan's side of the office. Tristan's witch box is tucked into the back corner, under a pile of papers meant for the recycling.

'Knock yourself out,' he says. 'They're not well organised, but there's a lot of material in there. I've gone through the kirk records and everything else I can find and then just printed out or scanned any other bits and pieces that I've stumbled across over the years. I think Iris has still got a few original sources in her office at the kirk.' He pulls a face.

'Council Iris?'

He nods. 'She's the reason that the trial records and paraphernalia have stayed in the kirk. It's funny, really. Mostly she and Father Lee go about things in unison. What Father Lee wants, Iris gets for him. One day she'll start acquiring the heads of heretics. Keeping the witch stuff is the only time she's ever really stood her ground. If Father Lee had his way, he'd have burnt the whole lot in a bonfire the day he took over the congregation.'

'What paraphernalia?'

He smiles. 'Free tomorrow morning? Around ten? I can show you.'

'Alright. Thanks.'

Luda pulls out armfuls of papers. She eventually finds reference to the women who'd met on Seannay. Five women had been charged – four had been executed. Their crime had been calling whales in from the sound and riding upon them like horses. A farmer who owned land near the sound brought the charges.

One of the women was his wife.

Luda sits back, rubs at her forehead. She is aware of Tristan, across the room, once again frowning and muttering at his computer, pecking at his keyboard with two fingers. Again, that fizzing delight at his indignation, at his petulance, at the way she sometimes senses that he's watching her, trying to work out what she's like.

* * *

Saturday dawns watery and slow. Light spills in from the window. It is the brightest morning the Managans have woken to since moving to Seannay. Min feels buoyed by it – the sun makes things feel more like home. The bright light, like so many other things, seems to irritate Darcy.

Across the table from Min, he scowls. 'We need a bigger place,' he says to Luda. 'If I have to listen to Min mouth-breathing for one more night I'm going to smother her.'

'How many times do we have to go over this? We can't afford it.' Luda studies her hands. Probably looking at those scars that Min can't see. 'This house comes with my job. We're staying here for as long as we can.'

Min ignores them. She finds herself searching the surface of the sea, as though if she watches – if she is *vigilant* – she might somehow be able to stop another stranding.

Darcy raises his voice. 'Do you know how weird it is to be sixteen and sharing a room with my *sister*?'

'If it bothers you that much, you're welcome to sleep on the kitchen floor and I'll have the bed.'

Darcy grimaces, picks up his mug of coffee. Outside, a gull calls.

'I'm going to have a look around the kirk this morning,' Luda says. 'You can come too, if you'd like. Tristan said he'd show us around, tell us about the witch trials.'

Min pulls a face. 'Why do you want to know about *that*?'

'It's interesting, don't you think?'

'It's depressing.'

'They started building the kirk a thousand years ago. It was under Norse rule, then.'

Min turns back to her toast.

Luda looks at them both. 'So, do you want to come?'

Darcy shakes his head.

'But you love that sort of thing.'

He narrows his eyes. 'No, I don't.'

'Well, suit yourself. Min?'

Min suspects that if she declines, her mother will perhaps not go to the church by herself. Instead, she will go outside for a walk where she will be crowded by thoughts of Joshua and then come back smelling of wine. Or else she'll come back all flushed and frenetic, ready to take more photos like the ones of Allie Reynolds. Perhaps it is something Min is imagining, but she finds herself nodding because Darcy won't. She finds herself nodding for the both of them. Darcy watches her with a sour expression. For a moment Min's breath catches with anger and she wants to hit him; pinch him; mark him. For making her feel small. For making her feel young and ridiculous for agreeing to go to a church with their mother on this still and milky day.

She looks at his face, wishing that she could see the scars Cassandra had mentioned. It would be particularly soothing in moments like these to be able to make out the ones she'd been responsible for over the years. The scratches and slaps and shoves and wrestling matches where she managed to catch him by surprise. She grits her teeth, gets dressed and meets their mother by the pitted front door.

* * *

The church is cold and still when they reach it. Min feels a prickling of something like winter rain down the skin of her back. The church back home in Narra had been a bustling building of blond brick near the petrol station and feed store. It had smelt of flowers and sugar and varnish. In Sunday school, they had rolled dough and talked about Jesus.

Luda hesitates at the entrance, pretending to examine the wood of the door, until Tristan appears from inside. 'You must be Min,' he says, and smiles, but his eyes shift quickly back to Luda. Min notices this; feels an odd warmth towards this man, who seems capable of recognising her mother's veiled panic. 'Think of the kirk crowd like a pack of wolves. They sense blood, so don't show them your wounds,' he says to Luda.

'My wounds?'

'Keep your chin up, avoid eye contact, walk with purpose, and chances are that they'll leave you alone.'

They follow Tristan inside the church. Luda immediately drifts towards a stained glass window bearing the words *Fiat Lux*.

'Let there be light,' Tristan tells them. 'If we don't move, Lee might not notice we're here,' he adds in a low voice.

'Funny.' Luda leans closer to the window.

Min wanders further down the aisle, where there are large stones propped up against the walls. Gravestones. There are skulls carved onto many of them – grinning and eyeless. When did we stop acknowledging death this way? She thinks of her father's funeral – all beige colours and soft music and sandwiches with dry corners. She didn't even see the body after the police came and took it away. The whole process had been so clean and neat and *tidy*. It had made all the messy, complex emotions she had feel completely out of place.

She reaches out and touches the cold stone.

'Tristan?' she calls.

He lopes over, arms crossed over his chest against the chill. 'Hmm?'

'What are these?'

'They used to be on the floor, but the stones were getting worn down by people walking over them, so they got put up onto the walls.'

'And the bodies?'

'Exhumed. Well, some of them. Don't think there's any way they could have got them all out.'

Min stares down at the floor. She shifts her feet backward and then forward again.

'Ah,' says a small, grey-haired woman stepping out of the custodian's office. 'We haven't officially met. Mon, isn't it?'

'It's Min.'

'Right.' The woman smiles. 'Come to worship, have you?'

'This is Iris,' says Tristan in a bored voice. 'She's on the local council. In her spare time she likes to track down sinners and convert them. Her main redeeming quality is her appreciation for island history.'

'It's lovely to meet you,' Iris says to Min, without really looking at her. Her gaze is fixed, quite coldly, on Luda. Min recognises the look – she thinks of it as the cliff look. That expression of disapproval that she hopes will eventually fade.

'Let it go, Iris,' Tristan says, following her gaze. 'Luda thought she was doing the right thing.'

Iris's expression hardens. 'Has a writer been in touch with you?'

Tristan scratches his chin. 'Any particular sort of writer?'

She looks at him. 'The one nosing around Theo,' she hisses.

'Oh! That one! Yes, he has.'

'And?'

'I told him to fuck off.'

Iris exhales through her teeth. 'Good. That's good.' She looks at Min, expectant.

'He hasn't been near me,' Min says. 'But there's no way I'd talk to him.' She is about to add that she and Theo are friends, but then thinks of the expression on Iris's face as she'd studied Luda. *Cliff look*. Min stays quiet.

'Still okay for me to borrow those books, Iris?' Tristan asks.

'I said so already, didn't I?'

Min follows Tristan across the transept. Luda stands a little way off, still gazing up at the windows. 'Why does Iris care so much about that writer?' Min asks.

Tristan raises an eyebrow. 'She adopted Theo, that's why.'

'Oh.' Min's footsteps slow. The strangeness of prim, sharp-edged Iris raising wild Theo. She remembers now that Theo had mentioned Iris's name when she'd met him in the ghost house. *We get along. Mostly.*

'Oh, I know,' says Tristan quietly. 'It's fascinating, isn't it? Can't see that much of her's rubbed off on him, though. Thank God.'

'How does he stand her?' Min asks.

'You'll have to ask him.'

Luda joins them, her shoulders hunched.

'C'mon, we'll start upstairs,' Tristan says, tilting his head pointedly towards Iris.

They begin climbing the tight, narrow sandstone staircase. *Kirk*, Min thinks. Not a church. A *kirk*.

'The women accused of witchcraft were put on trial here in the kirk,' Tristan says, as they reach the first floor. 'This is the dock.'

Min stays near the stairs, not liking how close her mother is to the wood of the dock; not liking how Luda reaches out a hand to touch it.

'And this is the hangman's ladder from the seventeenth century,' says Tristan, nodding at a double-width ladder leaning against the sandstone wall. 'Any idea why it's worn on one side more than the other?'

Luda's mouth twitches. 'Oh, is this the official kirk tour? I didn't realise. Should we be paying you?'

Tristan shakes his head. 'Such ungratefulness.' Min closes her eyes and wills herself outside. She can't. She is here. In the kirk. In her body, always. Being pushed up close – too close – to death. She is so sick of death.

'Well, the story goes that the hangman climbed up and back from the gallows platform. The condemned woman only climbed up. So the left side therefore got twice the wear.'

Luda spends a long time gazing at the dock, the hangman's ladder. She spends even longer lingering near the manacles that had bound the women. Min feels as though she's going to vomit.

They walk the perimeter of the upper floors of the kirk for a long time, Tristan pointing out windows and stone and rafters, until the kirk seems less a whole thing than it does a roughly stitched patchwork, constructed over a thousand years.

The kirk is empty when they return to the ground floor. Min and Luda follow Tristan to Iris's office. He begins rummaging in the bookshelves, passing Luda book after book until her arms are trembling. She sets them down and flips one open to a sheet of recorded denouncements.

'The witch hunts here started with a lass called Mary,' says Tristan. 'She was accused of having carnal relations with the devil at one of the farms on the south of Big Island. She had a deformed babe shortly after. Historians have pieced together that it was likely her father who raped her. But during interrogation – torture – she admitted to sleeping with the devil. Memory plays strange tricks when we're terrified or hurt. Happen she really *did* think she'd had sex with the devil.'

'*Unknown woman,*' Luda reads. She clears her throat. '*Unknown woman, accused of charming whales and children, and summoning storms. Hanged and burnt. Unknown woman accused of charming whales and promising fruitfulness in nature. Hanged and burnt. Unknown woman accused of charming whales and summoning a procession of the dead. Hanged and burnt. Unknown woman accused of charming whales and summoning a procession of the dead. Hanged and burnt.* They don't even give their names?'

'No. Not always. Recordkeeping wasn't the best to begin with back then, and a lot's been lost and damaged since.'

Luda shuts the book. 'Why are they all accused of charming whales?'

'Ah,' says Tristan. He takes the book from her. 'These are the Seannay witches. They were all executed on the same day, see?'

'Seannay witches?'

'The four women who were executed for calling the whales in from the sound. There's not a lot known about them beyond that.'

Luda frowns. 'What does promising fruitfulness in nature even mean?'

'That there'd be good crops, fine stock; that kind of thing. That's what makes these stories so bloody sad. So often they were executed over something so innocuous. Something so *good*.'

Luda nods, loading the books into her backpack.

'I'll show you Haaken's Hole, then we should get out of here – choir practice starts soon and they're good but they're *loud*.'

'What's Haaken's Hole?' Min asks, and immediately wishes that she had instead answered, *No, thanks*.

'It's where they kept the women accused of witchcraft before their trials,' says Tristan, walking slowly into the west transept. 'Only kirk in Britain with its own dungeon.'

He shows them the dark, narrow hole cut high into the wall and Min rears back. Tristan arranges the ladder and gestures to it.

'How awful,' Luda says, but she sounds fascinated. She climbs up to the mouth. She leans in, touches some of the stone. Min wants to drag her away from it. She thinks of the dead under the floor and takes a very deep breath.

'Is that a witch mark?' Luda asks, pointing to an *M* carving, oblivious to Min, her barely contained panic.

'Just a basic one, invoking the power of the Virgin Mary.'

'Wait,' says Min, frowning. 'Why would the witches make these markings here? Weren't they meant to be marks *against* witches? Why would witches make them?'

'Marks against *evil*, not marks against witches,' says Tristan gently. 'Marks against bad spirits. The women held here weren't bad people, Min. They would have invoked any protection they could.'

'Would the Seannay witches have been locked in here?' Luda asks.

'Suspect so.'

'How long would people have been locked in here for?'

'Weeks, sometimes.' Tristan's expression darkens. 'A few died waiting for trial. Some were stripped off before they were locked in. There's not a lot of air or warmth in there. And there's a drop-down door that would have left them in the dark.'

Luda shudders and steps back. She meets Min's watery eyes and reaches for her.

Min thinks that the red and yellow sandstone walls look like blood on sand. She wants to be outside, on the island. She wants to be staring at the photo of Father Lee in Kole's lounge room. She wants to be with Darcy. More, she wants to be with Harper and Sōta and Nico. She wants to be with Bramble her pony, with the dogs. Chasing chickens, the sound of a goose. Her dad. Her *dad*.

Anywhere but in here.

'You okay?' Luda murmurs, reaching out.

Min shrugs her away. 'They were alone, weren't they?'

'Well,' says Tristan, clearly puzzled by her distress, 'some of them. Yes.'

* * *

While Min and Luda wander the narrow passages of the kirk, Darcy puffs breath onto glass, traces one bird, then another. He thinks that the scars are like this. That the light here is just like a puff of air, warmed with heartsblood. Not that he can see them.

He wishes Theo would turn up.

He tries to read. He stares out the window. His heartbeat quickens when there's a knock on the door. He rises and opens it.

It's not Theo.

A tall, well-built man wearing a Barbour jacket waits on the flagstones. 'I was hoping to catch you!' the man says, his voice very loud. His accent is not from the islands.

Darcy stares at him. The man's face is flecked with old acne scars, a few scratches. The scars, Darcy thinks, of someone who has coasted through life. The man has the face of someone who has never been properly hurt. 'What do you want?'

The man is looking at him very intently, the way people often look at Darcy. Darcy waits for him to finish.

The man swallows. 'My name's Carter McGregor. Could I come in for a minute?'

'Not allowed to let strangers in. Sorry.'

Carter looks over Darcy's shoulder. 'Fine. I'm in the early stages of doing research on the boy that washed up on the beach ten years ago. Is he here?'

'No.' Darcy glances at the notebook, already out and in Carter's hand, bound with twine and full of notes and snippets of things that nobody here will admit to telling him. He hesitates. 'What sort of research?'

'It's for a book.'

'Have you talked to his family about it?'

Carter laughs. 'Have you met his foster mother? God. She makes Margaret Thatcher look like a kindergarten teacher.'

Darcy says nothing.

'You're friends with him, aren't you?'

'No,' says Darcy. He'd read to Theo for hours in the loft. Sometimes he's sure he's imagined the whole thing.

'Must have heard some interesting stories about him, though?'

'Not really.'

Carter studies Darcy with bright interest. 'Well, I was wondering if you could keep an eye out for him. Let me know if he turns up.'

Darcy crosses his arms. 'You'd better go.'

'Wait …'

Darcy shuts the door and slides the bolt. He breathes out, feeling shaken. Feeling how easily he could have slipped into sharing all the useless, precious things he thought and knew about Theo. Who he did not know at all; who somehow already felt familiar to him.

* * *

It is one of Father Lee's favourite tricks; turning up at Iris's little house by the water when he knows that she will be out. He always has some sort of vague excuse – dropping off notes, picking up a book.

Really, though, Theo knows that Father Lee has come for him.

Iris is sorting things at the kirk, as she often does on Saturday mornings. Theo is pulling shoes on, bannock in his mouth, watching a redshank prod its beak into the sand across the road. He is going to run to the barrows this morning and then maybe the Wailing Cliffs. Movement out the window. There is Father Lee's bullish form, his meaty hands unlatching the gate. His surprisingly short-strided walk up to the front door.

Theo groans around his bannock. He considers not answering, but Father Lee has a knack for knowing when he's being ignored. The last thing Theo wants is Iris coming home in a mood and tearing shreds off him for not showing Father Lee enough respect. (It has happened before. More than once.)

A thick-fisted knock on the front door. A brief pause. Another knock.

Theo kicks his shoes back off, fishes the bannock out of his mouth, and opens the door. 'Father,' he says.

Father Lee strides inside. 'Brought Iris the outgoings report from the last council meeting,' he says, smacking a small exercise book down on the hallway table.

Theo presses his hands into his pockets and then trudges into the kitchen after Father Lee, who is already sitting at the table.

'I just came from the Reynoldses,' he says. 'They're in a terrible way.'

'Oh, aye.' Theo puts on the kettle, not bothering to hide his pissy expression.

'How are you, Theofin?' Father Lee asks, hands folded on the table in front of him.

Theo knows from experience that Father Lee will extend his visit if he knows that he's keeping Theo from other things. 'Fine. You?'

Oh, Iris would scold him for that if she heard! He breathes out.

'Not so bad,' Father Lee responds. 'I was speaking to your mother the other day, and we were thinking it might be time for you to try coming to worship again.'

We. Aye, in those early days Iris had been keen for him to come to worship with her. But after that awful night when he was young, she had let it go. This was before Father Frank had retired. He'd told Iris not to worry – that there were many ways to worship the Lord. That Theo would find his own way and come to the kirk when he was ready.

Theo fucking misses Father Frank.

Father Lee watches him from across the table, large hands still folded. He's gelled his hair into spikes. Theo can't work out why.

'No, thank you.' Theo pauses. 'Father.'

The kettle whistles and Theo makes Father Lee a sickly sweet tea, adding lots of milk so that it is not too hot to drink. He tosses a bannock onto a plate and shoves it across the table. He leans against the sink with his hands on his head, feeling trembly with restlessness and trying hard not to show it.

'Your mother is a senior member of the kirk community,' Father Lee says, tea cupped cosily in his hands. 'When you were a bairn, not attending worship didn't matter so much. People were willing to give you time to adjust to things here. But now that you're nearly grown, people are talking and it undermines your mother.'

It undermines you, Theo thinks. Undermine. He had thought it was a fun name for a farm when he'd first heard the word. If his absence at services still bothers Iris, she has not mentioned it to him. And Iris is known for her bluntness.

'I can't …' He swallows, glances down, wills Father Lee to drink his tea faster; to eat his goddamn bannock. 'I can't stand being indoors with crowds, Father. I'd throw up and pass out and ruin the whole service.'

Father Lee pales visibly at the mention of vomit in his kirk. 'Surely we could work on that.'

Theo takes a deep breath. The trick, he's learnt, is to act as though this conversation is happening for the first time. 'The thing is, Father …'

'Aye?'

'The thing is … well … There was that night … and I haven't been able to face going back inside the kirk since then. That doctor I saw said I might never be able to. That I was going through a … a particularly vulnerable time, and that it has … unfortunately … become a … formative experience.'

'I've also heard that you've been spending time with the Managans.'

'Barely, Father.' He makes his tone sullen and a little bit petulant. He'd heard gossip about the Managans before that day he'd knocked on the door of the ghost house – the cliff photo, the father's death, the distant relation to Cassandra. He had watched them himself from the rocks and the ruins, as they came and went and bickered and were silent. He likes the way Min notices small rocks and pebbles and the light on the water, the same way he does. He likes the way Luda watches her children, even when they don't notice her. Especially when they don't notice.

And Darcy.

He had expected someone who looks like that to be an arsehole (had suspected Darcy might be, after that first meeting on the day of the stranding). But then he'd somehow read to Theo for hours without making Theo feel like an idiot. His voice, Theo has decided, is as hypnotic as his fine-boned face, with that mess of light brown hair and faint frown.

'They're not a good family for you to be spending time with, Theofin. A bad influence. Your mother's worried.'

Theo loves Iris, but she is not his mother. She has never claimed to be. He has always been Theo and she has always been Iris and he belongs to her, but she has never been his *mother*. Does Father Lee really think that calling someone a bad influence is going to stop him from seeing them?

'I'll be sure to let them know next time I see them,' Theo says.

Father Lee surveys him gravely. Then he settles back in his seat, as though preparing for a long, long stay.

* * *

In the kirk, Min rears back from Haaken's Hole. Luda does not say anything. She always seems to say the wrong thing when her children are upset. She gives Min's arm a pat. She peers up at the fine fretwork. She squints at the stained glass. Oh, she had come because the job had landed in her lap, because she thought it might be nice to see this place where her great-grandparents came from. But it is here, in this crypt of a church, that Luda feels the lilting sensation of something that has not yet happened. A quickening. *I am here. I am here. I am* here.

PART TWO

Chapter Eight

MAY (THEIR FIRST YEAR)

Late spring and Big Island bursts into a flurry of gorse and wildflowers. The rocks along the shorelines gleam like seal hides in lengthening sunlight. People linger on the streets to talk and to laugh, bowed against bright wind. There is still talk of the man writing the book; talk about how he seems to know people's names; their connection to Theo. He's clever, people tell each other. He comes at them sideways. He asks them about the old stories of the selkies. He asks them about seals and tides and whales and whispers. People try to outdo each other with the volatility of their family's refusals until it seems that Carter has been tossed out of boats and set alight and punched in the face countless times. Still, he lingers. Still, he comes at them sideways. Something that is known without words on the islands: that if a selkie goes into the water without their skin, they will die.

* * *

Sometimes, while at school, Darcy will see a flicker of Theo, through a classroom window. Seeing Theo is like catching sight of a seabird, shocking against cloud and sky.

But Theo never comes into the school grounds, even as he occasionally wanders their perimeter, pausing here and there, examining things that Darcy can't even guess at.

In this way, Darcy will occasionally miss whole chunks of class. The accents here can easily drift over him if he doesn't pay careful attention. The words turn themselves inside out and become tidal.

As Darcy watches, Theo jumps up onto a very high fence that blocks this road off from the main street. He stands, buffeted by the wind, and then drops lithely down onto the other side, out of sight.

Darcy lets out an uneven breath.

* * *

More and more often, Theo stands outside the school grounds as the final bell rings, waiting for Darcy and Min. Today, Darcy stays back late and it is Min who spots Theo, standing motionless at the entrance to one of the back lanes into town.

Although she is with Kole, is meant to be going with him to get some drink from the older brother of someone who had once gone to the island school, she hesitates. Stops. She wants to go with Theo. She gestures for him to come, pointing towards the town. He shakes his head once, disappears down the lane.

'Hey, I'll need to dash in a bit,' she says to Kole. He's meeting up with his friends soon anyway. The only part of this afternoon that will not be tedious is the part happening right now.

He looks confused and she's not sure whether it's because he can't fathom her not spending the whole afternoon with him, or whether she's accidentally used an unfamiliar phrase with her flat, Australian accent.

He looks at the laneway where Theo had been standing.

'People ask me things about him all the time,' she says, as they begin walking again. 'Like I should know all of his darkest secrets just because we hang out sometimes.'

She likes Kole best when they're alone. He softens, and moves more slowly. He is more likely to think before he talks rather than go straight for a spiteful joke.

Kole shrugs. 'Well, he doesn't really spend time with anyone. Never has. You and your brother are the first.'

'Do you know my brother's name?' A few weeks ago, she would not have asked, but since meeting Theo, she has begun to feel braver. Being alone, on the outer, feels less scary with both him and Darcy already there.

Kole glances at her. 'What?'

'My brother. Do you know his *name*.'

He flushes. 'What? Why?'

She stops walking. 'Do you know it or not?'

'What's that got to do with anything?'

'Because I know that your mum's called Lily and your dad's called Patrick. I know that you tell people you're allergic to meat, even though you actually just don't like the idea of eating animals. I know you lost a tooth playing football and you like the colour orange and you're mean when you're impatient. I know you want your parents to take more notice of you, and you think that hanging out with me is a good way to get them to do that.' She takes a breath. 'Now, what's his name?'

He begins to walk again, ears pink. She thinks that it's over; that she's relegated herself to the edges of the social world on the islands; then he speaks, still facing away, his words muffled.

Min swallows. 'What?'

Kole blows a breath out. 'I *said*, his name is Darcy.'

* * *

From the laneway, Theo goes to the barrows on the far side of Big Island. It's a place he has not yet taken Min; a place that is still his alone. Darcy rarely comes with them when they go tramping across the expanse of earth between one sea and the next. Instead, Darcy reads to him, in the loft of the ghost house with its crosshatching of spells, or else on the rocks by the water of the bay. Normally, the barrows soothe Theo as much as being on Seannay does. He sometimes feels so ragged in the town that he digs his nails into the palms of his hands and can't sleep deeply enough to ever feel properly rested. Today the steep grassy mound with its belly of crypts is not calming; whatever magic he usually finds there eludes him. It remains grass and wind and hidden bone. Another sort of magic, but not the sort he craves.

After, he trudges around the back of the hostel as he passes through the town on his way home. He wonders if Darcy might one day teach him to read – whether Darcy might be able to do this without making Theo feel small and worthless. Or whether it would be worse, somehow, if it were Darcy teaching him.

He hears footsteps.

Hands on his body, the smack of the cobbles against his cheek. He gasps and rolls over. Would fight, except that there are too many hands. A knee presses down on his chest and he swears and bucks, but the knee doesn't move. He thinks, wildly, that he will kill them. *Kill them.*

The men – so young, more like lads – laugh. Still, all larger than him; their breaths thick with the raw scent of spirits. The one that Min hangs out with (if Theo asks her why, she just shrugs). Theo knows better than to walk this way on a Friday afternoon, when a lot of them buy sixpacks of ale and bottles of island whisky to drink at the hostel (cheaper, everyone knows, than the Blue Fin). Theo had forgotten the day of the week. He had been thinking about words.

Splayed on the cobbles. Raw breath. They smell of diesel and fishing bait. His gloves are pulled off and tossed aside, his webbed fingers are splayed out until the skin between them burns. Their laughter gives way to quiet as they study the fine, translucent webbing between his fingers. He feels his cheeks flush. He is aware of the weight of the knee still on his chest. He is aware of his heart pulsing through his ears, his head, his limbs.

'No scales,' someone says, sounding disappointed.

'How freaky's the webbing, though?' someone else breathes, touching it with a damp finger. Theo wants to throw up.

He manages to work one arm free and he immediately swings it as hard as he can into the space above him. He makes contact with a shin, a stomach. There's a grunt and then the knee on his chest presses down still harder. Breathing immediately becomes an effort.

He should not have swung at them. The quality of the air changes, becomes more charged. A pause as something unspoken passes between the men (the lads) above him.

A snigger. Then there are hands on his belt buckle. 'Let's see what else is webbed.'

Theo forces himself to draw in one ragged, strained breath and then another. His whole body begins to tremble with rage. Fear. He will kill them. He will dig his hands into their flesh. He will –

'Hey!' A new voice. Sharper. Older. There is a scuffle, the sound of the men swearing, spitting. The knee disappears from Theo's chest. The sound of running feet.

Theo lies gasping for a moment. Air. *Air.* Then he sits up, ready to run – whether towards them in a frenzy of fury or away from them to safety, he can't yet tell. He's suddenly overcome with dizziness and presses his hands to his head, wincing at the pain in his cheek.

'That happen a lot?' the man asks.

'Sometimes.' Theo looks up at him. It's the man from the black car. The one, Theo is sure, who came knocking when he was in the ghost house. The man holds a hand out. Theo stands by himself and pulls his gloves back on. 'I can take two or three, but not that many.'

'I'm Carter.'

'I know.'

The man nods. 'Can I give you a lift?'

Theo starts walking. Stops. His head throbs; his feet feel very far away from the rest of him. His head must have hit the cobblestones harder than he'd realised. He rubs a hand over his eyes, trying to steady himself.

'Get in,' says Carter, gesturing to his car, and Theo does.

'Do you need the hospital?'

'No.' Theo rests his head against the window. He crosses his arms over his chest. 'Just take me home.'

Carter starts driving and Theo notices – but finds he does not care – that Carter hasn't bothered to pretend he does not know where Theo lives.

'What do you want?' Theo asks.

'To drive you home.'

'What *else* do you want?'

'I'm sure you've heard. I'm writing a book about you. Well, it's largely around media frenzies and the way falsities take hold. I'm sure you can see how your story fits in with that.'

Theo shakes his head. He is aware that Carter doesn't speak to him in that slow, loud voice that so many people use when they talk to him.

'I want to interview you.' Carter pulls up outside the house and neither of them move.

'I don't do interviews.'

Carter looks at him. 'Aren't there things you want to say? Things you want people to know? This is your chance, Theo.'

The way Carter says his name. Like they're friends. Like he *knows* Theo. 'I don't do interviews.'

Carter sighs. He stares out through the windscreen, his hands still on the wheel. 'I'm going to publish the book anyway. Just so you know.'

'I don't care.' Theo opens the door and pauses. A shudder passes through him – the future he had only narrowly avoided. Exposed and dizzy on the damp cobblestones; his gloves still out of reach. 'Thanks. For stopping them.'

* * *

Cassandra drinks whisky and pins a brooch to Wilhelmina's jumper. Iris watches, her ankles neatly crossed, a load of Cassandra's freshly purchased medicines on the table between them.

'You should hear the way Kole's voice changes when he thinks one of his mates is around. He makes himself sound …' Wilhelmina frowns.

'Oafish?' Cassandra offers.

'Yes! Yes, oafish. But when it's just us, we get along. We're *friends*. But I don't want to be friends with the person he is when his mates are around. You know the graffiti on that old dancing class advertisement near the newsagency?'

'No,' says Cassandra.

Iris clears her throat. 'I believe it involves a penis and a speech bubble.'

'Yeah – that one. Anyway, we saw it the other day after school and he said it was gross and sexist and everything. And then I heard him with his mates the next day and they were pissing themselves over how funny it was.' Wilhelmina looks down at a glittery dolphin brooch. 'This is terrifying, Cass.'

Iris almost smiles. 'Isn't it?'

'Alright, aye. That's enough out of you two.'

Wilhelmina glances at Iris. Cassandra can sense Wilhelmina's wariness; her curiosity. It blooms purple and cream. Theo. Wilhelmina is aware of how much he loves Iris; how different they are.

'Don't let the prayer beads fool you,' Cassandra says to Wilhelmina. 'Iris knows that our Father Lee is an unholy arse.'

'Cassandra, don't.'

'Well, he is.' Cassandra takes the dolphin brooch off and pins a cactus with dangly arms and sunglasses in its place.

'I'll admit his last –' Iris breaks off. Flickers of Father Lee's smug face, his large hand closed over something. Patting his pocket.

'What's he done now?'

Iris waves a hand. 'Och, nothing. It's nothing. He's just trying to help Theo get over his kirk aversion.'

'How this time?'

'He found a piece of sea glass Theo's very fond of and he's insisting that Theo pick it up from him at the kirk. That's all.'

'*Found* it, did he? In Theo's room? In his wallet?'

'Don't. He's trying to help.'

'Obviously, you're going to get the sea glass back and tell Marcus where he can shove his –'

Iris presses her fingers to her temples, gives Cassandra a look that communicates all of the arguments they've had over the years. Cassandra's impatience and temper; Iris's rigidity and stubbornness. It's a cloudy thing, their history. At once blurred and perfectly clear. Exasperation and necessity and love. *Please. Don't.*

Wilhelmina takes the cactus brooch off. She still has a sparkly parrot and a navy-and-cream rowboat. She begins to describe the colour of the seaweed she'd seen on the rocks. Cassandra finds herself charmed by this; how much attention Wilhelmina gives to the words she uses to describe the colour of the sea. She pauses, often, to think of the best words to use. As she inspects them, an impression flares of words skittering like silver fish, startled by the fall of a shadow.

'Like ... flagstones that aren't gleaming wet, but more than damp. That sort of soft, deep grey.' A pause. 'It makes the water look warmer than it is, somehow. It makes the cold a shock.'

Cassandra finds that the house already feels a little hollow in her absence. She relishes the raw edges. She had long thought herself past missing anyone.

Chapter Nine

MAY (THEIR FIRST YEAR)

It is a truth universally acknowledged on the islands that if a man has too much ale and he hurts someone, he cannot really be blamed. What man hasn't drunk a few too many ales with the lads and had things get out of hand? It is also a truth universally acknowledged that if a woman drinks too much ale and is the one being hurt, she has really brought the whole thing on herself.

* * *

Theo can't stop thinking of the damp finger touching the webbing on his hands. His cheek aches for days. He reaches for his sea glass over and over. His hand hits the bottom of an empty pocket.

Father Lee had told him to come and collect the sea glass at worship on Sunday. Theo fantasises about setting his maroon station wagon on fire.

Instead, he hangs out by the hostel, his body braced against the loud voices, the jokes he does not find funny, the occasional sound of piss hitting the walls of the alleyway nearby.

A couple of the quieter residents nod at him, smile. They carry wrapped packages of fish and chips or a bag of things to cook up in the communal kitchen. Theo nods back, heart pounding. He waits.

He remembers their faces. When he sees them again, they seem so much smaller than they had when he'd been pinned to the cobblestones. They appear in ones or twos. Freckled faces; windburnt faces; faces thick with acne. Five of them. And Kole, who Theo will find after. Or perhaps not. Perhaps he will leave Kole, because of Min. Because Min would not want him hurt. Probably.

The fifth one keeps him waiting. It's getting cold and his hands are throbbing, his wrists tingling in that way they tingle when he's spent too many hours working on his strange, formless drawings. The fifth one is larger than the others. He approaches warily, his fists clenched, his nostrils flared.

It does not help him.

Theo straightens a moment later, breathing hard, wincing at the pain in his hands. He cracks his neck, leaves the road near the hostel. He wants his shard of sea glass.

Some men are such animals.

* * *

Luda slowly makes her way through the contents of Tristan's witch box. Among the journal articles and scanned notes and the books that were too niche for the local library, she finds a scanned scrap of paper recounting the denouncement of the women who had called the whales in from the sound.

She discovers that the man who had denounced the women often visited Seannay with his wife to collect seaweed and shellfish. The man claimed that his wife, Magdalena, had made a pact with the devil. The man claimed that Magdalena could see the ghost-scars on his skin. That she and her sister could raise the dead. The man claimed that Magdalena met with a group of other women, including her sister Susan, on Seannay and called the whales in from the sea.

Luda sits back from the kitchen table, her neck knotted. She keeps thinking about what Tristan had said, about a photo being enough to bring about condemnation. Persecution. She will never forget the sight of the cliff collapsing.

She is tired of people looking at her with unsmiling expressions. She supposes she deserves it. She thinks, again (always), of that photo she'd taken of Darcy in the dam. It's doing the rounds again; a meme this time about exams and homework. It makes her feel nauseous. She thinks of the cool, still space of the gallery where the image should have ended up. Safe. It makes her want to wrap her arms around Darcy. She breathes out, imagines the steady, thrilling feel of her camera button under her finger.

She tries to focus on the documents in front of her. Another of the executed women, Elspeth, had lived on Seannay, in what was now one of the ruins across from the ghost house. She'd been a widow and, after her execution, the land had reverted to the earl, who ruled the islands at the time. She was accused of calling the whales. She was accused of promising fruitfulness in nature. Luda has found no record of who had lived in the ghost house nor why it had been preserved when the other houses on the island had not.

Luda peers down at her arms. Her own history, netted in the scars on her skin. The ones that extend down her arms and across the flare of her palms.

And, scattered like stars, like stories across the walls and eaves of the house, those witch marks. The more Luda learns about these women, the more she is certain that they are connected to the marks. It is a feeling, drawn from the same part of her that recognises the crosshatch of scars on her skin as being her own.

She wonders whether these women, who had been charged and tried and executed together, had been friends. She hopes they had.

A pang.

It is so easy to shape her imaginings of these women into people she would have liked to know. Canny and ferocious and powerful. Unruly. Perhaps people who would have seen and loved that hidden, hungry part of her. The wordless part that lives in a world of light and angles.

Just women. Just women. Just women.

Father Lee. That smooth, arrogant face.

Sometimes, when she's had perhaps too much wine, she will be certain that she can make out women near the pebbled beach; a single woman standing over her while she sleeps on her thin mattress near the Rayburn.

Luda has always had a vivid imagination.

She comes frequently back to the list of charges. Raising a procession of the dead. Fruitfulness in nature. Calling whales from the sound and riding upon them like horses. She thinks of briny fields and broken sea walls. The photos she's taken.

She does not, *will* not, think of the cliffs. She makes notes, drinks coffee.

Not that she believes in magic, but would such a spell – a spell of fruitfulness – be enough to save the islands? Would that be enough to calm the seas? These ghosts. They are so much safer than staring through the viewfinder of her camera at the hungry, moving sea.

* * *

The more that Min thinks about Father Lee taking something precious from Theo, the more enraged and restless she becomes. She asks Cassandra whether Father Lee will be keeping it at the kirk.

'The kirk, or in a pocket,' Cassandra says. 'He'll be expecting Theo to turn up to worship.'

And when Min asks Theo if he's going to see Father Lee, he glances at her and then away. He has a faded bruise on his cheek. 'I'm not going to the kirk,' he says. 'I'll figure out another way.'

'Maybe Iris will get it for you?'

'No.' His mouth twists. 'She definitely won't.'

So, on Sunday, Theo goes to the Wailing Cliffs to stamp and yell, and Min rides her rusted, buckling bike towards the kirk. The water is still today and she thinks of her father, lifting things up from the sludgy remains of the dams back home.

She focuses on peddling. She waits until Father Lee begins his sermon and then she enters via the side door she had noticed on her visit, weeks ago now, with Tristan and her mother.

The door opens next to a dim corridor that leads to a small amenities room, tucked in behind the custodian's office that Iris inhabits. Min thinks of how Theo moves across the tidal island, disappearing into shadows. She tries to imagine herself into this secret, shadowy Theo. She slinks into the amenities room with its single high window, narrow table, kitchen. A faded couch with a jacket tossed onto it. Min glances behind her at the hallway leading into the main body of the kirk, and then slips her hand into the jacket pockets.

Her fingers close on the shard of sea glass. It's red and worn smooth by the sea. Smiling, she heads back out the side door like shadowy Theo and rides, breathless and thrilled, through the town and along the roads that lead to the northern side of Big Island.

The Wailing Cliffs are on the edge of a wild, frothing, churning sea. The hiss and thud of waves against rock. She finds Theo glowering, cross-legged, a little way back from the cliff edge. He's damp and breathing heavily from running or raging. He offers her a flask of whisky when she sits down next to him.

She hands him the sea glass without speaking. His gloved hand closes over it and he looks searchingly into her face. 'How?' he asks.

'I stole it out of his jacket while he was giving his Sunday sermon,' she says, stretching her legs out in front of her. She takes a mouthful of whisky.

He smiles then, a slow, beautiful smile. He holds the sea glass up to the sun and then tucks it into his pocket. 'Thanks, Min.' He reaches for her hand. And Min thinks of Harper and Sōta and Nico, but the thought of them doesn't make her ache quite as much as it had when she first came here. She rests her head on Theo's shoulder, and soon they stand and throw stones into the churning sea until their arms are sore.

Chapter Ten

MAY (THEIR FIRST YEAR)

After Sunday's service, a woman had waited patiently near the confessional to speak to Father Lee. She could hear clanging, bangs, coming from somewhere behind Iris Muir's office. *Where the hell is it? It was right here!* More banging. More clanging. She glanced at her watch.

Finally, Father Lee emerged, red-cheeked, hair tousled. 'Oh, Isabella,' he said, his voice calm and warm, even as his chest heaved with exertion. He grabbed her hand with both of his (sweaty). 'What can I do for you?'

* * *

Cassandra is at the pub. She does not come as often as she'd like – it's a difficult journey for her in this papery body of hers. But she had not been entirely lying when she told Father Lee that it was her version of a sacrament.

While she truly craves the wildness of the shoreline, the sea takes something from her if she strays too close. The wind and the sun and the earth. The price it exacts is exhaustion – the vacuous kind, where she disappears inside herself for days, breath so slow that often doctors are called.

Despite the fact it is a slow and painful process getting Cassandra into a car and then out again and then into the plushest booth in the pub, she can normally convince Lorraine to take her. Lorraine has six lads, now grown, and on any given day one or two of them can be found at the Blue Fin, picking at a plate of hot chips or playing darts. They are the sorts of lads who are happy to give her a hug and a peck on the cheek in front of people and it always makes Lorraine glow with pleasure.

It doesn't hurt that the pints are cheap on a Monday, either.

Lorraine had dropped Cassandra off an hour or so ago and Ewan would be picking her up when he finished at the docks. She has a blanket over her legs. She drinks whisky.

Violet Reynolds sits across the room, nursing a soda water. Like Cassandra, she seems to find the pub comforting. She comes for the company, the sense of space being taken up by warm air (not empty) and the general bustle of normal people living normal lives. She does not drink. Cassandra wonders if it is because of Father Lee's aversion to women consuming alcohol, or whether it is because Violet Reynolds is aware that if she starts, she will not stop.

After a while, Violet moves across the room and sits down next to Cassandra and takes her hand. They sit like that. Cassandra lets the waves of numbing sorrow move from Violet's body to her own. She senses Violet's breathing come a little easier, the slightest squeeze of Violet's fingers. Cassandra nods to Louise, who brings over another glass of whisky. A plate of hot chips that Cassandra hopes Violet will pick at. Another glass of sparkling water that Louise never charges Violet for.

Violet closes her eyes, imagining Cassandra's small, narrow hand into the small, narrow hand of another. Cassandra sits very still, watching one of Lorraine's middle lads lean over the bar and say something to Louise that makes Louise throw back her head and laugh. Men from the docks, vaguely familiar but nameless in that peculiar island way, empty the rubbish from their pockets onto their plates for Louise to clean away.

Cassandra frees her hand and has a sip of whisky.

Later, Iris comes and sits down next to her. 'Ewan got held up,' she says, frowning.

Louise brings over a tea for Iris and Iris thanks her curtly. Iris will drink it (as she always does) because she hates anything to be wasted. And Cassandra will have the pleasure of watching Iris seated in the pub with a tea in her hand, simmering with indignation.

One of those with Lorraine's middle lad says something about Louise spreading her legs – something crude. An attempt at humour. Lorraine's lad swats at him, but he's laughing. Lads are gentle with each other in this way – laughing at the unfunny things their friends say.

'I don't know what you see in this place,' Iris says in a low voice, but she does know.

Cassandra does not need to touch Iris for the impressions to flare between them. Iris is thinking of the kirk. Of her mother, August. She is thinking of Haaken's Hole. Of how, when nobody else is in the kirk, she will stand by the yawning mouth of it and trace her fingers over the worn stone, feeling an ache of something as old as the kirk itself.

Iris gives her a venomous look. The impressions fade to a studied nothingness. She has another gulp of her tea.

'I hear that Carter fellow caught the morning ferry,' Cassandra says.

Lorraine's middle lad has gone to the toilet. His friend is bending low over the worn-out pool table.

'Aye.'

'Well, that's good news, isn't it?'

'If he's leaving, it's because he's got what he came for.' Iris sags a little. It's as close as she ever gets to slumping in her seat.

'Or because he's given up.' But Cassandra knows this is not true. Iris knows it, too.

Theo's pale skin mottled in a bruise. His cheek grazed. The stubborn jut of his chin, his silence. Iris doesn't bother shutting this one away. Her aching worry.

'You can't keep him locked up,' Cassandra says. 'He's nearly grown. We learn best from our own mistakes.'

'I'm well aware of that, thank you.'

Old, old wounds. The missing shard of sea glass that Father Lee has been both sullen and defiant about. *It was right here, in my pocket!*

'I suspect it's been returned to its rightful owner,' Cassandra says, sipping her whisky.

Iris's eyes narrow, but she doesn't look as displeased as Cassandra would have expected. 'Marcus is livid.'

'Good.'

They stare at each other.

'How does Violet seem to you?' Cassandra asks eventually.

'Shattered. Bryce has had to disable their internet. She's been compulsively looking at the photos that *relative* of yours took.'

'Aye, I've already said that those were misjudged.'

'Misjudged? They were barbaric.'

Cassandra shrugs. 'Ewan says it's got the attention of federal funding bodies.'

'I'm on the council, Cassandra. I'm aware.'

'Apparently, one big construction company has already offered to fund the upkeep of the dry stone wall up north.'

'Well, that's alright then, isn't it?' Iris sets her empty teacup down. 'As long as the funding bodies are taking notice.'

'No.' Cassandra considers her whisky. 'No, I don't think it is.'

Iris's thoughts turn to Seannay as they occasionally do. She scratches at her long throat.

'I hear Tristan's still mooning around the ghost house,' Cassandra says.

'The council doesn't support the research.' A snort. 'Not that it stops him.'

Cassandra turns her whisky tumbler slowly on the worn wooden table. 'It won't be there forever, you know.'

'I'm aware of that.'

'Are you? You think you'll be able to just walk across one day and hunt everything out for yourself? That's not how it works. The islands are being destroyed.'

Iris says nothing.

'One particularly ferocious storm and the ghost house could be as tumbledown as all the other places on Seannay.' Cassandra says. 'Just something to think on.'

Iris sniffs.

Lorraine's middle lad emerges from the toilets. Cassandra sits up straighter in her seat.

'You,' she says.

The lad bobs his curly head, rounds his shoulders and comes over to the booth. 'How are you, yourself?'

'Not so bad,' Cassandra says. She senses Iris watching her with narrowed eyes. 'I was hoping you'd do me a favour.'

He relaxes a little. Big, strong lad like him probably thinks she needs help out to Iris's car. 'Aye,' he says.

'There's an image stuck up in the men's toilets,' Cassandra says, her voice very pleasant. 'Of an upset young lad lying on cracked earth.'

Lorraine's lad says nothing, but he nods once.

'Someone has scrawled the words *bad fuck* over it.'

The lad reddens. Why do the young always think they have the only claim over foul language? She has been using foul language for longer than he's been alive.

'Fetch it for me, would you?'

The lad bobs his head again, disappears, and returns with the printout of Darcy in the dried-out dam. Cassandra smiles, thanks him. Then she rips it into tiny, tiny pieces and sets them on the saucer beneath Iris's teacup.

'If you see anything else like this in the toilets, or around the town, take it down, won't you?' Her voice is more threatening than she means it to be. The lad takes a step back, nods.

Iris lets her breath out. 'You shouldn't do that.'

'Do what?'

Iris shakes her head and stands. 'Finish your drink. It's time to go home.'

* * *

Theo begins meeting the Managans further from the school; further from the alleyway that runs past the hostel. Sometimes, he thinks he dreamt attacking those lads.

His knuckles are still stiff.

Sometimes he does not fall into step beside the siblings until they've reached the other side of town. Sometimes he's not there at all, and this rattles both Managans, although neither of them admits it to the other.

Today Min walks alongside Kole, who has been strangely quiet with her since she demanded that he tell her Darcy's name. They are not meeting his friends today. Instead they are walking to the small inland loch that had once been part of the bay. There are swans there, he'd said. And he'd shrugged with unfamiliar awkwardness.

It's a bright afternoon, the days slowly beginning to lengthen towards summer. There are no swans at the loch, just swan shit, a few pale gulls and a pattern of rubbish on the shoreline. So much rubbish.

Kole's ears go red. They stare at the shit-tinged water.

'I don't just want to hang out with you to annoy my parents.'

Min gazes out at the loch. The water of it seems to be made up of a different substance from the breathing, watchful sea. She thinks of Cassandra's stories, about the one that made it sound as though Cassandra had swum here when it was still soupy with salt and seaweed and starfish. She wants to swim where Cassandra has swum. She wants to share Cassandra's stories with more than just her imagination.

'Min?'

'What?' She glances up from the water, startled to find that Kole has shifted closer to her. Things suddenly make sense. The swans; the absence of his friends. *Jesus.*

He runs a hand through his hair, angling his jaw in a way that he must practise in the mirror. He sighs, reaches for her face and tips her chin up. 'You're hot, you know.' He says this softly and reverentially, as though he has paid her an unimaginably profound compliment.

Perhaps back home, before everything, Min may have glowed and leant in. She may have given him what he wanted. She has kissed boys back home; it had been light and giggly and they had all been her age. Standing in front of her, Kole suddenly seems very much older than she is. He seems very much like a man.

She considers the word *hot*. She thinks, *Aren't I strong? And fierce? And don't I notice people and care?* The words she would prefer to *hot* tumble over each other until her head is buzzing and her cheeks flush with the urgency of them all.

She moves her chin sharply from his hand. 'I'm sorry,' she says, and she is. When she confronted him over Darcy, she had not wanted this. She had wanted to be *seen*. Why couldn't he see her without thinking that he had to call her hot? Why couldn't he see her and make space for her, without the possibility of sex or something like it? Wasn't she worth that?

His expression shifts. 'Is this because of Theo? Because it wasn't me. I was just *there*. Us local lads wouldn't touch him. Not ever.'

Min frowns. 'What?'

His expression shifts again. Surprise, then feigned casualness. 'Nothing. It was nothing.'

'What about Theo? *What* wasn't you?'

'Nothing! It was nothing. Just some of the hostel lads mucking around with him, that's all. He slipped. He's fine.' That self-righteous, defiant jaw. The way each sentence lands hard against the next like pearls on a string. *Clink. Clink. Clink.*

'I didn't know about that,' Min says. 'Bloody hell, Kole.'

They stand like that for another moment, and then Min straightens. She gives Kole a look and begins to walk away. She thinks he might follow. That, having gone as far as to call her *hot*, he might fight for her now. But he doesn't and she is relieved.

On the other side of the loch, where the road begins to arc towards the sound, Theo falls silently into step beside her.

He is still bruised around the eye, his cheekbone grazed. Min tugs at his sleeve until he stands still. She keeps tugging until he looks at her properly. She raises a hand and brushes the raised patches of his skin. Darcy would sometimes come home from school with the same sorts of injuries. The same shuttered expression. Rarely, though. Even the country boys back home had mostly left him alone. 'Kole reckons his mates just mucked around with you.' She raises an eyebrow. 'And that you slipped.'

Theo pulls a face. She expects him to shrug away from her, to keep walking or else to run, but they stay standing on the quiet road. 'T,' she says, 'Kole wasn't just *there*, was he?'

'They were drunk.'

Min mulls on these words – the generosity of them, when she feels no generosity is deserved. 'Have you told anyone?'

He shakes his head. He catches her hand in his and pulls at her until they're both walking towards the sound and the causeway and Seannay.

'I want to rip their arms off.' She pauses. 'No. I want to make them eat their own eyeballs.'

'That sounds like a lot of effort.'

'True. Maybe we could just dump them off Ewan's boat.'

He smiles properly then, glances sideways at her. 'Thank you,' he says. He rubs at his knuckles and then she understands. She's *glad*.

She swings his arm for a moment and then pulls him into a run. He moves stiffly, as though he has other bruises in other, more hidden places. And then the water of the sound opens up below them. The wind curls and sweeps them along, faster and faster, until cupped chins and bruised cheekbones fade into the roaring, blurring background.

* * *

Darcy does not seem to like being alone with other people. Nor does he seem to particularly like crowds. Still, he's always willing to meet Tristan for a coffee at the cafe or at the ghost house. At the ghost house, Tristan will climb up into the loft to touch the witch markings, as though checking to make sure that they are still there. He knows that he is being fretful and clucky, but he can't help it. Tristan always brings something for Darcy: an old book, a printout of a journal article; the name of something obscure for Darcy to track down at the island museum or in the archives of the small library. Some days, Darcy's body betrays its tension. On these days, Tristan is careful to give Darcy more space, pressing back in his chair in the cafe; leaning against the sink at the ghost house or sitting down on the floor with his knees up under his chin.

Tristan can see flashes of Luda when he looks at Darcy and it fascinates him. Although Tristan would gladly spend hours quizzing Darcy on Luda, on who she'd been before she came here, he only occasionally brings her up. When he does, Darcy's face always drops. 'What about her?' he'll say.

And Tristan will try to make his questions sound offhand; what did she like to do, back home? What was she like then? Had she changed? Had they all changed?

'She used to laugh more,' Darcy says now, as they sit in the cafe. 'She liked to paint – although she was a bit shit at it, honestly. She and Dad ...'

'Were they happy?' It's one of those days when Tristan sits back in his chair, not even putting his elbows on the table.

'They were. Yeah. But not for a long time. They both got too obsessed with their own things. Dad ... it felt like he was gone a long time before he died.' Darcy shakes his head. 'She used to make jokes. She liked to go to the theatre. She used to always forget when our school concerts and stuff were on, but she'd spend hours reading to us and talking to us. She liked to dance.'

'Right. Do you think she'd like dancing now?'

Darcy's gaze sharpens. *God, he's quick. That brain.* Through Darcy, Tristan thinks that he might get to experience all of the academic heights he himself had failed to reach. Darcy's brutal intelligence and his strange, awkward tentativeness mean that Tristan never feels the sting of resentment or jealousy. He wants Darcy to succeed. He wants to see him *soar*.

'Maybe,' Darcy says, his expression suddenly amused.

'What?' says Tristan. 'What's happening to your face?'

Darcy shakes his head, tensing as the cafe door is suddenly opened.

'I just worked something out.'

'What?' Tristan frowns. 'What did you work out?'

Darcy smirks. 'Nothing.'

'Right,' says Tristan slowly. 'It's just good to know your colleagues.'

'Oh, I'm sure it is.'

'Anyway, what were we talking about? Before we got onto Luda?'

'Magic,' says Darcy.

'Yes. Magic. Continue.'

'Well, it doesn't exist,' Darcy says.

'You can't say that.'

'Can't I?'

'No.'

'Wow, strong argument. Did that get you through your doctoral defence?'

Tristan shakes his head, trying to look reproving, but giving it away by grinning. 'You're a savage beast when you want to be, Managan.'

'Not savage. Just right.'

'If a man is hexed by an enemy,' Tristan continues, 'and *believes* he's been hexed and dies from the stress of it all, how can you untangle his death from the idea of the hex? They're inherently linked.'

'It's not magic.'

'Maybe not, but there's still cause and effect at work. There's still an interplay.'

'Since when is magic about cause and effect?' Darcy frowns. 'Or an interplay, for that matter? It's such an academic's argument you're making, Tristan.'

Tristan snorts, but he's pleased. He's always pleased when someone calls him an academic. 'God, you're obnoxious.'

'Because I don't believe in magic?' Darcy is quiet for a moment; his expression changes. 'Do you see them?'

'See what?'

'The ...'

Tristan sighs. 'The scars on Seannay? Yes, I do.'

'How can science explain *them*?' There is an edge to Darcy's voice. Something close to desperation. 'I know there must be an explanation – there has to be. There's no such thing as magic.'

'Maybe you just need to broaden your thinking about what magic *is*,' Tristan says, after a moment.

Darcy frowns. 'Tristan.'

Tristan contemplates the flippant answer he usually gives about eyesight and whatnot. 'You might not like it,' he says instead.

Darcy inclines his head.

'I can see them,' Tristan says. 'And my theory is, well, I think that the people who can see them have been hurt. I used to think it was just people who've seen too much, or been traumatised. But now I think its people who've been badly hurt. Physically. I think it's people who've been hurt so badly that they're sure they're about to be killed.'

Darcy flinches. A fleeting expression; a moment of anguish before his face shutters. He's still flushed across his cheeks. Tristan can tell that Darcy knows what his face has done; that he knows that Tristan has seen it. Tristan wants to take the words back; he wants to reach across the table and hug Darcy, but knows it will not help.

Darcy looks down at the table, flushed now across the bridge of his nose; his forehead, his scalp too probably. 'You have ... you have a lot of scars,' he says.

'My dad was a bad drunk with a fondness for his belt buckle.

Knocked me out a few times tossing me into the walls of our house. Ma couldn't help, or she'd get belted too.'

Darcy looks utterly unsurprised by this. 'I'm sorry.'

'Aye, well. It's a common enough thing, isn't it?'

'Doesn't make it less awful.' Darcy hesitates, that oddly endearing awkwardness that makes him seem so young. 'Thanks for telling me.'

'Well, it's not a secret.'

'Was it? Ever?'

'When I was young, yes. Felt like a sort of failing; like it wouldn't be happening to me at all if I didn't somehow deserve it. But now I know the truth of it, which is that my father was a brute.'

Darcy nods, looking tired suddenly.

Tristan runs his hand around the back of his neck. 'Now, if you repeat what I'm about to say to anyone, I'll deny it.'

'Noted.'

'In all seriousness, those bloody scars are the closest I've ever come to giving up on empirical research and everything else. I can't explain them and I can't deny them – they're *there*.'

'What made you keep going?'

'I don't know, really.' Tristan glances sideways at him.

Darcy gives a small smile. 'Well, whatever it is, it's not bloody magic.'

Chapter Eleven

JUNE (THEIR FIRST YEAR)

Summer comes. The star-dashed evenings disappear. It is never full dark. The nights are short. They taste of salt.

* * *

Sometimes, Theo seeks out Darcy rather than Min. She suspects this has to do with staying as far away as possible from Kole and his friends. She also suspects that it has nothing whatsoever to do with avoiding Kole and his friends. Not that she spends time with them anymore.

She could stay in the ghost house with Darcy and Theo on these occasions, she knows. She could sit and listen to Darcy read and read and read. But she wants to be outside.

Instead of spending the early evenings at Kole's house or wandering Big Island with Theo, Min now goes out with Ewan onto the sea. Ewan knows Cassandra's stories too and he takes Min to the places Cassandra has told them both about, the places where Cassandra had swum when she was young. Min stares out at the water, the clouds and the sea-bitten edges of the earth. She braces herself against the gunwale and thinks that she will swim, as Cassandra had swum.

'You don't need me for that,' Ewan says, when she tells him. 'Just walk out from the shore like a regular person.'

'I want to swim *here*,' Min says. 'These places. Cassandra's places.'

Ewan sighs, falls quiet. He often does this, and then another thought will catch him – like an acrobat snagging the edge of a trapeze swing – and he will talk quickly and loudly about the tides or a recent haul or the council. He tells her lewd jokes about women behaving badly. He tells her about the lads at the pub – their boats, their families, their stories. Sometimes, Min feels like he has forgotten that she is not a grown man but still fourteen and a girl.

Other times, Min luxuriates in the surprising wonder of her own company. She picks gorse and flowers and arranges them in jars on the windowsill of the front room, where Cassandra seems to live out most of her life. They play cards and watch movies and Min changes Cassandra's bed and opens the windows to let the salty air in.

'Did you go swimming today, Wilhelmina?' Cassandra will ask.

At first, Min shakes her head. And then she nods with quiet pride – those chilly, awkward dips in the shallows. Theo refuses to go into the water; he stands on the shore if he's ever with her when she swims, quickstepping back if a wave comes too close.

Min soon realises that Cassandra wants her to explain what she's seen; what she's felt. She understands there is a ritual that comes with the sea stories. Sometimes they sit at the pub, but mostly they stay in the warm fug of Cassandra's front room. Min makes black coffee for Cassandra, to counteract the drowsiness of her pain meds, and weak tea for herself.

'I'm getting better at holding my breath,' Min tells Cassandra one afternoon.

Outside, rain splatters against the window. They talk about seaweed. About whales. About the tidal island. Min has brought custard pies from the bakery.

'Do you reckon Seannay's haunted?' Min asks. 'The girls at school all say it is, and Mum's getting really into all the witch history of it. It's creepy.'

'Oh, Wilhelmina – don't be silly.'

'So you don't believe in ghosts?'

Cassandra gives her a look. 'Of course I believe in ghosts. I just don't believe that Seannay is more haunted than anywhere else. All places have their ghosts.'

'Can you see the scars?'

'Aye,' says Cassandra.

'I can't.'

'And you want to.'

'Yeah.' Min thinks of all that is delicate and unspoken between her and Darcy – how, if she could see the scars, maybe she could finally put words to the things that needed them.

She thinks of the islands, the water.

'Nobody talks about the land,' Min says. 'All the talk about climate change and most of it's about people and property prices and houses. What about the actual *land*? The sea?'

'I don't know.'

'We don't matter more than the sea,' Min whispers.

'No, I don't suppose we do,' Cassandra says, and sighs.

They sit in silence for a while. Min nods at the cards on the side table. 'Who left them here?'

'They're mine, actually.'

'How do you make out such tiny numbers with your poor old eyes?'

'*So* rude. And they're tarot cards, not playing cards.'

Min stands up. This is not part of their ritual – their ritual is one of weak tea and strong coffee and stories of the sea.

'Oh, whist.' Cassandra waves at her. 'Come sit back down.'

'Put them away first.'

'Wilhelmina.'

Min frowns. 'I don't like messing with that stuff.'

'What *stuff*?'

'Just … ghost stuff. I don't think we should mess with it.'

'*Ghost* stuff? This isn't a séance. I'm not going to call on the spirits to give me mysterious messages.'

'Still.'

'Good Lord, Wilhelmina. The power of these cards doesn't come from some dark, witchy source. Their power comes from their ability to illuminate our most complex dilemmas and desires.'

Min pulls a face. 'You're laying it on a bit thick, Cass.'

'I could use a deck of playing cards or a Tesco catalogue. The cards don't matter, is what I'm saying. They're just pretty pictures, really.' Cassandra pauses. 'They can be the foundations of a story. If you let them.'

Cassandra shuffles them, offers the deck to Min. They stare at each other for a moment. Finally, Min sighs and takes one. 'I'm scared of ghosts,' she says, very quietly.

Cassandra's fingers brush Min's. 'I know.'

* * *

Luda wanders among the crooked headstones in the kirk yard until Father Lee's maroon station wagon disappears from view. Without Tristan's warmth – his careful attention – and his certainty that everything in the world is negotiable, the kirk seems foreboding.

Luda wipes her damp hands on her jeans, glances at her watch. She is due at the docks in an hour. She takes a deep breath of cool, salty air and steps into the dry stillness of the kirk.

I am here, she thinks, despite herself. Shivers. She moves quickly to the custodian's office, where Iris is sorting through pamphlets for upcoming community events. Iris raises an eyebrow when she sees Luda, but nothing else in her expression shifts.

'Can I help you?' she asks.

Luda swallows, reminds herself that she is a strong, clever woman in her thirties – that she is far beyond the schoolgirl nervousness she feels in Iris's presence. Perhaps if that first council meeting hadn't felt quite so much like being reprimanded in the principal's office.

'I'm trying to pull together a history of the witch trials,' she says. 'Specifically, the five women charged for calling the whales into the sound. In my own time, obviously. And people keep saying I should talk to you.'

'Cassandra's the one you'll be wanting.' Iris shuffles the papers. 'She might even throw in a tarot card reading if you ask her nicely.'

Luda shakes her head. She had asked Cassandra, and Cassandra had been frustratingly evasive. 'No. I need you.'

'I'm a good Christian woman, Mrs Managan,' she says finally. 'Don't mistake my willingness to preserve records and artefacts from this island's history for an affinity with the occult.'

'Of course not.'

'The world really doesn't need another gory rehashing of the same tired old story – women executed by men,' Iris continues crisply.

'I'm not interested in the executions,' Luda tells her. 'Or the charges, for that matter.'

Iris's expression seems to sharpen. 'No?'

'No. I'm interested in the women themselves.'

'The women,' Iris repeats.

'Yes.'

'What about them? Specifically?' Iris sounds bored now. Or like she's trying to sound bored. 'How long they were kept in Haaken's Hole? Whether they went mad before their interrogations? Because everything recorded about that is in the tourist pamphlet in the vestibule.'

'No. I want to know about *them*.'

Iris goes very still. 'Why?'

'Because they deserve to be remembered properly, don't you think? As more than a creepy story. For more than being locked away and killed.'

Iris gazes at her. Luda breathes shallowly, waiting.

'I don't know how much luck you'll have,' Iris says at last. 'But unexpected things do cross my desk from time to time. People clearing out their parents' houses and whatnot, finding old records and letters and that sort of thing.' A pause. 'I'll let you know if anything turns up.'

Later, Luda lies in front of the Rayburn in the ghost house. She's been brightened by Iris's delicate (reluctant) acquiescence. The women seem so solid to her in this moment – more than names scratched into old parchment. Women she might have called friends. Above her, the loft is dark and quiet – her children sleeping under the witch markings. She has not run today; has not drunk her customary glass or two of wine. She's not sure if sleep will come.

Had Magdalena known her husband was the sort of person who would betray her? Or had she trusted and loved him, just the way you were meant to?

Luda thinks of the moment when she'd pieced together what the police officers had not explicitly told her about Joshua's accident. Sole occupant. No signs of braking. The layers of horror, unfolding and unfolding and unfolding.

She tries not to think of him choosing to leave her. She tries not to think of it as the worst sort of betrayal.

Had Magdalena hated her husband, after?

Luda wonders this: had those women who met on Seannay to trace each other's scars and call the whales in from the sound ever thought of themselves as witches? Had they cultivated the identity for themselves as a way to make a living? To help? To damage? Or was it a surprise to them, the day they were charged and dragged to the kirk? Those heavy, metal manacles. The dock.

The cold mouth of Haaken's Hole.

Why, if they commanded magic, hadn't they been able to keep themselves safe? Surely, Luda thinks, *surely* a woman of magic would be unlikely to be caught and imprisoned and tortured and killed. Or maybe the magic – whether real or imagined – was as limited and unknowable as everything else in this world. The thought makes her feel sad, for a moment, until she remembers that she does not believe in magic.

Promising fruitfulness in nature. The islands, drowning.

Still.

Still. *I am here.*

She dreams of dark places.

117

* * *

The next afternoon, Min and Theo go out to the Wailing Cliffs, where the sound of waves on rock is a living, dangerous thing. Min stares out and wishes, for a moment, that she were under the water instead of gazing at it from the land. She has been spending more time out on the boat lately than she has with Theo. Still, she's glad to be here with him now. There is the steady thud and hiss of froth-topped waves. The rawness of it all. Even though it's summer and the air is bright and almost mild, it's still a forlorn place. Discomforting in a way that makes Min feel at once very small and very large. Apart from the indignant screeching of the arctic terns from their summer nests, Min and Theo have the cliffs to themselves.

Over the past few weeks Theo's face has healed, yet it still seems more fragile than it had before.

Theo is at his wildest along the cliffs, pacing close to the edge, yelling at the waves. It's the part of himself he has to keep in check everywhere else, where people watch him for signs of what he had been before. He needs to prove his humanness, over and over again. To prove his civility, his restraint.

Min paces and roars with him until they're both damp and panting. Until their hearts have settled into the rhythm of water against rock. Until they sit down on the tussocky ground with their legs stretched out in front of them.

'Someone took a photo of me here, once,' Theo says. 'A couple of years ago. It went all around the newspapers – how nobody knew who I was, how I was clearly dangerous, unhinged. That sort of thing.'

'I'm sorry, T.'

Theo shrugs. 'Iris won't take photos of me. I remember seeing that photo and thinking how much I'd changed. You notice more in a photograph than you do in a mirror.'

'I can't imagine not having photos of myself,' Min says. 'We've got piles and piles of albums of just Darcy and me. Mum was kind of obsessive about documenting our childhoods.'

'Are they here?'

'Yeah. At the ghost house.'

'Can I see?'

'Sure.' Min looks up at the clouded sky. 'If you want.'

* * *

Later, in the ghost house, she and Theo sit down at the kitchen table. Theo finds that he does not mind being inside the ghost house – not when it's just Darcy and Min there with him. The space feels as safe as the cliffs, as the bay, as his own sea-smelling bedroom.

Theo accepts the first album with both hands and a quiver runs through him. Min sits down next to him, watching as he turns the pages.

'I can't even remember when most of these were taken. Mum used to take photos of us every single day. Things started to take off for Mum after that photo of Darcy in the dam got published in all the papers. Darcy was thirteen, I think? Anyway, Darcy started to get funny about Mum taking photos of him after that. Made her promise not to do it anymore.'

The photos are of Darcy and Min when they are nine, maybe ten. Min in gumboots and her mother's slinky dresses. Min squatting to piss beside a big corrugated-iron cylinder. Darcy laughing, wrestling a dog in a dusty yard. Min covered in vomit. Wailing. The images are astonishing, but Theo's wonder quickly fades into something else.

'These are …'

'They're beautiful, aren't they?' She smiles at him, a forced sort of smile. She runs a finger around the edge of a photo in which she is five and naked, shelling peas at the kitchen table. Then she draws her hand back and her face falls. 'Well, I always thought they were. You want a tea?'

'Thanks.'

She gets up, and Theo forgets to tell her that he does not take his with sugar. That he likes it strong and unsweetened, so that it almost tastes like salt. The rituals of their friendship take place outside the ghost house. Inside, they falter. Inside, they trip into gaps.

He turns the pages of the album until there are no more, and then Min fetches another album and watches his slow progress through that one, too.

'So, these are published in magazines?'

'Some of them.'

Theo gazes out the window, thinking that the viral photo of Darcy was not a single intrusion but one of many – a chain of intrusions, linking back and back and back. 'Darcy really hates that photo your mum took of him in the dry loch.'

'It's called a dam,' Min says. 'He's never talked to me about it. He doesn't talk to me about anything. But I think mostly it's because he was really upset – like, you've seen it, right? He's really, really upset in that photo. And Mum just looked at him and saw a publicity opportunity for the drought. She didn't even tell him that she was there. She just took the photo and left him.'

Theo pushes the album away, begins on another.

'She didn't mean to hurt him. She probably didn't even really see him, you know?'

'Why was he so upset?' Theo asks. 'In the photo. Was it actually the drought?'

Min hesitates. 'That's what Mum's always said.'

Theo keeps turning pages until he's finished that album as well. 'You know exactly where you've come from,' he says, and the words feel raw. The absence of his own knowing, suddenly present like a fresh bruise.

After that day, he looks at every photo of Darcy and Min that Luda has brought to the islands. It takes him hours, days. Twice, he lets himself into the ghost house when nobody else is there and quietly turns the glossy pages of the photo albums until it feels as though his own skin is being peeled off.

Darcy's skin.

* * *

Darcy sometimes has a lovely dream where he's being privately tutored by someone who owns a very large, private library. In this dream, Darcy can pursue whatever fields he wants and his tutor exists mostly to answer any questions he has as he studies.

But, no. School. *School.* With its gossip and strange rules and the way that people either ignore him or giggle and whisper when he comes near. Once, he'd asked Min about it when she'd trailed into the library-gym-space during a particularly wet lunch break. 'Why are they always *laughing* at me?' he'd whispered to her, inclining his head towards a group of girls seated in the aisle behind him.

'They're not *laughing* at you.'

'Look at them! *Look!*' he'd hissed. 'They're giggling, Min. I hate it. It's distracting.'

'They're not laughing *at* you. It's because of how you look,' she'd said.

Darcy had run a quizzical hand over his hair. 'What? Have they done something?'

And she'd just rolled her eyes and left him sitting there with the *gigglers*.

He tries to ignore them, tries to imagine himself just passing through, on his way to the quiet library of his dreams. But today Min's name keeps snagging his attention. Min, going out on Ewan's boat. The things the older boys say make Darcy want to punch their faces in, which is an impulse he has only seriously had once before. It frightens him now. He goes straight to Luda's office after school.

'Hi Darcy,' she says, looking up from her computer. 'You here to see Tristan?'

Tristan sit backs from his desk and frowns. 'Your face looks weird. What's wrong?'

Darcy glances at Tristan and then back at Luda. 'People are saying things about Min going out on Ewan's boat.'

'What sort of things?' Luda asks, half an eye still on her screen.

'What things do you *think* they're saying?' Darcy snaps.

'People are always going to find things to gossip about.'

'That's all you've got to say?'

'Well, what do you *want* me to say, Darcy?' She looks at him properly now, her expression irritated. 'If I listened to even a tenth of all the crap people go on about, I'd lose my mind. I trust Ewan. Min's fine. That's that.'

Darcy feels his body tremble. Separate. Always *separate*. Luda has gone back to her laptop. Tristan is still watching him. 'Darce, let's get a coffee,' he says, standing, but Darcy shakes his head, gives his mother another look that he hopes stings her somehow, and then he leaves the office. Drawing in one deep breath after another.

* * *

Theo is flipping through the last of the photos at the kitchen table in the ghost house that evening when Darcy suddenly turns his chair to face Min's. 'What?' she says, not looking up from the photos. Theo's flipping slows.

Darcy takes a deep breath. 'Ewan ...'

'What about him?'

'People are ...' Darcy breaks off and Theo looks up. Despite the angle of Darcy's chair, Darcy is looking away from Min. 'People are talking.'

'Oh.' Min considers this. 'I actually don't care,' she says, sounding a bit surprised and pleased by this.

'Has he ... has he ... has he ever ... has ...' Darcy balls his fists up. He forces out a breath.

Min raises her eyebrows. 'Wow.'

'Can you just *listen*?'

'If you manage to get any clear words out, I will.'

Theo rests his head in his hands. 'You two make my head hurt.'

They both ignore him. 'Darcy, if you're trying to ask what I think you're trying to ask, just don't. I'd never be stupid enough to let something like that happen to me.'

Darcy goes very still. Min exhales. 'God, I just mean ...'

'Forget it,' says Darcy. He stands up, kicks his chair back and stalks outside.

'God he can be a dick,' Min says, both of them watching Darcy stride briskly down to the bay.

Theo turns slowly back to the last album. He looks at those final photos very, very slowly. Studying not only the Managans, but the landscape behind them. The albums document not only the Managans growing up, but the land around them slipping further and further into crisis.

It makes him feel panicked, ill. Finally, he looks up at Min and feels as though he now knows her story better than she knows it herself. Darcy's story. Even Luda's, for each photo is a sliver of her as well. Each photograph tells more about Luda than whatever it is that she has trained her camera's gaze on.

Min raises an eyebrow at him. Theo just holds out a piece of paper.

'What's this?' she asks.

'Someone sent it to me.'

She repeats the words written there until he has them memorised. *Call me if you change your mind. I've headed back south but can return any time. C.*

'Darcy still near the bay?'

'Probably.'

Theo looks out the window, standing so close to Min that he can feel the warmth of her arm. She nudges him and he nudges her back. Then Theo lets himself out into the night. It's late, but at this time of year it is not yet dark. Outside, the light is dim and gentle, the air unusually mild.

Darcy looks up at Theo from the rocks near the water. 'What?'

'I looked at all the photos.'

A pause. 'God. That must've been boring.'

Theo doesn't say anything. He presses his foot into the deep, green turf that collars the bay.

'What?' Darcy says again. 'What's up with you?'

Theo looks out to sea, where a fish, something silver, breaches briefly then disappears. 'The albums.'

Darcy straightens. 'It's called a drought,' he says. 'It's called *climate change.*'

'Darcy?'

Darcy looks up, but won't meet Theo's eye.

'Here.' Theo hands him the shard of blood-red sea glass. It's warm and damp from his palm.

'What's this?'

'The first thing I remember. I was clinging on to it when I was found.' Theo half-smiles. 'It's rare. Red sea glass.'

Darcy goes to give it back but Theo shakes his head, holds his hands up. 'Keep it.'

'I can't. It's … your first thing.'

'Keep it.' Theo presses his hands into his pockets.

Chapter Twelve

JUNE (THEIR FIRST YEAR)

A ringleted child waves at a short-eared owl, which is perched on a low fence. A bloody vole is clutched in its claw. 'Smile!' the child says. The owl stares, grumpy to find itself daylight hunting. 'You'd be so much prettier if you'd just *smile!*'

* * *

Perhaps it is the island summer; the days fanning open so wide that even the most unpleasant things lose their power. Perhaps it is just that it seems like a decent thing to do. Perhaps it's because Darcy has become sullen and snappy again, and Luda has no idea what to do about it. She thinks that, on balance, the Reynoldses are less scary than her seething, clever, complicated teenage boy.

She tells Tristan about it over their morning coffee; her plans for apologising to the Reynoldses. She expects congratulations, approval. She waits for his eyes to crinkle at the corners in that warm, surprised smile of his that she has come to quietly adore. His eyes narrow at her over his cup. 'So you're going to say sorry for taking the photos?'

'No.'

He sighs, twirling the cup in his hands. 'I don't think you quite grasp the concept of an apology.'

She glares at him.

'Alright. Then you're just a truly terrible apologiser.'

'If I'm going to apologise for something it has to be sincere.' She rolls her shoulder. 'And I'm not sorry about taking those photos. They did too much good.'

'Right.'

'God, Tristan. You *know* they did! They got more done in a few days than fifty funding applications and a media campaign could have.'

'Uh huh.'

She looks at him, feels her pulse quicken. 'This is war, Tristan. You know that.'

'Has anyone ever told you that you could really do with being a bit more dramatic?'

'I'm not being dramatic. Back at home we were being hit with once-in-a-lifetime weather events every couple of years. Every summer we were breaking high temperature records. And no rain. I know you don't get it because the farthest south you've ever lived is London, but no *rain*. Our complacency is going to kill us.' She swallows. 'I'm not sorry for those photos.'

He studies her, his expression softening. He knocks her shoulder with his. 'Alright then, Commander Managan. What *are* you going to apologise to the Reynoldses for?'

'For not giving them warning. I should have warned them.' She frowns down at her coffee. She hopes the Reynoldses are in less pain now, but she supposes they won't be (*knows* they won't be). Luda still feels winded by her own grief and she had not lost a child. 'For hurting them.'

'But not for the *thing* that hurt them, though. That's just going too far.'

'Can you stop being such an arsehole?'

'Yes, I'm the arsehole in this situation.'

She frowns, trying to find the words to explain to him that she will never regret her best work. That the vivid, quicksilver part of herself that lives, always, in shape and colour and light, won't let her regret them. It's how she can look at that photo of Darcy and feel guilt as his mother, grim satisfaction as someone suffering on the land, and a quiet thrill at the beauty of it. The power.

'Piss off,' she says, because it is easier this way.

'Right.' He pauses. 'How's Darcy? Have you mentioned the conference to him?'

'No, I thought you'd want to.'

'You *sure* you don't want to come? Sometimes the lunches at this venue include *pizza.*'

'I told you how I feel about crowds,' she says.

'Okay. No pizza for you, then. I'll stop by and tell him after work.' A pause. 'Is he doing okay, though? Do you think?'

'You tell me. You see more of him than I do.'

'He's been …' Tristan squints. 'Has he ever talked to someone?'

'If you mean have I ever sent my kids to a shrink to have their thoughts dissected, the answer is no.'

'You know, for someone progressive enough to view climate change as a war, that's an extremely backward way of viewing therapy.'

'They haven't needed it.'

'Oh, really?'

'What, exactly, are you trying to say?'

He sighs. 'Nothing you're going to listen to.'

'They're both fine. They're very resilient. They've had to be, living through the drought and then losing their dad.'

'Yes. Yep. Both perfectly fine. Not at all troubled.'

They walk back to the office in silence; Tristan eventually gives her a sideways look and she knows he's about to ask her about the witch trials. 'How are your friends?'

'Arsehole.' She strides ahead and he doesn't try to catch up.

* * *

Luda is not sure why she has waited so long to do this. Palms slick with sweat: she knows *exactly* why she has waited so long to do this.

Luda drives out to the Reynoldses' farm in Ewan's car with a bouquet of flowers on the seat next to her. She had not had much use for flowers after Joshua died (had asked for donations to drought relief efforts instead), but Violet is not her – and it is Violet she is going to see. As she drives, she is struck by the softness of the islands in summer; the changing quality of the light. The patterns of flowers and fresh growth, vibrant against sky and sea.

The Reynoldses live on a sprawling hillside property north-west of the town. From the pastures that snake up from the curve of the driveway, Luda is certain you'd be able to see Seannay, yoked awkwardly to Big Island by its rutted, weeping causeway.

She parks out the front of the house, struck for a moment by the sight of a child's swing set tucked along its flank, out of the wind. She swallows, climbs out of the car with her bouquet of flowers. She strides across to the house, veering sideways at the last minute when she catches sight of someone moving in the garden.

'Violet?'

The woman looks at her, expressionless and far gaunter than she had been that day by the cliffs. Her red hair is pulled into a tight bun that does not quite hide how long it's been since it was last washed. 'Mrs Managan.'

Luda swallows. 'I just … I brought you some flowers.' Luda waves them and then, wincing at herself, she hands them over.

Violet takes them, letting the bouquet hang at her side like a bag of shopping. She turns back to the garden bed, which Luda can now see is a small, overgrown vegetable patch.

'She helped me plant …' Violet trails off. 'Why did you come?'

Luda shrugs. 'The flowers,' she says. 'I … I didn't think about how much pain those photos would cause. I shouldn't have …'

Violet nods.

The back door bangs open. 'Who's here, love?'

Bryce Reynolds is a beautiful man – tall and muscular with high cheekbones, brown hair and large blue eyes. His mouth twists when he sees Luda.

'Bryce …' Violet says.

'You! You've got no business being here. Fuck off. Fuck off with you!' he says to Luda, and she tries to, but he catches her before she's reached the side of the house. He grabs her by the collar of her jacket and slams her against the pebble-dashed side of the house. She feels his fingers tighten around her neck.

'You've done enough.' His breath in her face, thick with the smell of whisky. 'Stay away from my wife.'

Luda gasps for air. Her vision begins to spot.

'Bryce,' says Violet, again.

He stares at Luda, the way one dog will stare down another when it has already got it pinned to the ground. She scratches at his hands with her nails, tries to lift a leg to kick at him.

'Bryce.'

And he lets Luda go so abruptly that she lands hard on the ground, biting her tongue. She tastes dirt, stays there, coughing and breathing in lungfuls of air that smell like rotting cow manure. She closes her eyes. Trembles there, just breathing.

Then she senses Violet turn towards the house, bouquet of flowers still hanging from her hand like an afterthought. The back door rattles open and, as it does, something heavy collides with Luda's side. A heavy booted foot, not as hard as a kick can be, but hard enough.

'Stay *away*.' His voice wobbles. And then he follows his wife towards the back door.

Luda sits there for longer than she means to. That wobble. If she weren't so busy spitting out mud and making sure she still had all her teeth, she might have felt sorry for him.

* * *

Darcy is alone in the ghost house when Tristan stops by that afternoon. Distantly, the chiming of the kirk bell carried from the belfry. Tristan kicks off his boots and takes off his jacket. He puts the kettle on and sits down opposite Darcy. 'You're looking particularly aggrieved this afternoon. You alright?'

'I'm fine.'

'Okay. Well, I was hoping to run something past you.'

Darcy closes his book. 'What sort of something?'

'One I think you're going to love,' Tristan says, grinning. 'I've got a conference next month in London. I've got an extra pass from a friend who's helping organise it and I thought you might like to come with me – have a look at the colleges, the museums, sit in on some of the talks. What do you think?'

'Take me to a conference in London?' Darcy looks bewildered. 'Why would you want –'

There's the sound of heavy feet on the flagstones outside. Min and Theo burst in, laughing. Their fingers are linked, their shoulders bumping. As always, Darcy aches at the sight of their easy closeness – the casual way Min tousles Theo's hair; the way Theo tugs on Min's arm when he wants to run. It is how Min had once been around Darcy, too – easy and playful and loving. Before everything.

Darcy much prefers Min getting drunk with Theo than being on the boat with Ewan.

'Oh God,' says Tristan. 'You two smell like a brewery.'

'We were just there! At the brewery! Declan gave us some of the stuff they can't sell,' says Min, flopping down on the couch. 'I like beer.'

Tristan sighs. 'Why are you wet, Min?'

'She went for a swim,' Theo says, apparently mystified. He stays by the door, as he always does when anyone other than Darcy and Min is present.

'Right.' Tristan stands. 'It's ten degrees out there and you went for a drunken swim. Perfect. You're going to soak the couch.'

Min looks down at the darkening fabric. 'Well, shit.'

Theo grins, but Darcy sits back in his chair and stares up at the ceiling wearily. He can tell that Tristan is trying hard not to smile as he makes four coffees and sets them down on the table. Darcy frowns at Min, but he's talking to both of them.

'You know that alcohol will destroy your brain, right?'

'That's a shame,' says Min, standing up from the damp couch in order to peel her clothes off in front of the heater. The flicker of scars on her arms and legs and torso.

'Hold it! If you're going any further than that, take it elsewhere,' Tristan says when she's down to her underwear. She shrugs and climbs up into the loft.

Darcy picks up his coffee and holds it with both of his hands. He turns to Tristan. 'Why would you want me to go with you?'

Tristan raises his eyebrows. 'Because you'd love going to a conference.'

'Well, I don't think I can.'

'Of course you can! I've already cleared it with Luda.'

'Is she coming too?'

'You know how she feels about crowds.'

Theo runs his fingers along the doorframe. 'A conference in London?'

'Darcy! You have to go!' Min calls down from the loft.

'I can't.' Darcy's voice cracks and he feels himself colour. He looks down at his book.

Tristan frowns and sits back in his chair. 'I thought you'd be excited.'

'I am! I want to go – it's just ...' He feels suddenly, impossibly, on the verge of tears.

Theo glances between Tristan and Darcy.

'Can I come too?' Theo asks.

Tristan looks dubious. 'Do you *want* to come?'

'I've never been to London.' Another quick glance at Darcy.

Darcy feels himself soften. Reaches for the shard of red sea glass in his pocket. Holds it tightly.

Tristan glances from Theo to Darcy. 'Well, it's fine by me, but we'll need to check with Iris.'

'What about me? I want to go with you!' Min says, coming down the ladder from the loft.

Tristan rests his head in his hands for a moment. 'Sure. You can all come. But no drinking, okay? And if you dive into the Thames, Min, I'm bloody well leaving you there.' He sighs. 'Where's your mother?'

'Out taking photos somewhere probably,' Min says. She sits down on the floor near where Theo's standing with her coffee.

'No,' says Darcy. 'She said she was going to the Reynoldses'.'

Tristan tenses. 'Shit. I didn't think she was serious about that. You sure?'

'Pretty sure.'

Tristan downs his coffee. 'Right. Well, I'm off. Behave yourselves,' he says to Min and Theo. Adults have never needed to tell Darcy to behave. He's always done it all by himself.

* * *

Being in the same room as Theo. It's something that feels hot, at first. As though Darcy has sat down too close to the Rayburn. It travels down his body, makes him clammy. It settles in the pit of his stomach, lodges there like something clawed and heavy.

Theo. Impossible, strange, luminous Theo.

Darcy notices this abstractly. He and his body. Sometimes he can forget the uneasiness between them – the fact that they exist alongside each other, but separate. He and his body. Amicable, mostly. They make it work. But right now he feels particularly removed from it.

He is aware of the shard of red sea glass in his pocket.

Outside, he can see Theo pacing among the rocks. The idea of London has set off something charged in him. Sometimes he blends so entirely into the landscape that he seems to disappear for a stretch of seconds – minutes. Then he'll recommence his pacing, tossing rocks into the sea.

Darcy looks down, watches his hands pick up a mug of cold coffee. He watches his feet square up under his chair. He takes note of his eyes blinking, his throat swallowing. He watches his hand press against his stomach. The memory of curtains sliding closed.

He still hates the smell of fresh mown grass.

* * *

Tristan drives too fast across the causeway, wincing at the sound of sharp rocks grating against the underside of his large, grumbling car.

On Big Island, he floors it around the top of the town and onto the main road leading towards the north part of the island – the cliffs, the Reynoldses' farm.

It's on this lonely road, through drywall-edged pasture filled with fat, contented cattle, that Tristan spots Luda driving towards him. He pulls off near the crumbling wall of an old byre. His car engine ticks as he jumps out onto the gravel shoulder and waves.

Luda pulls over. For a moment she just sits there, motor still running, and then she turns it off and climbs out.

She's muddy, her neck marked with welts from thick, angry fingers. They look at each other. Tristan takes one step towards her and then another. When he's only a couple of steps away she gives him a long, bewildered look. And it comforts him, this look. Because it makes him think that perhaps she's never been hurt before. Perhaps the possibility of being hurt like this by another human had never before even entered her head. Comforts him and tears him open.

She leans into him and he wraps his arms around her, his chin resting on her head. He can feel every shuddery breath, can feel her wince when his arm presses too tightly against her ribs.

'That fucking bastard,' Tristan mutters into her hair.

'It's my own fault.' And he can hear the tears in her words. He stays like that, holding her, wanting to go and rip that bastard Bryce apart. Wanting to lay into him with his fists, his feet, his teeth. His belt buckle.

Luda stays pressed against him, breathing unevenly, her face buried against his neck.

'Luda, Luda, Luda,' Tristan murmurs, rocking slightly on his feet without really meaning to. He presses his lips to her hair and closes his eyes.

Finally, she pulls back a little. 'What are you doing here, anyway?'

'Oh, nothing much.' He would like to bundle her back against him, but doesn't dare to. 'Just thought I'd make sure you hadn't been cut up into tiny pieces and dropped into an old crypt.'

Luda shudders.

'You could press charges.'

'Against a man who's just lost his child?'

'He shouldn't have touched you.'

'I shouldn't have gone there.' She steps away then.

'Luda ...'

They regard each other.

'I'll drive you back to Seannay.'

She shakes her head. 'It's Ewan's car. I'll only have to come and pick it up later ... and I don't ... I don't want to have to come back out this way.'

'I'll leave mine here.'

'I'm fine, Tristan.' She rubs at a smudge of mud on her cheek, her expression set. 'Really, I'm fine.'

* * *

Bored by Theo's stillness near the water and by Darcy's silent reading in the kitchen, Min pushes her bike across the damp sand to Big Island, then she rides to the docks. She clambers onto Ewan's boat as he's about to cast off and he rolls his eyes at her. As they cross near the sound, Min points wordlessly at a huge chunk of earth that has subsided from Seannay into the water. They hadn't noticed it from the land.

Ewan rubs at a spot on his chin. 'Erosion.'

'They'll disappear eventually, won't they?' Min says quietly. 'The islands, I mean.'

'Aye.'

Min wraps an arm around her knee and says nothing. She thinks of Theo, washing up there. Theo, who still spends long stretches of time perched on the rocks, staring out to sea. 'I think I'm going to London,' she says.

'My condolences.'

'Tristan's taking us – Darcy, me and Theo.'

'Theo too? That'll be interesting. Don't think he's been off the islands since the day he washed up.'

Min thinks about this. 'I can't imagine that.'

'I can.'

'You have a boat!'

'Aye. That I use to fish in the same waters.'

'You've never been off the islands either, then?'

'Once, to the mainland coast for a wedding.' Ewan straightens his hat. 'Got too pissed to remember much of it.'

'What a beautiful story.'

'Aye. Well, it was a beautiful wedding. I think.'

Min picks up a piece of rope and runs it between her fingers. 'So, people have been … talking.'

'Aye.'

'You know about it? What they've been saying?'

He raises an eyebrow at her. 'Aye. You think the lads at the bar keep those bits of gossip to themselves?'

She twists the rope. 'I guess not. Anyway, you don't have to take me out anymore.'

'Is that what you want?'

'No. I love coming out on the boat. You know that.'

He's quiet for a while and then he moves closer to her and holds out a hand. She passes him the rope. 'Then fuck them,' he says, finally. 'Although, if you keep doing that to my ropes, I might have to throw you overboard.'

'Fair enough.'

He jerks his head towards the cabin. 'C'mon. I'll show you how to knot properly.'

'Like a self-respecting sea woman?'

'Like a self-respecting sea woman.'

* * *

Luda is alert to every sound that night. She dreams sweat-soaked dreams of men breaking through the door. Of booted feet. Of hands clenched around her windpipe.

It all feels very familiar, as though the separate pieces of this moment have happened to her before. As though she has, until now, lived her life in anticipation of these pieces falling together into a moment of horror.

But still, she had not expected it. Not really.

Min and Darcy had both been upstairs when she'd come home, Darcy probably reading and Min doing last-minute homework. They'd called goodnight to her, but neither had come down from the loft. She'd showered and curled up in bed, trembling with self-loathing.

The scars on her skin are brighter than ever.

Eventually, she sets a chair under the knob of the front door. She surveys it, goes back to her makeshift bed on the floor. When she next wakes, the impossibly early summer dawn has come and pearly light spills across the floor. Darcy watches her, not from the table, not from behind a book. He's seated on the floor next to her, studying the marks on her throat. She raises a hand to them, swallows. His eyes flick to hers.

'I'm fine,' she says, her voice casual and calm, and she hates herself a little bit for how easily the lie comes to her. 'Really.'

His worried expression disappears. He looks irritated. He hands her a glass of water and pops some painkillers from a blister pack into the cup of her hand. Then, so quickly that later she'll be sure that she's imagined it, Darcy brushes some stray hair behind her ear and stands up, as though he's flustered himself. He glowers as he walks away.

'Thank you,' she says, and her voice trembles. Undone by his startling, gruff gentleness.

* * *

Across town, as the morning brightens, it turns out that Iris does not want Theo to go to London. Her reluctance is reinforced by the fact that Theo had come home unusually drunk the night before and by the fact that it is Tristan who wants to take him there. 'Absolutely not,' she says, and closes the door in Tristan's exasperated face.

'What on earth were you thinking?' Iris asks Theo, as they watch Tristan cut across their narrow front garden to where his car is parked on the street. 'That man couldn't organise himself out of a paper bag. You'd probably end up in New Zealand.'

Theo paces the room. 'I want to go.'

'No, Theofin. It's a terrible idea. You've never even been to the mainland. London would eat you alive.'

'And whose fault's that?' He does not often use this tone with Iris. It surprises both of them. He takes a deep breath. 'I'll be fine. It's not like I'm going there alone.'

'And why would I let you go to somewhere like London when you're rolling home drunk as it is?'

'I wasn't ... I just had a bit of ale.'

'Aye sure, and Father Lee's hobby is tap dancing.' Iris turns to him. She is backlit by the bright light of the window. 'Why do you want to go?'

'Because I want to see more of the world than this damn island!'

Iris studies him, unmoved. 'Why do you want to go *really*?'

Theo does not know how to answer. He does not know how to explain the photos of Darcy, the way Darcy slips away from them all sometimes. He doesn't know how to explain what he simply *knows*.

After a long moment, Iris turns back to the window. He has the sense, one he has often had with Iris, of being seen. Of being understood, even if she is disappointed in him, or wary of what it is that has passed between them.

'Alright,' she says finally. 'There will be conditions. But you can go.'

A burst of something like summer clouds lit up with sun. Theo takes a deep breath, frenetic with it. 'Thank you.'

Chapter Thirteen

JUNE (THEIR FIRST YEAR)

It rains and rains and rains. In the tearoom of the kirk, Father Lee sits in a marriage counselling session. He waves a hand to quiet Mimi Hargraves. 'If David doesn't want you to get your own bank account, you need to respect that,' he says. 'You're united in the eyes of the church. He's your husband; through honouring him, you honour the Lord.' On the windy farm north of the town, Violet Reynolds dreams of wreathes made of gorse. She makes one and lays it where Allie had died. Bryce tells her not to go there again. For her own good.

* * *

The rain is loud in the office above the laundromat. It makes Tristan feel extremely sleepy, even as he peers at Luda and frets about Darcy and thinks about funding applications and wonders if Iris is hiring a thug to remove parts of his anatomy until he agrees to rescind Theo's invitation to London. Luda frowns down at her laptop, doing the new thing she does, rubbing her palm impatiently up and down her throat, as though trying to erase the marks there.

'We don't have to go,' Tristan says.

She looks up from her laptop. 'What?'

'London. I can cancel.'

'It's all you've been talking about for weeks, Tristan. You have to go.'

Tristan sits back in his chair, taps his finger on the edge of his desk. The idea of Luda alone on Seannay is revolting to him. 'It's really all too much of a hassle, anyway …'

'Tristan!' Her voice is exasperated. She touches the skin of her throat. 'You're going.'

'But …'

'You have to go! I can't … I can't rely on other people to be okay. I've been there, done that. I'm not doing it again. You all need to go, just like we've planned. It'll do the kids good to get off the island for a bit, and Darcy would be crushed to miss out on the conference. I'll be fine.'

He swallows. He wants to cross the space between them, wrap his arms around her and feel her face pressed against his neck. He wants to explain to her that it's normal and human and *good* to tell other people that you're not fine. To tell other people that you might actually need things from them from time to time. He thinks of that bewildered expression on her face. He wants to tell her that pretending bad things haven't happened doesn't make them go away. He hopes it's not a lesson she'll have to learn the hard way. God, that stubborn way she tilts up her jaw.

'He's a shark,' Luda says, 'and when I went to their house I was in the ocean. It was a mistake.'

'How poetic and misguided.'

'I've never felt unsafe here.' It's a lie. Tristan knows it's a lie. He's never known a woman who has felt entirely safe where she lives. But she's looking at him very intently. 'I can protect myself, Tristan. Not that I'll need to.'

'But …'

'God, Tristan. Let it *go*. I'm done talking about this.' She goes back to typing, but he can tell she's just typing the same words. He knows what they are – he's seen them on her screen sometimes, when she's been too distracted to notice him moving to the door.

We're safe. We're safe. We're safe.

* * *

Theo runs. And he feels restless, no matter how far he goes; no matter how much he yells into the waves at the Wailing Cliffs. He finds himself thinking more and more about the webbing between his fingers. The lads from the hostel stretching it out. Touching it.

He shudders. Spends long hours fretting over it, picking at it. Wishing, more than anything else, for it to be gone.

He tries to do it himself. He tries with scissors and secateurs and Iris's sharp butcher's knife. But he always shakes too badly. He can't bring himself to slice his own flesh.

He would go to see one of the island doctors, except they've already tried to unfasten his fingers, and failed; the skin has always grown back. The idea of going again into the cramped examination room with its too-bright lights and smell of antiseptic is enough to make him wince.

He does what he has begun to do whenever he needs something he has no words for. He seeks out Darcy at the ghost house.

'How's your mum?' Theo asks, although all he can really think about is his fingers.

'She's okay,' Darcy says. 'She's not telling anyone she got hurt. I can't decide if it's really kind or really stupid.'

'Can I talk to you?' Theo asks.

Darcy stiffens. 'About what?'

'My fingers. I don't …' Theo hesitates and takes off his gloves with trembling hands. 'I want you to cut them. The last two.'

Darcy stares at Theo's face, but Theo can tell how badly he wants to look at Theo's normally hidden hands. Those endless, wearying stories of scales and green and fur. 'Go to a doctor, Theo. A surgeon. I'm not doing it.'

'I've had them cut twice by surgeons.' He can feel his face go blank. 'It doesn't hold.'

Darcy swallows.

'I know it can … I know it can work. I had webbing between all of them when I … when I came here. Ewan sliced them before anyone could see.'

'Ewan did?'

'I've been trying to cut them myself but I can't. I don't want to be running around London with' – he forces a laugh – 'you know.'

Darcy grimaces and holds out his hand. Theo breathes out slowly and rests his own hand, palm up, in Darcy's. Darcy's skin is warm, his fingers precise and detached. Darcy inspects the webbing and Theo looks away.

'There are veins through it,' Darcy says.

'I know.'

'It'll bleed.'

Theo rubs at his nose with his other hand and then jams it deeply into his pocket. 'I know.'

'Why does going to London matter? I don't … I don't get any of this. What does London have to do with getting rid of the webbing?'

'I don't want to … I'm …' Theo makes himself breathe. His hand clenches into a fist against Darcy's palm. 'I stand out enough without having webbed fingers, okay? I just … I need the webbing *gone*.'

'There's hardly anything there. Nobody will even notice.'

'Except they *do*. They do notice. Because it's me.'

'No. Because you keep them hidden.'

Theo tugs his hand free. 'Had you heard about me? Before you came here?'

'Yeah. Of course. I mean, everyone's heard about you.'

Theo gives him a hard look. 'It's not about the gloves, Darcy.'

'Why don't you at least *try* a surgeon again? They'll do a better job than me.'

'Because I can't … I hated it.' He swallows. 'I hated the smell of the place and the colours and the lights. I hate how … I just can't.'

Darcy looks at the webbing. 'Why are you even going to London, then? If it's stressing you out this much.'

'You know why I'm going to London.'

Darcy looks at him and then away.

'I'll see if I have a scalpel,' says Darcy finally.

'Can't you use scissors?'

'The skin's too thick.'

'A knife, then.'

Darcy cracks his neck. 'I think this is a bad idea. But I'll do it.'

Theo looks at him. And then he nods. 'Okay.'

* * *

That night, Darcy reads late. Articles on the anatomy of hands. The complex alignment of nerve and tendon and muscle. He ignores Min's pointed huffs for a long time before he switches off the light. He lies down, feeling unsettled. In the dim midnight sun, he can make out the witch marks. Their sharp corners and graceful arches.

'Tell me something,' Min says.

A pause. 'Theo wants me to cut the webbing between his little fingers. He doesn't want to look like a freak in London.'

'Oh.' Min pauses. 'Are you going to?'

'I said I would.'

'You don't want to, though.'

'Of course not.'

'Darcy?'

'What?'

She exhales. 'Is Mum okay?'

'Yeah. She's fine.'

'You said she went to the Reynoldses … Did she?'

'Yeah.' Darcy feels that stony part of himself. The one that he was not born with. It has developed with time, a culmination of awfulness, both large and small. Sometimes he feels as if sinking into that detached, cold place is the only way he can survive. 'She did.'

* * *

That night, Cassandra wakes up to the strong scent of August's particular collection of herbs. Just so. She does not move, letting her mind float. The flickering of old memories.

August drawing circles in damp sand around the quivering, impossible bodies of dying whales. Scarred skin. August bundling Iris up in herbs and trinkets. August showing Iris how to chant, how to pick the right herbs to cure blocked noses and fevers and headaches and nausea. August braiding Iris's hair. August pressing a line of delighted kisses along Iris's cheek.

Cassandra sighs. She imagines Iris across town. Iris in her nightgown and lavender-scented bed. Iris pressing her face into her pillow. 'No,' Iris is saying. 'No. No. *No.*'

* * *

The next day, Darcy has no classes in the afternoon so he walks to the docks and waits for Ewan.

He grimaces when Ewan climbs off his boat. He looks hard at the water. 'I need your help.'

Ewan raises an eyebrow. 'Do you now?'

* * *

Luda is still in her office above the laundromat, running her hand across the skin of her throat. Min sulks through an afternoon maths class at school. She's trying to ignore the rude comments about how she's screwing Theo; about what she gets up to on Ewan's boat. The teacher can hear what's being said, Min knows he can, and yet when she finally cracks and turns to flip the boys off, it's Min's name that gets written up for detention. While Min is plotting how to remove six pairs of testicles with her pencil sharpener, and Luda is trying to erase the marks on her throat, Theo makes his way across the damp sand to Seannay. His shaking hands are pressed into his pockets.

When he knocks on the door of the ghost house, Darcy answers with an unusually grave, almost arrogant look on his face. Theo is momentarily taken aback until he sees a shimmer of something deeper. Worry. A little bit of fear, maybe. Ewan is behind him, looking disapproving.

'Ewan said he'd help,' Darcy says, glancing at Ewan and then back at Theo. 'It's the only way I'm doing it.'

Darcy sets up a basin, plate, disinfectant and gauze in the bathroom. He pulls in two kitchen chairs and sets them next to the bathroom sink.

Theo watches these preparations. He swallows. 'I don't remember this many things last time.'

'There weren't this many veins last time,' Ewan says.

Darcy hands Theo a roll of bandages. 'Cut this up so we can put it straight on.'

'Alright. Pass me the hand knife,' Theo says to Ewan.

'The what?'

'The hand knife. The …' Theo frowns. 'The scissors. You knew what I meant. You *knew* I meant scissors.'

'Hand knife,' Ewan says, and smiles. He passes the scissors, and Theo begins to cut up the bandages.

Darcy inspects the scalpel, his lips thin. He carefully straightens the bandages and gauze and disinfectant.

Ewan pours Theo a generous serve of whisky. 'Drink it.'

Theo does and then Ewan hands him a belt.

'What's this for?' Theo asks.

Ewan says, 'To bite down on. Prefer you use that rather than my hand this time.'

Theo does not smile.

'Right, well. Not that you'll need to, but just in case. Ma always used to give me something to bite on when she dug splinters out of my fingers. It stopped me fidgeting.'

Theo accepts the belt.

Darcy takes a deep breath. He reaches for Theo's hand and stretches the fingers out, inspecting the webbing. Theo can barely stand it.

'Do you even remember when you bit me?' Ewan asks Theo. 'Still got the scar.'

Theo frowns. 'I *bit* you?'

'The day I found you on the beach at Seannay. I thought you were a dead porpoise or something.'

Darcy glances up at Ewan.

'Got the fright of my life when I realised you were a naked lad,' Ewan continues. 'I watched you roll in with the tide. When I saw your hands … the webbing … I was worried some of the older folk might think you were a changeling or a faerie. I panicked and sliced the skin with my gutting knife. I didn't get a chance to do the final two fingers.' Ewan sighs. 'I was still a lad. Didn't know any better. I scared you half to death, I think.'

Theo gazes at the pearly mark on Ewan's skin. He says nothing.

'Are you sure you want me to do this?' Darcy asks.

'Yes.' Theo runs a finger over the belt buckle as Darcy sets his other hand down on the plate. 'Just do it.'

Ewan stands behind Theo, where he cannot see Theo's face. Theo is grateful. Darcy gives Theo one more searching look and then bends his head. Theo gasps and fumbles to get the leather of the belt into his mouth.

Chapter Fourteen

JULY (THEIR FIRST YEAR)

A plump pony gelding escapes his paddock and is found in a neighbouring byre, gorging on grain that is not his. That is not needed at this time of year, when the days are long and mild. At the loch, a group of lads laugh hard as they try to windsurf on the still water. The swans watch on, heads tilted. On the other side of town, a woman dishes up fish for her family's dinner. In the house next door, a young lad watches his father sort washing, and tries to thread the blush petals of a flower into a skirt for a faerie.

* * *

Theo is sullen and red-cheeked when they meet at the ferry terminal for the first leg of their journey south. From the mainland they're flying to London, where they will stay for three nights before flying home.

Ewan gives the Managans a lift from Seannay. At the terminal, Luda stands a little apart from her children, the wind whipping hair into her eyes. Min hugs her, then tightens the hug and keeps hanging on, long after Luda expects her to let go. 'Will you be okay?' Min asks.

'Of course!' Luda makes herself laugh. 'I managed for twenty years without you two, didn't I?'

Min pulls back to stare at her, and Luda knows Min is looking for the marks on Luda's neck. Luda tugs up her collar, even though they had faded quickly. 'I'll be fine,' she says. 'You behave yourself, okay?'

'I will.'

Luda swallows. 'I'm looking forward to some quiet time, honestly. I might even sleep in a *bed*.'

Min looks stricken. 'Maybe I shouldn't …'

'I'll look in on her,' says Ewan, holding Min's gaze. 'She'll be sick of the sight of me by the time you two get back.'

Min studies Ewan, her expression serious and searching. And then she nods, hugs Luda again, and hurries onto the ferry without looking back.

Darcy gives Luda the sort of hug that she'd expected, quick and light. 'Stay away from the Reynoldses,' he says, not quite looking at her.

She laughs, like he's made a joke, but it comes out sounding too high-pitched.

He cocks an eyebrow, exasperated, then turns towards the ferry.

Luda exhales. She's trying to be a regular sort of mother. The sort who doesn't still have the dull ache of bruised ribs. The sort who doesn't know the taste of mud or the feel of a hand closing around her throat. The sort who doesn't very badly want to cry at the sight of her nearly-grown children going away without her. She watches Tristan and her children disappear onto the ferry. Theo is slower. He has his hands tucked up under his arms. He stares at the ferry, which he has spent so long watching from Big Island.

'How are you feeling?' Ewan asks Theo, his voice gruff and impatient.

'Fine.'

Ewan helps Theo loop his bag over his arm. He stares at the sea. 'It's going to be a rough crossing,' he tells Luda, as Theo, too, boards the ferry.

She can tell Ewan is eager to leave; craving his boat, the ocean, his work. But she waits until the ferry casts off.

They don't talk on the drive back to Seannay, and when they get there, she smiles at him, feeling oddly tremulous.

'Thanks.'

'Welcome.' He hesitates. 'I wasn't just saying it – I'll stop in and see how you're doing.'

'You don't need to. I'm a grown-up.'

He grunts and she knows he'll be turning up whether she wants him to or not.

She stands in the doorway of the empty ghost house. She is filled, suddenly, with the terror that had gripped her the night after she'd visited the Reynoldses. She steadies her breathing. The flagstones under her feet. The stones. The sound of water splashing and hissing. Flickers of women. A face through the glass. She braces herself against the wind for a moment, and then lets herself be swept inside, the door shutting roughly behind her.

* * *

The air outside the boat is thick with sea spray. Min watches the waves. Their trip from Australia had been made in the dark.

Darcy stirs in his sleep.

Min thinks of how Ewan has explained currents and tides and waves and the motion of the wrecks at the bottom of the flow. She sees it now. Had caught glimpses of it on the islands. The waves off the Wailing Cliffs. The tug of the currents outside of the harbour. She feels herself go loose. There'll be no nasty things whispered into her ear about her and Ewan here. No questions about what hidden parts of Theo's anatomy are webbed.

She tries not to think of her mother, alone on the tidal island.

She stares through the misted windows and imagines diving into those waves – being carried by them – and a shudder passes through her. A strange feeling that exists on the knife edge between bliss and terror.

* * *

Theo's hands throb. His stomach heaves. He wonders if he's felt this before. A boat this large; the swell of the ocean this far from the islands.

He can't tell. He can't fucking tell. He'd thought he'd be able to. The blur of before feels solid.

A particularly large swell sends Theo grabbing for the guardrail by the window. He gasps, feels the stickiness of fresh blood soaking into the bandages around his hands. He knows they're watching him. Tristan and Min. The other people on the ferry. That even when he's still, his energy is wrong and not like theirs. He needs to run and draw and sit by the pebbled shore of the bay. And now he's moving further and further from Seannay. His salt-sweet room, crammed with things from the sea.

Iris.

He needs to get away from all these people.

He's pitched again into the guardrail and this time he hears the metallic sound of his flask hitting it. He exhales shakily. He positions himself so that he can drink from it – drain it – without anyone seeing him.

Darcy sleeps. Or feigns sleep. Darcy has gone, as he occasionally does, far away from the rest of them.

Theo swallows, closing his eyes against it all until he feels the alcohol kick in. His breathing evens out; the pain in his hands dulls. Then a strong, warm arm loops around his back. Min's head rests on his shoulder. Her fingers drum against his ribs. The ferry. The ocean. The plane. London. He can do this. He can do *this*.

* * *

It's late by the time they get to London. Darcy is bright-eyed but oddly absent, Min quiet and Theo utterly exhausted. He had very nearly lost his mind on the plane – only Min keeping a hand on him (even when he told her to leave him alone, almost mad with panic), only Darcy (awake now, thank Christ) quietly reading to him, only Tristan watching, had gotten him through without shattering.

* * *

They're in a small hotel fifteen minutes from the conference venue. The hotel smells of fabric softener and cigarettes. In the reception area, Darcy gazes out the window at the busy street, unfazed. Min huddles close to him without realising it.

'They screwed up the bookings,' says Tristan. 'Or, more likely, *I* screwed them up. Anyway, draw straws. Someone's going to have to share a room with me.'

Theo looks up. 'I don't mind.'

'Do you snore?'

'No.'

'Good. I can't deal with snoring. If you snore, I may end up smothering you.'

Darcy glances at Theo, who looks particularly out of place in the hotel. He looks less human than he ever has before. Theo, who knows so little of what humans are capable of. It brings Darcy back to himself, out of the stony place. 'No, I will,' Darcy says.

They all look at him. Theo shrugs. 'Okay.'

Tristan narrows his eyes and points at Min and Theo. 'The door between the rooms stays open.'

Min laughs. 'Seriously?' She glances at Theo and Darcy and then back to Tristan. 'Are you blind?'

'Why does it have to stay open?' Theo asks.

'Use your imagination, Theo. And if I get even a *whiff* of alcohol from you two …'

Min rolls her eyes. 'We *know*.'

* * *

London in summer. They wear t-shirts. They eat dinner at a cramped, noisy pizza restaurant across the road from the hotel. Theo doesn't eat much. He gazes at the crowds. The mixed accents and unfamiliar languages. The sense of motion sickness has not left him.

Words tangle themselves into meaninglessness on street signs and billboards. Quietly, Darcy begins to read things out to him in an undertone, so that Tristan and Min do not hear, but half of the words that Darcy reads out don't make sense to Theo. In London, he is a foundling all over again. He is nothing. He is lost. He can't stand to take the elevator – sprints up the stairwell instead. He can't sleep, aware of people above and below him on other floors, listening to the sound of each passing car. He wishes the windows would open. He drinks the vodka and craves the roughness of salt.

* * *

During the day, Darcy uses Tristan's extra conference pass to get into lectures on debitage and electron scans. He makes sure to take notes at two talks that touch on things related to the periods that have so entranced his mother. Her witch stories. *Women*. He is captivated by the talks, by this first true taste of what the world beyond school could be like for him, but part of his mind keeps circling helplessly back to Theo. The way Theo studied the London crowds hopefully. His silence. His palpable disappointment. How is it possible, Darcy thinks, that they can work out what a man ate five thousand years ago and yet still not know where this living, breathing boy came from?

In one lecture, and then the next, he sits next to an academic named John, who's from the medical school at King's College. He's a professor who's here because he's fascinated by forensic pathology. They walk together to the main hall during break, John listening intently to Darcy. They are joined by a woman from Inverness who is an expert in Pictish language and a man who has worked for four decades on various stone circles.

'Where are you studying?' John asks Darcy once they've settled with cups of fruit salad in the noisy main hall. Tristan sits across the table, eating his way through several slices of pizza.

'I'm still in school.'

Eyebrows are raised, glances exchanged.

'I wouldn't have guessed that,' the stone circle man says.

'He's very clever,' Tristan says, and smiles.

'Tell them what you were saying about your friend,' John says.

Darcy feels giddy. He tells them about Theo. They have all heard of Theo. Everyone's heard of Theo. Darcy tells them that he's going to find out where Theo came from.

They nod, like it's possible. Like it's something that he can *do*.

Tristan doesn't say anything else, but he watches Darcy closely from across the table. It feels like a dream. Darcy is handed business cards. He is given email addresses. He and his body, working in unison. Ears and thoughts and fingers and eyes. He stops obsessing over the stupidity of agreeing to cut the webbing of Theo's fingers. Sitting in the domed function room, listening to the hum of people's talking, discovering Theo's origins feels suddenly vital, necessary.

Wildly, dizzyingly possible.

* * *

Cassandra always has the sense that Father Lee drops in not out of some misplaced sense of duty, but as one used to battle always does with one they suspect to be an enemy.

'To what do I owe this delightful surprise?' Cassandra asks when Lorraine leads Father Lee into the front room. Lorraine tries not to smile, but says nothing. Lorraine attends the kirk with her rabble of grown sons, mostly because she can sometimes imagine Father Lee's figure at the pulpit into Father Frank, particularly if she doesn't wear her glasses.

Besides, it never hurts to remind energetic lads like hers about hell.

Father Lee smiles at Cassandra, pats her hand very gently, and sits down on the couch opposite her.

'Just wanted to see how you are. Is there anything you need?'

'Och, a younger body would be nice.'

He laughs, although it's not a particularly funny joke.

152

Cassandra tilts her head. She misses Wilhelmina's easy liveliness. In her absence, Cassandra feels particularly insubstantial. Slow.

She straightens as best she can, looks Father Lee in the eye. 'Have you spoken to Bryce Reynolds lately?'

Father Lee's smile stays in place, but she can see his eyes harden. 'We're all praying for them.'

'That's not what I asked.'

'Aye, I have. He and Violet aren't doing so well. It's unimaginable, isn't it? Losing a child like that. It's early days yet, though. I keep reminding them that the pain will lessen.'

'I don't imagine it will.'

'Of course it will.'

'In my own quite extensive experience, the pain stays the same; we just adapt to it. Our capacity grows, the pain doesn't lessen.'

Father Lee looks thoroughly uninterested. 'Regardless, it's only been five months.'

'Aye.' Cassandra smooths her skirt. 'Are you aware Luda went out to their farm?'

For a moment, they just stare at each other. He does this sometimes. As though expecting her to drop her gaze or to become frightened. But it's been a very long time since the Father Lees of the world have been able to scare Cassandra.

'Aye,' he says curtly.

'And you're aware Bryce attacked her?'

'She wasn't welcome.'

'You might want to give him a What Would Jesus Do bracelet, *Father*. Or some remedial sermons. I don't think he's quite got the gist of things.'

Father Lee flushes. 'He was within his rights to protect his family.'

'From a five-foot-five skinny woman who'd gone over there to apologise? Come on, Marcus.'

He stiffens. 'He's grieving and he was provoked. The Managan woman understands she was in the wrong, or she would have pressed charges.'

'The Managan woman is it now?' Cassandra folds her hands in her lap.

Father Lee glances at the door. 'Aye. She's not a parishioner.'

'She might've been, if you weren't such a painful bastard, Marcus.'

Father Lee blinks at her, and then quickly recovers. He glances at the door, as though to ascertain that Lorraine is out of earshot. 'You make things very difficult, Cassandra.'

'Aye.'

He looks on the verge of saying something unpleasant, and then catches himself. He stands, pats her hand. 'I'll pray for you.'

* * *

It rains softly in London that night. The sound of a siren. Someone calling down on the street. The drip of water landing on the windowsill. Tristan comes out of the bathroom and lies down on his bed, yawning. Darcy scrunches his eyes shut and takes deep breaths. He touches his hand bones through his skin. Phalanx. Metacarpus. Lunate. He had seen them cast up on the projector screen today, illuminated by a new radiography technique.

The light is switched off. 'Bed, you two!' Tristan calls, thumping the wall separating their room from Min and Theo's. Then Tristan speaks more quietly, in a voice intended only for Darcy. 'You don't trust me.'

Darcy says nothing and burrows further under his blanket. *Triquetrul. Hamate.*

'I hope you know that ... you can.'

'I'm sorry.' Darcy feels his ears redden in the dark. His panic at the invitation to the conference; his stepping in to take this space in Tristan's room.

Tristan sighs and it's a resigned sound; a sad one. 'You've got nothing to be sorry for, Darce.'

* * *

Theo had told himself not to expect anything. That if he had no memory after ten years, a trip south would hardly bring everything flooding back to him. And yet.

He's quiet at breakfast. He is quiet as Darcy and Tristan walk to the conference and he and Min head to the library and museum. He cannot stand the idea of the underground and so they walk and they sprint. He has run out of vodka. His hands throb constantly. He feels scratchy-eyed and scratchy-throated from the air of the city. Even breathing here is different.

He searches. Even a fragment of something.

Please.

Anything.

The disappointment of it quickly turns molten. He cracks his knuckle joints. He flexes his fingers hard, making them bleed. He knocks them against bicycle racks and light poles until Min grabs his wrist and holds it firmly in her own warm fingers.

* * *

Cassandra is at the Blue Fin, staring down at her whisky, letting the bubbling late-afternoon chat and laughter and sense of people in motion wash over her like the tides. The smell of deep-fried fish; oily dressing; stale beer and aftershave and sweat. She ruminates on Father Lee, his fickleness, his unpleasantness. She marvels that he has the power to rouse her ire like this. She is secretly pleased – the last time she had been this irritated by somebody was a very long time before Father Lee.

'You're looking particularly morose,' Iris says.

'It's Sunday.'

'Aye. We agreed I'd pick you up, remember?'

'Oh, aye. But I thought you might burst into flames entering a pub on the Sabbath. I thought I'd have to sweet-talk a young lad into carrying me out in his arms.'

'Picked one out already, had you?' Iris sits down opposite her.

'Aye.' Cassandra waves at Louise's cousin, a strapping young red-haired lad who's come up from Glasgow. He blows her a kiss and Cassandra makes a show of pressing it to her heart. He grins and goes back to wiping down the bar.

Iris's mouth tightens, but she's not paying much attention to Cassandra. She looks quite grimly pleased with herself.

Louise brings her over a tea.

'Thank you,' Iris says. 'You make surprisingly good tea, Louise.'

'I know you mean that as a compliment,' Louise says as she walks back to the bar.

Cassandra raises an eyebrow at Iris.

'I had a discussion with Bryce after mass today.' Iris studies her cup of tea. Knowing Louise, it's likely still too hot to drink comfortably, but Iris has never minded too-hot tea.

'Oh, I see.' Cassandra has a sip of whisky. 'A productive talk, was it?'

'Aye. Quite.' Another sip.

Cassandra imagines the kirk office. Bryce. Iris shutting the door behind him. Violet watching from the transept, pale-faced. Her clothes hanging too loose on her. Bryce's rough-edged shirt in Iris's fingers, holding so tightly that Iris could feel the pulse of her own blood in them.

'I reminded him – very politely, of course – that there will be severe repercussions if I ever hear of him touching anyone ever again.' Another sip. 'The thing about being a woman and getting old, I told him, is that nobody really sees you anymore. You become invisible. And when you're invisible, you can do all sorts of things. It's amazing, I told him, what nobody notices when you're an old woman.'

Cassandra imagines Iris's face very close to his. Bryce staggering out of the custodian's office, eyes wide. Violet catching Iris's eye, her expression dark but not hostile. Cassandra glances down at her whisky, trying not to look too pleased. Iris is always irritated if she pleases Cassandra too much.

Expression carefully in check, Cassandra looks up. She can't help it; she immediately feels her whisky-slick lips curl up into a grin. 'Sometimes, Iris, you're so like your mother.'

* * *

On their last night in London, Tristan goes out to have a late dinner with a friend he hasn't seen in years. Min falls asleep quickly, exhausted by the rush of the city. She sleeps clutching an old flannel shirt of Joshua's. Tristan had made each of them swear not to leave the hotel and has called to make sure they are still there and behaving themselves.

In the other room, Darcy and Theo sit on separate beds. Theo cracking his knuckles, frowning out the window. Darcy watches the action movie playing across the screen on the opposite wall.

Darcy pauses the movie mid-explosion. 'You don't like action movies?'

Theo blinks. 'What?'

'You don't like this movie?'

'I don't really like any movies,' says Theo. He glances at the screen. 'Or television shows. I've never really gotten the hang of them.'

Darcy lies down on his stomach, his chin propped up in his hand. 'How do you mean?'

'I can't follow the stories properly. It's like I'm too aware of each frame and where the actors are and how they're moving and I get disoriented when the shots change.' He shrugs. 'Iris doesn't have a television and I'm not the sort of lad people invite over for a movie night.'

'Interesting.'

'Is it?'

'I don't like them much either.' Darcy studies Theo. The way Theo sits with his hands resting palm up in front of him, tense and exhausted and lost. Darcy feels mostly relaxed in London. Softened in a way that makes him feel generous. His mind hasn't stopped

157

ticking over; making connections between the different things he's learnt. Always thinking, *Why? Why? Why?*

He stands up and moves across the room. 'I *am* going to find out where you came from, Theo,' he says, his voice low and intent. 'I promise.'

* * *

Further down the river at a small restaurant in St James's, Tristan settles back in his chair and tilts his glass of pinot up towards the light. 'Dear Maria, that was truly the finest salmon I've ever had.'

The woman opposite him laughs. 'I'm happy to hear it. Ruby's strictly vegan these days – says this place doesn't have enough options.' She waggles her fingers.

'Outrageous. Dump her immediately.'

Maria shakes her head. 'If only I weren't so fond of her.'

'I'll be thinking of you.'

'Appreciated,' says Maria, looking at Tristan over her wine. 'Now, I said I'd let you know if I heard of any job openings.'

'You did, yes.'

'Something's come up. Associate lecturer position in the school of classics. We're interviewing, but if you want it, it's yours.'

'Where?'

'King's College. Obviously.'

'Really?' He blinks quickly, clears his throat. 'Figured I was too dried up these days to be considered hireable in academia.'

'You've always been a very gifted researcher.' Maria folds her napkin. 'You burnt out. It happens.'

'I flunked out of my post doc.'

She shrugs.

Tristan tilts up his glass and laughs. 'God bless nepotism.'

'Is that an acceptance?'

Tristan has a large mouthful of wine and sets the glass down on the table. He has dreamt of this moment for so many years. Some archaeologists thrive in roles like his but he has always burned for the academy. He swallows, meets Maria's gaze.

'I can't,' he says, and his voice comes out a little bit hoarse.

'It won't take you long to catch up on things.'

'No, no. It's not that.' He runs his hands along the edge of the table. 'It turns out I don't want to leave the islands after all.'

She cocks an eyebrow. 'I thought you hated the islands. The last time we caught up you expressed your regret that there weren't enough trees on the islands to set them on fire.'

'I've never *hated* them.' He sniffs. 'I've … tolerated them.'

She chuckles.

'And now …' He breaks off, thinking of the Managans; of Min's easy laugh and the stubborn tilt of her chin. He thinks of sitting in the cafe with Darcy, on the days when Darcy flinches at sudden sounds and movement. Mostly, he thinks of Luda's lips and cheek and nose pressed into the crook of his neck; the way she narrows her eyes at him when he says something dickish. Her scars on Seannay. Her skin, her skin, her *skin*. 'Now, I love them.'

Maria smiles slowly at him. 'Oh. I see.'

'Shut up.'

'You love the *islands*.'

'Dr Sanchez, that's enough.'

She holds up her hands and laughs and gestures to the nearest waiter for more wine.

* * *

Darcy sits down next to Theo on the hotel bed and crosses his long legs. He holds out his hand, his gaze steady on Theo's face. 'Show me,' he says.

Theo stiffens, slowly rests his hand in Darcy's outstretched palm. He looks away thinking, *Darcy has promised to find out who I am*. He gives himself a moment to feel warm and thrilled and nervous. And then he shuts the idea away. He lets Darcy unwrap the bandages from one hand and then the other. Darcy's breathing changes.

Theo waits for Darcy to reprimand him. He's stupid. He's an idiot. Why the hell did he ask Darcy to *do* this? Theo braces himself for it as Darcy bows his head to inspect the wounds more closely.

And then Theo feels Darcy's lips press to the skin of his hand. It is a touch tempered by guilt, by remorse. It makes Theo feel woozy. Darcy shivers and lifts his head, letting go of Theo's hand.

He moves back to his own bed just as the door creaks open and Tristan comes in, smelling of wine and cologne. He smiles at them both. 'Bed,' he says, glancing at Theo's ragged hands and then away.

'Did you bring disinfectant?' he asks.

'Aye.'

Theo looks again at Darcy – who has lain down and closed his eyes very tightly – and moves slowly across to the room that he's sharing with Min.

* * *

There's a knock on the door of the ghost house in the early evening. Luda, home alone, goes very still. She peers through the kitchen window until she can see the shadow of a woman cast upon the flagstones and turf.

She opens the door cautiously, almost shutting it again when she sees that it's Violet Reynolds.

'Please,' says Violet, and Violet has lost her child and you can't shut your door on a woman who has lost her child, and so Luda leaves the door open, even as her entire body whirrs with tension. She keeps thinking of that day at the farm. She can't stop replaying Violet walking away from her. Violet leaving her alone with Bryce.

Luda tries to take deep breaths without being obvious about it. She waits for Violet to speak, but she doesn't. Luda notes dully the fact that Violet has walked over from Big Island. That her hiking boots are coated with mud and damp. Luda knows that she should invite the woman in, but she can't bring herself to move.

'I just wanted to thank you – for not pressing charges.' Violet fiddles with the cuff of her jacket. Her hair has been pulled back into a braid. Her face and hands are heavily scarred. 'And to see how you are after …'

Luda slowly steps back from the door so that Violet can enter. 'That's kind of you.'

She puts the kettle on and then she and Violet stare at each other across the small kitchen. 'I appreciated it, just so you know,' Violet says. 'You coming over like that.'

'I should never have taken them.'

Violet swings her head from side to side impatiently. 'Probably not,' she says. 'But really, it doesn't matter, does it? Allie's gone either way.' She blinks rapidly. Her fists bunch on the surface of the table. 'It was easier to blame you for everything. It … is easier.'

Luda nods.

After a moment, Violet pulls a crumpled piece of paper out of her pocket. 'Allie made this welcome card for you. We were going to drop it off once you'd had time to settle in. We can see your wee island from our farm.'

Luda takes the card. There's a smiling seal and some fish on the front. *Welcome to the islands! You will love it here! What's Austrailya like. Love from Allie.* She presses a hand to her mouth. 'Thank you.'

The kettle clicks and Luda rises, putting the card down on the table.

'She was worried about animals becoming extinct,' Violet continues. 'She was worried about things going hungry and being too hot. She was *kind*.'

Luda nods like she had known this, like it's a very important fact. It *is* a very important fact. She makes Violet a black tea and Violet drinks it. And Luda can see a bruise on Violet's wrist, faint against the newly visible patterns of bone.

A lot passes between them as they drink their tea. When Violet rises to leave, Luda rises too. She hugs Violet to her and can feel the woman's heart, the sharp lines of her shoulder blades. Violet smells of tea and salt and unwashed hair.

After she has gone, Luda pours herself a wine. The sound of a gull calling in the dusk. She studies her marked skin and tries to steady her breathing. She stares down at the crumpled card and then carefully sets it upright in the middle of the table.

* * *

There is nothing in London to remind Min particularly of Joshua. But it is a city of shifting moods and colours and smells and feelings. Min finds that Joshua is nowhere and everywhere in London. Every man. Every smell of food they'd eaten together. Someone's laugh. Cigarette smoke. It seems utterly removed from the wide, dusty plains of the home they'd left in Australia; removed from the ghost house, tucked onto the flank of Seannay. She thinks about how she will describe the colours to Cassandra when they get home. To her mother, whom she misses with surprising ferocity.

Min thinks of the ocean. It had taken her coming here – leaving the islands – to make her realise how much she loves them. How much she feels as though she belongs there, pitted by wind and salt. The thud and hiss of wave on rock. Cassandra's stories of the world beneath the frothy, churning surface of the ocean. As she and Theo cross a road in Bloomsbury, she decides that she will learn to dive. As they shelter from a sudden burst of summer rain under the awning of an antique store, she decides she will learn to dive *deeply*. She will go where Cassandra cannot, if only to bring her stories of the colours that she finds there.

PART THREE

Chapter Fifteen

OCTOBER (THEIR FIRST YEAR)

It is autumn on the islands. There are bushfires in Australia. Spring there. Not bushfire season. The catastrophic fires, in this time that is supposed to be wet and damp, are terrifying. Min catches Luda reading the news on her laptop, but she shuts it before Min gets close enough to read the details. Min goes outside and launches herself into the water of the bay.

* * *

Darcy had started emailing John from King's College about articles he'd come across on the topics they'd both found interesting at the conference. It had felt a bit presumptuous at first, but John always seemed pleased to receive them. Eventually – and Darcy is not sure how it happened – Darcy began writing to John about Theo.

Sometimes things about his search for Theo's past. Mostly things about Theo's drinking and the fights he sometimes starts and always finishes. Theo's eyes and hands and how he looks when he runs. And John sometimes writes back or else doesn't, but that never matters. He is an idea, a figurehead, and Darcy pours out his heart.

* * *

The cormorants here are black. The spirits of drowned women come back onto land. Luda tries not to think of Min – who, over the past few months, has gone from paddling and splashing to holding her breath and diving. Luda tells herself that it's no different from Min disappearing on her pony for hours on end. She drinks wine and scrolls through the information she has gathered so far on the women who met on these islands. It's patchy, factual. With the exception of Magdalena, she doesn't even know their names. All Iris has passed on to her is a list recording supernatural sightings on the islands – ghostly figures and strange lights. And that had been months ago, and the sightings themselves were far too modern to have any bearing on the women who called in the whales.

It hadn't mattered what other people thought of them. Until it had.

Broken sea walls and salt-drenched turf. Imaginings of the women. *Promising fruitfulness in nature.* Luda yearns for them more than she yearns for Leanne or anyone else in Narra. Luda wonders what shape the spirits of dead women back home will take. The ones who have died from earth and fist.

Just women, she thinks. *Women.* And drinks.

* * *

Theo carries his own whisky around, now. Theo starts fights at the pub. When he's warmed by liquor, the crowds of people don't seem to bother him. He no longer hovers by doorways and paces along the walls like something caged and fretting.

Pissed, he's just like everyone else. Even with his goddamn hands. Theo still visits the Wailing Cliffs. Theo still dreams of Darcy.

* * *

Tristan hunches at his desk and reads a short press release, announcing the recent publications from the new lecturer in the school of classics at King's College, London. He holds his breath, wondering if this is the moment where regret will suck him under, but it doesn't. He's where he's meant to be. With them.

There's a knock at the office door and he rises to open it.

Darcy lets himself in and does not shrug off his jacket. 'I found this list of supernatural sightings that Iris gave to Mum and I think it's related to where Theo's come from. I need you to help me track down some old parish newsletters.'

Tristan sighs. Darcy has been doggedly pursuing Theo's origins since their trip to London. 'Lord, Darce. I'm an *archaeologist*. Would you ask a cardiologist to bandage a scratch on your finger?'

'If he was there and I needed it done.'

'Why, *why* would you want to go looking through that drivel? What on earth's going to be in there?'

'If you're going to get all pissy about it …' Darcy turns back towards the stairs.

'Fine. Alright. Wait.' Tristan sighs. 'You really need to do it?'

'Yes. I really do.'

* * *

Min likes to stand on the very edge of the Wailing Cliffs, staring out at the sea. She no longer tries to make sense of things in school. She no longer sees Kole and his friends, although she is aware of his eyes on her occasionally. Resentful and yearning and curious. He is taking a year off to work before heading to the mainland to study next year.

The gap in their ages seems more pronounced now that he's finished school.

Instead, she has the water, Cassandra, Ewan. She has the unexpected wonder of her own company. The deep.

Min sits at the stern of Ewan's boat and licks her salty lips. Min has never seen a whale in a single one of her dives. Just their blurred and shifting shapes, heavy on the shoreline. The endless ghosts of them. Holding her breath until her body roars and bucks.

Peaceful, now. She has seen starfish and flounders and pale, sun-flecked sand. She has seen large silver fish and crabs. She has seen birds, diving for fish the colour of shadows. Anemones.

She collects pieces from the deep to put on Cassandra's windowsill. They have replaced the flowers and gorse. She collects rubbish and grimaces at the sodden weight of it. Min will sit in Cassandra's too-warm front room. They will drink tea and eat scones and Cassandra will tell her stories about the water. 'I've never been down as deep as you,' Cassandra says, her voice wistful.

Min tells Cassandra about every dive. Every sensation of her body, the play of light across the sand and the shimmer of small, wary fish. Min sometimes struggles to find the words for the world under the water. 'I'm not me,' she says finally. And Cassandra nods. 'Go on.'

As Min speaks, Cassandra always closes her eyes and listens. Sometimes, Min has the sensation that the words themselves are unnecessary. That she could perhaps sit here and think her thoughts and that Cassandra would somehow know them.

Cassandra. The water. Min finds a steadiness. She no longer thinks of the sound of metal against wood. The tang of blood on dry, Australian air.

Near the stern of the boat, there is the sound of a body landing in the water, the flap of fins, a seal face peering up at them and then disappearing beneath the spangled surface.

'How far down do you actually go when you dive?' Ewan asks, over the sound of the anchor sluicing through water.

'I've told you, Ewan. To the bottom.' Min pulls her pants off and her flippers on.

Ewan makes a noise.

'What? I do.'

'It's ...' He glances into the cabin. 'Sixty-one metres down to the floor here.'

Min shrugs. 'You asked.'

'There is no way you get down there without a tank. And how the hell do you get back up?'

Min turns to the water and breathes carefully – the way she's read and practised. She pulls on her fins and then she's in the water. Packing air, little sips.

She knows because Cassandra knows.

The sea is clear today. She pushes down, down. Waiting for that moment when the weight of water helps her draw herself deeper and deeper. Her lungs burn, but she's used to that. She can ignore it. She listens to the sound of the ocean, the clicks and whooshes and the creaking, restless sound that sometimes comes from the wrecks.

It's so dark.

At the bottom of the sea, she waits, listening to the thud of her heart in her ears. In the water, she forgets. She is Min. She is not Min. In the water her words all disappear. She becomes sound and shadow. Memories skitter away like schools of small, uneasy fish. In the water, she becomes like Theo's Before.

There is no Narra. No scattering of birds, no sound of metal against wood. This deep in the sea, there is no space where her father once existed.

Hazily, she reaches down to the sand. A shell. She pushes off and swims. Drags herself up. She's read about hypoxia. She's read about fizzing, bubbling blood. Embolisms. Death. She forgets these things, these words. She forgets that she should not be able to dive so far down. The water makes her forget. The water, in these moments, is everything.

At the surface she takes a deep breath, right near the stern of Ewan's boat. The shock of air. She holds up the shell, treading water. She will smile, soon. But not yet. This fresh from a dive, she has forgotten about smiling. Ewan stares at her. She realises then that another boat has pulled up next to his, and that the man on it – a man who had once told Min stories of whales and dolphins while she waited at the docks for Ewan – is also staring at her. Min tosses the shell onto the deck of Ewan's boat and hauls herself up after it.

Ewan glances at her and then the man on the other boat. 'Where'd you get that shell?' the man asks.

Min tries to answer, but her words have not come back yet.

Ewan tosses a towel at her. 'Get dry. You'll freeze.'

She methodically towels herself off and then drapes the towel around her body and shimmies into the pile of dry clothes she'd left for herself.

The man shakes his head, gives them another uncertain look, and starts the engine of his boat.

Ewan picks up the shell from the deck and runs his fingers around the edge of it.

'You shouldn't be able to do that,' he says unsteadily. 'Fucking hell, Min. You were gone for fifteen minutes. I'd flagged Collin down to help me because I thought you'd …' He closes his eyes and exhales through his nose. 'And how would I tell your mum about that? What would I say to Darcy? And Cassandra. Lord, she'd murder me. She'd rip me to pieces if I let anything happen to you out here. Nobody can hold their breath for that long.'

Min stares out at the waves. 'I can.'

He hands her back the shell.

'You don't have to bring me out anymore if you don't want to.'

'No, I like bringing you out.' He looks at her. 'I just … I don't understand.'

'There's nothing to understand. I can hold my breath. I can dive.' She closes her eyes for a moment. 'Cassandra says that everyone has things they're good at.'

* * *

'It's not much to go on,' Tristan says to Darcy, sitting back from the microfilm in the archives room at the Big Island library. The parish newsletters had yielded a name that Darcy is almost insufferably smug about. He had made a call outside and returned with a wide smile. He is utterly convinced that he's right. That a jagged, lonely island north of Big Island is where Theo had lived before being found on Seannay.

'It makes sense, though, doesn't it?' Darcy had abandoned the microfilms an hour ago and has since been poring over tidal maps, trying to interpret the numbers and lines. He'd started swearing under his breath so emphatically that someone had taken pity on him and run him through the basics. Lost in data and records, Darcy has relaxed. 'It makes sense that this is where Theo could have come from.'

'I suppose,' says Tristan. He glances down again at the notes Darcy has brought in with him. 'But then why didn't Carter work it out?'

'Because Carter doesn't care about finding out the truth as much as I do,' Darcy says, and looks down as though he has given something away. 'Anyway, Ewan's taking us out there tomorrow.'

'You already organised it?' Tristan grimaces. 'Then why the hell did you subject me to the horror of the parish newsletters?'

Darcy shrugs. 'I was pretty sure and now I know.'

'It's a nice idea, Darce. But that doesn't mean it's true.'

'Of course it is! It *fits*. We're going out tomorrow and I'm sure Theo will recognise something there.'

'Well, if you're sure,' says Tristan, picking at one of his nails. 'If you *know*.'

'What? You don't think I should? You think I'm wrong about it?'

Tristan glances up, looking tired. 'Shit, Darce. I think you're probably right. You're always right. Does Theo know you've been looking into all of this?'

'Yeah, of course. I told him back in London that I was going to work it out.'

'And he believed you?'

'How the hell would I know?'

'What does your mum think about all this?'

Darcy flicks at the curling corner of a map. 'Don't know.'

'You haven't told her? About any of it?'

'She didn't ask.'

'Would you tell her if she did?'

Darcy stares at him and then half-smiles. 'I don't know. Maybe.'

Tristan presses his fingers together. 'Does it bother you?'

'I didn't realise this was a therapy session. Are you charging a fee?'

'Darce.'

'No, I don't care.'

'And what do you reckon taking Theo out there is going to do to him?'

'It'll be fine. Ewan's taking me out this afternoon so I can check … so I can make sure there's nothing … traumatic there.'

'Right. Shove the bodies into a closet before the prodigal son returns home.'

Darcy ignores this. He stares down at the map. 'And Theo's nosediving anyway. This might help him level out.'

'You think so?'

Darcy begins packing the maps away.

Tristan leans forward. 'Have you told him about the island?'

Darcy looks up. 'If I tell him, he's going to freak out, then spend the next God-knows-how-long in a neurotic, self-destructive spiral, giving himself alcohol poisoning and …' Darcy frowns. 'I thought I'd save us all that and just take him straight out.'

'You don't think taking him out there with no warning is a bit … cruel?'

'It's not cruel.' Darcy shuts the folder of maps. 'It's logical. It's necessary.'

'You know Theo better than I do.'

'I know.'

'Well, if you're sure.'

Darcy appears suddenly aged and wise and very, very young. 'I am.'

* * *

Theo stares at his hands. Since Darcy sliced through the webbing between his smallest fingers, the webbing between the rest of his fingers has begun to regrow. It fills him with a strange sort of shame. He wears gloves. He tries to press the webbing down so that it is less obvious. Sometimes, he bandages them. He's been so caustic about the whole thing that he is rarely asked about them anymore.

It makes it so hard for him to draw. To eat with a knife and fork.

Still, he can hold a pint and throw a dart. He's grateful for that, at least.

'Another one, thanks,' he says to Louise.

He can see her calculating how much he's had. She pulls him another and slides it across the bar.

'You're an angel,' he says.

She narrows her eyes.

Theo turns and spots Cassandra sitting in her usual spot. It's late for her to be here. He sits down opposite her and she smiles, lifts her whisky in greeting. 'Theofin,' she says.

'How are you?'

'Oh, as well as can be expected at this age.' She pauses. 'I can't help you, Theofin. I wish I could.'

'Help me with what?'

She looks at him intently. 'I don't know where you came from.'

'I wasn't going to ask anything.'

'Aye. You were.'

Theo stares down at his hands. Rain begins to fall on the pub roof – only lightly, but they can hear the roar of it becoming heavier in the distance. 'You really don't know?'

'No, lad. I wish I did.'

Later, he goes outside and smokes a joint in the flickering light streaming from inside the pub. He spots Ewan crunching across the gravel car park and waves him over.

'Heard you're taking Darcy and me out tomorrow,' he says. 'Something about a crypt on Doolay he wants to look at?'

Ewan grunts and Theo offers him the joint. Ewan takes a long drag and passes it back to Theo. 'Min can hold her breath for fifteen minutes.'

Theo gazes down at the lit end of the joint, considering this. 'Shit. That's not normal, is it?'

'No.' Ewan nods at Theo's hands. 'They're still giving you grief?'

'It's fine.'

'You should see a doctor.'

'No.'

'Why?' Ewan's impatient voice.

'I shouldn't have tried to get rid of those last ones.'

'Maybe they would have grown back anyway.'

'Maybe.' Theo takes another deep drag on the joint. 'I was hoping they'd settle down, but they haven't.'

'Just go to a doctor.'

Theo looks at him and butts out the last of the joint.

He can sense Ewan watching him, exasperated, as he walks towards the door of the pub, his hands pressed deeply into the pockets of his winter jacket.

* * *

Min falls into a doze on the couch that evening, and when she wakes up it's dark and Darcy is typing something up on his laptop. Min listens to the clack of the keys and then she stretches and stands. She spends so much time in the water these days, dreams of the water so deeply, that it always takes her a moment to adjust to land when she wakes up.

'What time is it?' she asks.

'Midnight,' Darcy says, not looking up from the screen.

Although Darcy has taken to sleeping in an old caravan, he still seems to prefer studying in the ghost house. The caravan has been pulled up on the hillside near the ghost house. He'd bought it cheap and Tristan had towed it across the causeway for him with great difficulty and a lot of swearing. Upstairs, Luda shifts in her sleep.

'Ewan said he took you out on the water today, and that you're taking Theo tomorrow,' Min says. She picks her words carefully, trying to sound flippant. Sisterly. 'Since when do you like boats?'

'I don't.' He keeps typing.

'What are you doing, Darcy?' she asks, more quietly. She knows he talks to Tristan, but sometimes Tristan looks at Darcy with such intensity as they talk about degrees and doctorates and scholarships and fellowships that Min wonders whether Tristan sees Darcy at all, or whether he instead just sees some alternate version of himself.

'Trying to study.' Darcy frowns. 'Some of us are in our final year.'

She closes her eyes and for a moment it feels like she's swimming. Diving. 'Darcy …'

Darcy snaps the laptop shut. 'What?'

'Why are you taking Theo out on a boat?'

'Hasn't Ewan told you?' His tone becomes mocking. 'Anyway, you'd know if you ever bothered to ask me about anything I've been doing.'

'I do ask you and you bloody ignore me!' She waits for him to say something, but he's opened his laptop again. 'Where are you taking Theo?'

'Piss off, Min.' His tone is exasperated, careless. Min, who has been feeling so calm and grown-up lately, who has been imagining herself into a sort of sea creature, reaches across and pinches Darcy hard on the arm.

'Ow!' Darcy looks at her, wide eyed. 'You *pinched* me!'

She does it again.

'Shit, Min! Don't!'

'You can't lock me out of everything and then have a go at me about not knowing what you're doing! Never mind that you don't give a flying fuck about anything that I'm doing. You're such a *dick*!'

They stare at each other, Darcy holding his arm. It's the first time he's properly looked at her in months. 'You finished?'

'No!' She goes to pinch him again but he catches her wrist. 'Tell me about what you've been doing! Tell me about Theo!'

'If you do that *one* more time …'

'Goddammit, Darcy! Just tell me what you've been doing!'

A weariness passes over Darcy's face. He lets go of her wrist and he shuts his laptop and piles up his books. He bundles them up under his arm and turns to leave.

Min exhales. So much spun between them. 'Just ... tell me something.'

He turns at the door, looking tired and worried and annoyed. 'Not tonight,' he says and leaves.

* * *

The next day, Theo and Darcy walk to the docks, finding Min perched at the stern of Ewan's boat.

'What the hell are you doing here?' Darcy snaps.

Min smiles. 'You're up to something and I want to know what.'

'It's just a crypt,' Theo says. He's wearing sunglasses, a hat pulled down low over his face to protect his eyes from the sun. He smiles at Min and bumps his shoulder against hers once he's on the boat.

'T,' she says, and loops an arm around his middle, tugging him up beside her. 'You really reek of smoke.'

'Get off the boat,' says Darcy.

'Tried that already,' Ewan says, leaning out of the cabin.

Min brushes at an oil stain on her jacket, ignoring them both. 'Done any new drawings lately?' she asks Theo.

Darcy moves closer and Ewan ducks inside the cabin, muttering, 'Oh boy.'

'Get. Off. The. Boat.'

'Make me,' says Min, but Theo can feel her tensing next to him.

'I wouldn't try it,' says Theo to Darcy. 'She's burly.'

'I am not burly,' says Min. 'I'm ...'

'Sinewy,' Ewan calls from the cabin.

'I am not sinewy.' She crosses her arms. 'I'm strong.'

'I don't care!' Darcy snaps.

'There's no way you can get me off this boat unless I let you,' Min says, 'and I'm not going to let you, so let's just go.'

'This has nothing to do with you, and you weren't invited, so piss off.'

'Suck. *Shit*. I'm staying.'

'Classy,' Ewan calls.

'Oh, you swear worse than anyone!' Min yells back.

'What's the big deal?' Theo asks, his hands in the pockets of his jacket. He looks at Darcy. 'It's just an old crypt.'

Darcy rests his hands on the gunwale and doesn't answer.

'Let's go,' Min says to Ewan, moving to help him cast off.

They head towards the west face of a ragged spit of land north of Big Island. It had been inhabited once, but now the place feels broken and mournful.

'The only people who come here are the farmers who graze their sheep,' Darcy says, his voice sullen. He stands with his arms crossed, resting against the side of the cabin.

Theo and Min sit cross-legged in the hull, Min using Theo's leg to practise her knots. They don't talk. Theo offers Min his flask and she considers it and then shakes her head. Theo has a swig. He glances at Darcy more than he usually would, safe behind the reflective lenses of his sunglasses.

'So, what's this crypt?' he asks.

Darcy pretends not to hear him.

Ewan stays in the cabin and ignores them all, although a few times he glances at Min as though to confirm she has not flung herself into the sea.

Finally, Ewan docks the boat at a pier that has clearly been mended many, many times. Darcy moves towards the edge of it and glances over at Theo, waiting for him to follow. Min makes a move to join them and Ewan puts a hand on her shoulder. 'Leave them be,' Theo hears him mutter.

'He's up to something.'

'Leave them,' Ewan says again, and Theo pushes his sunglasses up and, squinting, tries to catch Ewan's eye. Ewan mutters something under his breath and goes back into the cabin. Min's eyes narrow and Theo expects her to ignore Ewan but instead she turns away from them, leaning over to inspect the water off the far side of the boat.

Theo watches Darcy wrap his jacket more firmly around himself. Watches him swallow and breathe in deeply so that all the muscles in his neck seem to flicker and stall.

Theo is first off the boat. He balances on the broken wood of the pier and leans into the wind. He watches Ewan open the cabin door to say something to Darcy, who nods. The wind snatches the words before Theo can make them out. Then Ewan says something to Min and she points out to sea and Ewan starts the boat engine up. Min doesn't turn to look at them as the boat moves away from the sunken pier.

Theo studies Darcy and smiles a little when Darcy stiffens and turns.

'This way,' Darcy says, and begins to navigate the ruins of the pier.

There's so much wind that Theo finds himself almost unable to draw breath. They move into the shadow of the hill and the world quietens. Hidden almost completely by the crag of the hill is the opening of a small crypt. From the far side of the island, they can hear the sound of the waves crashing violently into rocks.

'This is it?' Theo asks.

'Yes.'

'So, what are we doing here?'

Darcy takes a deep breath. 'You know Luda's been bringing home all sorts of weird articles and research and other bits and pieces that could help her find out more about the executed women.' Darcy steps up onto a small rock, squints away from Theo. 'I go through them, sometimes. The papers. And a few months back I found this anonymous record of supernatural sightings on the islands that only stopped a few years ago. It turned up in a car boot sale and someone passed it on to Iris who passed it on to Mum. A lot of the reports seemed to happen when people were pissed and on their way home from the Blue Fin, but there was one that stuck out. A farmer on the edge of Big Island reported regularly seeing flashing lights coming from the direction of Doolay. He keeps his sheep here and knows the island like the back of his hand. He figured it couldn't be people, that it *had* to be magic. And then the flashing lights stopped at around the time that you were found.'

Theo has gone very still. Darcy ploughs steadily on. 'I managed to track down the full name of the farmer through the parish newsletters and got in touch with him. I wanted to make sure the lights had actually stopped, not just that he had stopped reporting them to whoever was keeping the records. He confirmed that they had – he explained that this side of the island is the only place anyone in their right mind would dock. He told me that he can see it from his own pastures on Big Island, if he gets out his binoculars. He tends to keep an eye on things – just to make sure nobody's getting up to any funny business, like taking his sheep or anything.' Darcy swallows. 'He also told me that the only structure on the island is an old crypt built into the hillside. A barrow, I guess. He fenced it off decades ago to keep his sheep from getting into mischief and hasn't bothered looking at it since. I've done the research, and you *can* dock on the other side of the island – it's just incredibly dangerous. There's a small bay, but it's surrounded by cliffs. You have to get the timing exactly right to get into the narrow harbour mouth or you'll be smashed into the rocks. But if you make it, you can dock here without being seen.' Darcy takes a deep breath and steps closer to Theo. 'Theo, I think this is where you came from.'

Theo glances around. Somewhere, a cormorant calls. 'What?'

'I think you and your mum lived here, Theo. Well, for a while. I think she was … transient. And I think … I think she was trying to get out of the bay. Or get back in. And something went wrong.'

There is only the sound of the waves. Neither of them move. Theo's blood thumps too hard. Everything suspended. The way the grass flickers in the wind, the shape of the sheep silhouetted against the grey day. Then, quite suddenly, everything seems to crash over him and he's overcome with a sort of recklessness. He lunges at Darcy and kisses him. For a moment Darcy is stunned into stillness. For a moment, Theo thinks that he may kiss back.

And, for a moment, he does.

But then Darcy pulls away, takes one step back and then another, his expression bewildered.

'How do you know that I came from here?' Theo asks, his voice uneven. He begins to crack the joints of his knuckles, resisting the impulse he has to close the space between him and Darcy and kiss him again and again.

'I *don't* know,' says Darcy. He takes a deep breath.

They stare at each other and then Theo turns away, suddenly damp with sweat. 'Have you told Carter already, or did you want to wait until you'd brought me out here? The rights have already been sold around the world – you'd be famous.' Theo's voice is acidic. 'You going to go tell him that this is … this is …'

'Bloody hell, Theo.' Darcy rubs at his jaw. 'Of course not.'

Theo's voice is raw, too loud. He feels giddy with pain and confusion. 'Why the fuck would you just … *bring me here?*'

Darcy steps closer. 'Is it familiar?'

'Fuck you.' Theo stomps further onto the island and Darcy follows him. Theo vaults over the old stone wall barring the entrance to the crypt. He stops there, glancing back at Darcy, knowing that he probably looks frightened and young and furious.

Theo hovers near it, dragging his hands through his hair. 'I can't …' He cracks another knuckle, starts pacing backward and forward in front of the tomb's mouth. He wants to claw the webbing from his fingers. He wants to touch Darcy, who has reverted to his default don't-fucking-touch-me energy.

Darcy climbs over the wall and holds out a torch. Theo stops. 'You've been here before,' Theo says, his voice trembling. God, he hates that tremble.

'I had to check.' Darcy bites down on his lip. *Check for bodies.* Unspoken between them. *Check for bones that are not ancient.*

Theo pushes the torch away, keeps pacing.

Darcy leans against the wall. 'There's a wooden door inside,' he says. 'Just past where the passage twists out of sight. There's what looks like an old air mattress, bedding, some women's clothes, rusted cans of food, a gas heater.' Darcy pauses. 'Do you remember anything?'

Theo gives him a look. 'Fuck you,' he says, more quietly this time. And then he turns away from the crypt.

* * *

Min dives in the waters near Doolay, while Ewan fishes with a rod. When she reaches the surface, when she comes back to herself, Min watches him from the water. 'No self-respecting fisherman would sit in their boat with a rod.'

'Aye, and no self-respecting fisherman would spend all his time chauffeuring your ungrateful arse around,' he says, without looking at her.

Min smiles, backstroking to the stern of the boat. 'Touché.' She climbs back onto the deck. 'Fishing's getting harder, isn't it?'

'Well, it's never been the easiest way to make a pound.'

'You know what I mean.' She wraps a towel around her shoulders and they both stare towards Doolay, Ewan tapping a finger against his chair.

'Caught another triggerfish the other day.'

'Umm … good for you?'

'They used to be unheard of this far north. Now they're just … here.'

'Oh.'

'Aye,' he says, curtly. 'We should go pick them up.'

'Alright.' She works her way into dry clothes on the deck behind the cabin while Ewan guides the boat back towards the sunken pier. Min sees them before they've docked, Darcy sitting with his chin cupped in his hands, looking thoughtful and annoyed while Theo paces up and down the shoreline near the pier.

'Oh, this is going to be a fun trip back,' Ewan mutters to Min, as he cuts the engine.

Theo almost sprints across the pier, nimble enough to be startling. He begins to pace on the deck as he had been on the shore. Darcy is slower, picking his way carefully across the submerged planks. 'Thanks,' he says to Ewan, and follows him into the cabin.

Min sits down in the hull with the rope, keeping an eye on Theo as he paces and paces and paces. Finally he stops, just in front of her. She tugs one of her ropes free from under his shoes.

'You dived,' he says.

'Yeah.'

A pause. He takes a ragged breath. 'Did you see any ... any wrecks?' He begins pacing again before he's finished speaking.

Min rises and watches him. She waits. Eventually he comes back to her and stands very close, his breathing uneven.

'No. Should I have?'

'You knew about this, didn't you?'

'About what, T?' She glances towards the cabin and then back to Theo. 'I have no bloody idea what today was about. Darcy wouldn't tell me.'

Theo begins to crack his knuckles again, viciously, one after the other. Min watches him for a moment and then puts her hand on his and stops him. 'Do you want to talk about it?' she asks, quietly.

He shakes his head, keeps moving. Min goes into the cabin, which is very noisy and seems very small with her and Ewan and Darcy all inside at the same time. 'What the hell have you done to him? I've never seen him this worked up before!'

Darcy stiffens but says nothing. He traces a finger along the back of a seat.

'Darcy! Bloody hell! What *happened*?'

Ewan minutely shakes his head at her over Darcy's shoulder, his own expression confused and a bit pissy. Min considers poking Darcy, or tackling him to the floor of the cabin and pulling his hair until he tells her what happened. Instead, she makes a rude gesture at him and goes out onto the deck.

Back on Big Island, they all head off in separate directions. Min heads towards the flow, that wide-open bay south of the town that is – for now – almost unruffled by wind. It has a narrow neck and a stretch of white sandy beach where she leaves her clothes in a pile. There are shipwrecks in its belly and she dives down to them, again and again. They creak and groan. Down here, she can forget about Theo and Darcy.

Down here, she is mesmerised by the play of shadow and light, in just the way her mother would be. She presses her fingers to rusted iron and brings up armfuls of rubbish. Old shoes and crushed plastic bottles, thick with goose barnacles. Packing tape and endless, bright shards of broken plastic.

After, she walks along the main street of town, hair dripping down her back, rubbish carried in sacks and squashed into her schoolbag. She pauses when she spots Kole, his arm looped around the shoulders of a young woman with short, dark hair and a wide, easy smile. She could have had that. She could have *had that*.

She breathes out. She did not want it. Does not want it. She walks home with rubbish in her bag.

* * *

When they get back to Big Island, Theo goes straight to the Blue Fin and then, when he's about to get kicked out, he goes home. He's sober enough to get inside without waking Iris. He lies down on his unmade bed, surrounded by the things he's brought here from the edge of the sea. He clenches his fists until his hands begin to throb. He drinks whisky until everything loses its precise shape. He pulls out one old sketchbook and then another, until the little piece of paper he'd been looking for flutters out.

He pulls out his mobile phone and then lies back on his bed and waits.

'Hello?' The voice on the other end of the line is groggy and confused. A little bit afraid.

Theo glances at the time. It's nearly two in the morning.

'Researcher Carter?' he asks.

'Who is this?'

'It's Theofin Muir.' He rolls onto his stomach. His words blur. 'I've been considering your offer.'

Chapter Sixteen

NOVEMBER (THEIR FIRST YEAR)

Outside the Blue Fin, a frost lies on the grass. The snow will come soon. The men speak of a lass who can dive to the bottom of the ocean. They make sure the foundling is not there, first. He has punched more than one of them in the face when they've said the wrong thing about the Managans. It is agreed that he's a bleeding heart. Almost as emotional as the women.

He is not at the Blue Fin tonight and so they speak of the lass. Not a selkie, not a spirit. 'Cold fish,' someone says. 'You'd ken all about that, eh, Collin?' Someone spills their ale as they laugh.

* * *

Luda has just come back from walking the edge of Big Island with Violet, who comes by now and then and rarely speaks to Darcy or to Min. Darcy comes inside as Luda is making herself a cheese sandwich. He nods over his shoulder at Ewan's car, slowly crossing over the causeway.

'You expecting him?' Darcy asks, flicking the kettle on.

Luda shakes her head. They wait for Ewan, who steps into the room tentatively, wearing odd socks. 'Do you have a few minutes?'

'Which one of us?' Darcy asks, for Ewan has not looked particularly at either of them.

Ewan looks at him, then.

'You.'

'Right,' says Luda, sticking her sandwich into her mouth. 'I'll be outside.'

They watch her go. 'Is it about Theo?' Darcy asks.

Ewan shakes his head. 'I haven't seen much of him since he sprinted off the boat. Have you spoken to him since?'

'He won't speak to me,' Darcy says. 'What's this about then?'

'Min. Her diving.'

Darcy pulls two mugs from the shelf. He still feels utterly deflated by everything that happened on the lonely island with Theo. The same old pattern – being clever enough to find the pieces of things that other people miss, but failing in the execution. He feels as though he has unleashed something in Theo that was better being contained.

'What about her diving?' he asks, not really paying attention.

Ewan sits down. 'I've been thinking about whether to bring it up or not. But I have to. She shouldn't be able to do it.'

'Do what?'

'Most people can free-dive a few metres, if they're lucky. Even with a scuba-diving tank and all of the equipment, if you're diving more than forty metres, it's classified as technical and you've got to have all these logged hours and certifications and things before any of the dive companies will take you out.'

Darcy studies the plastic Christmas tree that Tristan had inexplicably set up on top of the piled photo albums. It wasn't even *December* yet. 'Min doesn't scuba-dive, though.'

'No,' Ewan agrees.

The kettle boils and Darcy makes two instant coffees, black.

'She's diving down with just her flippers and goggles. Yesterday, she came up with this.' He puts the shell down on the table.

Darcy picks it up and examines it. 'I don't know what this is.'

'It's a dog cockle from the sea floor.'

'How far down's the sea floor?'

'From where she dived for this? Fifty-five metres. But I've clocked her up over sixty.'

Darcy looks at Ewan properly, then. 'Sixty metres?'

'Sometimes she's gone for fifteen minutes, Darcy.' Ewan looks up, his expression almost desperate. 'She shouldn't be able to do it. The water's freezing. There are all sorts of risks diving that deep.'

Darcy taps his fingers on the table. 'Why are you telling me this? Tell *Mum*.'

Ewan winces. 'I thought you might tell her. If you thought she needed to know.'

'You don't want to tell her?'

'Not particularly.'

'Why?'

Ewan shrugs.

'Because Min asked you not to? Or because Mum's been such a shit to you about Allie?'

Ewan's whole body flinches this time. 'You really can be quite the prick.'

Darcy scowls. 'I don't want to *know*.'

'She's your sister and you should.'

Darcy frowns.

'She … she shouldn't be able to do it.' Ewan gnaws on his bottom lip for a moment and it makes him look oddly boyish. 'I keep thinking I'm imagining it somehow. But even Collin saw her a few weeks back. Been saying things down at the pub about her being strange.'

'She *is* strange.'

'You know what I mean.'

'There're always rumours floating around about someone or other.' Darcy gazes down at his coffee. 'Maybe it's not as deep as you think.'

'I look at the fathometer. It *is* that deep.' Ewan shakes his head. 'I don't understand.'

Darcy sits back, turns the shell over in his hands. 'I still don't get why you're telling me this? What do you want me to do?'

Ewan's eyes narrow. 'Nothing.'

'Because I can't fix everyone! All I do is make things worse.' He draws in a long, shaking breath. 'I don't want to hear anything else about her diving, okay? Call me if she's hurt or turns into a squid, but ...'

Ewan stares at him, one eyebrow cocked.

'I don't want to hear,' Darcy says, and he can feel the tremble in his own words.

* * *

Theo is restless, waiting for the time when he'll ride his newly acquired, very old bike to the pub on the far side of Big Island to meet with Carter. He goes to the pebbled beach and drinks vodka and smokes a joint. By-the-wind-sailors have been cast up onto the pebbles, blue and gleaming. Dozens of them. Theo has only ever seen them in spring and in summer. It makes him suck harder on his joint.

Theo had expected Carter to come to the islands straight away, but Carter had deadlines. Carter had *meetings*. It has been weeks since Theo had called him and it is only now that he is finally scheduled to arrive.

Theo inhales thick smoke; half-hoping Darcy will see him and come out. He has been avoiding Darcy since Doolay. Goddamn Doolay. Nothing about it had been familiar to him. Not the stones nor the contours of the earth nor the very particular sound of the wind. His memories remain wordless – colours, water, the sense of being carried by many hands.

The disappointment of this latest, unexpected failure makes him feel skinless. He studies the tidal island, wanders across the beach. He spots a woman with pale hair kneeling near the gorse as though in prayer.

It is not the first time Theo has seen women here like this. And so he does what he always does and makes himself invisible to her. Stills himself so that his body sinks into the rocks and air and water.

'Theo?' Darcy's voice.

Theo blows out another mouthful of smoke, acutely aware of the sound of Darcy's footsteps coming closer. The woman stands, tugs her jacket more firmly around her, and begins to walk towards the causeway.

Theo turns. Darcy's standing a few feet away, his fists balled at his sides. He's breathing shallowly, as though he wants to say something, but he doesn't. Can't. 'That will rot your brain.'

'Not much to rot.'

'Bullshit.'

'What do you want?' Theo asks.

'Are you … are you okay?'

Theo studies the end of the joint, feeling like the world is shifting. He has to be careful not to set his gloves alight. 'I'm grand.'

'Do you …' Darcy hunches his shoulders. 'Do you want to come in?'

'No. I'm only here killing time before I meet Carter.'

For a moment, Darcy looks confused and Theo feels a lurch before bracing against it. *The island. The island. He took me to that fucking island.* He can't quite hold onto the rage, though. Just the idea of it. He wants, absurdly, to giggle.

'You're … meeting *him*?'

'Sure.' Theo glances up at the clouds, struck, for a moment, by how close they seem.

Darcy's fists clench tighter at his sides. 'Why the hell would you meet him?'

Theo bites down on the impulse to laugh, butts the joint out on a nearby rock and retrieves the remains of his vodka. He is careful not to avoid the by-the-wind-sailors. 'Because I can.'

'It's not a good idea.'

Theo smirks. 'Just because you hate everyone on the planet, doesn't mean I do.'

Darcy rubs at his forehead. 'Really? You're going there?'

Theo tucks the vodka bottle under his arm. He'll stash it among the rocks before he crosses onto Big Island. 'Bye,' he says, taking a couple of unbalanced steps. 'I'll say hi to Carter for you!'

Theo rides to the other side of Big Island – a smaller town than his own, one built around the ruins of the old bishop's palace. Theo comes here when he's sick of the Blue Fin back in the main town, even though it takes him twenty minutes to get here. He rides more slowly than he usually does, every part of him dulled by alcohol and pot.

He and Carter are the only ones in the pub. Carter looks the same as he had the last time Theo had seen him. He grins and stands. The pub has been decorated with tinsel and a plastic Christmas tree. A battered nativity is set up on the mantle over the gas heater.

'What changed your mind?'

Theo shrugs. Carter orders them both a pint of ale. 'Make it three,' calls Theo, and the publican grunts from behind the bar.

'Can I record this?'

'No.' Theo sits down and props his head on his hand and studies Carter. 'Where are you up to with the book?'

'Still working on it,' Carter says. He glances at Theo's gloves and then away. 'Actually, once I've incorporated whatever we talk about today, it'll be pretty much finished.'

'You waited. You *knew* I'd call.'

'I hoped you would.'

'Just so we're clear, I'm not here to spill my guts,' Theo tells Carter. 'I'm here to listen to you spill yours.'

'Oh? Is that right?' Carter raises an eyebrow and smiles. 'So you've got me all the way out to the islands to find out what's going to be published in a few months, anyway?'

'Hard for you to buy me drinks if you're all the way down in London.'

Carter's smile broadens.

'I want you to get this book right,' Theo says. 'I don't need another load of garbage inflaming everything again.'

'Tell you what. I'll run you through what I have,' Carter says. 'You confirm or give me details as we go along. If you give me what I want and if there's anything you really don't want in there … we can negotiate. Okay?'

Theo tilts the last of the ale into his mouth. 'I need this book to stop things. I need this to be the end to it all.' He wipes his mouth on the back of his glove and inclines his empty pint glass towards Carter.

Carter's voice changes, becomes deeper and more rounded. 'How old were you when you were found?'

'You tell me.'

'I have it written down that you were officially estimated to be seven years old. Correct?'

'Aye.'

'So you agree?'

Theo glances at Carter. 'I don't know. Do I look seventeen now?'

'I'd say you look a bit older than that. Eighteen, at least.'

Theo reaches for his second pint.

Carter clears his throat. 'What are your first memories?'

'Lying on the shore on Seannay with the waves still reaching my feet. Being found there by Ewan. Him cutting the …'

'Cutting the what?'

'Seaweed off me.' He digs his fingers into the flesh of his leg. 'Then ending up with Iris. Getting bundled off to the police station and then the hospital.' He has another mouthful of ale.

'So Ewan found you on the western edge of the tidal island Seannay.'

'Aye. I just said so, didn't I?'

'And how'd you end up with Iris?'

'He must've called her. She …' He frowns, trying to remember. 'She was waiting on Big Island. She and Ewan argued. I think about going to the police.'

'She didn't want to take you?'

'She wanted to … she wanted to take me straight back to her place.' Theo shakes his head. 'We've never discussed it, not really. And I didn't know what they were saying. I didn't really know … English then.' He looks away. 'But I'm sure that's what they were arguing about.'

'So Ewan drove you and Iris to the Big Island police station. Peter Calvin was on duty. Correct?'

'Suppose so.'

'My records say you were there for about an hour. Relevant bodies were notified on the mainland' – Carter slides a list of agencies across the table – 'and then Chief Inspector Peter Calvin and Constable Will Setiawan transported you, Iris and Ewan to Big Island Hospital. It seems that they initially wanted to airlift you to the mainland for assessment, but Iris argued strongly for you to be taken to the local hospital. You were admitted at 9.03 am and remained there in a private room on the general ward from the eighteenth until the twentieth of November. The pediatric ward comprises three beds on one ward, and it was decided you needed privacy.'

'How did you find all this out?'

'Records.'

'Aren't medical records private?'

'Sensitive things get leaked to the papers all the time,' says Carter. 'And then they're in the public domain. Besides, people are normally pretty happy to fill you in on details if you ask them the right way.'

Theo reaches for his drink.

'Iris stayed with you at the hospital. The police exercised powers that allow a child to remain subject to police protection for up to seventy-two hours. You ceased to be subject to police protection on the twentieth. Your care was at that stage formally handed over to Sutherland Family Services. They wanted to place you with an experienced emergency foster carer, but Iris kicked up a fuss. It seems that Calvin pulled some strings to fast track relevant procedures to accredit Iris as a foster carer with Sutherland, which came into effect on the twenty-fourth.'

Theo shrugs. 'I don't know about any dates.'

'The media got a hold of your story. On the nineteenth, Doug Tiernan, the editor of the *Big Island Gazette*, published this image of you on the front page, accompanied by seven hundred words of his own copy, detailing the situation and highlighting your unusual appearance.' Carter flips open another folder. 'Have you read the article?'

'No.' Theo glances down at the image. He's seen it before. Iris, cradling him. All you can see is one hand curled onto Iris's sleeve, the webbing. He has his face turned away from the camera, so that only his mess of water-darkened hair can be seen. Ewan walking alongside Iris, looking frightened and confused and excited.

'By the time you were released on the twentieth, the story had been picked up by five mainland mastheads. By the twenty-first, the first television crew from down south arrived.'

Theo stares down at his ale. All of these things he'd never known about his own goddamn life.

'*The Sun* ran a front-page story on the twenty-third. On the thirtieth, they offered a ten thousand pound reward to anyone with information on where you'd come from. At this stage, media on the ground were becoming problematic. Iris only allowed Calvin and the local priest Frank Rendall in. One of Iris's windows was smashed by a man who fancied himself a bit of a gonzo journalist. He was charged with vandalism and fined. Calvin organised a police presence outside Iris's residence from the first.'

Theo remembers the closed curtains and electric lighting. He thinks he remembers the window being broken – the noise, the sudden drop in temperature. He remembers opening his mouth and screaming. Or perhaps he doesn't remember anything at all.

'Walter Mage, who owns Gazette Corp, offered a two-hundred thousand pound reward for anyone with information.'

'I need to piss,' Theo says, although he doesn't. The bathroom is cool. He rests his head on the wall near the toilet and takes a few deep breaths. Cracks his knuckles. Breathes and breathes. On his way back to the table, he collects another two pints. 'Why?' he asks, when he sits back down. 'Why did people *care*?'

'Is that rhetorical or are you actually asking?' Carter glances at the pints. He's only halfway through his first.

'I'm asking,' Theo snaps.

'I think the answer's three-fold. Firstly, it's a good story. Wildling waif with webbed fingers washes up on an abandoned tidal island in the middle of the North Sea and is found by a young fisherman. It reads like a fairy tale.'

Theo grunts.

'Secondly, when you were found, a lot of the more right-wing outlets were in damage control after corruption allegations involving the Tory prime minister, hence the huge reward and coverage. At the same time, a lot of the more left-wing outlets were covering the slashes to family services in the latest budget, and they pounced on you as a poster boy for vulnerable children in care. With all the big media outlets in the UK covering you, the global interest followed.'

Theo drains the pint.

'Thirdly …' Carter hesitates. 'There'd been five young boys kidnapped across the UK in the eight years leading up to your appearance. There were international campaigns to try and find each of them. Three were murdered, one was being kept in a basement and the other one … he's never been found.' Carter looks at Theo's expression and shakes his head. 'Nothing to do with you, I promise.'

'How do you know?'

Carter exhales. 'He was eight when he went missing, and that was seven years before you were found.' He pauses. 'He was my youngest brother.'

'Shit. I'm sorry … I …'

Carter waves a hand at him, swallows. 'The general public,' he continues, 'followed the stories of these boys. They donated, they marched, they went out and searched the streets, and they followed the trials in the cases where charges were laid.' Carter exhales. 'By the time you were found, I think everyone was ready for a story like yours. No matter what had happened to you, you survived it. You were *alive*, Theo.'

Theo coughs on a mouthful of ale.

'People thought you might *be* one of those missing boys, at first. Zachariah Clements. I think that's why you stayed under police care for the full seventy-two hours before being released to Sutherland.

Clements was ten-years-old and had been missing for four months when you washed up.' Carter sits back in his chair. 'But you weren't him. And then he was found locked up in his uncle's basement.' Carter's expression hardens.

'What happened to him? After?'

Carter shrugs. 'He went back to his mother.' A pause. 'He'd be twenty now.'

Theo cracks his knuckles. 'I don't want to talk about this anymore.'

'Alright. Do you remember anything from before you were found?'

Theo blinks. That lonely, ragged island. He swallows. The island is *his*. Darcy had given it to him, whether he wanted it or not. 'Colours. Blues and greys and greens. That's all.'

'What sort of colours? What sort of blues and greens and greys?'

'The sort you might find in the sea, Carter.'

'Nothing else?'

'No.' *The hands, those carrying hands.*

'There's been a lot of speculation about your genetics. Have you ever had a genetic test done?'

'I've had six mail-out genetic tests done under false names. They all came back as inconclusive. Too much saliva. Errors in collection. There was always an excuse.'

'Those aren't the most reliable tests. Would you ever get detailed sequencing done? I'm sure there are lots of researchers out there who'd –'

'No.' The only reason the tests he'd sent off had been bearable was because they had felt like they still belonged entirely to him – hidden by his made-up name. If the tests had revealed some vital information, that information would have also belonged only to him.

'You've never been to school. Why is that?'

Theo shrugs.

'Go on,' Carter says.

'I don't want this in the book.'

194

'Alright.'

Theo looks at him. 'I mean it. You know those lads who beat the shit out of me in the alley that time? I tracked them all down. I made them *hurt*.'

Carter crosses his arms. 'Understood.'

'School. I don't … I couldn't be in rooms for that long with other people. If the classes were taught out in the schoolyard I might've been okay.'

'Who taught you how to read and write?'

A pause. 'Nobody.'

'You taught yourself?'

'No.'

Theo might be imagining Carter's jaw tightening. 'So you can't read or write.'

Theo says nothing. He looks up at the wood panelling on the ceiling and then motions to the publican for another drink.

Carter clears his throat. It is strange to Theo that it is this that makes Carter uncomfortable. Perhaps because it represents a sort of power imbalance that cannot easily be corrected. What are the ethics of writing a book about somebody who can't read what you've written?

'Some of the people I interviewed around here are convinced you're a selkie,' Carter says.

Theo leans forward a little bit. He bites his lower lip for a moment and then lets his voice soften. He's become so good at getting people's attention when he really wants it. 'And what do *you* think?'

The corner of Carter's mouth twists, as though he's trying not to smile. 'I think that old people will always have their superstitions.'

Carter picks up his pen. 'What's it like when you swim?'

'If you'd done your research properly, you'd know I never swim.'

'Why is that?'

'Selkies die if they go into the water without their skins. Common knowledge.'

'So you think you're a selkie?'

'You clearly know more about me than I do myself, Carter.' Theo rests his elbows on the table. Again, that flickering glance at his hands. 'What do *you* think I am?'

For a moment, something troubled passes across Carter's features. He takes a gulp of ale and wipes his mouth with the back of his hand. 'You know, I started this book because I wanted to dispel all the myths about you. To document each outlet's coverage of you, to lay out how the media can sensationalise an event into a huge, global phenomenon. This book was never meant to be about *you*. It was meant to be about the media and the power of stories.'

Carter pauses and Theo thinks suddenly of Luda's photos – of that image of Darcy, curled up in the cracked bed of the dam.

'I wanted to pull your story apart piece by piece until it was completely ordinary.' Carter presses his hands together and stares down at them. 'That's what I *do*. But you know what? I still have no fucking idea where you came from. And even knowing what I know about the political landscape at the time and the lead up of tragic news … I don't know why your story erupted the way it did.'

Theo doesn't know why this admission makes him feel like shit, but it does. He thinks of Doolay and the crypt. How Darcy had found what Carter had not.

His voice turns needling. 'So you're saying I *could* be a selkie?'

Carter looks suddenly annoyed. 'No. I'm not saying that. I'm *saying* that I have no idea whether you've fallen off a boat near the mainland coast or whether you've floated in on a pile of plastic from the Pacific garbage patch. Selkies aren't real.'

'Are you sure about that?' Theo feels gripped by something he has no words for – which exists in the same space as Darcy's cleverness and his lips and Doolay and the memory of water and carrying hands – Theo pulls his gloves off and holds his flesh out in the dim pub light.

Carter's breath catches. 'Mary, Mother of God.'

'What's your theory about *these*?'

'I thought …' Carter swallows, straightens. His voice settles into its usual timbre. 'I thought it was just the skin between your little fingers.'

'What else have you got wrong?'

'I've never … I've never seen … nobody I spoke to had seen …' Carter reaches out a hand and touches Theo's scarred skin.

Carter calls to the publican, orders them both a whisky.

'Slàinte mhath,' Theo says, and throws it back in one swallow.

'That was eighteen years old,' Carter says. 'You're meant to *savour* it.'

Theo's mouth feels numb. Carter tries to pry more information from Theo and Theo refuses in a way that makes them both flushed. Finally, Theo tugs his gloves back on. 'It's snowing. You going to give me a lift back to town?'

Carter studies him. 'Alright.'

'My bike'll have to go in the back. It's dirty.'

'That's fine.'

Carter takes his time finishing his whisky and then they walk out into the windy night. Theo watches Carter fit his bike awkwardly into the back of the station wagon he's hired. He's very tender with the bike.

Theo moves towards him without really thinking about it. He's drunk enough for the flat ground to feel sloped. And when Carter turns around, Theo's there – inches from his face.

'I'm sorry about your brother.'

Neither of them moves. Theo tries to think clearly, but everything is fractured, tilted. He steps forward, that last inch. Carter grabs him roughly around the back of the head and kisses him hard on the mouth.

They end up in the ruins of the palace, the sky thick with stars. The crumbling, incomplete walls are like fingers reaching, curling. After, Theo throws up on the tourist information sign. They drive back to town with the windows open and the heating on high.

* * *

Later that night, Theo thinks about everything he'd told Carter –
showing Carter his hands – and everything Carter had told him.
He throws up again on his bedroom floor. He stares blankly out
the window at falling snow. He thinks about the abandoned
island, the crypt he could not bear to enter. He cuts the skin
between his own fingers with Iris's sewing scissors and then sits
and cries on the bathroom floor, his hands wrapped in towels.

Theo blearily hears Iris mutter 'mother' into her pillow. An
unhappy yearning in her voice. Iris does not wake.

Chapter Seventeen

JANUARY (THEIR FIRST YEAR)

There is talk at the pub and on the street that Carter, the journalist, the writer, the one who's *doing that book*, had come back to Big Island a few weeks ago for a single night. On her fifteenth birthday, Min swims naked in the icy water of the flow. The one man who notices her averts his gaze and thinks of how strong and graceful she is. The kirk choir continue to be very good but very loud. On the hillside near the main road out of town, someone carves a giant mer-woman out of snow. Her eyes are made of beer cans. Someone carefully arranges seaweed into long, sweeping strands of hair.

* * *

Theo finds work on a farm east of the Wailing Cliffs. The farm is owned by a man called Gerald, who has a penchant for weed and peated whisky. As early winter darkness falls, the two of them relax into a pattern of listening to 1950s rock. Theo sometimes drinks until the world blurs. The weed makes him feel disjointed. It takes him out of his skin, but not in the heady, pleasant way that alcohol does. And the full-time job at Gerald's gets him out of the house.

Sometimes they fuck. The first time takes Theo by surprise, but he meets Gerald's advances with a sort of shocking enthusiasm. He thinks of Darcy, hotly. Furiously. *Fuck you, Darcy Managan.*

He never stays. Gerald never asks him to. Theo rides his bike or else runs unsteadily home along the road that goes by the Wailing Cliffs.

Today he stops. Snow on the ground. The red-hot pain of his hands where he has picked at the cut webbing.

He takes his gloves off, but not even the icy wind, the snow, is enough to dull the ache of them.

He doesn't scream into the wind anymore. Instead he drinks whisky or vodka and watches the waves and thinks, *I came from those waves*. The rhythm in his bones. Gerald's sour breath. Darcy, always just out of reach. Clenched fists. Theo closes his eyes.

He may never know his story, but he knows this: one way or another, he has come from the sea.

* * *

Luda spends weeks at a time on the smaller islands, capturing the broken landscape, the fierce, determined communities. Some islands are down to five inhabitants. They have started carving witch markings onto their seawalls and the eaves of their houses. The sight of those markings makes something inside Luda ache. She senses that the community has forgiven, if not forgotten, the photos she took of the cliff collapse. She thinks, often, of the women. *Her friends*, as Tristan puts it, sometimes with a bite in his voice, but mostly not. The more familiar she becomes with the landscape of the islands, the more she thinks of the women. They are bound up in the very bones of the place.

Ewan drops her back at the docks in the afternoon. 'Thanks, Ewan,' she says and he thumps her on the back.

She finds Tristan waiting for her, blowing warm air into the curve of his bare hands. 'Figured you might like a lift.'

'Thoughtful,' she says. 'Thanks.'

'Your hair is looking …' He squints. '*Not* very nice, actually. Did you stand at the bow the entire time you were on the boat?'

'You know, I wasn't going to comment, but you have an enormous sauce stain on the front of your shirt. I can see it in the dark.'

'Well, shit. I video-conferenced the head of a government department today.'

'Before or after lunch?'

'After.'

'Ouch.' They fall into step together. 'Do you want to have dinner with us?'

'Depends. Are you cooking?'

'I'm getting pizza, Tristan.'

'Then, yes. Yes, I would like that very much.' He glances back at the boat as they reach the car park. 'What does Min do when she's out on the boat?'

Luda smothers a yawn. 'Swims, I guess.'

Tristan straightens. 'You haven't gone out with them? After all that stuff people have been saying?'

'It's crap, Tristan. All of it. You know that as well as I do.'

'But you didn't even ... when's she going out with him again?'

'Tomorrow, probably. Why?'

They reach Tristan's car and climb inside. Luda buckles her seat belt.

'We're going out with them,' Tristan says, starting the car. 'Actually, it's meant to be a bit drizzly tomorrow. *You're* going out with them.'

'No. I'm not.'

Tristan sighs. 'Luda.'

'What? I'm not ... I've never been ... one of those helicopter parents. I don't hover. They wouldn't know what to do if I started now.'

'It's not hovering, it's showing an interest.'

'If she wants me to, I will. Otherwise, I'm giving her space. It's what teenagers need.'

Tristan sighs.

'What?'

'Nothing.'

* * *

Theo smokes in the narrow yard behind Iris's house, cracking his knuckles, thinking about the crypt, about Carter. About those missing, murdered boys. When he comes back inside, Iris looks at him closely, her mouth thin. 'Set the table.'

'What for?' His voice is slow. He straightens.

'Father will be here in ten minutes.'

Theo notices the tablecloth, then. He notices the pots simmering on the hob. Iris watches him, frowning. 'Theofin.'

He thinks of running, straight out the door. He thinks of running to the cliffs, or to the barrow. He thinks of running to the Blue Fin or to Seannay. But he will have to come back, after. And the idea of leaving the islands entirely makes him flinch.

'I'm actually feeling a bit sick ...' he says.

'Father is coming specially. You will eat with us, you will be polite, and you will listen to what he has to say. If you try to leave, with God as my witness, I will tie you up.'

'Sure,' he says, backing away. 'I was just getting changed.'

'Then setting the table?'

'Then setting the table.' He goes into his room. His bandaged hands make it difficult to dial. He dials Min's number, but she doesn't answer. He dials Ewan and he doesn't answer either. Swearing, he dials Tristan's number and speaks low and urgently into the phone. God, he's regretting that joint now. .

Father Lee arrives precisely at six. Iris hangs his jacket up and brings him a tumbler of whisky. Theo sets the table slowly, trying to concentrate, trying not to panic at the sound of Father Lee's voice in the next room. Normally alcohol, smoking, soothes him enough to be able to be inside with other people. But nothing is soothing him tonight.

The doorbell rings. 'Iris! I know you don't like wine, but I brought some anyway. It's a bit shit, though. Sorry.' Tristan strides into the dining room, shedding his jacket and draping it on the back of one of the chairs. 'Something smells wonderful!'

Iris comes into the room, glancing at Theo, at Tristan, and at the extra setting at table. 'I told you Tristan was coming,' Theo mumbles. 'Didn't I?'

For a moment, Iris's fists clench but then she takes a deep breath. 'I must've been distracted.' She narrows her eyes at Tristan and speaks through gritted teeth. 'Can I get you a drink?'

'Anything but the wine.' Tristan catches a glimpse of Father Lee in the living room. 'Actually, the wine is fine. *Whatever* is fine. Just alcohol. Please. Thank you.'

Iris goes back into the kitchen. Tristan raises his eyebrows at Theo. 'Sorry,' Theo mutters. 'I can't … I can't get through a dinner with them. Not at the moment. I panicked.' He frowns. 'Is that a giant stain on your shirt?'

Tristan covers it with a hand. 'You owe me, Muir,' he mutters. 'I was going to have *pizza*.'

'You don't have to stay.' Theo closes his eyes for a moment, telling himself that the walls aren't *really* creeping in closer and closer.

'That whole Doolay thing's really thrown you, hey?'

'You know about it?'

'Not much. Darcy roped me into trawling the parish newsletters.' Tristan grimaces. 'Honestly, Theo. I wanted to gauge my eyeballs out. There was a piece where Father Lee called himself *illustrious*.'

'Darcy shouldn't have done it.'

'No,' says Tristan, more quietly. 'He shouldn't have.'

Iris strides back in and shoves a glass of wine towards Tristan.

'Thank you. Oh, we're just going to drink that at room temperature, are we?' Tristan says. 'Lovely. Room temperature sparkling wine is really *not* served enough, is it?'

Iris appears to spend a moment deliberating whether or not to tip the wine over his head. Theo steadies himself on the back of a chair. His hands ache.

'Go speak to Father Lee,' Iris says to Theo. 'It's rude, leaving him in there alone.'

'I'm not the one who invited him,' Theo says. They stare at each other until Theo has to close his eyes again.

Tristan takes a deep breath before heading into the living room. 'Marcus!' he calls. 'It's been too long!'

'Tristan,' Father Lee says.

Theo takes one deep breath and then another until he can manage walking slowly into the next room and collapsing onto the couch. 'So, how's life at the kirk?' Tristan says, downing half of his wine in one gulp. 'Given any good sermons lately?'

'I like to think all of my sermons are good, Tristan.' A pause. 'Which you'd know, if you ever came to worship.'

'You know, I really admire your self-confidence. You just don't see *enough* of it in older, white, male members of the clergy.'

Theo snorts. Father Lee frowns, trying to work out whether he's been insulted.

'Another drink, Father?' Iris calls.

'Oh, I'm fine. Thank you.' Father Lee looks at Theo. 'I hear you've been getting into trouble, Theofin.'

'Pish! Trouble! What lad doesn't get into a bit of trouble at this age?' Tristan says, giving Theo an awkward punch in the shoulder. 'I'm sure you got up to all sorts of things when you were a lad.'

Father Lee looks at him blankly.

'No? Well, slàinte mhath! Never too late to start.' Tristan finishes the wine and grimaces. 'Good *Lord*, that's bad.'

Father Lee looks at Theo again. 'Your mother's extremely worried about you, Theofin.'

Theo imagines sinking into the couch.

'Starting brawls, drinking, staying out until the wee hours.' He drops his voice. 'Is that really how you repay the woman who took you in?'

Theo begins to sweat.

'So, how'd you decide you wanted to join the clergy?' Tristan asks, glancing quickly towards the kitchen before reaching for the bottle of whisky that Iris only brings out of the locked cupboard for Father Lee. He unscrews the lid and pours some into his wine glass. 'I mean, did you always know? Were you drawing crucifixes with crayons in P1? Or did you have a transformative moment?'

'I always knew I was …' Father Lee looks thoughtful. 'I suppose I knew I wanted to lead, but it wasn't until I reached about fifteen that I knew the church was where I belonged.'

'That's beautiful,' says Tristan. 'I had a similar experience at fifteen.'

'Oh? Powerful sermon?'

'Bad mushroom trip, I think.'

Tristan stays close to Theo throughout dinner and dessert, only pausing in his endless chatter to quickly devour the stew, bread and whatever alcohol is in arm's reach ('Oh! Father! Sorry – was that yours?'). When Iris finally gets up to see Father Lee off, Tristan sags down into his seat. 'I am now very tired and very drunk.'

'Thank you,' Theo says. 'They would've spent the whole night going on about … everything. All the ways I'm screwing up. I couldn't have got through it … I would've …'

'They'll have another go at their little intervention. You know that, right?'

'I don't need an intervention. I'm okay. I just … I just need to get my head sorted.'

'Question,' says Tristan, leaning his head back on his chair. 'Who'd you call before me?'

'Min and Ewan.'

'Darcy?'

'No.'

'I think this would've been his worst nightmare,' Tristan says. 'I mean, between our illustrious Father Lee and that terrible wine, it would've been a lot of people's worst nightmares. But he would have come, Theo.'

Theo breathes out. 'I know.'

* * *

At the ghost house, Luda opens her laptop and stares at the most recent images she's caught of earth, cracked and dry, on one of the more far flung islands. Sometimes she's so preoccupied by the islands and the women that she barely hears what anyone says around her. Tonight she is pulled from her contemplations of erosion and drowned sheep and broken slate by the shape of Darcy lying on the couch, staring up at the ceiling.

Her muscles tense. She tells herself there's nothing wrong – that there's nothing wrong with her nearly grown son lying on the couch, thinking his unknowable, nearly grown thoughts.

'You okay?' she asks.

He ignores her. He always ignores her.

She sits down on the floor with her back against the couch. She is aware of Darcy studying the scars on the arm she is resting on her propped-up knee; her neck, the profile of her face. He has still never made any mention of being able to see the scars, but she knows that he can.

He says something that Luda doesn't catch.

'Sorry?'

A sigh. 'I *said*, tell me about the women.' A hesitation. 'Please.'

'Really, why?' When was the last time Darcy had said *please* to her? Had asked anything of her other than to pass him the milk for his morning coffee?

'I like the idea of them. Of all these strong women who didn't give a fuck.'

'It's more complex than that. Some of them weren't strong – they were victims of poverty and abuse and had no say in any of it.'

'Story. Not a lecture.'

She is losing him, tension creeping back into his body. This fleeting moment, as precious and unknowable as her best work, and she is letting it get away. 'What story?' she asks, her voice quieter.

'The ones who called in the whales.'

'There were four of them executed for that. One was also charged with summoning storms, another one with promising fruitfulness in nature. And the last two women, Susan and Magdalena, were also charged with raising a procession of the dead. What does that even *mean*?' She sighs. 'Maybe in the ruined cottages. I keep wondering, were they ghosts? Bodies? Bones? What does a procession of the dead *mean*?'

'Maybe it was just a feeling,' Darcy says, almost to himself.

That sense of being watched in an empty landscape. Sounds with no source. She shivers. Faces through glass and fingers on her face. Sometimes she is sure she can hear their voices. They call her back from the darkest of her dreams.

She is about to ask him what he means, but she knows. Swallows the words. Joshua flares up between them like a struck match.

'You want a coffee?' she asks.

He's quiet and she thinks that he's ignoring her again. She stands up, moves into the kitchen, and then his low voice. 'Warm milk with honey?'

Luda's mother had made warm milk and honey for Luda when she was young and unwell – a cold, a headache, a bad day at school. Luda had made it for both her children, too, but she cannot remember the last time she made it for Darcy; or, rather, cannot remember the last time it had been drunk. The sight of congealed milk and honey in a cold mug had been enough to make her eyes prickle.

'Sure,' she says, like it's no big deal. Except that it is. Except he is suddenly a newborn, mewling into her damp skin. He is a toddler, pointing out letters before his second birthday. Older; he is studying other children at church, stroking baby Min's hair.

Curled up in that fucking dam. Luda's camera in her hand.

She makes the drink and takes it to him. He sits up, mutters thanks, and does not look at her.

She wants to stroke the hair off his forehead; she wants to rest her head on his shoulder and breathe in that smell of his neck, like she had when he was young. Biscuits and playdough and paper and *boy*.

He has so many unknown scars. She wishes she could drink in every mark of his skin until she knows it properly again.

He has the skin of a stranger.

Darcy cups his hands around the mug, flushed as though embarrassed. He *is* embarrassed, she realises. He is embarrassed over needing her. She wants to sit down next to him, she wants to ask him about what he's feeling, how she can help him; she wants to tell him that she shouldn't have taken that photo and that she should listen more when he talks. She'd ask him what he felt about Joshua. Whether Joshua still snuck into tiny moments, or whether Darcy had somehow left him behind in Narra.

But there is nothing for Luda to clutch at. Nowhere to find purchase. Soon this time – which feels so infinite – will shrink to a flicker. Will become something she's convinced she made up. *Darcy never asked me for milk and honey!*

She thinks, instead, of the women who met here. She wonders about ghosts.

* * *

Cassandra is dozing in her chair when Iris stomps into the room, drops a bag of cans onto the table and flops down onto the couch in a very non-Iris-y way. Cassandra blinks, feeling dulled by her medications.

'You're here unusually late, Iris.'

Iris casts Cassandra a withering look. 'Food delivery from the kirk,' she says.

'I see. Didn't you have Marcus for dinner tonight?'

'Aye.'

'And how did that go?'

Iris scowls. 'Tristan turned up.'

Cassandra grins. 'Oh, did he? So, you, Marcus, Tristan and Theo. That must've been *fun*. Was it fun?'

Iris's pulsing worry. Father Lee, letting himself be pulled off track by Tristan, over and over again. 'Tristan was there for Theo,' Iris says, reluctantly.

'Aye. Polite to Father Lee, was he?'

'He did that *thing* he does where he's extremely, repeatedly rude in a very pleasant voice.' A swell of anger. Iris wanting to claw at Father Lee's skin (that pearly, barely marked skin). 'Father Lee's a good man, underneath it all,' Iris says, her voice unwilling. 'He's just young.'

'He's not *that* young, Iris,' Cassandra says, yawning. 'He'll never be Father Frank. Father Frank may have been a cocky little bastard when he first came here, but he always had depth to him. Father Lee ... he doesn't have that.'

Iris picks up a can of soup and slumps back against the floral fabric of the couch.

'You need to stop fighting his battles for him. He hasn't improved since being here on the islands. He's got worse. Surely you can see that.'

Iris sniffs. 'I don't fight anyone's battles for them. I fight my own.'

'You let Tristan stay for dinner.'

'Theo invited him, I could hardly throw him out.'

'Hmm.' Cassandra yawns again. 'You want Tristan to keep researching the ghost house, don't you?'

'No. I don't care.'

'You want to know if there's anything there,' Cassandra continues. 'You're *curious*.'

Iris frowns, says nothing. That choking suspicion; that wariness of anyone outside the kirk. Even Cassandra, who has known Iris for longer than anyone else.

'Aligning yourself with the Father Lees of the world isn't the answer. It never has been.'

Iris turns the soup can over in her hands. They both think of the darlings in the gorse of Seannay. The darlings – the tiny remains of unbaptised babies, brought to Seannay to be buried. Iris had imagined them into friends when she was the lonely child of a wild, wayward mother. Between them, blurred and imagined, clouded with fear, the island sinking beneath the sea.

Iris places the can back down on the table and stands up.

'Iris.' Cassandra shakes her head and sighs. 'At least get me a dram before you go!'

Chapter Eighteen

FEBRUARY (THEIR SECOND YEAR)

A woman scoops her child up from a tumble onto the cobblestones. She mops blood and kisses a salt-damp cheek. 'Shh, don't cry,' she murmurs into the child's hair. 'C'mon, my brave lad. Deep breath.' She wipes his tears. 'There's no need to cry.'

* * *

That evening, Luda agrees to go to the Blue Fin to celebrate Tristan's birthday. She smiles over her Australian chardonnay, as Tristan gets more and more emphatic with his gesturing; louder and louder in his passionate diatribe about the shortcomings of *anthropologists*. She watches Tristan roll up his shirtsleeves and play darts (very badly) and inexplicably take off one shoe. The others there to celebrate Tristan – erratic, generous, impatient Tristan – drift off and join other groups. It's often this way at the pub – the way it had been back in Narra. People knowing each other; gatherings and catch-ups spilling over.

Luda sits down with Cassandra, who drinks whisky in a corner booth, pausing to blow kisses to Louise's red-haired cousin, Angus. He always blows them back, making Cassandra laugh. She and Cassandra rarely talk. A comfortable silence exists between them, as though all the necessary things have already been said (although Luda is sure they haven't been).

'You've been here a while,' says Luda.

Cassandra blinks. 'Aye. A wee while.'

'I keep seeing women in the gorse on Seannay ...'

Cassandra looks sad and unsurprised. 'Women used to bury dead bairns there. Decades ago.'

'Why?'

'I don't know, hen. The babes weren't baptised so weren't allowed to be buried in consecrated ground. Happen Seannay's always felt like a woman's place. A place that would hold that sort of grief.' She pauses. 'Not all places do.'

'No. They don't.' Luda turns her place mat over in her hands.

Tristan sits down with them. 'Iris came by the office today,' Luda tells him.

Tristan rests his cheek in his palm and looks at her. 'Do *not* mention that name to me. Iris *or* Father Lee. I experienced more psychological suffering at that dinner than any decent person should be subjected to.'

'And to think you could have had pizza. She wants you to tell her if you find anything in the ghost house. She said it was what her mother would have wanted.'

'I thought she hated me nosing around the ghost house,' Tristan says.

Cassandra shrugs.

'Happy birthday, indeed.'

'Yes! It's my birthday, isn't it? I am *forty*-four. How'd that happen? I mean how'd that *happen*.' He sinks down in his chair. 'It's pretty old. Practically pension age.'

'Not quite,' says Cassandra dryly.

'What are you?' He squints at Luda. 'Like, forty?'

'Thirty-eight.'

'Jesus, so *young*.'

'You're *both* so young,' says Cassandra.

'Well, sure. It's all relative and you're ... what? God, how old *are* you, Cassandra?'

'Old enough to know it's dreadfully rude to enquire about a woman's age.'

Ewan appears by the booth. 'Your chariot awaits,' he says.

'Och, how grand.' Cassandra holds her hand out to Ewan and he helps her up. 'Have a good night, you two,' she says to Luda and Tristan.

'How old was Joshua?' Tristan asks Luda.

Cassandra blows kisses generously to everyone in the pub as Ewan helps her towards the door.

'Three years older than me.'

Tristan rests his chin in his hand. 'What do you miss about him?'

'Joshua?'

Tristan nods.

'Him. Just him.' Luda sighs. 'Really, we weren't well suited. And things were over between us a long time before he died.'

'What else do you miss?'

'Oh, sex. I think. I can't really remember.' She frowns. 'And … feeling like someone noticed when I came home at night. Or if I was stressed. Although he got so caught up in schemes for the farm by the end that he wouldn't have noticed if the house caved in.' Luda blows a stray piece of hair away from her face. 'I don't miss him like I thought I would. And then I feel guilty.'

'You shouldn't feel guilty,' Tristan says, sounding almost sober. *Almost.* He leans in closer. He gazes intently at her. 'I didn't want to like you, you know.'

'Oh, we're at the drunken sharing stage of the evening. Wonderful.'

'After you took that photo of the cliffs and were so bloody stubborn about it, I wanted to not like you. But I don't not like you.'

Luda yawns. 'You just needed to keep me on side so you could get in to see the witch marks. I can see right into that rat-cunning brain of yours.'

'Well … yes, alright. At first. But then' – he looks bewildered – 'I just *liked* you.'

'I like you too, Tristan,' Luda says, watching the flickering orange and blue of the gas heater in the fireplace. 'You're just about the only friend I've made since we came here.'

'No … I mean …' He exhales, suddenly agitated. 'I need air.'

Luda considers staying inside and watching the flames of the gas heater, but then she thinks of how much Tristan's had to drink and tries to calculate the likelihood of him passing out and losing vital appendages to frostbite. She follows him outside.

Snow dusts the ground. She wraps her arms around her body, her breath misting.

'You really should be wearing a jacket,' she says.

Tristan turns to face her and they stare at each other. The air seems to shimmer with snow and cold. Luda looks away.

'I'm glad I didn't take the job,' he tells Luda.

'What? What job?'

He waves a hand at her. 'I like you,' he says. 'And that's not just the alcohol talking. I *like* you.'

'I know,' she says. 'I like you too. You ready to come back inside? It's freezing.'

'Luda … you can be so bloody obtuse.'

'About what exactly?'

He hesitates. And the way he hesitates is unfamiliar. Luda considers going back inside, the fire, the remains of her wine. And then Tristan steps towards her until they're nearly up against each other and things rearrange themselves. 'Luda,' he says, and his voice is exasperated and rough and warm. She looks into his face – thinks of the crosshatching of too-many scars when he's on Seannay – and realises that the beat of her heart has quickened. It's racing.

He presses his lips against hers and Luda feels her body respond as though she has not been actively avoiding this sort of thing since they came here, and long before.

He smells like the islands. He smells like whisky and earth and salt. Kissing him erases everything. Kissing him, she feels young again – before Joshua and the drought and the children. She pulls away a little, rests her forehead against his. She squeezes his arms through his shirt. 'Wait.'

He closes his eyes.

'I …' She swallows.

'I'm sorry.'

'Tristan …'

'I get it. I just *wanted* to …' He rubs at his nose. 'I wanted to choose *happy* for once in my life.'

'Kissing me is you choosing happy?'

He nods, loops an arm around her neck. 'You're exasperating and stubborn and obtuse and obsessive and remarkably good at lying to yourself. But yes. You're my happy.'

'I'm your happy,' she says. Had she ever been Joshua's happy? 'You're my happy too, Tristan. You know that.'

'Desperation and lack of other choices doesn't make me your happy.'

'Well, you are. It's just …' She exhales in a rush. 'I'm sorry. I'm sorry that I can't … not yet … I'm sorry.'

He gives her a small smile and steps away from her, back towards the pub. 'You're still my happy, Luda.'

She watches him go. The hunch of his shoulders, the way his hair sticks up. She takes a step forward. 'Wait!'

He turns to face her, but doesn't come closer.

'Can we try that again?' she says.

He walks back across the snow. 'Which part?'

'This part.' She leans in and kisses him and feels his surprise. Then he cups her face and kisses her back and she can feel him smiling. For a moment, she wants to run. She wants to curl back into the life she's already made for herself. But no. She kisses him, touches his face, his hair.

'Oh, about fucking time,' Tristan says against her mouth.

Luda marvels at the feel of him, the taste. How he kisses her as though she's something precious. She is his happy.

She is his *happy*.

* * *

Things that Theo did not tell Carter: in that first year, he would wander the kirk yard as though he'd lost something, peering at the weathered inscriptions beaten into stone. Words he couldn't read, even if he could make them out. Sometimes, he'd startle and latch on to whoever was closest to him, dragging at waterproof pants and skirts and jeans and jackets as though he were drowning. In these months, people looked at him, long and quizzical, and it felt as though he would never belong.

He had started drawing in Iris's kitchen. From that first day, when he picked up a discarded pen and began making large, sweeping shapes on the yellowed paper of an old notepad. Doctors spoke about amnesia and concussion and trauma and repression. There was talk of cults and abandonment and torture. There was talk of shipwrecks and refugees. 'Your drawings are grand, but you need words,' Iris had said, when he became frustrated with the letters in the books that she made him repeat again and again. Sometimes, halfway through writing a word, his hand would spiral off and draw curving shapes. 'You need words.'

Sometimes, he'd slip away from Iris's pebble-dashed house on the south edge of the town and wander along the roads, peering into any uncurtained windows and watching the people inside. How they read and stared at their televisions and pressed up against one another. Into one another. They hadn't often noticed the lad watching through the window, but when they had, they'd been shrill and unhappy about it.

Once he'd learnt to speak, Theo told Iris that in those early months everyone had looked the same to him. People were little more than a smudging of faces and arms and legs and hair that seemed always to be kicked up by the wind. But, somehow, he always knew Iris.

* * *

Iris is waiting for Cassandra in the living room, stacked cans of soup on the table. 'Did you manage to set yourself on fire? You reek of peat.'

Cassandra allows Ewan to settle her into her chair and then smiles at him warmly, pats his arm. 'Thank you, lad.'

He drops a kiss onto her head and lets himself out.

'That skirt is truly hideous, Iris.'

'You've been at the pub more than usual lately.'

'Aye. So I have.'

A pause. 'And?'

Cassandra shakes her head, frowns. Between them is this: an understanding that there is tension building in the town. An understanding that something, soon, will happen.

Chapter Nineteen

MARCH (THEIR SECOND YEAR)

Joshua had been fireworks and impossibility and never quite making things work between them, no matter how much they wanted to. They did not understand each other. Had never understood each other.

Tristan is different. His hair sticks up. He still types with two fingers. He touches her, always, like she is something miraculous. He links his little finger with hers when they walk down the street to the cafe. He beams at her with delight as he does his rubbings and measurements of the witch marks. In the evening, they drink cans of beer on the grass. 'I thought I was done,' Luda tells him.

'Done?'

'Done. I thought I'd just be alone from now on. And I was okay with that.'

He snorts. 'Oh, you *flirt*.'

'I'm paying you a compliment, Tristan! I wasn't … I wasn't looking for anything. I was okay. I'm with you because I want to be with *you*. Not because I just don't want to be alone.'

He thinks about this for a moment, picking at a piece of grass. 'A lot of people are scared of that, aren't they?'

'I think so.'

He turns and cups her face. 'We're lucky then.'

'We are.' Luda leans in and kisses him.

* * *

Earlier in the day, Theo had said *breath-steam* and Iris had mouthed *breath-steam* to herself and then smiled. Theo knows that the phrase will be penned into the green notebook that Iris doesn't know he occasionally tries to read. Sometimes he will ask Min what something means. Words and phrases he's said that aren't quite right; that amuse Iris or shock her. He likes to keep track of the list so he knows what to never say again. One day he will rip every single page from the skin of green cover. He will throw them into the wind and all of it, this record of his idiocy, will be gone.

Breath-steam. The word rumbles around and around Theo's mind as he works in the chilly, dim day. Spring is late this year, the ground still heavy with frost.

Theo works as well as he can with his bleeding hands, mulling over the green-skinned book. Gerald pretends not to notice how slow Theo is in his pain. His cursing. Theo can't tell if it's a kindness, this silence, or an unusual sort of cruelty.

'You going to stay back?' Gerald asks him, his voice even. Gerald's voice is always even. Theo knows exactly how Gerald will be each day. Can tell, just by glancing at him, whether they'll fuck that night.

'Not tonight,' Theo says. And Gerald looks surprised for a moment and then he glances at Theo's hands and nods. Theo is careful never to let Gerald see the extent of his damaged, scarred flesh in anything more than the softest of lights. To be rejected by Gerald Rendall would be a sort of wrongness that Theo cannot even contemplate.

Theo has heard nothing from Carter since the night at the pub on the northern tip of the island. The stars spangled above the ruins of the bishop's palace.

After work, Theo rides to the Blue Fin and plays darts. He drinks and drinks.

At one point he looks up and sees Min carrying a large sack, her expression fiery. 'What?' he asks, but he's really quite drunk and had thought she was walking towards him, when she is actually striding into the middle of the room.

'Christ,' Ewan mutters, leaning against the wall next to Theo.

'Sorry, Louise!' Min calls, her face determined. She then briskly upends the sack into the middle of the pub. Everyone stares at her. In the background, Cher keeps singing about believing.

'I collected this from the water in a single *day*,' she says.

Everyone continues to stare, except for Louise, who is moving swiftly from the bar to Min and the garbage pile.

'I see people dumping rubbish off their boats,' Min continues. 'I see people laughing when their bin gets blown over *again* and all their shit goes flying down the street. And do you know how many cans of Corrigan's I've found in the water? This is the only place on the islands that sells it. How hard is it to just drink what's on tap?'

Louise reaches her. 'Out.'

Min glowers. 'Do fucking better,' she says to them all, balling her sack up and storming out of the pub.

There is a moment of quiet, once she's left. Everyone stares at the rubbish, at the cans and bits of plastic packaging and condom wrappers and plastic forks. A ripple of shame, Theo thinks, but perhaps not.

'Garbage girl,' someone says, and there is laughter. People break back off into chatter.

'Everyone grab a piece of rubbish,' Louise says. She would not speak to her patrons like this during tourist season, but it's all locals tonight. '*Now.*'

And, because even the hardened men from the oil rigs are secretly terrified of Louise, everyone helps dispose of the rubbish.

Ewan finishes his pint, wipes his mouth with the back of his hand and thumps Theo on the back. 'Goodnight,' he says and Theo says something garbled and well-meaning in return. He stands frowning near the dart boards, feeling weird about all of it – about the quiet, about Min and Louise and the sack of rubbish. He strikes up a conversation with a girl about his age, a relative of someone who lives near the loch, but his heart's not in it. If he'd wanted to fuck, he would have stayed late at Gerald's. He continues to drink until Louise won't give him any more alcohol. He sings raucous songs with the football team and shares their jugs of ale, instead. He drinks until Louise rings Darcy.

* * *

The phone's gentle vibration cuts through Darcy's dreams. He knows it's late. He thinks, *Louise*.

'It's Theo,' she says as soon as he answers.

Darcy yawns. 'Fighting or passed out?'

'Neither, but he's currently throwing up in the bathroom and he's about to do one or the other.' She sighs. 'I've brought his bike inside.'

Darcy dresses and pulls on his boots and latches the door of the caravan shut. He rides to the pub, careful of the frosty roads. He almost enjoys slicing through the dark streets. His breath a puff of silver. He finds Theo sitting in the doorway of the pub, his eyes closed, his head resting against the doorframe.

'Theo,' says Darcy.

Theo doesn't respond.

'Theo!'

Theo squints at him. 'Darcy.'

Darcy looks away. He wishes the smell of alcohol didn't make him feel sick. Life would be easier for him if it didn't. Things would be easier with Theo.

Theo staggers upright and gazes at him.

Darcy shifts. 'What?'

Theo shakes his head and then unexpectedly rests it against the crook of Darcy's neck. He smells of alcohol and sweetly of vomit. Darcy wheels his bike towards the causeway, Theo leaning heavily on his other side.

The tide is out so they cross to Seannay over sand made silver by the moon. Darcy does not bother going into the ghost house. Theo is a loud drunk and neither Min nor Luda like being woken in the middle of the night. Not that Darcy particularly likes it either. He stuffs Theo into the caravan and turns to find him sitting on the end of the bed, studying Darcy intently. 'Your scars,' Theo says, lifting a hand as though to touch Darcy's face. 'You've got so many *scars.*'

Darcy flinches.

'I don't have any,' Theo adds, his hand dropping. 'I don't have a single one.'

'Or maybe you've got more than anyone.'

'What?'

'Nothing. You shouldn't drink like this.'

Theo pulls his gloves off and surveys Darcy solemnly. 'I can be around people when I drink.'

Darcy takes Theo's hands in his own.

'Shit, Theo,' he breathes. Theo's hands smell like iron and warm skin. They are streaked with old blood. The webbing between his fingers has been savagely, crookedly cut, over and over. The flesh is puffy, colourless. Theo's beautiful hands. Between them, London. Darcy's lips pressed to his fingers. 'Shit.'

Theo turns his head into Darcy's shoulder, lets Darcy keep holding his hands. Darcy sighs, nudging Theo up onto the pillows. He pulls the blankets over Theo and then sits back down at the end of the bed.

In another world Darcy may have slid into the bed, pressed his cold body to Theo's (always) fiery one. Slept like that. Enjoyed it, even. In another world, it may have meant something or not, but the meaning was not important – the closeness was. The absence of it, now.

Darcy swallows and slides down onto the floor.

The blankets rustle. 'Darcy.'

'Use the bucket if you need to throw up.'

'Don't need to throw up.' A pause. 'Darcy?'

'Go to sleep,' Darcy mutters, tilting his head back against the edge of the bed.

'Why are you on the floor?' Theo seems genuinely perplexed by this and sits up to stare. 'Darcy?'

'Because *you're* in the bed,' Darcy snaps.

Theo climbs unsteadily to the foot of the bed and sits back on his heels. 'It's a big bed.'

'It's really not. Go to sleep.'

'You must be cold,' Theo says, in that warm caramel voice that Darcy has overheard him using with attractive strangers at the Blue Fin. Theo likes the ones just passing through. The ones who are drunk enough not to realise who he is. Darcy *hates* the Blue Fin.

'I swear to God, Theo.'

Theo flings himself onto his back, his head off the end of the bed and suddenly very close to Darcy's. 'You're beautiful, you know,' Theo says, still in that cloying, caramel voice.

Darcy feels every part of his body tense and it is an unpleasant sort of tensing. The memory of Theo wildly, angrily kissing him on the lonely island rears up. 'If you don't shut up, you can sleep outside.'

'Don't want to sleep outside,' Theo murmurs.

'Then. Stop. Talking.'

The caravan creaks. Something small skitters past and away. Theo continues to stare at him, and then he begins to drowse, his breathing made heavy by too much whisky and beer and God knows what else.

The night feels hazy. Darcy tugs a cushion down from the little seat at the other end of the caravan and curls up on it as best he can. *Beautiful.* Darcy considers the word as he sometimes considers Theo's sea glass, running it through his fingers over and over again.

* * *

Here is another story that Theo had not told Carter: when Theo was young and without words, some of the local children dragged him into the kirk and locked him in one of the cupboards on the second floor. Iris had spent all night looking for him – the whole island did. Boats and cars and torches flashed along the roads and paddocks and out across the dark plain of the sea.

It was Ewan who found him, curled up in a ball at the bottom of the cupboard, one hand hitting the side of it. *Thump. Thump. Thump.* Theo's fingers were bloody from clawing at the wood. His face was caked with snot and saliva. The cupboard smelt of piss and tears.

Theo looked up at him, wide-eyed. He reached out trembling arms and Ewan scooped him from the cupboard and hugged him for a moment. 'It's okay now,' he said at last. 'It's all okay.'

Ewan was well-built, even as a teen. And Theo was only young and a tiny, fragile thing, easy to carry down the stairs and down the aisle and out into the bright morning sunshine. When Iris joined them in the kirk yard, she snatched Theo from Ewan and held him tightly to her. 'Oh, my lad,' she murmured into his hair. Theo stared at the kirk, at the sandstone walls. When Iris tried to carry him back in, to wait in the office until the doctor came, Theo screamed.

'I don't think you're going to get him back in there any time soon,' said Ewan.

'Don't pressure him, Iris,' Father Frank had said, smoothing Theo's hair. Father Frank had always been able to soothe Theo. 'He'll be ready to go inside one day, or he won't.'

The next day, Iris left Theo with Cassandra and went to visit the homes of each of the children who had left Theo there overnight. There were four of them. All gone from the islands, now. One in Aberdeen, one in Yorkshire and two in North America. The parents were apologetic, but the children were not. Iris had waited in each house until the children were alone and then leant in very closely and hissed, 'If you touch him again – if you hurt him again – I'll destroy you.'

And then she'd smiled, like it was a funny thing she'd just said. But all the children saw the hardness in her gaze and told each other in whispers that Theo needed to be left alone. Selkie. Faerie. Changeling.

* * *

In the morning, Theo stirs with a groan, blinking in the pale, slatted light slipping in from outside. Darcy watches as his eyes flit over the caravan, taking in the bed, the ceiling, the glass of water on the small bedside shelf.

Then his gaze settles on Darcy, who is leaning back against the sink. Theo winces. 'Shit. I'm sorry.'

'It's fine,' Darcy says. He looks more upbeat than he usually does the morning after he's had to drag Theo home from the Blue Fin.

Theo winces, swallows and winces again at the sour taste in his mouth. He inspects his bleeding hands and pulls his gloves back on. 'I can barely ...' He rubs at his head. 'Where'd *you* sleep?'

'Floor.'

Theo swallows. 'Did I throw up?'

'I think so. Not here.'

'It better not have been on the pool table again. Louise will bar me for life.'

They go into the kitchen of the ghost house.

Min jumps down from the loft. 'Good morning,' she says.

'Is it?' Theo mumbles, sinking into a chair and resting his head in his hands.

Min fills the electric kettle and Darcy starts pulling butter and spreads out of the fridge and cupboards.

Luda looks up from her laptop and raises her eyebrows at Theo. 'You look like you had a big night.'

'Sorry.'

'Don't be sorry.' Luda grins. 'It's not me you woke up.'

Theo glances at Darcy and then away.

Tristan arrives then, cafe coffees in his hand for Luda, Darcy and himself, and a hot chocolate for Min. He's also carrying a small satchel of tools and is red in the face, his hair all stuck out. 'Didn't know you were here, Theo! Have mine.'

'I'm fine,' Theo says. 'Thanks though.'

Tristan points a finger at Min. 'Stop smiling. You're lucky Louise didn't murder you on the spot.'

'What happened?' Luda asks, glancing from Min to Tristan.

Min settles back in her chair, still smiling.

'Word in the cafe is that Min deposited a large amount of rubbish in the middle of the Blue Fin and then started yelling at everyone about drinking what's on tap.'

Luda looks at Min. 'Are you drinking again?'

'No,' Min snaps. 'And I barely drank anything when I *was* drinking!'

'Why does it smell like a brewery in here, then?'

Darcy arches an eyebrow and glances pointedly at Theo. 'I'll shower,' Theo mutters.

Luda frowns at Min. 'What were you doing at the Blue Fin?'

Min's chin tilts up. 'Making a point.'

'About people drinking what's on tap?'

'Do you know how many Corrigan's cans I find in the flow? They should just drink what's on tap. That was one of the *many* points I made.'

Luda closes her eyes. 'Oh, Wilhelmina.'

'What?' Min's eyes narrow. 'You know, I get so sick of everyone wandering around, acting like we're victims of climate change when we've *done* this. We're doing it. It's all connected.'

'I *know*,' Luda snaps. 'My whole job is trying to address climate change.'

'*No*,' says Min, speaking slowly. 'Your job is to scrabble around trying to bucket water out of a ship we've busted wide open to the sea. It's pointless. We need to *fix* the damage we've done and work out how to stop more damage happening in the future.'

'Bucket water out of a ship?' Luda says, rising from her chair, her hands pressed to the table. *'Bucket water out of a ship?'*

'Right, well,' says Tristan, hurrying around the table. 'Probably a bit early for this level of existentialism.'

Theo mouths the word existentialism.

'Let it go,' Tristan murmurs into Luda's hair, and she takes a deep breath and places her hand on his back, and it's such an unfamiliar gesture between them that Min's eyebrows shoot up. She exchanges a look with Darcy and Theo and then swivels around more fully in her chair.

'Are you being safe?' she asks, her voice heavy with mock concern.

Theo snorts into his gloves and Tristan mutters, 'Jesus Christ.'

Luda lets her hand drop. 'Wilhelmina!'

Min widens her eyes. 'I ask because I *care*.'

Tristan covers his face with his hands. 'Please. Stop.' He surveys them through his fingers. 'How do you two, er … feel … about your mum and I dating? A bit.' He is asking both of them, but it is Darcy his half-covered eyes are fixed on.

'Honestly,' says Darcy, reaching for another bit of toast, 'I'm surprised it's taken you two this long.'

'Yeah, the only pair more glacial is Dar— *Ouch*! Darcy! Don't *kick* me!'

'Don't kick,' Luda says, without any conviction. 'Bucket water out of a ship,' she mutters.

Tristan glances from Luda to Min, who's got her chin jutted out again. 'Let's talk about something else.' He squeezes Luda's shoulder. 'Please.'

Luda takes a deep breath. 'Okay, well.' She pauses, cracks her neck, gives Min another grumpy look. 'Leanne called me last night.'

'How is she?' Min asks. 'Did she say anything about Dad?'

'Why would she say anything about Joshua?' Luda says, a little petulantly.

Min sits up straighter. 'Well, why wouldn't she?'

'She didn't say anything about your dad. Just that everyone misses us. Also that the bank manager died – the one who wouldn't give us the loan.'

Min frowns. 'Who?'

'I forget his name. He managed all the banks in the district. He had that huge house on the main street, remember? Darcy did all that work in his garden to butter him up so that he'd give us that last loan.' She sighs. 'But he had Darcy over there for months and months and then he rejected our application anyway.' She sips her coffee. 'Bastard.'

'Oh, that guy!' Min sits back in her chair. 'Yeah, I remember him. I think.'

'In hindsight, I don't know how much discretion he had, really.' Luda sighs.

'How did it happen?' asks Darcy. He sits very straight and still in his chair, his eyes fixed on his mother.

'Didn't ask. Maybe a heart attack or something?'

Darcy looks at her. Then he looks at Theo. And then he strides quietly out into the bright, white morning and vomits into the turf.

* * *

Darcy lies on the bed in the caravan, staring up at the white-painted ceiling. The bed smells of Theo. Of salt and vomit and stale beer. Blood.

The door cracks open. 'You okay?' Min asks.

'Gastro.'

Min sits on the end of the bed. 'Can I get you anything?'

'No. Thanks.'

She touches his leg, trying to be comforting, but the unexpected contact makes Darcy startle so violently that he hits his head on the windowsill. 'Shit.'

'Sorry!'

He presses a hand to his forehead and closes his eyes. 'I agree with you, by the way,' Darcy eventually says.

'About what?'

'That repairing sea walls and … getting water trucked in when there's a drought and donating generators and things isn't going to solve the problem.'

'Thank you,' she says, quietly.

He sighs. 'I'm going to sleep now.'

'Okay.' She raises her hand, like she's going to touch his leg again, but doesn't. 'Sorry about your head.'

Darcy doesn't reply.

Later, Luda comes to the caravan on her way out to do the grocery shopping. 'I'll get you some lemonade,' she says, hesitating and then reaching down to brush his hair from his forehead. He tenses at the touch, but doesn't flinch. 'You won't want any milk and honey.' She hesitates. 'Are you really okay with ...'

'I like Tristan, Mum. You know that.'

'I know it hasn't been that long since your dad ...'

'It's been over two years,' Darcy says. 'And, no offence, but from the outside it looked like your marriage was over way before he died.'

Luda winces. 'Thanks. I think?'

He lets her touch his hair again and can tell that she notices and is buoyed by it.

Later still, Theo stumbles into the caravan to collect his ratty old jacket.

'You should probably get antibiotics for your hands,' says Darcy, not opening his eyes.

'I'm allergic.' Theo doesn't move.

Darcy isn't thinking about Theo's hands. Not really. Every thought, every sensation, has disappeared. His body is thirteen. His body is in Narra. *They're counting on me. They're counting on me. They're counting on me.*

No.

The head of his body bowed in the Narra Church. *Please, God. Let him die.* Because even at thirteen he'd known he could not ask God to kill someone. Even if they really deserved it. *Please, God.* Min catching hold of his fingers, squeezing them.

He feels a shudder run through him. He is in Narra. His body. He will always be in Narra.

'I just meant to have enough to take the edge off,' says Theo. 'I didn't mean to have ...'

Darcy's words are choked. 'I can't do this anymore, Theo. I can't watch you slowly destroy yourself.' *Fresh-mown grass and closing curtains.* 'I *can't*.'

Theo swallows. 'I'm sorry.'

Chapter Twenty

APRIL (THEIR SECOND YEAR)

The days are lengthening. The puffins are beginning to nest on the cliffs. A large amount of rubbish is dumped on the beach near the docks. Laughter. Many hands shaping the cans and plastic and Styrofoam to shape two words. *Garbage girl*. More laughter. A high tide. The rubbish is swept away.

* * *

Luda sorts through all of the photos she's taken since arriving on the islands. Scrolling back and back and back. Bucketing water out of a boat. She clenches her jaw.

'You look very fierce when you concentrate,' Tristan says from across the office.

Luda bites back a smile and says nothing.

'I tend to look confused and a bit dim,' he adds.

Luda scrolls absently all the way back to those ones she'd taken at the cliffs.

Shit.

She'd done her best to ignore them. But here they are, filling her screen. She frowns. She'd forgotten about the ones she'd taken just before the collapse – in those minutes when she'd been struck by the light on the cliffs; how tiny the two figures looked, striding over stone and sand.

She zooms in.

Allie, turning to beam at Violet. Allie, reaching her arms up. Violet tackling her in an easy, silly hug from behind. Allie's face, screwed up in a shout of laughter, her fingers gripping her mother's arms tightly.

How could Luda have missed these photos? How could she have forgotten taking them?

A flooding of shame.

Tristan looks over her shoulder. 'Oh,' he says.

He drops a kiss on her head when he leaves. She stays up late that night, cropping and fussing over colour levels. She loads them onto a USB to get printed tomorrow. She feels thick with tears. What a bittersweet gift she is about to give to Violet Reynolds.

* * *

Theo's hands scab over, although he can't resist picking at them fretfully. The days are lengthening quickly, now. Hands less painful, he once again slips easily into the work on Gerald's farm. Smoking too much. Drinking too much. Fucking probably just the right amount.

His hands don't draw the way they used to. There's something finer required, with drawing, than is necessary for farm work. The animals follow him around the fields as Theo chews at his lips, thinking about paper and pencils and ink and the very precise way he can no longer pull them all together.

Sometimes, he'll see someone at the Blue Fin. Someone who smiles at him a fraction longer than they need to. In these moments, he relishes the freedom of alcohol. He relishes his ordinariness. He thinks of buying them a drink, asking them questions, paying attention to them.

The idea gives him a headache. Better Gerald. Solid, reliable Gerald. Sometimes, Theo spends most of the day inside Gerald's house with Gerald instead of out in the byre and the fields. Gerald still pays him.

Theo does not let himself think too hard about this.

He dreams of gnawing the bones out of his fingers with his teeth.

Darcy. *I can't do this anymore.* He's lost weight. He's sharper than usual if Theo risks talking to him.

Even after that bullshit with Darcy blindsiding him with the trip to goddamn Doolay, Theo had never even thought of saying it. *I can't do this anymore.* What was *this*, anyway? Darcy taking two steps back for every one step Theo took towards him.

Theo takes joints to the pebbled beach on Seannay when he knows the Managans will not be home. He sits with his back to the rocks, out of sight. One day, one of the rocks seems to move and Theo tenses for a moment before recognising the shape, the erratic movement, of a young, grey fur seal.

'Fuck,' he mutters. He butts out the joint, as though a child has just caught him smoking. They study each other. It's a very young seal. Theo knows that the mothers will often leave their young on land while they hunt, but this seal has a hungry, underfed look about it. Its neck should blend seamlessly into the curve of its skull, but it's shaped more like a dog – head and neck and shoulders sharply delineated.

Had he been hungry when he'd washed up on this beach?

Theo sucks in a tremulous breath and stands up. It will be safe enough here. There's shelter. He decides to check on it tomorrow. Then he heads in the direction of the damp expanse of sand that will take him to Big Island. For a moment, he imagines that the seal pup is following him, but when he looks back, he can only see the water and the rocks and a buttery yellow slice of spring sky.

He goes back to Gerald's. He can't shake the sense of desolation that has crept into him, clouding everything else. Even as the entire room seems to rattle and shake, he feels removed, watching. They smoke after. Watch some of the game on the television. Gerald glances at him a few times, but doesn't ask if he's alright. Instead, he wordlessly hands Theo a joint and a bag of tomatoes from his glasshouse to take home. Then Theo tugs on his boots, climbs onto his bike, and rides it unsteadily back towards the town.

* * *

Min rises out of the water near Ewan's boat, her sack filled with rubbish. He watches her from the cabin. He has learnt when to keep his distance. Min pushes her hair out of her face. 'I'm the one bucketing water out of the ship,' she says. Theo had told Ewan about the conversation she'd had with Luda; or else Luda had, herself. Either way, he knows what she means now.

Ewan peers at her from the doorway of the cabin. 'You're not bucketing water.'

She waves her arm at the overflowing sack and doesn't speak. She sits at the stern of the boat as they go to check Ewan's traps. She glares out at the foaming water behind them.

* * *

Theo trips twice as he makes his way across the causeway to Seannay. The lights in the ghost house are off but there is a soft glow coming from the one remaining window on this side of Darcy's caravan. Theo slows down, staring at it. For a moment, he forgets about the seal pup.

But no. He needs to check on it. The roaring wind. He won't sleep otherwise.

It's dark and he's sore from tripping on the sharp rocks of the causeway. He thinks that of course the seal has gone. That it's beyond stupid to have staggered all the way here this late at night.

Then he sees something shift near the rocks. The gleam of an eye in the dim light of the low moon. He sighs and squats down next to it, not too close. All of the island children have had it drummed into them, Theo included. Do not feed the seals. Do not touch the seals. The baby seals are left safely on the land by their mothers.

The mothers come back for them. Seals bite, even ones as young as this. They might be frightened into the water if you get too close. They can easily drown.

He and the seal regard each other.

'What the hell are you doing?' Darcy's voice is like the icy water puddled along the causeway, filling his boots, making him gasp. 'It's nearly one in the morning.'

Theo loses his balance. The seal huddles more closely against the rocks.

Darcy is wrapped in a jacket, his arms crossed over his chest. His boots are unlaced. Theo can make out the constellation of scars across Darcy's disapproving face. So much of Darcy has pulled away since the night he'd last collected Theo from the Blue Fin. Theo had not meant to come here again like this; drunk and loud. At night. Shit.

The scars on Darcy's face are particularly bright in the moonlight.

'How'd you know I was here?' Theo asks, his tongue feels very thick.

'Half the town probably heard you swearing and shouting. What are you doing, Theo?' Darcy asks, his voice sharp.

Theo looks away from him and swallows. 'Baby seal.'

Darcy looks searchingly towards the rocks. 'Oh.'

'It's young.'

'It's fine. Its mum will come back for it soon.'

For a moment they don't speak, and then Theo takes a deep, frantic breath. He begins to sob.

Darcy shifts but doesn't come any closer. 'Come and sleep in the caravan, then.' Darcy is already moving. 'Just c'mon.'

Theo trails Darcy across the grass.

'The sheets are clean,' says Darcy, pulling the door shut behind them both and pouring Theo a glass of water in the tiny sink. 'I changed them today.'

Theo wouldn't have minded sleeping on sheets Darcy had slept in for weeks or for months, but he's not quite drunk enough to say so. Instead he says, 'There's a book coming out about me, you know.'

'Yeah. I know.'

'He told me all about it.' He pauses. 'There's so much stuff I didn't know, Darcy. Even though I *lived* through it. He still had to tell me my life story like a picture book at bedtime.' A sigh. 'I told him so much stuff. *So* much.'

'When did you meet him?'

'Oh, *ages* ago. After you took me out to …' He grimaces.

'I'd hoped you were lying about that.' Darcy sighs. 'Does Iris know? That you spoke to him?'

'No.'

'Is this what you want?'

'I don't *know*.'

Darcy looks at him, and then he wrinkles his nose slightly and turns away.

'What?' Theo asks. His voice becomes louder. '*What?*'

'Nothing.' Darcy sets the glass down next to the bed. 'You just smell like him. Like pot and whisky.'

Theo clenches his hands. It hurts.

'Goodnight,' says Darcy, moving towards the door.

'Wait,' says Theo. 'Please?'

'Please what?'

'Please.' He reaches out a hand towards Darcy and they are back in the hotel room in London. They are in the ghost house. Darcy is reading to him in the loft; in the kitchen. Darcy is sitting on the floor of the caravan, watching Theo sleep.

Except that things have shifted. Except that he smells like another man's sweat. Except that Darcy has been strange, even for Darcy, since Theo last ended up here, drunk. Theo hazily remembers trying to coax Darcy into bed. *God.* He's sure he even used that voice he uses on strangers at the pub. It was not a voice he'd ever meant to use on Darcy.

Theo should not have come here.

'Goodnight, Theo,' Darcy says, more gently.

Theo supposes that he imagines the hesitation, the brief flicker of something vulnerable and uncertain across Darcy's face.

The door of the caravan snaps shut. The sound of Darcy's quick strides towards the ghost house.

* * *

Min is woken by the sound of Theo's yelling, his stumbling across the causeway and turf. Luda is at Tristan's.

Min wraps a cardigan around herself and climbs down onto the ground floor. She looks out the window as Darcy walks Theo across the turf. As Darcy follows him into the caravan. The snip of the door behind them.

She smiles and turns to the ladder and then her smile fades as she hears the door of the ghost house open and close. The rush of wind.

Darcy, sour-faced, moves into the kitchen.

'What's up?' Min whispers.

'Theo being Theo.'

'I thought you might stay out there with him.'

'Don't.'

'Darcy …'

He shakes his head violently. 'I don't want to hear it, okay? He's in the caravan, I'm going to sleep on the couch. End of story.'

'Oh my *God*. How long are the two of you going to *do* this?'

'Do what?'

'You know what.'

Darcy swears under his breath, throws himself down onto the couch. 'Go to bed,' he snaps.

* * *

Theo wakes. For a moment he expects the cream-coloured ceiling of his bedroom and then blinks and wonders if he'd fallen asleep at

Gerald's. He sits up and recognises Darcy's caravan. The tiny table and bench seat at one end, heavy with books. The bed at the other with the kitchen cupboards, and a tiny sink crammed in between.

No Darcy leaning against the sink this time.

The seal. The beach. He's wearing only his underwear, his wet clothes in a pile by the bed, his muddy footprints on the laminate floor. He drops his head into the naked, raw skin of his hands then inspects himself as he slowly peels off the sheets and blankets. His bright, empty skin. His knees and shins are grazed and bruised.

He finds an old pair of Darcy's pants and a jumper and tugs them on over his underwear. The nausea grips him and he bends forward, swallowing air. He thinks of Min diving. *Sipping air. Just little sips of air.*

When had Min slipped away from him? When had Min been claimed by the sea?

He unlatches the door. Something moves and Theo's knees buckle. The seal pup looks up at him with liquid eyes from near the caravan steps.

They are still staring at each other when Darcy emerges from the ghost house, a mug of coffee in his hand. 'What are you doing?'

Theo points at the seal and Darcy considers it, his head tilted. 'You brought it up with you?'

'No. I just found it here.' Theo is affronted. 'I've never touched a *seal.*'

Darcy crouches down, looking – as he always does now – as though his thoughts are far away. 'It looks skinny. Min might have a wildlife number to call. I'll ask her.'

Theo barely hears him.

The seal pup; faint marks in its hide. Perhaps new scars or old ones. So young. It's difficult to say.

He extends a trembling hand towards it half-expecting to be bitten. Thinking that his hands hurt so much these days, it wouldn't really matter if he were. The seal takes an ungainly step forward and rests its head in Theo's scarred and aching hand.

* * *

Luda wakes to the feeling of Tristan's even, dream-drenched breathing across her neck and shoulder. His arm looped over her waist.

She stays like that, warm and safe, gazing out at the slither of sky visible from the high window. She thinks that she could spend a whole day like this; a week; a month; forever. But it's getting late. She rolls over to face him, touching his nose until his eyes flutter open.

'Cruel,' he says, still half-asleep, bundling her up more tightly against him.

'Sleep well?'

'I did.' He buries his face in her neck, yawns. 'You're not still going out this morning, are you?'

She wiggles away from him. 'I've got to print the photos and get to the kirk before worship's over.'

'I am very furious about this.'

She aims a kiss onto his cheekbone, but he tilts his head up and kisses her mouth. 'No!' she says. 'No. I've really, *really* got to go.'

He heaves a huge sigh. 'So cruel,' he mumbles, and drops back off to sleep. Luda prints the photos, careful not to let anyone else in the library see them. They are for Violet only.

She tucks them into a folder and walks to the kirk. She waits near the kirk yard fence, listening to the sound of the bells tolling in the belfry. When worship is over, the kirk doors are opened and people flood outside, chatting and milling and filling the nearby cafes.

Bryce leaves with a group of other men. He does not notice Luda, and she's grateful. Violet comes out a little bit later, pushing her red hair behind her ears, nodding as Father Lee says something to her. Iris calls Father Lee into the vestibule, and Violet spots Luda and crunches over the gravel to her.

'I've got something for you,' Luda says. 'Can we go somewhere?'

Violet dips her head towards the kirk and, after a moment's hesitation, Luda follows her inside. It feels like a room after a party, the air still ringing with the sound of voices and organ notes. Iris has sent Father Lee off somewhere and nods at them before heading off to the custodian's office.

The kirk itself is empty.

Violet leans against one of the pillars, her arms crossed. She's wearing jeans and a windbreaker and a worn pair of boots. Luda hands her the folder and sits down on one of the pews.

'I forgot I'd taken them,' she says, very quietly.

She watches Violet's face. The carefully cultivated blankness crumpling. Violet sinks slowly onto the floor, her breath catching. Luda is aware of Iris striding out from her office, but Iris stops near Luda.

'She's so beautiful,' Violet says, her voice stilted. Tears run down her cheeks. She spreads the photos out on the kirk's stone floor, side by side. She crouches over them, running her fingers over Allie's laughing, radiant face.

Luda glances at Iris, as inscrutable as ever. Iris meets her glance, gives her a quick nod, and then goes back into her office.

Finally, Violet looks up. 'Thank you,' she says, reaching out a hand to Luda. 'Thank you. Thank you. *Thank you.*'

* * *

At dusk, the rescue woman Min had called arrives on Seannay in a white four-wheel drive. Ewan arrives with Luda and Violet, who clutches a folder to her chest. The island feels very full of people.

'No,' Theo says. 'What are you doing? It needs to stay here.'

'It needs proper care. The mother hasn't been back for it,' says the woman. Nobody can remember her name. Nobody can be sure she'd even mentioned a name. 'It's not well. That's probably why it followed you. Come on. I've got to take it.'

'No!' A catch in Theo's voice. He sounds like a small boy. 'Please,' he says. 'It needs to stay here.'

'I'm sorry,' says the woman.

In the end, Luda, Min and Ewan have to wrap their arms around Theo to hold him while Darcy and the woman coax the seal pup into a large animal carrier and settle it into the back of her car. Violet clutches her folder, tears streaming down her face.

As the woman drives away with the seal, Theo howls. It is Ewan who clasps his shoulder. Who can still so vividly remember the slight, slick feel of Theo's tiny body on the day he found him on the beach. 'It's alright,' Ewan says gruffly. 'It's for the best.'

* * *

That night, Darcy dreams of Theo disappearing into the waves. It upsets him so much that he snaps back from Narra. In the moonlight, he is vividly, sharply on the island. He is *here*. He flings himself out onto the grass in front of his caravan before he's properly woken up. The cold shocks him, like being doused in iced water.

Darcy stands for a time on the grass. Breathing. He listens to the sea and the call of a harassed seabird from the nearby gorse. He half expects to see Theo pacing along the lip of the pebbled beach, but the island is quiet and empty.

In his dream, Theo had been a selkie.

In his dream, Theo had been reclaimed by the sea.

Chapter Twenty-one

MAY (THEIR SECOND YEAR)

Occasionally, Luda still notices the women who cross the causeway to stand among the gorse of Seannay. Very quiet. Very still. Luda watches the women. She knows they would work, these images. That they would likely be the rare sort that makes people's breath snag in their throats. The type that have been eluding her since she took the photos of the cliff collapsing and alienated everyone. This tidal island, this place for women and secret loss, sinking slowly into the sea. Yet some things are not meant to be captured on film. She knows this now – has learnt it twice over. Some things are too precious and fleeting to exist beyond memory. She thinks these words and then she thinks of Tristan, the island smell of his breath. She is his happy.

She sighs. She thinks instead of Darcy and the dam and that photo she took that sent him spiralling away from her.

Except.

Except, he had asked for milk and honey.

She is thinking in photos now. Fetches her camera, like responding to a voice or reaching up to brush her fingers at an itch. She studies the loads of rubbish Min has pulled from the sea. She loosens some from the sack, feeling her attention sharpen at the contrast between the faded crisp packet and the flagstones. She thinks of bucketing water out of a ship; of Min standing in the middle of the pub, upending a sack of rubbish onto the floor. She lifts her camera slowly, and holds her breath while she works.

'What are you doing?' Min asks, coming out of the ghost house.

'Bucketing water.'

'Mum! I didn't *mean* it like that.'

Luda turns to her. 'Can you get me more rubbish?'

'Yeah. There's not exactly a shortage of it.'

'Where are you going now?'

'The flow.'

Luda looks back down at the rubbish on the flagstones. 'Try to get me different things,' she says, 'Different colours and textures.'

'It's not a shop.'

'Min,' Luda says, her voice unexpectedly sharp. 'This is me trying to listen, okay? Bring me rubbish and I'll do what I can.'

Min stares at her for a long moment and then she nods. 'Alright. I will.'

* * *

Theo smokes and drinks and studies the pale skin of his hands. He runs – not as far as he used to. He grows puffed and nauseous much more quickly now. Everyone knows about the book. *The Salt Boy.* Carter has been giving pre-release interviews. People have been begging Theo to appear on television; on the radio; to be interviewed alongside Carter.

Theo doesn't respond to any of it. He drinks. He smokes. He studies his skin. He thinks of the baby seal. Seal pup. He tries to draw but his eyes are blurred and his hands don't work.

'What's all this about the book coming out?' Iris asks one day, when Theo trudges in from a short, frustrating run.

'Nothing.' He expects her to rear up. Instead, her face softens and she holds a hand out to him.

For a moment he wants to punch a wall. He wants to stalk back out and scream on the edge of the Wailing Cliffs. He wants to run. But instead he leans against Iris's shoulder, his eyes suddenly hot and throbbing. Iris strokes his cheek and holds him and Theo sobs into her shoulder.

* * *

Iris has always been secretive when Theo is sick. At first it sprung from a sort of furtiveness – a fear that it would be decided Iris was not fit to take care of him, after all. That the virus – the cold, the flu, the inflamed tonsils – were a sign that she was an inadequate caregiver.

Iris appears at Cassandra's door, a bag of cans in her hand. 'Theo,' she says, sits down on the couch and closes her eyes.

Cassandra looks closely at Iris and then gets up on unsteady legs and slowly pushes her walking frame to the kitchen. She makes Iris a tea.

'He won't leave his bed. Won't eat. I've been dragging him up in the morning and washing his mouth out with salt water.' Iris's voice is dull.

Cassandra nods at the cup. 'Drink.'

'I haven't been enough for him,' Iris says and her voice cracks.

'Oh, Iris.' Cassandra reaches for her hand, her own clammy and trembling from the trip to and from the kitchen. She focuses all of her thoughts, all of her energy, on Iris and on Theo. 'You *have*.'

* * *

Later that day, Luda and Violet wander the western edge of the island, where the sea is deep and often green. They search for puffins, hunt the light, talk to each other about everything and nothing.

'It's a relief, being around you,' Violet tells Luda. 'Everyone else knew me before. And when I'm around them I feel like I've got to pretend to be this person I'm just not anymore. You – you just like me the way I am now. I don't feel like I'm letting you down just by being myself.'

'You're not letting anyone down by being yourself,' Luda says. She is still thinking about rubbish. 'Nobody would expect you to be the same as you were before. How could you be?'

'You'd be surprised.' Violet pauses, scooping up a piece of driftwood, incongruous on the cliff top. 'Mostly people have never lost more than an elderly relative. They think grief is something you just work through and then somehow complete.'

'Please tell me you haven't had people say the word "closure" to you.'

'Several times.'

'Oh, Vi. Such bleakness.'

Violet almost smiles. Then she frowns. 'I think I used to be interesting.'

'You're still interesting.'

Violet shakes her head. 'I'm not. I'm *really* not.'

Later, Luda meets Tristan at his flat on the other side of town. She thinks that she has *people* now. She loves the women still; her lost friends, but the urgency has dissipated. She knows they'll wait patiently for her. Tristan looks harassed, bent over a stove that is too low for him and cutting up greens on an old plastic chopping board. Luda watches him, bemused. Making dinner, drinking wine. Tangling in his bed with its book piles and article clippings.

Tristan, tracing the lines of her face with the same reverence as he traces the markings of the ghost house.

* * *

Min walks home from the flow in the dim evening light. She has a sack of rubbish flung over her shoulder and is thinking of Theo and the book and wondering when he stopped being someone whom she could ask anything. When he had shifted away from them all.

Perhaps she'd left him first. She knows she has changed since she began diving deep into the sea. Perhaps she'd left him without even realising it.

That seal.

She is garbage girl. She shivers, crossing the road near the Blue Fin. The sound of laughter from inside. She clenches the neck of her sack. She had spent the morning out on the boat with Ewan. She'd ditched him as soon as they were back at the docks for the peace of the flow by herself.

It's a drizzly Wednesday night and the rest of the town is very quiet. She is nearing the end of the main street, where the road veers off towards the causeway, when she becomes aware of footsteps behind her.

She tenses but doesn't increase her pace. She has always been told to be alert to people walking near her like this. She knows it will most likely be nothing – it always is. Except, she knows, it is not. Not nothing.

'Stop,' the voice says, and it's a man's voice and it's drunk and Min breaks into a sprint.

A heavy arm drags her down behind the drywall that runs alongside the road. Her sack lands next to her, spilling blue and orange and black and yellow across the ground. From here, she is invisible. Min tries to fight, but the man pins her easily.

Bryce Reynolds.

'Let me go,' she says, her voice very calm.

His grip on her wrist tightens.

'I thought I'd made myself clear that time she came to stir shit up at the farm,' he says. His breath makes Min's eyes water. 'My wife's been crying for days because your bitch of a mother had to twist the goddamn fucking knife. Does she get off on torturing us?'

'I don't know what you're talking about.'

'I found the photos she gave to Violet. They've broken her goddamn heart.'

'Okay. Okay.' Min tries to swallow. 'I'm sorry, alright? But this has nothing to do with me.'

Bryce looks at her intently. She feels his fingers on her neck. 'Just listen! Fuck. I need you to *listen*.' His fingers tighten and Min gasps, digging her nails into his flesh. She will die now. She will *die*.

The deep. The deep. Little sips of air. The tug of the tide. She draws the air in, tiny little bursts, until her lungs are full. And then she disappears. She goes into the curl of blues and greys. She dives into salt, even as his fingers stay tightly around her throat.

His fingers tremble. He does not let go.

Min thinks of deep water; of shells from the ocean floor. Her hand reaches. She feels the edge of a rock, grabs at it, brings it down as hard as she can against Bryce Reynolds's head.

His hands release her neck. He rocks, cradling his head. He begins to sob quietly. 'I'm sorry,' he says, dragging the brightly coloured rubbish back into the sack. 'I'm so sorry.'

* * *

Theo's life feels fractured. 'It's amazing what can be slept off,' Iris would tell him those times when she was sick with a cold or the flu. 'Leave me be, lad.'

And so he sleeps. And sleeps. And he dreams of the world moving as slowly as treacle being poured from a cup. He dreams of Gerald. Lost boys. The sting of vomit. The book. A curlew regarding him from a tilted eye. The seal. The seal.

A flutter of hands, of wordlessness. The rush of water. Stones under his feet.

He recoils from it. All of it.

And he sleeps.

Chapter Twenty-two

MAY (THEIR SECOND YEAR)

Cassandra wakes in her chair to bright morning light, her hand around her own throat. She feels bruised. She thinks of whales and churning water. She has been so focused on Iris and on Theo. Now she thinks, *Oh Min*.

* * *

Min knocks on the caravan door, straightening when Darcy opens it. 'We're going to see Theo.'

'No. No, Min.' His expression turns grumpy. 'I told him. I can't … I can't sit in the front row while he implodes. I won't.'

'Darcy.'

'I'm studying.'

'Ewan says he's not well.'

'He'll just be hungover. He's always hungover.' Darcy looks at her more closely. 'Your neck … Jesus, Min. What happened?'

'Get your shoes on' – she coughs; grimaces – 'and I'll tell you.'

Darcy frowns and Min takes hold of his arm. Darcy swears and tries to push her away, but Min is strong from diving and working on Ewan's boat and riding her bike. She thinks she would no longer go wherever Luda and Darcy tried to drag her too. She senses this shift and doesn't know how she feels about it.

Her grip tightens. She does not let go, and after a moment Darcy yields.

'It won't do any good.'

'It will. Come *on*.'

Darcy walks towards town with his arms crossed. The drizzle last night has turned into rain. 'Tell me what happened.'

'Bryce Reynolds happened.'

Darcy swears under his breath. He pulls Min to a stop alongside the drywall. 'What the fuck do you mean by that? What did he do?'

She takes a deep breath, runs a hand around her throat.

Darcy swears and then looks at the road that leads towards the northern part of the island, where the Reynoldses live. 'Where is he now?'

'Home, probably.' She tugs at his arm until he starts walking again.

Min smiles at Iris when Iris opens the door. 'Theo in?'

'He's not well.' Iris frowns at her. 'Are you alright, Wilhelmina?'

'I'm fine. We'll just pop in quickly then. We brought something for Theo.'

'I can give it to him.'

'Iris,' says Darcy. His voice is heavy, tired. Iris moves her gaze from Min to Darcy. She sighs. 'Be quick.'

Min is immediately disoriented, although the house is not a large one. It is certainly much smaller than Cassandra's, which Min moves through without thinking. Darcy strides across the living room, past the kitchen and into the back room where Theo sleeps, as though this is a job he wants over with as quickly as possible.

Theo is curled on his side, his back to the door. The curtains are drawn and they can only see the part of him illuminated, sliced, by light from the hallway.

Darcy gives Min a very un-Darcy look. Panicked, almost. He shakes his head. Min rolls her eyes, crosses her arms, and perches next to Theo. She prods him.

'Min!' snaps Darcy. He places the red sea glass on the bedside table, then moves back to stand in the doorway.

'What?' She prods Theo again, and Theo rolls onto his back.

'He's got a virus!' Iris calls from the kitchen.

Min studies Theo. 'I don't think he's got a virus.'

Darcy says nothing.

Min tugs Theo up, the way Iris does when she rinses his mouth with salt water. She pulls him up and wraps her arms around his chest. His cheek rests against her cheek. She thinks of the sound of her father's car hitting the tree. Birds taking flight. Bryce's weight, pinning her to the ground. Hands around her neck. She feels a burst of anger, squeezes Theo so tightly that he gasps and pushes her off.

'Get up,' she says hoarsely, her voice shaking. 'You've got to get up.'

He rolls back onto his side. He has been picking and cutting at the skin between his fingers again. 'Get up!' she yells, and she is kicking him and hitting him with her fists, like she's administering CPR, with all the desperation and fury of someone trying to get a heart to beat.

'Fucking *get up*! Theo! Get up!'

She is aware of him crying, of Iris appearing and dragging her out of the room. She thinks Darcy has stayed with Theo, but finds he has joined her out in the cool, bright day.

Min's hands are wet.

'You're crying,' he says.

'I'm not! Theo was crying.'

'Min ...' He reaches out to her and she stiffens for a moment, as though she's about to run. And then she lets him hold her. 'I thought I was going to die,' she whispers into his shoulder.

She can feel the pulse of rage in him still.

Her fists sting. She feels ferocious and teary. The weight of Darcy's rigid arms around her is like a sort of miracle.

* * *

Luda leans against Tristan's kitchen bench, staring out at the rain. She nurses a coffee, watches Tristan curse and mutter and hop around as he tries to wedge his foot into his boot.

'You're very graceful,' Luda says, and he waves a cranky hand at her.

They climb into Tristan's car and begin the short drive into town, Luda watching the rain and clouds cast patterns across the rolling fields. When they pull up, Darcy is waiting out the front of the laundromat.

'You need to answer your damn phone,' he says.

'Why? What's happened?'

'Bryce went after Min.'

'*What?*'

Darcy pushes wet hair out of his face. 'She's alright. She won't talk about it, but … I think he tried to choke her.'

'Where is she?'

Darcy shrugs. 'Who knows? It's Min. She might be swimming across to the mainland or something.'

'*You* need to get to school,' Luda says.

Darcy looks pale and tense. He doesn't move.

'I've got this, Darcy,' she says, more gently. 'Go.'

Luda thinks, *I will kill him.* She glances at Tristan and he nods, his expression black with rage. Tristan moves towards the driver's side of the car, but Luda snatches the keys from him. The rain starts to fall more heavily. She sits for a moment, her hands on the wheel, then she starts the ignition, her heart beating calmly.

'What are we going to do?' Tristan asks quietly as she drives off.

'Whatever it takes to make sure he never dares to hurt anyone again.'

A pause. 'They don't change, you know. Men like that.'

'Some must.'

'No. They don't.' Tristan turns his head towards the water. 'Whales,' he says, and sighs.

Luda slows down and can just make them out through the rain, as the road rises and snakes along the edge of the sea towards the north of the island.

'Beautiful,' Tristan murmurs. He presses his hand to the glass.

For a moment, they travel slowly, entranced by the slice of black dorsal fins through rain-dimpled water. And then Luda feels a stab of urgency. Bryce. *Min*. She accelerates, flipping the windscreen wipers on full. Luda turns the wheel, following the curve of the road, but the car doesn't respond. She hits the brakes and the tyres squeal. The engine roars.

Tristan yells. And then they are lurching towards the water. Luda gasps. So much sound. And then, water. Water.

Her fingers snag on her seatbelt until Tristan leans over and unbuckles her. The car is sinking. 'What the hell do we do now?' she asks, her voice catching. 'Tristan! What do we do?'

Tristan's head is bleeding. He rubs at it with the heel of his hand. 'Open the windows. We can try and get out that way.'

'It's not working!' Luda takes a deep breath. 'Shit. It's filling so fast.'

The water is icy, up to her chest. She looks at Tristan, so calm. Covered in blood. She starts trying to break the windows, smashing them with anything that she can pull free from the cabin of the car.

Then, then. The water keeps rising. Her throat. Her chin. She feels Tristan reach for her, touch her hand, her face.

Then they are under. Pinned there by an impossible weight.

* * *

Min rides her bike in the rain, her hood pulled up. She cannot stand the idea of a classroom, not when she's still a little bit stuck in whatever place she disappeared to yesterday. Someone had mentioned a pod of orcas moving across the west side of the island. She hopes to catch sight of them from the Wailing Cliffs, although she doubts she'll be able to make them out in rain this heavy. She feels oddly panicked, like it matters – seeing these whales.

She notices a crowd of people gathered by the side of the road, peering into the water. Muddy tyre tracks leaving the road. She knows that sort of crowd. She's seen it before. She's seen it in Narra. She'd seen it after their father died on the road near their farm. She begins packing air, even as she drops her bike and runs across the wet road, even as she kicks off her gumboots and shucks off her anorak.

She veers sideways, to the place where the cliff angles out enough to haphazardly climb down to a shelf of rock. She slips a few times, grazing her knee, her shins, the palm of her hand. She keeps packing air. The water is wild here – this is not the still and haunted waters of the flow or the large swell where Ewan takes her, far out from land. This is water eating furiously away at land. This is water at its most perilous. She can hear more voices now. 'Min!' 'Managan!' 'Garbage girl!' She blocks them out and prepares to dive. Still, she hesitates. Until a large wave sends a spray of water over her skin and she gasps and calms. She bends and plunges into the rough, grey water, made blurry with run-off from the rain and bubbles from the waves. She draws herself deeper down, where the sea becomes more steady; more herself. She strikes off towards the place where the car hit the water. She thinks only of reaching whoever it was who went over the edge of the cliff.

PART FOUR

The-in-between

The whales move from the Wailing Cliffs to the shallow water of Seannay. They beach themselves. Two of them. It takes a long time for anyone to notice. After, it is noted that their insides are full of bright plastic and the grey flesh of tangled carry bags.

* * *

Theo wakes up and finds that the grey roaring has eased, and in its absence repeats a single word. *Darcy. Darcy. Darcy.* His fingers tremble as he turns on the shower. His legs tremor as he walks out the front gate.

* * *

Luda can piece together exactly what happened in the water. She can piece together being in the car *before* the water. The sound of the car leaving the road. Tristan's coffee upending on her thigh. Burning her. The way they scrabbled for seatbelts, could not open the door. They could not smash their way free. She can piece it together neatly. Completely. She can examine it dispassionately. Tristan's nearly dead body. The cracks in the windshield. Blood turning the water rust-coloured.

She can piece together the feeling of Min's hands, warm and strong, working her from the car.

She knows she had not been conscious. Could not have been conscious. She had been technically dead.

And yet.

Those firm, fierce fingers.

* * *

Luda rips into her skin with her fingernails. As though she is searching for something, making something. It goes on and on, the faint sound of it throughout the ward. Like the sound of the tide rushing in. Like breathing.

'I'm so cold,' she tells them. 'I can't *breathe.*' Her arms are strapped to the bed. She is sedated. 'Now then,' a nurse says, patting her cheek.

* * *

The shard of red sea glass Darcy had returned to Theo appears on the bed of the caravan, set neatly right in the centre of his pillow.

* * *

Luda is a marvel. Her recovery. The parts of her that survived what should have been death by drowning. She is a marvel.

She is no longer their mother.

Min realises this slowly. Tiny, sharp fragments. They fracture Luda until she feels like a different creature entirely from the one who lives with them now.

The doctors at the mainland hospital to which Luda was airlifted speak to Min and Darcy about brain damage, oxygen deprivation. 'It can manifest in all sorts of ways,' they explain.

Luda is tested. She is scanned. She sings on the ward, when her intubation is taken out. She smiles at the empty chair next to her bed. 'Oh, I thought you were dead!'

She has weakness in her left side. Executive dysfunction.

Min picks at her lips until they bleed and tries not to think of Tristan, who she had pulled from the water too late. He is in a coma, may not ever wake. The whales had been there. As Min wrenched at the car door, she had seen their shadows. Enormous. They had not come close. All of those stories about whales and dolphins rescuing people in distress. Fucking bullshit.

'He hasn't finished his rubbings of the witch marks,' Luda says in a quavering voice to Darcy, who drinks too much coffee. Then she will turn to the room, her gaze settling again on empty air. 'You haven't finished your *rubbings*!'

* * *

Darcy closes his books and does not open them again. He throws out anything that includes the phrase 'Advanced Highers'. He sits by Tristan's bed at the small island hospital, thinking about not very much. He talks about what he's reading, but sometimes he can hardly remember. Other times he sits by Tristan's bed silently and waits. In these moments, he wills Tristan to wake up. To step back into this living and impossible world. The focus of his attention feels like a blade; he is surprised that Tristan does not wince.

Sometimes, filled with a very particular kind of remorse, Darcy will lean in towards Tristan's bed. He will take Tristan's hand. 'I do trust you,' he'll say, as though they're still in London, Darcy rucking his blankets up like armour.

PART FIVE

Chapter Twenty-three

MARCH (THEIR THIRD YEAR)

A group of girls, home from university for the weekend, sit at the Blue Fin. 'He said he's not interested,' the girl with dark hair says. 'And he hasn't been replying to my messages.' The girl with the buzz cut smiles. 'That just means he's intimidated by how much he likes you. It just means you've got to be *persistent*.'

There are flowers lain in the place where the car had left the cliff, as though someone had died there.

* * *

Cassandra thinks that, when she dies, there will only be the sea and the air. And that she will disappear into both at the same time. And that when this happens it will be the most wonderful and terrifying thing imaginable.

There is a knock on the door and Cassandra yells to come in. Her mother told her never to yell, but her mother is long dead.

It is Iris, her face set. 'Cassandra.'

'Iris. To what do I owe the pleasure?'

'Delivery from the kirk.' She puts a canvas bag down on the table. It clunks with the unmistakable sound of canned soup.

'Oh, thank goodness! I was about to starve.'

'Cassandra.'

'Thank you for the tinned soup.' Cassandra pauses. 'It is soup, isn't it? You get old and people stop believing that you can handle things as solid as tinned carrots.'

They stare at each other.

'How are they?' Iris asks. 'Really?'

Cassandra shrugs. 'Min tells me Darcy's dropped out of school, and he needed the Advanced Highers for medicine. He's working at the brewery, now.'

'Aye. I'd heard that.' Iris sniffs.

'Violet's officially moved into the ghost house with Luda and the bairns.'

'Don't you think it's …'

'Healthy? Strange? Toxic? Who's to say. Min likes having her there, at any rate.'

More and more, Cassandra always has a sense of where Min is: restless in the ghost house; elated on the boat; mesmerised and barely human under the surface of the water. Sometimes, if Cassandra really concentrates, she can almost taste the sea.

'Hmm.'

'How's Theo?'

Between them, impressions of him laughing, gloved hands digging into dark soil, polishing the spokes of a bike. 'He's come back to himself.' Iris gives Cassandra a wry smile. 'Happen Violet's not the only one who was yearning for someone to nurture.'

'Darcy, you mean?'

Iris says nothing. She's still smiling.

* * *

Darcy wakes up in his caravan. He'd been dreaming of the hospital again. The smell of disinfectant and ripe fruit. In the dream, he'd had a maths exam in the room, but it was hard to concentrate – his mother wouldn't stop singing and Tristan's body was decomposing. Nobody had noticed him slipping finally from the world of the living.

He tries to shake the dregs of his dream away. He clutches the shard of red sea glass. He often wakes up with it pressed tight in his fist.

He does not have to be at work until the evening. He has grown used to the smell of alcohol. He still refuses to drink it.

He cocks his head at the sound of Min's breathing. She sometimes comes out to the caravan, deep in the night. She sleeps on the floor, pressed close to the base of his bed. She says it's because her own bed base has become uneven and hurts her back. Darcy thinks (knows) that she comes here because of their mother's ghosts. Still so much that is wordless spun between them. It both comforts him and fills him with an odd despair.

Waves on rock and sand. The wind finding the angle under the eaves that makes a noise like a boiling kettle. A gull. Min is already awake, staring up at the ceiling, gripping the blankets very tightly.

'Nightmare?' Darcy asks, propping himself up so that he can see her.

Min rolls onto her side, points to his cheek. 'That crooked one. There. That was me, wasn't it?'

It's hard to describe the despair he feels when Min asks him about the scars that she can, since the day Bryce hurt her, see on his skin. Sometimes she'll lift her hand to her neck when she asks him, her eyes fixed firmly on his face.

'I can't remember.' *Just focus on the future. The past will tear you apart.* These words are their mother's.

Min keeps studying him. 'You've got more than me. I wouldn't have guessed that.'

'Can we not?'

'Why do you always pretend they're not *there*?'

'Min …'

Min stands up. 'I'm going to find Mum.'

'She said she'd be digging for clams if it wasn't raining,' Darcy says. 'You'll be late for school.'

They still pretend Min goes to school – that she doesn't now spend all of her time with Ewan and Cassandra.

'Why don't you see Theo anymore?' Min asks, and it is a violation of what should remain unspoken. But he senses a shift in Min – a wearing down of reticence and fear. She is less enervated these days, seems preoccupied. She hardly ever dumps bags of rubbish at the doorstep. Sometimes her face looks completely blank. It frightens him.

'We just grew apart.'

'Bullshit.'

'Friends grow apart. It's normal.'

She grunts, as though she knows exactly why he doesn't see Theo anymore, even as Theo makes tentative moves to approach him if they see each other in the street: Darcy is ashamed. Ashamed of how much he had wanted to get away from here. Ashamed of how badly he's failed his exams.

He reads *The Salt Boy*, the book about Theo, with Theo's shard of sea-dulled glass warm in his fingers. He highlights and folds pages. Theo. Luminous and wild.

'Drop it,' he snaps, certain that she's going to keep needling him. Instead, Min shrugs and slams out of the caravan. He breathes out slowly. He and his body. Study hard, get the fuck out of here. That was his goal. Without it, he's rudderless.

* * *

Luda stands outside, considering the sky. High clouds. She's forgotten the word for them. She will collect razor clams from the shallows of the bay. She's become good at it, although she promises her doctor that she doesn't go into the water.

Sometimes, Joshua turns up. He sits on the rocks, looking as he had before he died on the road near their farm in Narra. He does not have scars.

None of those who visit her do.

He sits and watches her burrowing her hands into the silty sand for the razor clams. Sometimes, her fingers will catch their sharp edges and Joshua will laugh.

Luda does not like to be laughed at.

She eats crumpets – she likes crumpets – and gazes at the scars on her skin. Some of them are new; many are still puckered and red and visible without the necessity of the tidal island (its curse; its light; its shared hysteria). These, the ones that she can't remember, she knows that they must be from the accident.

She marks them on her list with an A. A for accident. *Do you see, doctor? I remember the alphabet. I'm fine.*

The biggest scar she has is across her scalp. The place where the doctors had removed a piece of her skull, to deal with the swelling of her brain. Tristan, unconscious.

She knows that she's changed, from the tentative way that people often treat her now. But she's not sure *how* she's changed. She asks her children, sometimes. They look at her with large eyes. *Oh, Mum.*

Violet says she'll keep improving; that brains are inherently complex and unknowable things.

Sometimes Tristan visits her, too, when she's rummaging around in the rock pools. The part of Tristan that has been shaken loose from his body – Tristan-from-the-in-between. He never laughs at her. And when she goes burrowing for razor clams, he only watches. He winces if she cuts herself. He tells her stories about some of the digs he's been on to distract her if she doesn't find any. Tristan has always been kind like that.

She had been his happy.

Today she finds a clam much longer than her hand. She's pleased and puts it in the bucket. Its little leg comes out and starts stumping around the blue plastic, searching for an escape. Searching for a way to burrow deeply back into the sand.

Luda had not realised that she hadn't taken off her shoes or rolled up her pants until she feels cool hands on her arm. 'Mum.'

She looks up at the young woman with short hair, strong shoulders and a gap between her two front teeth. More than that – a feel of something larger than a human body, something that Luda had never before been able to see or feel or recognise. For a moment, Luda is disoriented. And then she remembers.

'Min,' she says.

'Your boots are soaked.' A sigh. *Oh, Mum.* 'Come on.'

'I caught a clam ...' Luda turns to the bucket, her finger extended in an excited point, but it's empty.

* * *

Min's world has shifted. When people ask her about her diving, about how she managed to free her mother and Tristan from the wreckage of that car, she shakes her head, looks down at the ground. 'Just a rush of love,' she says, trying her best to look girlish. And if people still talk about it – well, that's none of her business.

Nobody calls her garbage girl.

Fingers around her neck. Violet had pressed charges against Bryce so that Min did not have to. He is on the mainland now, serving some sort of community order where he has to talk about his feelings. He writes long letters to Violet that make her weep at the table of the ghost house. She always seeks out Luda, after. To brush her hair or paint her nails or tell her stories of unicorns and faeries and mermaids, pausing patiently when Luda mutters things to her ghosts.

Cassandra. Min closes her eyes. A flicker of soup and wilted flowers. Cassandra, who believes in ghosts.

Min doesn't worry about the ghosts when she's diving. When she's submerged, they cease to exist. She still feels the pull of the water, but she doesn't feel swamped by the whales, by the memory of bodies in water. She is not swamped by her father's crushed car. Birds taking flight.

A breath caught in a gasp. Fingers around her throat. No.

* * *

Sometimes, Luda's mother-in-law turns up. Glenda. In her floral shirts and sensible shoes. She tells Luda about all the things that she's doing wrong. How Luda should wash the forks before the knives and the bowls before the plates. How she does not have the water warm enough. How she should *never* boil water from the hot tap.

Luda can drown her out, mostly. She had years of practise when she and Joshua first came back to Narra from the coast. It was meant to be a brief trip to support his mother after the loss of his father; to ease Glenda's transition into this strange, halting life where she often looked up for her husband and found only air; empty rooms. Yes, Luda has perfected drowning Glenda out. Although sometimes they get into arguments at the market, when Glenda tells Luda that she's picked the wrong zucchinis, the wrong brand of butter.

'Go fuck yourself!' Luda bellows, and finds herself escorted out of the store by one of the local police officers – someone young and solid who still calls up the newly retired police officer Mathers to make sure she's doing the right thing, following the protocols when she must and deviating when she should. Luda is given a referral for a mental health worker. She is escorted back to Seannay, where the ghost house is quiet and dusty. She still has a zucchini clenched tightly in her hand.

* * *

Darcy walks home from his work at the brewery. Along the waterfront, he notices witch marks carved above doorways. He's not sure whether he's just never noticed them before, but he's fairly certain that they're new: that maybe there are people here who are beginning to feel frightened of the sea. The weather.

He no longer writes to John.

He's nearly reached Seannay when the young police officer calls him. He has her number programmed into his phone. 'I dropped Luda home about fifteen minutes ago.'

Darcy sighs, quickens his pace. 'What happened?'

'She got agitated at the market. It's fine, though. She's calmed down now.'

'Thanks,' says Darcy, a headache building behind one eye.

He finds his mother out with her bucket, collecting seaweed and clams that she won't want – won't remember – to eat.

'No, it was you,' Luda says. 'You'd had too much to drink.' A pause. 'It was. It was.'

It unsettles him, seeing his mother suddenly obsessively pre-occupied with every past hurt and whisper.

'Why don't you come see Tristan with me,' he suggests. He realises that his copy of *The Salt Boy* is poking out of the bag he has slung over his shoulder. Luda will not notice it, though. And even if she does, she will not make the connection with Theo; will not read into Darcy's unspoken longing and weariness.

She waves a hand, not looking up from the water. 'Why? Why would I bother sitting in that awful room when he's *here*?'

'He's not here. He's in that awful room. *By himself.*'

Luda looks up, her face soft. 'He's not,' she says, very patiently.

'You know, it's amazing you can go through what you did and somehow come out the other side still completely self-involved and fucking *selfish*.' Darcy kicks up a spray of water but his mother does not flinch. He turns away; waits to feel better. Him and his traitorous, pointless body.

Chapter Twenty-four

MARCH (THEIR THIRD YEAR)

Violet has moved into the ghost house, which both puzzles Min, when she thinks of how many people with proper houses would welcome Violet into their families, and does not puzzle her at all, when she watches Violet caring for Luda with all the gentleness and ferocity of a mother. Min likes to listen to the sound of Violet breathing in the other bed of the loft. She sometimes thinks that they lie there in the feathery summer evenings, under the constellation of witch marks, each comforted by the song of the other, *alive*. Violet's skin is heavy with the marks of farming; of working with her body. Of being married to Bryce. Violet does not like being in her house at the farm by herself. Even Bryce, who – unable to describe his pain and his yearning and his hopelessness – would control every part of her life that he could, had made the house feel like home. Had made it feel, at least a little bit, the way it had felt when Allie was there.

Bryce had not been like this before Allie died.

'The worst he ever did was throw me onto the bed,' Min hears Violet telling Luda. She forces a laugh. 'He was so gentle, before. Such a gentle, kind man.'

But to Min, who had felt Bryce's fingers around her throat, his weight pressing her into damp earth, his ferocity had felt well practised. The grief may have ripped it out into the world, but Min is certain it had been in him all along.

'Throwing you onto the bed isn't okay,' Min says.

Violet just smiles and makes Luda a sandwich with the edges cut off.

Sometimes Luda wanders to the market or the kirk, where she paces around, muttering to her ghosts. Luda has started collecting ritual objects – the sorts that are mentioned in the papers she'd unearthed in the Before, about the witchcraft and trials of the seventeenth century. She stores them in the ghost house, her stones and sieve and bones and iron. Also, her cans and condom wrappers and fractured pieces of plastic – the rubbish Min had once brought with her from the deep. She does not like it if Darcy or Min get too close to them. She presents them to Violet, though. It's one of the rare occasions when their interactions feel like two grown women, neither responsible for the other. Luda. Conversing impatiently (sometimes mournfully) with the dead.

* * *

Theo sits back on the rocky shore of Seannay. He stares down at the illustration he's finished – the same sort he's always done, full of nameless things. His back's sore from work. He's taken up a position at a larger farm on the other side of the island. He's good at working with difficult animals; with the well-bred bulls that have been mistreated, the dogs that bark and snap. It's a step up from smoking joints on Gerald's back steps.

He's stopped picking at the flesh of his hands and the pain has eased. His fingers once again move how he wants them to. Mostly, he doesn't even notice the webbing between all of his fingers. He wonders what would have happened if Luda had not driven the car into the water, shocking them all into something new. *Darcy. Darcy. Darcy.* He wonders if he'd still be in that place, that place of sleep and tidal dreams.

He suspects that a part of Iris liked him like that; reliant on her. Childlike. Curled safely in his room while she plied him with oatcakes and cups of strong tea, and glasses of salt water when he would not brush his teeth.

He shudders.

The chaos of his life before is like a fever dream. If he's careful, if he stays away from the pub, he might have enough money to move out in a few more months. The owner of the farm, Marcia, never mentions *The Salt Boy* – that bestselling book about him by Carter McGregor. Giving that interview, the book itself, has not dampened people's curiosity about him but made it flare bright and hot.

As far as books go, it's a good one. Even Theo can admit that, from what he's gauged when he's listened to parts of the audio recording. Carter had sent him a box full of copies of the book at about the same time that Luda and Tristan went into the sea, but Theo – still in that giddy, strange place – had set them on fire.

After, he'd had to wait months to borrow an audiobook from the library. The book outlines all the facts of Theo's appearance. The times. The dates. The weather. It lays it out like a story. Carter then meticulously details all of the theories about his origins, using snippets of interviews with locals and with experts across all sorts of fields, from anthropology to psychology and genomics and folklore.

It is nothing that people had not already known. Carter had never worked out what Darcy had worked out – that Theo might have come from the crypt of that abandoned, lonely island. There is a power in his story being bound up in a book, though, particularly the parts of him that exist beyond the words. Even Theo – who still cannot read – recognises this.

The burning of his unremembered childhood has faded to an ache. Those carrying hands. Or perhaps those flickers of something he can't quite grasp are not actually his. Perhaps they are unreal; the childhood of Min and Darcy that he has imagined, has experienced through stories and the thousands of photographs, wedged into photo albums and dragged here from the other side of the world.

He prefers the story of the selkie. He prefers the stories of washing up from the deep and shedding his skin.

These days, it is proximity to Darcy that draws him to Seannay. An excuse to be where Darcy sometimes is.

Before him, in the shallows, Luda is holding half a conversation. Luda does not eat much anymore. Not because she resists, but because she forgets. The idea of mealtimes and hunger has fallen away from her. Theo knows this feeling. It had taken weeks for him to feel properly hungry after he'd been pulled from the water as a child. And she is more Other than he is. He looks at her and thinks that she's a dead thing now. Or a half-dead thing. That she had moved on to wherever it is we go after life, and that somehow she has been pulled back. Altered.

Sometimes, Luda looks into his eyes and smiles at him. She offers him tea, which she makes laboriously – sometimes forgetting how to dunk the teabags or pour the milk. She asks him about Iris. She never remembers his job, but he's unbothered. Other times she is in the middle of frantic, fractured conversations with people who are not there. Often, it's about hexafoils and debitage. Other times it's about cows and water and bruises.

Occasionally, she seems to stop breathing. Everyone that Luda talks to in these moments, her eyes searching the air as though reading a complicated expression on a familiar face, is dead.

Theo treats these moments as though Luda is in the middle of an important phone call. He smiles, waves and takes his leave.

He sees how it affects Darcy and Min, though.

Theo hears the caravan door open and close, as he always hopes it will. He bends back down over his sketchbook, oddly comforted by Luda's voice coming in from the water.

Darcy stops near him, arms crossed, staring out at his mother, as though she is the reason he has come out. She might well be. Theo opens a new page; begins drawing something else.

'She won't visit Tristan,' Darcy says, and the sound of his voice, wary and awkward, emerging of its own volition, almost makes Theo slip off the rock. He looks up, and is surprised again; Darcy is looking back at him. God, he's still so beautiful it makes Theo actually *ache*. As his unremembered childhood aches; a different present (a future) that he mourns.

Her voice carries to them, raised in irritation. Darcy winces. 'Those goddamn voices. You know she's convinced that Tristan comes and visits her? That's why she won't go to the hospital to actually see him.'

Darcy's voice is raw. Theo wants to close his sketchbook; wants to drag Darcy to him so that he can feel Darcy's body pressed against his own; wants to keep him there until Darcy stops hurting, even if that takes the rest of their lives. But, more than that, he wants to be what Darcy needs, and what Darcy needs is stillness. What Darcy needs is for Theo to keep his distance.

'I know how much you miss him,' Theo says instead. And from the corner of his eye, he sees Darcy react to his words, his arms tightening, his knees bending, his chin tucking inwards, as though weathering a blow. Fatherless boys recognise this about each other: the value of a man who loves you.

'I trusted him,' Darcy says after a moment, sounding confused.

'I know. I know you did.'

For a moment they watch Luda brushing her fingers along the sun-spangled surface of the water.

Darcy draws in a breath and it catches, and that catch undoes Theo. He tosses his sketchbook aside and stands. A splash as Luda clasps a small stone for inspection and then returns it to the sea.

Theo reaches for Darcy, and Darcy's expression collapses. 'Don't.'

'Darcy ...'

'Don't!'

Distance. Distance. Distance. Theo tries to be still, to be patient. But everything he wants makes it too hard. 'Why?' Theo's voice is loud, and trembles. And he expects Darcy to bite back, to say something cutting and cold, but Darcy just walks away.

* * *

Darcy wishes he'd thought to ask Tristan about Theo. About all sorts of things beyond academia and the islands and ethics and exam prep. Darcy wishes he'd explained what happened when Theo was close to him. How sometimes an hour could pass in which he thought of nothing else, his eyes skirting over the same sentence in the page of a book again and again and again. He wishes he'd had the guts to lay it all out for Tristan, methodical, empirical, like a paper he wanted edited. 'So, what do I do now? What do I do *next*?'

But Tristan is not here anymore. Not really. And Theo belongs more to other people than he ever has, ever will, to Darcy.

* * *

Luda stands in bright sunshine. For a moment, there is a woman next to her. A fine-featured face that shifts like sand in wind. Dark hair.

'Did you call the whales?' A pause, she bites at her lip. 'Is Tristan there where you are?'

'Of course not,' says Tristan-from-the-in-between, furious now. 'Of course I'm not *there*, wherever the hell there is. I'm here. I'm here with *you*.'

He pokes at her arm, but she feels nothing.

The woman watches them. Sand in wind. 'Can you help him, at least?' Luda asks her. 'He's not very happy here. Please.'

There is a gust of wind, the sort that makes Luda stagger in this unfamiliar, strange body of hers in the After. She is sure, though, that the woman has spoken into the wind. Words Luda has not been able to untangle into meaning.

'Go and see me,' Tristan-from-the-in-between says.

'I can see you *now*.'

'The rest of me. For Darcy. Go for Darcy.'

There is a raised voice. She and Tristan-from-the-in-between both look towards the shore. Theo and Darcy. Darcy striding away, Theo watching him and then throwing a rock hard into other rocks. Kicking at the water. He looks like the Theo she remembers from the Before – all sharp edges and fury and bloodied hands. She waves at him, this long-lost friend. But he's still raging and does not see.

Luda leaves the bay, Theo's wordless frustration. Away from the water and the ghost house, she finds gorse woven into wreaths, left on the hillside in the place where she had seen women (the living, breathing kind from Big Island).

Before.

Luda shivers, suddenly cold. Hands. She can't breathe.

Later, Violet gives her a lift to the hospital so that she can visit the rest of Tristan. She clings to the underside of the passenger seat and finds, when they arrive, that she's been crying silently for the whole drive.

Violet does not come inside. Violet pulls out her whittling knife and settles back into the seat of her car.

In Tristan's room, Luda takes out a sewing needle and carefully carves a hexafoil into his skin. She has become unaccountably worried about others from the in-between finding their way to this space/body that he has left behind.

It may not *be* Tristan, but it belongs to him and she will protect it. Him. She sits for a very long time. She presses more deeply, is contented in her work.

'What the hell are you doing?'

Luda looks up, smiles at Darcy, who is enraged into stillness by the door.

'Jesus, don't smile right now, Luda,' Tristan-from-the-in-between says. 'He'll yell more if you smile.'

'Nothing.' She lets her hands drop, but Darcy moves quickly across the room and Luda hears his breath hitch when he sees the marks that Luda has carefully added to the flesh of Tristan's arm.

Darcy looks away from her and dashes his hand across his eyes. Luda brushes Tristan's hair from his face. How can she explain to Darcy that the marks are a gift? An act of love? How badly she wants him to understand that she is getting closer to untangling the magic of it all.

* * *

Iris's mother had cast spells – nights of candles and August muttering under her breath. She had tried to teach Iris, but Iris had never wanted to learn.

Even then, right at the beginning, Iris had had a sense of how it would all end.

Iris still joined in, though, when Cassandra and the others came over and told stories among themselves. The woman who could rein in raging wind and thick curtains of needling rain. August knew the stories of Athena and Artemis; Aphrodite and Persephone and Hera. Women, all women. All women, fierce and powerful.

August and Iris would sometimes go to the kirk and Cassandra often accompanied them. Sometimes for worship and sometimes to poke around the echoing space, the upper levels, and the belfry with its view all the way to the sound.

In the kirk, August would survey Haaken's Hole and the hangman's ladder and the manacles and the dock. Sometimes, if nobody was looking, August would take out a knife and carve symbols into the wood of the ladder and the dock. 'Stop it,' Iris would say, terrified of damaging anything in a place of God.

Cassandra knows that, even then, Iris had known all about hell. That she could imagine it vividly and fretted about August and Cassandra and the others unleashing something of it with all of their candles and incantations.

'There's no hell, Iris,' August would say.

But that would mean that there is no heaven.

Cassandra knows that Iris had tried to channel the power of these women whose tales she had fallen asleep listening to. When a wind roared, she told herself she had called it up, like a friend. When a particularly unpleasant man was blown off the cliffs and drowned by the tides, she had thought, *Aye. Aye.*

The stale, chalky smell. Each Saturday, Cassandra would watch as Iris and her mother wore blacks and greys, made wreaths of gorse and seaweed, and left them around the tidal island, weighted down by rocks.

* * *

Min often seeks out Cassandra. That old, old ache. She can't explain the tug she feels, no matter where she is – the awareness of Cassandra on the other side of the island. Exhaustion. A memory stretching back and back and back and back. Sometimes, Min is aware of the sharp physicality of her pain.

Min tells herself that her mother does not see ghosts, and yet the idea of them existing terrifies her in unnameable ways. Cassandra did not tell Min that she was a hero for diving into the water after her mother and Tristan. She did not ask Min how she did it or what it was like. Instead, she had pushed herself up onto her narrow, unwieldy legs and held out her trembling arms.

'Oh, my darling,' she'd said, and Min had almost cried. Cassandra. Holding Min tightly, rocking her. Or maybe it was just her trembling. Trembling, trembling. 'My darling, darling Wilhelmina.'

Min had flooded Cassandra with her memories of the water that day, and memories of the night before, until she worried that Cassandra could not take the burden of her sorrow and her horror anymore. But Cassandra was unyielding, willing to sit with Min in long silences or engage her in light chatter. Always, beneath everything she did. *My darling, darling Wilhelmina.*

* * *

That night, Luda wakes to a woman leaning over her. Dark hair, a face that shifts like sand. Luda has an impression of great longing, of impatience. *Soon.* And then the woman disappears.

Chapter Twenty-five

APRIL (THEIR THIRD YEAR)

It is Violet who tells Luda about the photographic exhibition sponsored by an offshore drilling company; it is Violet who suggests that she enter it. A photo depicting the islands; an aspect of island life. They sit in the empty kirk, as they often do, because Violet likes it here and Luda doesn't much mind where she is, most of the time.

Luda considers the idea. She studies the fall of light through the kirk window. 'I haven't taken proper photographs in a long time.' She frowns. 'Don't even know if I could still work a camera properly.'

Violet rolls her eyes. She rubs cream into Luda's hands. 'Of course you can!'

Luda touches her fingers to her head and frowns. She feels as though she can perhaps still operate a camera – the memories of working them are vivid and full, the sort that she has found will act as a guide for her now. Her confidence in herself has been worn away like an island shoreline, a little each day – and occasionally a huge chunk – disappearing into frothing water. How people talk to her; how they *don't* talk to her – instead talking about her, across her, as though she isn't there. How people don't broach anything complex with her anymore. Don't ask her what she thinks.

Violet tells her it's a little like being trapped in grief. People talk to you as if you're no longer one of them. As though some vital part of you is gone and they don't know how to treat you without it.

'How are you, Violet?' Father Lee comes out and drops to his knee and takes Violet's hands in his.

She raises an eyebrow, but she has always been devout and he is still a man of God. She inclines her head. 'Oh, not so bad, Father. And yourself?'

'Fine, fine. This time of year's always been my favourite.' He smiles at Luda. 'It's cheering, don't you think?'

'Yes,' says Luda, although she doesn't much mind what the weather's doing. The only type of weather she really takes proper note of now is the gale force wind that springs up more and more frequently around the islands. All these rare weather events, happening more and more. A flicker of her own voice from the Before: *this is war.*

'Tell me, Violet, have you heard from Bryce?' Father Lee asks, still holding her hands.

'Aye, he writes to me. Beautiful letters.'

'Grief does terrible things to a man.'

'Aye.'

'He loves you very much.'

Violet smiles, but there's steel under it. 'Aye, and I him.'

'He should be home with you.'

'And maybe one day he will be, Father. That's up to the good Lord to decide.' Violet stands and Luda stands with her. Father Lee is left on the floor for a moment too long and rises hastily, straightening his shirt.

'I wish Father Lee would stop pressuring me,' Violet says as they walk slowly from the kirk towards Violet's car. 'I shouldn't say it, but he really is a bit of a knob, isn't he?'

'Will you go back home with Bryce?' Luda asks.

Violet shrugs. 'If it was just me he'd lashed out at when he was missing Allie, then aye. But it's not just me he's hurt.'

Luda considers this. 'No, it's not.'

'When I was a lass, I thought love was enough – that if you loved someone, things were simple. But it's never simple, is it?'

'No.' Her ghosts. 'No, it's never simple.' She pauses, struck by the fall of light near the car. Violet pauses with her, as she always does.

'That day you came out to the farm and he lost his temper was the first time I realised I was scared of him. I wanted to stop him, but I couldn't.'

Luda's finger twitches as she looks at the town. Twirling the focus of an imagined camera. A car rumbles past, too close. Luda does not like cars. She gasps and flails at every bump or dip in the road.

The dark. The cold.

She and Min, backing away from cars and flinching at the sound of loud engines. If Luda had thought to notice this, she might have called it kinship.

* * *

Darcy drinks coffee in the little kitchen of the ghost house, Theo's sea glass on the table in front of him. He watches his mother through the window, pacing with her camera. She had said it was work, but he knows that she has no work to *do*. Her sudden fervour makes him uneasy.

Min is off with Ewan. She has grown pale, since the accident. Looks nauseous any time Luda mentions a ghost or starts those twisted, one-sided conversations.

'Not real, not real, not real,' she'll mutter to herself. Damp palms. Caught breath.

Over the last few days, Luda has started taking photos the way she had up until the cliff collapse: without thinking about anything other than what's in front of her. Without delineating flesh from earth. It's what had made her so good – so awful – at her work. It scares him, this sudden circling back. He thinks of the dam photo. His sprawled limbs, cracked earth.

He swallows bile.

It is not the fervour on its own. It's also her growing collection of stones and animal bones and ale and stale bannocks. Little bundles of straw and water kept in glass bottles. Cloth. Herb. Salt. Thread. Rubbish that Min had pulled from the deep in sacks before the accident.

At first Darcy had thought that his mother believed herself to be a witch. Lately, he's realised that she's studying the objects – puzzling over them and how they fit together. It is nothing like the clutter of Theo's room; things frantically clawed from the sea to be sorted over later. Luda's objects are carefully ordered. She discards what she deems of no further use. There is something scientific in how she fits them together, and this unsettles him more than anything else.

Darcy tilts back in his chair, watching. Watching that pause. Soon, his mother will begin crouching and shifting, coaxing the scene, drawing it out into something beautiful. Something deserving of enduring on gelatin silver, beyond itself. She will be impatient with the scene, Darcy can tell. It will not yield to her the way that living things do. He knows that this new Luda will grow tired of the landscape, of old bones and cairns and frost on thick grass. He senses that she will soon come after them, as she has always done. She will demand that they yield to her and the cold eye of her camera. Softly, quietly, and in the very precise way that eroded beaches and flooded turf and wind-pitted whalebone cannot.

* * *

Ewan takes Min out to the reef off the eastern edge of Big Island. He studies her, takes in her pale face, her overly bitten lip, swollen in the sunlight. He can read her now – she knows this. He can read her like the surface of the sea.

She always seems somehow *less* when she emerges from the water. As though the most important parts of her have been washed away. The parts that make her most human.

Min touches Ewan's arm as she often does after diving; snaking her fingers up his sleeve if he's wearing a jacket. His skin always feels burning hot and it brings her back to herself. Flickers of Cassandra's front room. Her breathing changes. She hands him a piece of coral without a word. Next it may be a shell; a stone; a bone. Ewan will keep them all in his cabin, stowed in a small, dusty drawer. It is the same place where he keeps his grandfather's compass; the rope he learnt to tie knots with as a lad.

* * *

The small ones are fascinated by the razor clams. That's when Luda feels them the most. It's why she often forgets the buckets, sometimes leaving them to be swept out by the rising tide. She does not see them the way she sees Tristan-from-the-in-between and the others. She does not hear their voices. They do not have words. But she feels them. The prickle of gorse. The memory of tremulous hands.

Her mother does not visit her on the tidal island. Her grandparents do not visit. The woman that is faceless; made of sand. She scowls up at the pinpricked night sky, and if Luda gets too close, she disappears.

'Do you know how to capture the scars?' Luda's voice carries through the air. Her camera is comforting in her hands. The darlings in the gorse, the small ones, are fascinated by the camera. The woman looks up, studies her in that very particular way that those no longer *here* have of studying those who remain. For a moment, Luda thinks that she might answer, but the woman turns towards the water and promptly disappears.

Luda realises that she's become cold. That Darcy is standing next to her, staring.

'Mum,' he says, and tugs her inside.

* * *

At first, Cassandra is surprised to find Father Lee on her doorstep five minutes after Iris has arrived with cans of baby carrots. It is clear from Iris's expression that she had not been expecting Father Lee. Between them: a licking seam of red.

'Oh, you're both here! Wonderful, wonderful,' he says, as though he has run into them at the local cafe, instead of following one of them to the other one's house. 'Make myself a tea, shall I?' he says, raising his eyebrows at Iris, who does nothing but sip hers and look back at him.

Luda, Cassandra thinks, watching Father Lee's back as he heads to the kitchen. *This is about Luda.*

Iris drinks her tea. 'I still don't know why it has to be in the kirk,' she says, as though nothing has happened; as though Father Lee has not turned up on this rainy spring night to pressure them.

'It's a photography exhibition, Iris, not a Satanist convention,' Cassandra says, but there is no heat in her voice. Her focus, like Iris's, is trained on the sounds coming from the kitchen.

Father Lee comes back with a sweet and milky tea. He has also unearthed some stale oatcakes from a cupboard and put them on a plate. He is immensely pleased with himself.

'Right,' he says, spreading a napkin across his knees. 'I was hoping to talk to you about the Managan woman.' He addresses only Iris, and then Cassandra understands why he's come here and what he will say. How wrongly he's intuited everything. She reaches for her tea, relaxing a little bit.

'What about her?' Iris asks, clearly not understanding. She casts a quick glance at Cassandra and seems comforted by Cassandra's sudden calm.

'I don't think this island can really cater to her needs. Poor Violet Reynolds is caring for her and those children – after everything she's been through.'

'It's my understanding that Violet quite likes Seannay – and the Managans, for that matter,' says Iris.

'The Managan woman has been wandering.'

'Och!' says Cassandra. 'Since when is a bracing walk a crime, Father?'

'She's turning up to my parishioners' houses without invitation, agitated and insistent.'

'Same could fairly be said of you, Father,' Cassandra says.

All the muscles in Father Lee's neck tense. 'She's dangerous,' he says at last.

'She's really not that bad, Marcus,' Iris says, voice weary. 'And they're expecting her to keep improving. Is that really all you've come here to say? May as well have brought the cans yourself and saved me the bother.'

Father Lee blinks rapidly and Cassandra has another sip of tea. Iris has always made a very good cup of tea. 'Iris, I hate to ask, but I need you to help me find her somewhere more suitable to live,' he says, suddenly intent upon her. 'Before she hurts someone. Or herself.'

'Pish!' Cassandra snaps. 'Good Lord, Marcus. What a performance.'

Iris glances at Cassandra, and Cassandra knows that she now understands.

'Can I count on you?' he asks Iris, his voice sorrowful.

Father Lee, who had thought Cassandra's presence would fence Iris in. Father Lee, with so few friends of his own, does not truly understand the depths that friendship can reach. Father Lee, who has never recognised the connection between Iris and Cassandra as anything other than antagonistic. He had thought Iris would be eager to side with him against Cassandra; would welcome the opportunity, as she has done in years past, to present a united front.

Poor, lonely Father Lee.

'No, Father. Unfortunately you can't.' Iris sighs, like it's a very heartbreaking thing for her to say. Cassandra reminds herself that it is, really. Iris has invested an awful lot in Father Lee. 'I just don't see what danger Luda Managan poses. She's strange, but she's always been strange, hasn't she? And it's truly up to her family and the doctors to decide where would be best for her.'

'The council will evict them from the house, then,' he snaps.

Iris sighs again. 'No, the council won't.'

'Of course we will, if it's what's best for the community.'

'It's my property,' Iris explains. 'The council maintains it and runs it, but it's mine.'

He stares at her and Iris stares back. Cassandra considers the tins of carrots and wonders exactly how hungry she'd need to be before willingly ingesting them.

'Right,' he says, red-faced. He thumps his tea down next to the oatcakes on the table. 'I see.'

He leaves his napkin scrunched on the floor. They watch him striding off down the garden path.

'Sadly, not the end of it,' says Cassandra.

'No,' agrees Iris. 'But quite satisfying.'

* * *

As Iris and Cassandra discuss Father Lee's visit, Theo knocks on the caravan door and Darcy opens it. They have been avoiding each other for weeks now. Since Darcy stormed off from the bay.

'Can I come in?'

Darcy stands back from the door.

The caravan feels too small for the both of them, as it always has. Darcy clears his throat and sits down on his bed. He shuts his laptop. He's wearing blue jeans and an old, green jumper that's much too big for him. He pushes the sleeves up his arms and rubs at his cheek. He hasn't shaved. These days, he often hasn't shaved. 'What do you want?' he asks. And then, more tentatively, 'Do you want a coffee? I have instant in here.'

Theo shakes his head and then glances at the closed laptop. 'You researching something?'

'No.'

A corner of a book is visible from beneath Darcy's cream-coloured pillow. Theo frowns. 'Is that *The Salt Boy*?'

'No!'

Theo reaches for it and Darcy does not move quickly enough to stop him. The pages are folded down, the cover creased and marked. The red shard of sea glass tumbles out with it and Darcy tucks it quickly out of sight.

Theo puts the book back down on the bed and clears his throat. 'Your mum ...'

'I know.' Darcy runs his fingers around the edge of the laptop. 'Gerald was at the brewery today.'

'Oh.' Theo shifts. 'Was he?'

'He was asking how you were.' Darcy picks some fluff off his sleeve. 'Guess you're not seeing him as much these days.'

'I haven't seen him ... like that ... since the seal.'

'You really don't need to tell me about your sex life.'

Theo exhales. 'I just mean ...'

'It's not my business.'

Theo reminds himself: *Distance. Stillness.* 'Do you remember when you used to read to me?'

Darcy breathes out. 'Of course I do.'

Theo passes Darcy *The Salt Boy.* 'Will you read a bit?'

Darcy takes the book. For a moment, he says nothing. Then he pushes his sleeves back up his arms. 'Just a few pages,' he says. But the sky's beginning to darken and his throat is stinging by the time he finally sets the book aside.

* * *

In the evening, Ewan gives Luda a lift to the hospital. Ewan does not comment on Luda hanging on to the passenger seat with both hands or how she insists on her window being wound right down, even if it's hailing or snowing or sleeting. He does not comment on her suddenly wanting to go there, when she has until recently been completely uninterested in visiting the place.

Ewan, towelling off the inside of the passenger door. Sighing, but never saying anything about it to anyone.

This afternoon, Luda sits next to Tristan's bed, alone. She holds his hand (the rest of him). It's papery and the same temperature as the room. Unscarred skin. The scattering of half-healed wounds, spun into the shape of hexafoils. Witch marks.

She stares down at her own hands. She wants to capture the scars. Seannay, with its people-from-the-in-between and shells and whales and secrets. Joshua would not be able to see the scars, she is certain. She has asked the Joshua that visits her now, but he never tells her one way or the other.

Joshua had called her hysterical whenever she got upset. Even if she didn't cry or raise her voice. No matter how reasonable she was, how calm, he always threw that hateful, belittling word at her.

'Don't get yourself worked up,' he says now, appearing at the other side of Tristan's bed. 'I didn't say you were hysterical *that* often.'

Chapter Twenty-six

MAY (THEIR THIRD YEAR)

When Darcy wants to do something, his body may or may not let him. It is a fickle and unknowable thing. Some nights, curled up on the floor of the caravan, Min will talk about the water. About holding her breath.

'I don't want to hear about it!' Darcy snaps.

Min ignores him. Keeps talking.

He is not scared for her. He knows this. But he tells himself that he is. That he does not want to hear of her swimming, of her diving into that wild, cold ocean, because he is scared for her.

He is not scared.

'Do you ever feel like ... like your body won't do what you want it to?' he asks.

Min frowns. 'No,' she says. 'What do you even mean by that? We *are* our bodies.'

Darcy shakes his head in the darkness. Reaches for his sea glass.

Min talks about her diving. On the edge of sleep, her words will become muddled. Flames and stones. Whales in the sound. It makes him shiver; it makes him acutely aware of the witch marks in the ghost house.

That night, Darcy tries to dream himself into the sea. Into the filtered, shadowed impossibility of it. As though sensing it, Min stirs in her sleeping bag. 'You need to go into the sea, Darcy. You need to *swim*.'

He ignores her. Tries, instead, to dream himself into the deep. When he does finally fall asleep, he dreams of two Darcys. Him and his body, walking together through dust and dirt under a wide and pearly sky.

* * *

The wind the next day becomes so wild and animal that Luda is frightened and backs away from the windows. A cyclone out to sea. Sea spray and rain. The waves become more urgent, the high tides higher than they've ever been before. Tristan-from-the-in-between sits on the edge of the couch where Luda sleeps. 'Something happened to Darcy,' he tells her, over and over. Outside the weather roars. Luda holds a cushion over her head, trying to drown out his voice. She can still hear him, just as loudly. As persistently.

'Something happened to *Darcy*.'

And she realises that he doesn't know what he's talking about. Darcy – clever, beautiful Darcy. *Something happened to Darcy.* Nothing has happened to Darcy.

The wind. The wind. The wind.

Violet watches her from the kitchen. 'You alright, Lu?'

'I can't *think* in here.'

Violet folds a tea towel very precisely on the edge of the sink. She adjusts one of the photos of Allie that she has had framed and placed on the kitchen bench. 'Go outside for a bit. Take your camera.'

Luda stares at Violet. Tristan-from-the-in-between stares at Luda.

'My camera.'

'The exhibition, remember? They're holding the opening night at the kirk. Come on, Lu. You were going to take some photos of island life for it.' Violet does not use a loud, slow voice with Luda.

She scolds her often. Sometimes she strokes Luda's hair, as though Luda is very young.

Luda stands, thinks that she *will* go outside with her camera. She remembers loving it; the world through her viewfinder. Rocks and ocean and the stretch of ever-changing island sky.

A gust of wind shakes the panes of glass in the window. She hears the caravan clatter a little on its perch near the ghost house. Luda knows this: that sometimes leaning into the wind is the only thing that takes away her fear of it.

Why does she so often think that she sees that dark-haired woman, the set of her face oddly like Iris's, threading gorse and seaweed into a wreath?

* * *

Min and Cassandra do not always speak. Their voices are tidal things – blazing and guttering. Sometimes, Min can't get the words out fast enough. Stories of the sea. Whales. Sometimes Cassandra will tell Min stories. Other times they sit in silence, surveying the landscape visible through Cassandra's front window. Sometimes, Cassandra's mind will wander and Min will have impressions of scarred skin and a clear sky and the tidal island by candlelight. The slick feel of whale oil. Snow scattered bright and shocking on green grass.

An orca rising from the sound in moonlight, its face flickered with scars.

* * *

How many times has Min told Darcy to dive into the water? To swim? She was convinced, had always been convinced, that it would soothe him. He thinks of going into the sea, but something stops him. Something animal. Something that shies away from the cold, the tides, the wildness of the world beyond land.

Him and his body. Maybe the water will bring them together – maybe that is the real reason why Min seeks out the deep. Darcy checks that he cannot easily be seen from the ghost house or the track from the causeway. Over his shoulder, he can see only ruins. He begins to strip, the cold summer air like something solid. His mother's ghosts. He shudders, drops his socks, his shirt, his jacket. He weighs them down with rocks so the wind does not take them out to sea.

He takes a step into the water, then another. Rocks, sharp against the tender arch of his foot. He thinks of razor clams. Makes himself breathe (his body breathe). The thud of his body's heart.

The water reaches his knees, his waist, the tight muscles of his stomach. He takes a breath and contorts down under the surface. Again and again he ducks his body down, trying to understand what it is that Min finds here. Trying to claim a piece of it for himself.

But there is only the sound of the sea, the murmur of his own tired thoughts.

Him and his body, both in the water.

* * *

Theo walks across the causeway, loaded with food from the market. The wind makes him stagger. He finds Luda taking photos of the flagstones of the doorway, so entranced that she does not notice him as he steps around her. Violet is sitting at the kitchen table, whittling driftwood into the shape of a small, human figure. She watches Luda with an indulgent expression. 'You're heaven sent,' Violet says when she sees Theo. She rises to unpack the shopping bags. 'Drink?'

'Oh, I'm fine. But thank you.' He nods at Luda. 'Nice to see her back out with her camera.' Although he's not entirely sure that the flagstones in the doorway constitute being *back out*.

'She's going to enter the photography exhibition,' she tells Theo. 'She says the flagstone there has a surprisingly lovely texture.'

'It does,' Luda murmurs from the open doorway.

'Where're the others?' Theo asks Violet, because Luda will not know.

'Min's at Cassandra's, I think.' Violet sweeps her wood shavings into a neat pile on the table. 'I guess Darcy's in the caravan. Although I don't think it'd be much fun in there with all this wind.'

Theo thinks of Darcy's caravan, of being in there with Darcy. Darcy's voice unspooling *The Salt Boy* with such care that the words don't feel like so much of a violation. He might not have minded at all, if it had been Darcy who'd written the book.

Theo steps outside, thinking to head for the caravan, but something moves in the corner of his eye, near the bay. *A seal*, he thinks. But no.

Darcy. Darcy, wading out into the water, hands cupped forward slightly as though in supplication. The low sun catches him and the sight of him naked in the water is something Theo wants to remember for the rest of his life. He ducks under as though he's searching for something long lost.

Darcy.

Theo walks towards the bay, still thinking of Darcy reading him *The Salt Boy* in the caravan. Trembling a little, Theo takes a deep breath and begins to strip.

* * *

Darcy's body breaks the surface of the water, lungs burning, vision glittery at the edges. He winces at the sight of Theo naked on the edge of the bay. He immediately turns away. Bewildered by Theo's easy nakedness. A dazed thought: it is Theo's hands that Theo keeps private, and he has always shown Darcy his hands.

'Darcy.' The word is snagged between them. Beseeching, almost.

Darcy does not turn back, but something in his body must soften, because he can sense Theo stepping forward from his own pile of clothes. Darcy turns away from Theo because no good has ever come from it; this skin.

Then he does look at Theo, the skin of his throat the colour of a scar. Those impossible, slate-coloured eyes. Theo glances away as Darcy climbs out of the water. With his fiery body, he does not, has never, seemed to feel the cold.

It starts to rain again and a flock of cormorants take flight from the beach. Theo's old shirt is taken by the wind – he does not think of things like weighing his clothes down with stones on windy days. 'Darcy!' he says, and points, so struck with the wonder of it that he does not realise that Darcy is already watching. The buck of its shape above the wind and rain-ruffled water. Darcy shivers. For a brief and flickering moment, he and his body are merged. Neither he nor Theo moves. They watch the shirt. They hold their breath. Then Theo reaches out a hand to touch Darcy's cheek. Darcy flinches and turns towards the house. It is a while before Theo is calm enough to follow him.

* * *

Hail Mary, full of grace. The Lord is with thee.

Sometimes Iris enters the kirk at night and the flickering impressions always rouse Cassandra from her patchy, restless sleep. Cassandra half-dreams of Iris pacing down the aisle. The cold. Smell of dust. Iris's pale, narrow hands. Iris likes the kirk at night. She sometimes imagines the sea rising up to claim the islands and the sinners. She likes to imagine the strong, the just, the *true* packed in here as the rest of the world is washed away. A sort of Noah's ark, but the kirk is all that survives. Fanciful, she knows. Still, she feels safe here. It's always been a place of final refuge.

'Oh, Iris,' Cassandra will mutter crossly, and begin the slow process of rolling over in bed.

Blessed art thou among women, and blessed is the fruit of thy womb, Jesus.

Iris goes through the rosary. After, she wraps her jacket more firmly around her, for the kirk always feels colder on this side of the transept. She gazes up at the mouth of Haaken's Hole.

Holy Mary, Mother of God, pray for us sinners, now and at the hour of our death. Amen.

If she ever senses Cassandra's exasperation, her impatience, Iris never gives herself away.

* * *

Luda thinks of cold, dark places. Sometimes the thoughts are like waking nightmares, in which she forgets the sun, the ground, the breeze. There are hands in the dark. The women come nearer when her thoughts shadow themselves like this. They don't ever speak, but they draw close. They watch her. Often, she sees her distress mirrored on their faces.

Sometimes, when this happens, she makes a high-pitched noise. Darcy will shake her shoulder and Min will less gently thump her on the back. Or else Min will be gentle and Darcy will be rough. Her children switch roles. They are never gentle at the same time.

'Do you remember it?' she asks Tristan-from-the-in-between. 'Do you remember being under the water?'

'I remember the whales and the cold.' A frown. 'I remember you holding my hand.'

Chapter Twenty-seven

JUNE (THEIR THIRD YEAR)

Summer. Pale arms exposed to the slow, lazy sun. Someone submits a photograph to the exhibition of Corrigan's cans spelling out the word *Garbage Girl*. Iris rips it into little pieces and nobody says anything about it.

* * *

Min had briefly considered wearing a dress, but she doesn't own any dresses and she feels strange about going through her mother's things. Her mother feels too much like a stranger now. Instead, she wears a pair of black leggings and a clean, warm jumper that's a sort of dusty blue. She looks in the mirror and is startled. She looks older, her face thinner. She tries to think back to the last time she'd studied herself closely in a mirror but can't.

Theo puts his chin on her shoulder, inspecting her reflection. 'Beautiful,' he says, very gravely. And she turns to rub her nose against the side of his face, smiling.

'Your mum already gone across with Violet?' he asks.

'Yup.'

'And Darcy?'

'Not coming. Let's go.'

Theo pulls Ewan's old beanie down over his hair and puts on the thick-rimmed glasses that he sometimes wears when the islands swell with tourists.

'Oh, what an elaborate disguise,' says Min.

Walking across the causeway, Theo and Min both feel young and a little enthralled by everything. For a moment, it's like they're about to run to the Wailing Cliffs to drink stolen whisky and rage at the sea. Instead they link arms and walk steadily, like adults, to the kirk.

The stairs leading up to the kirk entrance are lit with small lanterns. The tree is strung with fairy lights. Theo pauses as they get close. Finally, he stops. Min glances at him. 'What?'

'I haven't been inside … Not for years.'

'I thought you wanted to come.'

'I did. I do.' He exhales.

'I hate it in there,' Min says in a quiet voice. 'I hate that there are people buried under the floor. And I hate the hole and I hate the dock. Ghosts, Theo. I can't … I can't stand the idea of ghosts.'

Theo nods, puts an arm around her shoulders. His own hands tremble a little inside their gloves. The crowds; the kirk itself. The *noise*.

Wordless, bound in wildness. The two of them approach the doors – thrown open, revealing a glow of candles. Theo glances around before stepping more fully inside. He clasps Min's shoulders tightly and she can feel the change in his body, like something electric, as they're engulfed by the crowds of noisy, moving people. Violet, not far from the door, wide-eyed, one hand touching the cross she wears around her throat, as though she has been swept there by mistake.

Theo's voice is tight. 'Where are your mum's photos?'

'I don't know, T.' She looks at him. 'You alright?'

His cheeks are flushed, but he nods. He lets go of her and tugs his beanie down over his ears. 'I'll be okay,' he says. He begins to move across the room to the photos, staying as close to the walls as he can. Min goes to follow him but feels an urgent tug on the back of her jumper. She turns to face Ewan, who looks shocked; his brows drawn low over his eyes.

'What?' she says.

'Is Darcy here too?'

'No, he's not coming. Why?'

'Get Theo out of here.'

'What? Why?'

Ewan grabs her arm and drags her around the back of the space. 'Ouch!' Min snaps, wrenching free. 'What the hell is wrong with you?'

Ewan nods at the wall and Min looks up, still irritated. Luda's work spreads across the back wall. Min gasps.

There are photos of the byre and the house and the land bitten hard by the sea. There are images of an old whale vertebra. The vertebra is like a tiny, curled-up child. Vulnerable and disquieting. Once, Darcy had looked up the proper names for the different parts of the whale bone and told Min. The shapes that are so like wings, flaring on either side, are called transverse processes. *Whale wings*, she thinks.

And then.

Min feels the world tilt, rage rising in her. Despair at the damage these images will do. The blurred shapes of naked bodies, frozen on gelatin silver. She thinks that it was always going to happen; her mother taking photographs of bodies on the island. Scarred skin.

'Oh, Mum,' says Min softly. Then she straightens, turns to Ewan. 'We need to find Theo.'

* * *

Cassandra had bribed Lorraine and Iris into bringing her to the kirk for the exhibition, mostly to watch Father Lee's slow implosion over the whole thing. She accepts a third glass of champagne and smiles up at Lorraine. 'You're an angel,' Cassandra tells her.

'So you keep telling me.'

Iris grips her crucifix. Runs it backward and forward along the chain. There is nothing between her and Cassandra here.

She is keeping it all to herself. She blinks quickly, catches Cassandra watching her and pulls a childish face.

'August would have loved this,' Cassandra says lightly. 'The kirk filled up with photos. Imagine!'

Iris says nothing, just gives Cassandra another look and goes off to inspect the images on the far side of the kirk. Cassandra knows that Iris has been thinking about August a lot lately. That it unsettles her. Iris has always preferred to keep her mother tucked neatly into the box Iris has in the back of her mind labelled: *A BAD WITCH*.

Cassandra squints, but cannot see what Iris is seeing. Iris pulling the rosary beads from her pocket. *Hail, holy Queen, Mother of mercy, our life, our sweetness, and our hope.*

The devil's scars that August used to trace with coal and marvel at and weep over; the scars that Iris has always, much to Cassandra's exasperation, done her best to ignore.

Luda has captured them. Cassandra drains her glass of champagne. *Of course she has.*

* * *

Luda stands resolutely on the upper level of the kirk, touching her fingers to the hangman's ladder. The dock. Her fingers finding shapes carved there that she has never noticed before. The whale-shaped witch marks she knows from the walls of the ghost house. She can see Haaken's Hole from here, but cannot reach it without going down into the crowds.

There are those from the other place everywhere tonight, drawn from wherever it is they dwell by the swell of noise and flickering light. The figure Luda sees so often is not among them for she does not leave the tidal island.

The women. Summoning the whales. Her hand drops. She looks down at the bright, full kirk. *See what I have done. See what I have done.* It is not hysteria. She thinks of the women from the other place, the witch markings, Tristan. Tristan. Tristan.

'Uh-huh,' says Tristan. The Tristan-from-the-in-between, watching with his hands clasped behind his back. Luda doesn't look at him. Mutters at him to go away, if he's going to be like that. He doesn't go anywhere. Doesn't smile. He is extremely disappointed in her.

* * *

Min follows Theo onto the street and finds him leaning with his head against the rough-cut stones of the building's outer wall. She's relieved to be out of the kirk. That place of death and spirits. She places a hand on his arm and feels the warmth of his skin.

'Theo? T?'

He backs away, nostrils flaring, as he had in those early weeks of the Managans being here. For a moment, Min is mesmerised. She had forgotten the precise shape of his wildness.

'No one will know it's you two,' she says.

'You did.'

'Only because it's *me*.'

'Darcy's so ... so private. Being naked in a photo ...' He closes his eyes. 'Ewan?'

Min exhales. 'Ewan recognised you both, too. But that doesn't mean anyone else will.'

He shudders and turns away. For a moment he's still, his whole body poised for flight with the glare of the bright summer night behind him. Then he runs.

She stands, staring after him. The empty road. Damp, even in summer. She counts her breaths and then goes slowly back inside, heart uneven. A tremor.

* * *

Would Luda have done it if she were well?

She already had. The dam. The drought. The cliffs. But, if she were well, would she have done it *again*?

Chapter Twenty-eight

JUNE (THEIR THIRD YEAR)

In the rush that follows the closing of the kirk for the night, the image of Theo and Darcy is taken down from the wall. It is carried resolutely into a dark, windy place. It is set alight.

The clink of rosary beads and the memory of gorse.

It becomes ash and is blown by a sudden gust of wind out to sea.

* * *

The air is raw in his chest now. His heart is thunder. Theo stops his headlong run just outside the caravan and catches his breath. Then he opens the door without knocking.

'What are you doing here?' Darcy asks, his voice softened by sleep. He is still dressed, lying under just the top blanket of his bed. Face down next to him is his tattered copy of *The Salt Boy*.

He thinks of the book. Of Carter. Of the bishop's palace all lit up with stars. Of how the scars on other people's skin become more vivid to him the more that he's been hurt.

'The photos,' Darcy says. He looks searchingly into Theo's face. 'What's she done?'

'She took a photo of us.' He is back on the shoreline, without words, without any sort of knowing. He is in the alleyway. He is locked in the cupboard at the kirk. He is windswept and staring

into the maw of the crypt on the lonely island. He thinks of Darcy –
Darcy's naked body. Darcy's skin. Darcy. But everything else, too.
The sea-drenched flickers of his life, before. Being wordless. Being
submerged in a world he does not know.

'When?' Darcy asks sharply.

Theo doesn't look at him.

Darcy lets out a shuddering breath. '*When*, Theo?'

'When we were on the beach.'

'That … that was only a few seconds!'

'I know.' Theo makes himself look up at Darcy then. Darcy's
face is coloured with panic, his pupils very large. He runs a hand
through his hair, making it stick up oddly. Then, like a switch, his
expression goes carefully blank and he reaches up to smooth his
hair back down, his eyes fixed on the other side of the caravan. It's
fascinating and awful to watch.

Darcy stands up. 'I'm going to get it taken down.'

'Now?'

'Yes. Now.'

'I can come with you.'

Darcy shakes his head. A flare of panic like a starburst. 'No,
it's … no. Thanks.'

'Well, I'm sorry I woke you,' Theo says. He makes a small,
involuntary move towards Darcy, and Darcy moves quickly away,
every line of his body tight with tension.

Theo sighs.

Darcy's voice is dull. 'I'm sorry.' He pulls his shoes on, a jumper.
'I'm sorry.'

* * *

It's late by the time Darcy gets to the kirk. There are still some
people in clusters near the kirk yard gate, like flotsam left behind
by the tide. The summer nights are hard to leave. Darcy strides past
them up to the kirk's main door. It's locked, so he goes around to

the side door. This handle, too, is unyielding beneath his fingers and he feels his throat thicken.

He sinks down, back against the door, his breath coming hard and fast. Flashes of things he does not want to think about. The curtains of that goddamn room sliding closed. The scent of freshly mown grass. The image of him in the dried-out dam plastered across all the lockers at school. Bursts of blue and red lights. The wreck of their car disappearing on the back of a flatbed truck. The cliff giving way. The keening of Violet Reynolds.

He pinches his legs through his pants until he feels more present. He tries to slow his breathing, but can't stop gasping. Gulping air, as though he is sinking into the deep, like Min on one of her dives.

Chapter Twenty-nine

JUNE (THEIR THIRD YEAR)

Here is a secret that only Iris knows: that on the day of the car accident, she had stood near the wild, rushing water and she had murmured the words of that long-remembered spell – *to raise a procession of the dead.* She was flooded with memories of her mother and Cassandra. How much had she learnt from Cassandra in this way? From the others? Listening on the edge of things, pretending that she wasn't. All those spells.

On the day of the accident, Iris murmured it whole for the first time in her life – those fractured pieces of magic woven back together. *Save them. Save them. Save them.* It was all she could think of to help and, in that moment, all Iris wanted was to help.

She felt a jolt, a warmth, a shiver. Iris had no altar; no circle. She had not properly grounded herself. But still she murmured the spell, again and again, as Min dived into the water. As Min saved Luda, and then Tristan, from the sea.

* * *

Luda wakes to the sound of footsteps across the kitchen floor. Violet, making coffee. Luda sits up from the couch, her head and back both aching. For a moment, she's not sure where she is. Narra; here; *other.* Luda is freezing cold. She shivers. Her arms hurt.

Tristan-from-the-in-between watches from across the table. 'What are you looking at?' she snaps.

'You didn't listen,' Tristan-from-the-in-between says.

'What?' says Violet to Luda. She glances at the empty kitchen table and back at her.

Luda looks away from Tristan-from-the-in-between. 'Nothing.'

Violet notices her shivering and reaches over to switch on the electric heater. 'Your kids are furious,' she says.

'They're always mad at me over something.'

'You shouldn't have taken that photo.'

'You told me to take them!' Luda looks at Violet, exasperated. 'It's about the scars! I've proven that they're real. It *matters*.'

Violet looks at her, drops her voice still further. 'They love each other, Luda.'

'She's right,' says Tristan-from-the-in-between.

'No one's asking *you*,' Luda snaps at him before turning back to Violet. 'Theo and Darcy?'

'Aye. Theo and Darcy.'

For a moment Luda looks puzzled, then happy, then puzzled again. 'Why aren't they together, then?'

'Luda,' Violet says, sighing. 'Love isn't always enough, is it?'

Luda lifts up her chin. 'Well, they're not recognisable in the photo. It could have been anyone.'

Violet sighs. 'But it's not anyone, Luda. It's *them*.'

* * *

Darcy blinks his eyes open, squinting against sunlight. He is still against the kirk's side door, his body stiff.

A shadow moves. 'Sleep well?'

Scars. The photo. His skin. The unyielding locks of the kirk's thick doors. He sits up, ready to claw his way through the side door behind him if he has to; to interrupt mass. Anything to get that photo out of sight.

Min frowns. 'You okay?'

Darcy stands up. 'No.'

'Where are you going?' she asks.

Darcy stalks around to the front of the kirk. A couple of people from the Art Society give him startled looks. Then he sees Iris and she sees him. Her expression gives her away; she knows about the photo. Knows that it's him in it. Recognises the horror of what his mother has done.

'Where is it?' he says.

'Where's what?'

'Where's the *photo*?' he says through gritted teeth.

'It's gone missing.'

'Missing?'

'Aye. Wasn't here when we opened up this morning.'

He leans against the pew.

'What?' he says. 'I don't understand.'

'It's gone,' is all she says, and then someone he does not know presses a chipped mug of water into his hands. And Min sits down next to him and he shakes and shakes – everything from before the accident spilling over.

Why had his mother never told them how impossible it was to hold the past at bay?

* * *

By the time they're back on Seannay, Darcy has stopped replying to Min and his face is set in that stubborn, immovable way of his. She follows him into the caravan and watches as he packs clean underwear and socks and his laptop and clothes into his backpack and zips it up.

'Where are you going?' Min asks. She wishes that Tristan were here; except if Tristan were here the accident wouldn't have happened and their mother would still be safely ensorcelled in stories and dusty records, not speaking to ghosts and hurting Darcy in this brightly awful way. *Again*. Again, again.

'Iris and Theo.' He slings his backpack over his shoulder. 'I can't be on this island right now. You can come too, if you want. They won't mind.'

Min pauses. The creaking house. Their mother. She shakes her head. 'I might sleep in here while you're gone.'

'Will you be okay?'

'Sure, I'll be fine.' She stands up, loops her arms around his neck and pulls him in for a hug. Her eyes have filled with unexpected tears. She does not want to be alone with Luda and her ghosts. She wants to follow Darcy to the Muirs' place. He stiffens for a moment, and then he hugs her back.

* * *

Later, the members of the parish council, Iris among them, meet in the community centre near the kirk.

The others are talking about the exhibition, the missing print. The scars that the photos had caught.

'She must have manipulated them in some way,' says Jackie. 'It's amazing what you can do with technology these days, isn't it?'

'We should pray for Luda,' Father Lee says. Bran looks up. Iris does too. Their eyes meet across the table. Father Lee's voice is gentle, his hands pressed tightly together in his lap. 'We should pray that she finds the light.' He pauses. 'That she finds peace after that awful accident.'

'Aye,' says Jackie, nodding.

The others nod too. They have all seen Luda, wandering and muttering and pausing in the middle of the narrow streets, damp up to her knees with sea water.

Luda is lost in darkness. Pitiable. Suffering.

They pray.

Iris lowers her head. She prays for Luda too. Fervent, remorseful.

* * *

When Darcy appears on the Muirs' doorstep in the drizzle with the hood of his raincoat only half on, Theo smiles. His expression softens; his eyelids drop so that he is regarding Darcy through his eyelashes.

Darcy wonders where he has learnt that look; who he has looked at with that sultry, lovely expression. It is caramel, the same way his voice used to go sometimes. Darcy swallows, does not think of Gerald or Carter or anyone else. 'Can I stay here?'

Theo hesitates for only a moment. 'Of course.'

Inside, sharp-edged, there is suddenly nothing between them but still air. The couch is too narrow and the lounge room too cluttered, so they carry the couch cushions into Theo's room, which had once been Iris's study. Theo fidgets. He looks away from Darcy as he swings the door of his room open.

Darcy gazes around the space. The trinkets and sea things. The smell of dust and salt. He has been here before, it is true. But the last time Theo had been almost comatose on the bed, Iris looming in the hall. He had not noticed the room itself, its contents.

It is not like a human's bedroom; a human's place. Theo's bedroom is as wild and animal as a sea cave. The sheer presence of *things* startles and unsettles Darcy. What he thinks is, *I don't know you*. The boys at school had always whispered about Theo's room – how it was like a tip; like the tideline after a storm surge. For Darcy, it seems like the frantically accumulated pieces of a broken, unsolvable puzzle. The buckets and boxes and bags of scraps from the sea make him feel unaccountably sad. And the sadness does not temper his fury, but fuels it.

He is aware of Theo leaving the room, coming back again. But he feels hollowed out. He barely notices.

* * *

Darcy is here. Darcy is *here*. Theo watches as he lies down on the floor and sighs, staring up at the ceiling, which Theo has plastered with drawings he's done of the islands. Shapes and colour. Darcy runs a finger absently across Theo's discarded pillow. For a moment, Theo forgets how to breathe. How often has he dreamt of this exact thing?

Except there is nothing inviting about Darcy's sprawl; he is preoccupied, frowning faintly. Theo clears his throat, stands up. 'Listen, I'll get you a blanket. Stuff ... ah ... stuff for your bed.'

Darcy looks up a little absently. 'Now?'

Theo swallows. 'Just so we don't have to do it later.'

He takes his time. He hears the clatter of the front door opening and closing and the sounds of Iris removing her shoes. Then voices – Iris and Darcy talking. When Theo goes back into his room, his face damp with cold water, he does not look at Darcy. He carefully tugs a sheet over the cushions and then folds another one and two blankets on top.

Darcy is now sprawled on Theo's bed. The sight of him there, where Theo *sleeps* and wanks and dreams and frets and everything else, makes Theo feel almost dizzy. Darcy had come to him. Darcy is *here*.

Chapter Thirty

JUNE (THEIR THIRD YEAR)

Cassandra would often find August on her doorstep. Cassandra taught August to read palms and weave stories from the beautiful images on tarot cards. August taught her about herbs and the meanings behind dreams.

They drank ale and Cassandra sensed in August a deep yearning for more; for other. For something greater than what she'd been given. And all the while, small and petulant and wide-eyed, Iris watched and she remembered.

* * *

Theo tells him about the trip to the lonely island as though he is expecting Darcy to resist. Theo is all too aware of their last time there – how Darcy had given him no warning; how he, Theo, had screamed and railed like a child; how he had pressed his lips to Darcy's. Reckless and aching.

They are by the front door, shoes in hand. Darcy doesn't look at him. 'Alright.'

The trip to Doolay is longer than Theo remembers. He wonders, with an echo of his old desperation, how he might have reached Seannay from there. The stretch of water feels impossibly vast.

Darcy sits at the prow. As Ewan and Theo watch, he climbs partially up onto the gunwale, leans forward and spreads his arms out, the wind wild in his hair.

Ewan flings open the door of the cabin. 'Fucking Managans,' he mutters. 'Darcy! Get down from there – I thought you were meant to be the sensible one!'

Darcy pretends not to hear.

Ewan anchors and ties the boat off at the sunken pier. 'Don't be too long,' he says.

Darcy looks at Theo. For a moment, Theo's certain he's going to ask a flood of questions that Theo has no answer for, but Darcy doesn't say anything. He makes his way along the underwater pier to the shore. Theo pauses, he looks at the cabin, but Ewan is studiously ignoring them, eating crisps with his eyes closed.

Theo follows Darcy onto the island. It's stiller than it was the last time they were here. Darcy crosses his arms and starts walking towards the crypt. Theo follows, almost having to jog to keep up with Darcy's long-limbed walk.

They reach the moss-clotted stone wall. The bay is out of sight. A sheep bleats. A bird calls. Darcy takes a deep breath and turns towards Theo. His expression is not a familiar one, and Theo almost steps back.

Darcy closes the gap between them, pressing his lips to Theo's. For a moment, Theo's mind goes completely blank. He has no idea what has prompted this. Darcy, bridging the gap between them without immediately shying away from him. Darcy's intoxicating breath filling his throat. Theo feels lit up; burning. Drunk. Darcy kissing him like this is unlike anything else he's ever experienced. Darcy kissing him is better than every good fuck he's ever had, combined.

Darcy's tongue, touching his. Theo's knees nearly buckle. He pulls away enough to speak, resting his forehead against Darcy's. 'I don't … I don't …'

'You don't want this?' Darcy's voice is unnaturally light, his breath in Theo's face is warm. That light voice is like a warning bell. It is like watching a wave rear up, knowing it's about to crash and flood the beach. *No*, Theo thinks, mournful. *Shit. Can't we just have this? Can't we just? Can't we just? Can't we just.*

'Fuck! Of course I want this!' Theo snaps. 'I just don't get why …'

'You told me I was beautiful once,' Darcy says, glancing away from Theo's gaze.

'You *are*. You are beautiful.'

Darcy's expression flashes and he straightens. 'Everyone on the islands has seen a photo of us naked,' he says, his voice still wrong. 'If everyone thinks we're fucking, we may as well actually do it.'

Theo exhales. 'That's what this is?'

'Yes.' Darcy steps towards him. Theo thinks that he sees Darcy tremble then, bracing himself like this is a difficult rather than wonderful thing. 'Does it matter?'

And there is so much that Theo wants to say. That it *does* matter. That he doesn't want it to be like this – Darcy hurt and insolent and more self-destructive than Theo has ever seen him before. But it is Darcy and he's looking at Theo with such an unfamiliar and intoxicating mix of yearning and defiance that Theo can't help but reach for him.

'I should have let you fuck me last time we were here,' Darcy continues. His whole body is tense.

'Don't. Please.' Theo's head begins to ache. His brain is short-circuiting somewhere between roiling want and confusion and concern. It's like Darcy is trying on a costume; seeing if it is less painful than his own skin.

'We could fuck in the crypt,' Darcy continues. 'Would you like that?'

Theo steps away then, heart pounding as though he's in danger. His mind such a blur that he can barely form an articulate thought beyond the wrongness of everything. *It shouldn't be like this.* He sits down on the stone wall, looks towards the crypt and feels a sudden longing for Tristan; Tristan would know how to help Darcy right now. Tristan would know how to stop Darcy slipping away from himself like this. But Tristan is inert in a hospital bed on Big Island, and Darcy is here and so is Theo.

'I never thanked you,' says Theo. 'For bringing me here.'

Darcy snorts. 'Why would you? It was a terrible idea.'

'It wasn't,' Theo says. 'It wasn't a terrible idea, okay?'

'It *was*. Because the first thing you did when you got home was call up Carter and give him the interview, and I bet you fucked him.'

Theo exhales. 'Darcy …'

Darcy waves a hand at him, impatient with himself or Theo, Theo can't tell. Theo is about to stand, but then makes himself stay where he is. *Distance. Stillness.* Even if Darcy is recklessly close and moving. Especially then.

'And then Gerald and all the others,' Darcy says, his voice oddly strangled. 'Bringing you here … everything that came after … it made me lose my goddamn mind.'

Theo remains quiet, his cheeks reddening with embarrassment and frustration and a longing to close the gap between them and kiss Darcy again. He had not thought that Darcy would care about what he did with other people. Darcy, who had rebuffed him over and over again. Darcy, who kept his skin covered and winced at any mention of scars. Those photos. The press of Darcy's lips on his wounded fingers in London. The flashes of everything reconfiguring. He experiences a moment of blinding frustration with himself. He forces himself to take a deep breath and then another. 'Darcy, I didn't mean to hurt you.'

'Right.'

'I thought …' Theo's voice fractures almost to a whisper, but he knows that Darcy can still hear him. 'I thought you didn't care.'

Darcy has his back to Theo. They stay like that for a while. Theo staring at Darcy, and Darcy staring off towards the sky and sea, his strange, brilliant mind doing whatever strange, brilliant minds do.

'Do you want to go into the crypt?' Darcy asks finally, turning around. His face is blotched. There is something stiff about his breathing. Theo wants to howl in frustration over how difficult this is; how difficult it has always been. How much he wants to tell Darcy what he has seen; what he knows. How much he wants to convey to Darcy that none of it matters to him. But he knows it matters, very much, to Darcy. Whatever it is that Darcy has been through. The reason he can see the scars so clearly.

'No,' says Theo, knowing from Darcy's tone that Darcy is not talking about fucking; that he is talking about the ruins of lives once lived here.

Darcy turns away again, starts walking. 'Let's go then.'

* * *

Iris and Cassandra sit in Iris's car, staring across the sound towards the tidal island. Iris's hands rest on the steering wheel. Cassandra's hands rest in her lap.

'Darcy's staying with us,' Iris says, as though them being here, their staring, is to do with the Managans and not themselves.

'Och, those lads.' Cassandra shakes her head. 'I take it Theo's pleased.'

'Walking around like he's won the lottery.'

'Darcy …'

Iris's fingers tighten on the wheel. 'He's not okay.'

'No,' says Cassandra after a moment. She extends a hand to touch the glass of the windscreen, hovering over Seannay and the house and ruins. 'I can't imagine he would be.'

'Is there anything to find there? In the house?' Iris asks suddenly, her voice small.

'I don't think there is.'

'Tristan …'

'He would have found anything if it was there.'

'You think so?'

'Aye, Iris. I do.'

* * *

Later that same night, in the narrow house where Iris and Theo live, Darcy stares through the open window at the starless grey light and is blinded by tears that come suddenly and silently. The betrayal of everything. How the accident had broken his mother. Changed her.

That photo. His *skin*. The way he had spoken to Theo on the lonely island; it makes him want to vomit. He has learnt to cry silently. In all the years he has shared a room with Min – as closely as she always watches him – she has never noticed his tears.

But Theo does. Darcy hears Theo's breathing change as he wakes. Then Darcy hears the creak of the bed. There's a beat of silence, and then the weight and warmth of Theo dropping onto the floor next to him. 'Move over.'

They lie like that, each half on the cushions and half on the floor.

'I'm sorry,' Darcy whispers after a moment.

'Don't be.'

Darcy feels Theo shift and then Theo's warm, sweet breath fans across his face. Darcy can make out his lips in the strange grey light. His anger and sadness, so raw, bring up the shadow of other, older griefs so that he's crying for so many things that his body feels suddenly too small to contain it all.

Darcy keeps crying, humiliated. Soundless. And Theo threads his strange fingers through Darcy's and presses a kiss to his forehead. 'I've got you,' he says and rests his forehead against Darcy's cheek. 'It's okay. I've got you.'

Chapter Thirty-one

JUNE (THEIR THIRD YEAR)

A newspaper lies open on a table; a story there about a lost boy (a man now) with a writer brother, who'd finally, *finally* found his way home.

* * *

Min walks home from the docks, teeth clenched. Her father's Holden. The sound of –

No.

She walks across the causeway, puddled – as it often is now – at high tide. She considers diving into the sound. Still, she's scared of the tides here. Knows enough to fear them.

The Holden.

The dry dam.

Fingers tight around her throat.

For a moment, she's sure she hears someone moving behind her and takes a single bad step. She stumbles. She swears and her hands graze the rocks as she lands. Her ankle throbs hotly, sickly. She can already feel it swelling under her fingers.

The stretch of road and gorse and wall behind her is empty.

She lurches up onto her good foot and eyes the distance between where she is, near the causeway, and the front door of the ghost house. She swears under her breath and begins hopping across the thick grass, pausing repeatedly to push tendrils of wet hair out of her mouth.

She groans, thinking she'll have to wait until Luda comes home, when the door opens and there's her mother, hair piled untidily, cardigan falling off one shoulder. Those new hollows under her cheekbones.

'What on earth have you done to yourself?' She sounds almost like her old self.

'I tripped,' Min says and finds herself almost teary.

Luda eyes her wet hair and bathers but says nothing. 'Where does it hurt?'

For a moment, Min can barely breathe. Oh, how many times has her mother asked Darcy that over the years? He was always moving stiffly – walking, sitting, lifting.

'My ankle.'

Luda helps her into a chair and then bends down to inspect it. 'Well, you've done a good job on it.' She sits back on her heels. 'Tristan says we'll need to get it looked at.'

Min glances around. 'What?'

'He says I'll need to take you to the place.'

'What?'

Luda looks exasperated. 'Where they fix you. The *hospital*.'

Ewan drives them to the island hospital and offers to stay. 'We're fine,' Min says and he studies her for a moment and then nods and leaves. Min sits with her head resting on her mother's shoulder. It's been a long time since she's been this close to Luda. She smells the same. Feels the same. Min closes her eyes, her ankle throbbing and throbbing. Luda strokes her hair. Luda mutters to someone in the empty seat next to her. 'She'll be fine,' Luda says, her voice sharp. 'I'm taking care of it.'

She seems the same, except that she's not.

* * *

That night, Theo rolls onto his side and can see Darcy awake in the moonlight. He stares, dry-eyed now, at Theo's bedroom ceiling. Darcy had spent the day working at the brewery and Theo had worked at Marcia's farm. Darcy had already been in bed when Theo got home and Iris was still at a kirk meeting. Darcy had left a meal wrapped on the stove for him.

'You okay?' Theo asks.

'Yes.'

Theo hesitates for a moment. Across the room, Darcy seems like he always does – distant and completely unobtainable. He is not goading Theo about fucking in a remote crypt or weeping in his arms. He has become detached again.

This version of Darcy is intimidating. Still. He had kissed Theo. The thought of Theo with other people had made him lose his *goddamn mind*.

Theo slides from his bed and into Darcy's. Darcy lets out a long breath. Every part of his body is rigid next to Theo's. His heart beats too quickly beneath his skin. Darcy's breath catches and Theo waits for him to retreat, to say something gaudy and provocative. Instead, he brings up one long-fingered hand and runs it through Theo's hair. The feeling of his hand is exquisite. Those fingers.

Slowly, tentatively, Darcy wraps his arms around Theo, pulling Theo in against his chest so that their bodies are touching, Darcy's legs and arms so much longer than Theo's. Darcy kisses Theo, a sort of desperate, hungry kiss that takes Theo's breath away. It feels different from the lonely island. Darcy doesn't feel jagged and out of control. He feels like he always has in those fleeting moments when Theo's been close to him.

Darcy tugs Theo's t-shirt off and then pulls off his own. Darcy feels cool against Theo's skin. He runs his hands over Theo's body and Theo holds his breath, his brain blank. Wordless. Darcy kisses a tentative line across Theo's ribs. Darcy, who is so self-contained that a single finger trailing across Theo's skin is almost enough to make Theo pass out. Theo reaches for Darcy, cupping his face, and Darcy stops breathing. His body, suddenly poised for flight.

Theo recognises it – his own body still reacts the same way if he is trapped indoors with too many people. 'Darcy …'

'Shh.' Darcy's hand slips beneath the band of Theo's boxers and Theo stares at the ceiling, shocked and insensate, as Darcy's hand finds an exquisite rhythm; as Darcy bends low over him. His lips brushing Theo's cheek, his forehead, his lips. Darcy, in his room. Darcy, lying next to him. Darcy, fucking *touching* him. *Darcy.* This is *Darcy.*

'God,' Theo mutters, the impossibility of it. Darcy presses against him, achingly hard. Theo's fingers drag at the couch cushions, the pooling sheets. His fingers drag at Darcy's hair, his back, his face. That face. Darcy's face.

For a time, there is only sound. Their heavy breathing, pounding hearts. The rustle of small, frenzied motion. And then he finds himself cresting, unable to hold back. He shivers, biting down on Darcy's shoulder to stop himself from crying out. For a moment, his vision wavers. He has no thoughts. He slowly becomes aware of Darcy sitting a little distance away on his bed, one hand held to the place on his shoulder where Theo had pressed his teeth.

Theo's breath is still coming hard. He props himself up on an elbow. Can see Darcy's pupils huge in the half-light of summer night. Theo sits up more fully, trying to force his stunned and sluggish mind to work the way that he needs it to. 'Why are you up there?' he asks, although as he speaks, he knows. *He knows.* And he hates himself for being so careless; for treating Darcy like anyone else; someone without Darcy's scars.

Darcy slowly brings his hands to his face, his whole body shuddering with the echoes of something that he cannot voice. Will probably never be able to voice. There is, Theo thinks, a certain way in which the past casts shadows into the present. And right now they're both sitting in the cold and the dark of the thing that they have never discussed aloud, but which Theo knows. Which Darcy *knows* he knows.

And Theo had fucking *bitten* him.

Theo rises from the floor and sits on the bed, with that particular distance between them. The same as always. *Distance. Stillness.* The sadness that hits Theo then is bruising and endless.

'I thought I could. But I can't.'

'It's okay,' Theo says. He sits on his hands, desperate to draw Darcy to him. To soothe those unfathomable, wordless hurts. 'I'm so sorry. I shouldn't have ... I didn't think ...'

'My brain's broken,' Darcy whispers then, his voice suddenly tremulous. It's a voice Theo has never heard him use before.

'Your brain's not broken,' Theo says forcefully. 'Please. Come here. Can we ... I want to ...' Theo swallows, his voice dropping into a whisper. 'Come back to me.'

Darcy rises. He picks up his phone from the bedside table. A moment of stillness before he throws it across the room. It breaks. He reaches for his wallet, next – still in the back pocket of his jeans. He reaches for his shoe. Theo does not stop him. Finally, Darcy curls up on his cushion-bed, his back to Theo. Theo counts the vertebrae of Darcy's spine. The narrow body, all sinew and bone.

Theo reaches out to touch Darcy's back, those delicate bones, but Darcy jerks violently. Theo runs his hands through his hair. 'Darcy ...'

'Just don't. Just ... leave me alone. Please. Just leave me *alone.*'

'Is that really what you –'

'Yes!' Darcy snaps. 'I shouldn't have come here. I can't stay.'

Theo closes his eyes. 'Of course you can.'

'No.' A shuddering breath. 'I *can't.*'

* * *

It starts when they're still waiting to be triaged. The nurse explains that it will be a long wait – her injury is not life-threatening – and that the accident and emergency department is unusually busy. Min tries to call Darcy, but he doesn't answer. She sends him text messages but he doesn't answer those, either.

They sit. Min considers, in great detail, all the things she's going to do to Darcy when she gets her hands on him. Darcy and his inability to check his *fucking* phone. Luda gets them crisps from the vending machine. She sits down next to Min and then quickly stands up. 'Stop it,' she hisses. A few people look around.

'Mum,' says Min. She tugs at Luda's sleeve. *'Mum.'*

Luda looks at her, sits back down and opens the packet of crisps. 'I've always liked salt and vinegar best,' she says. 'I *have*. Why would I lie? Answer me that. *Why would I lie?'*

'Mum,' says Min. 'You can't talk like that. Not here.'

Luda looks at her, surprised. 'Like what?'

'To … Tristan or whoever.'

'It's not Tristan – it's your father,' Luda says. Then she turns abruptly to the empty corner of the room. 'I'm *not!*' she says, very loudly.

'She's fine,' Min says, to the others in the waiting room. 'She's fine. I promise. She's fine.' She says it until her throat feels raw. The taste of her own swallowed terror. *It's your father.* 'She's fine,' she says when the nurses come out to triage her mother. 'She's fine,' she says as she explains her mother's accident – the water, the brain injury, the disturbances she'd experienced since. Luda is triaged. Her meds are reviewed.

Min's ankle throbs.

'She's fine,' Min says and finds herself swallowing hard, feeling almost on the verge of tears. A shimmer, in the corner of the room. Imagined. She's sure. Imagined. Imagined. For a moment, she can't breathe.

* * *

Tristan-from-the-in-between sits on the arm of Cassandra's chair. Or perhaps it is a dream. Tristan's voice is grave. 'You can't get there, can you?'

'Where?'

'To Seannay.'

'No. I could, long ago. But not anymore. Not for a long time.'

'So … no trips to London?'

'No trips to London.'

He frowns. 'What about boats?'

'The boundary is the water line. No boats.'

'Are you ever going to tell me?' he asks.

Cassandra smiles at him, eyes half closed. 'I don't know. Am I?'

'Please. Enough. What do they *mean*?'

'You're the one who decided that they were whales, Tristan,' she says.

'What?'

She cracks an eye open. 'Women back then were not taught how to write. Not even our own names.'

Tristan-from-the-in-between nods once, grimly.

'We never called in the whales,' says Cassandra. 'They just came in sometimes, same as they still do. The signs in the house were our version of signatures turned into witch marks. We kept ourselves safe.'

'From what?' Tristan-from-the-in-between asks.

'What do women always need to keep each other safe from?'

Tristan nods sadly. And he reaches for her hand. It is not a physical touch, but she feels the boundaries of him. Dreaming, imagined, or otherwise. They don't say anything else.

* * *

Darcy comes back to the ghost house with his bag slung over his shoulder. The feel of Theo's teeth. The sudden flood of warmth against Darcy's wrist. Darcy had known, deep down, that this was not something he could ever have. But he had hoped (God, he had *hoped*) that being with Theo would be enough to make it feel like something utterly different.

Seannay feels hazy and unchanging. Luda wades after razor clams in the water. Min's sitting at the kitchen table, watching their mother through the window.

'She says that Tristan's keeping an eye on me,' Min says. She glances around the empty room and shudders. 'That he'll fetch her if I need her. I can't stand it, Darcy.'

Darcy stares at Min's ankle. 'How'd you do it?'

'I tripped.' Min looks at him.

'Is it hurting?'

'Not really. Not now. As long as I don't bang it around too much.'

'I'm sorry I didn't answer.'

'It's okay.'

'My phone's broken.' He holds it up. The shattered screen. She looks at his clenched fist; notes the way one of his feet taps on the floor. He can feel her looking at his scars. 'What happened?' she asks.

Darcy runs his hands over his face. Leaves them there, over his eyes.

'Did you …'

'Don't, Min.'

'What *happened*?'

Darcy glances up at her. He can tell from her puzzled expression that his own is hard to read, even for her, who has spent so much of her life reading his face. Or trying to. '*Nothing*. Nothing happened,' he says, his voice wretched. 'Nothing will ever happen.'

'God, Darcy. Can't you just …' She waves her arms around. 'He *loves* you.'

Darcy looks at her, then. At her frowning, serious face. He can feel his eyes growing glassy, stinging. 'What does that even *mean*?' he whispers.

'I don't know. I don't know what it means. I just know that it's true and that it means *something*.'

He shakes his head, startling at the feel of Min's hand suddenly resting on his back.

'He loves you,' she says again, a little helplessly.

'I'm not ever going to be enough for him,' Darcy says, so quietly and quickly that he's not sure Min even hears him. He squeezes his eyes shut, forcing out the words. 'I can't … and he wants … he *needs* …'

'Do *you* want …?'

'God, Min!' He shrugs her hand off. 'Don't, okay?' A long pause. He drags his hands back over his face, so that his words are muffled. '*Yes*, I want … but I *can't* when … It's too much when I …'

He jumps when he feels Min's arms around him. A *hug*, he realises. 'I'm sorry, Darcy,' she says into his hair. She holds him like that and, exhausted, defeated (grateful) he lets her.

* * *

Theo would keep fighting for Darcy, but what's the point of that when Darcy does not want him to fight? Does not want *him* at all. What's the point of fighting when all it ever does is drive Darcy further away? Perhaps this deep connection he's always been so certain of is imagined. And that last time … Perhaps Darcy had just wanted to see what it was like. And maybe – Theo swallows – maybe he just didn't want Theo.

Theo wants Darcy to have everything, even if it's not with Theo. He's just not sure how to help; what to do. His mind blurs and fogs the more he tries to think of what comes *next*.

He slumps onto the couch in the little house he shares with Iris. He drinks cola, wincing at the bubbles and chemical taste. Makes himself a tea instead. Dark, like salt water after a storm. How the hell is he meant to do anything useful when Darcy won't let him close enough to try?

* * *

Min's ankle keeps her awake. She sleeps in the caravan because the ghost house is too full of voices and movement. She can tolerate it during the day, but at night the sounds startle her too much for sleep. Luda talking to her ghosts. Arguing with them. Three broken bones. If Min falls asleep and moves her ankle while she dreams, the pain is sharp – white-hot. She sleeps in short patches.

Darcy sleeps in the caravan with her. She sleeps in his freshly made bed at one end and he sleeps on the bench seat at the other. It is like the loft, with its spill of witch marks, warding off the dark.

'Min,' he says.

She is roused easily from her shallow, restless sleep. 'What?'

A pause. 'I've been shit to you, haven't I?'

She frowns, props herself up on the pillows. 'What?'

'Just … in general.'

She considers this, blinking. 'What?'

'I was … I don't even know if you're seeing anyone. Or who you're friends with. Or if you're still in touch with that dickhead you were going out with when we first moved here.'

'Kole.'

'Kole. It's … I only ever think about myself.'

Min thinks about trying to lever herself up and crossing the caravan, but she decides this is probably a conversation that's easier to have at a distance. 'Yeah, look,' she says. 'I'm not going to argue that you're not a self-centred arsehole a lot of the time, but I think you've had reason to be. With Dad and everything …'

'That was all my fault.' His voice is rigid.

'What? What was?'

'Nothing. Forget it, okay? It's nothing.'

'Alright.' She pauses. 'I never went out with Kole.'

'It's not that I'm not interested in your life, Min. I just …'

'Jesus, where's this coming from?' But she knows. She knows. Darcy, listing all of the ways that he is terrible and unworthy. Darcy, listing all the ways that make it impossible for Theo to actually love him. Min feels a flare of anger at this. It's always about Darcy. Even when it's not.

'Are you seeing anyone?' he asks, his voice small.

For a moment, Min feels disoriented, like she's accidentally started a conversation with a stranger. Her anger gutters. She lies back down on the bed and stares up at the curved ceiling. 'No.'

'Is there anyone you …' He trails off. She can practically *feel* him reddening from across the caravan. She's never encountered anyone who flushes with awkwardness the way Darcy does.

'No,' she says. 'I don't … want that.'

There is a silence as he processes this. 'None of it?'

'No.'

'Oh.' A pause. 'So Ewan …'

'Darcy! No! He's my *friend*.'

'And Kole told everyone that you …'

She sighs. 'Of course he told people that. But I didn't. He told me I was hot and I got pissed at him and he thought it was because of what he'd done to Theo.'

'Theo's black eye?' Darcy asks, his voice pained. Of course Darcy remembers. 'That was Kole?'

'Well, him and a bunch of hostel boys, I think.'

'So … hang on. You got pissed because he told you that you were hot?'

'It was *how* he said it, okay?'

Darcy begins to laugh, loudly and helplessly. 'Hot,' he gasps out, and then collapses into full giggling. It's as unfamiliar as everything else, the way he'd laughed when he was very young. It is edged, now, with hysteria. And yet Min finds herself bursting into giggles too. At the absurdity of everything. At the simple joy of Darcy wanting to know her.

Chapter Thirty-two

JULY (THEIR THIRD YEAR)

Darcy checks the vats of barley at the brewery without properly seeing them. Thinking about Min, who doesn't want what he is tearing himself up over. His mother, who is a half-dead thing.

Thinking, mostly, of Theo. Thinking of everything he wants. Wanted. Thinking and hating himself and working and working and not stopping until Tyler, the red-faced brewery manager, touches his arm. 'Your shift finished an hour ago.'

* * *

Min tries to hold on to giggling with Darcy in the caravan, but it slips away like a dream. She loses the feeling of it within a day. Things sliding into place in a way that makes her whole body shudder.

She hadn't realised.

She hadn't *known*.

She is engulfed by thoughts of her mother's ghosts.

The Holden. The echoing crack. The birds against the sky. And if she manages to press all of that away, she is instead engulfed by the car, the shadow of whales.

The sound of metal on wood.

The birds.

The white-hot pain of her ankle. The ghosts. The ghosts. The ghosts.

Her father's incandescent rage that day. They had been driving to the bank manager's house. Sometimes her dreams bleed into wakefulness and she finds herself blinking up at the caravan's ceiling. She wants Cassandra.

A shimmer. Her throat. The birds. The stony pain of a broken bone.

* * *

Min asks Ewan to drive her to Cassandra's house on the hill and he does, muttering under his breath. Inside Cassandra's warm front room, Min just about flings herself into Cassandra's lap. 'I didn't know,' Min says. 'I didn't *think*.'

She feels tiny, burrowed desperately against Cassandra's blouse. She is terrified that Darcy will hate her and that it will hurt so much more after these brief moments of connection. Wounded and laughing in the midnight sun. 'I didn't see what I should have seen, Cass. I didn't see any of it.'

And Cassandra lets Min trail tears and snot across her blouse and her cardigan. She strokes Min's hair. And Min talks and feels the passing of knowing between them. She senses the moment when Cassandra understands. The bruising sorrow for them all comes after.

'I've never told him,' Min whispers, sitting up and wiping her nose with the back of her hand. 'I've never thought to. I was so ashamed …'

'You've nothing to be ashamed of, Wilhelmina,' Cassandra's voice is firm. 'Nothing at all.'

* * *

Luda stands in the shallows, hands deep in the sand, seeking the hard edges of razor clams.

'The water's not safe,' Tristan-from-the-in-between says. 'Not anymore. There are storms coming. Can't you feel them?'

Luda ignores him, but she *can* feel it. A shift.

His voice, slow and sad. 'You shouldn't be here, Luda.' And she knows that he means *alive*.

Luda digs her hands deeper and deeper, listening to the sound of water splashing against her scarred, narrow wrists. The small ones come, a lightening. A sigh.

'You hurt them,' he says, his voice quieter.

'Who?'

'Darcy and Theo. You *hurt* them.'

She resists the urge to leave the water, which suddenly feels so hostile.

'Luda.' Tristan-from-the-in-between's voice hits her like cold water. She shivers. 'You shouldn't be here.'

* * *

Darcy comes home from his shift at the brewery, frowning and sullen. He hesitates at the door of the ghost house.

'Mum's not here,' Min says, without looking up.

Darcy acts like he hasn't heard her, but she sees him soften a little. He sits on the couch and pulls out his copy of *The Salt Boy*.

'Have you spoken to him?' Min asks.

'*Don't.*'

Min rolls and unrolls the diving magazine in her hands. 'Darcy.'

He looks up. 'What?'

'Dad ... he didn't suicide.' She senses the immediate sharpening of Darcy's attention. The weight of it fully on her is unsettling.

'How do you know that?'

'I was with him.'

'He was alone.'

'No. He wasn't.' She opens her eyes, blinks very quickly. 'Darcy, I'm sorry. I only just ... I didn't realise ...'

Darcy looks very young and cross. 'Are you finished?'

'He was angrier than I'd ever seen him.' Min's voice is a whisper. 'What he found out ... he didn't kill himself over it, Darcy.' Darcy is so tense that she worries – ludicrously – that he will shatter as she speaks her next words. 'We were driving to the bank manager's house.'

Darcy goes absolutely still. His hands are so tight on his book that his knuckles show through his skin like bare bone. Their eyes meet. Spun between them: the gun that had been in the back seat of the car when it crashed into the pole.

'How could you have been with him when he died?' Darcy whispers, almost pleadingly.

'Because I was too scared to let him go alone. And he was too impatient and out of control to try to argue with me. Darcy, I swear I didn't understand any of it – I thought he was just angry about the loan application being turned down. But that wasn't what he was mad about.'

'How are you ...'

'Alive? I don't know. I was there ... when he died. I held his hand, Darcy.' She swallows. 'But then I ran. I ended up in one of our paddocks. I was concussed, I think. I had scratches all over my face. Glass kept working its way out of my face. Nobody noticed. Mum was so focused on her work even on a good day ...' Min's voice thickens with tears. 'I left him alone in that wreckage.'

Darcy stares at her, his expression changing and changing and changing. 'Your face ...' he says and Min startles, because she knows immediately from his tone that he's talking about the scars. 'I can see where the glass ...'

Min realises that she's crying. 'All this time you thought he killed himself because he didn't get that loan approved but he didn't. It was an accident, Darcy. It was an *accident*. He loved you so much.'

Min organises her limbs and clunks across the room, wanting to touch Darcy. He shies away from her, suddenly furious. 'Why didn't you tell me earlier?' he hisses.

'I didn't think it had anything to do with you,' she says. 'I thought he was mad about the loan application. And I was … I'm so ashamed I left him alone.'

'You let me think he'd suicided.' Darcy's voice is unrelenting.

'I'm sorry.'

'You're sorry? *God*, Min. You have no idea what …' He breathes hard. Rakes his hands through his hair. 'It's too late now.'

'What is?'

'Everything!'

Outside, they can hear Luda's voice rising louder and louder. Arguing with her ghosts.

* * *

Cassandra listens to the wind. She is sure the weather has never been this raw before. It had seemed like a monster when she was younger. A wild, thrashing thing that pummelled the islands. Then it had seemed to ease. To become something in the background as she grew into adulthood.

She aches for Wilhelmina – for all of them. She senses Wilhelmina's pain, her regret at not speaking sooner. *You spoke when you could*, Cassandra thinks. *Wilhelmina, you spoke when you could.*

These moments of feeling so small and so frail. She misses so many people. Perhaps most keenly, she misses August. Her beautiful, fiery and clever August. She frowns at herself. *Stop it.* She thinks of the weather. It is the same as it has always been, she tells herself. And yet, it is not. The weather feels different now. She's sure of it.

* * *

Darcy walks around the side streets of the town, hands jammed into his pockets, head throbbing. He has never craved the wilder places of the islands. Still, he finds himself trudging the long and winding road towards the Wailing Cliffs. It's a long walk and he's sweating by the time he reaches them.

The boom and hiss of the waves is like a pulse, a heartbeat.

He and his body, always.

He thinks of his father. He bends and grinds a handful of dirt against the cup of his palm. Swallows back the taste of salt. He tries to unpick this thread from the others, but he can't. He does not stay long, but feels a little bit lighter as he begins walking back towards the town.

Soon, he hears the clatter of a bike on uneven asphalt and looks up. Theo, riding back to town from Marcia's farm. The night on Theo's bedroom floor still feels like a wound. Darcy wants very much to dive off the road and hide.

Theo slows. Darcy pretends not to see him. After a moment of hesitation, Theo lets him pretend. He pedals on.

Chapter Thirty-three

AUGUST (THEIR THIRD YEAR)

Theo chops up carrots for a soup. He can't read recipes, but he's found a few cooking videos that he's learnt by heart. Iris's delighted surprise the first time he'd made a dish she hadn't taught him.

Iris comes inside, kicking off her sensible shoes and hanging up her bag. For a moment, she stands there, one hand resting against the wall, and Theo has a moment of terror (he has them sometimes) when he realises that she will get older and older and that one day she will die and leave him, and that it is natural and the way of things but also deeply wrong.

'Someone called for you at the kirk today,' she says.

'Someone's always calling at the kirk for me,' he says moodily.

'Well, this one's different.' She sits down at the kitchen table. 'He's some professor from King's College. He and Darcy have emailed for years, apparently, but he hasn't heard from him in months.'

'Oh.'

'He knows that Darcy's a friend of yours, Theo. He just wanted to find out if he was okay.'

'Right. And you told him Darcy's fine?'

'Aye,' she says slowly.

'Right. Good.' He dumps the carrots in a saucepan. Stops. 'Iris?'

Iris raises an eyebrow at him.

'Did he leave a number? This King's College man?'

'Aye, it's in my notebook at the kirk. Why?'

Theo stares down at the carrots. 'Good,' he says. 'That's good.'

* * *

There are moments that Iris does not let herself recall. Moments that come to life and engulf her like cold water if she lingers on them for too long. Like all living things, they crave light, and Iris pushes them back hard into the dark.

Sometimes, though. They pick their way out into the brightness of her life and she is flooded. Her mother weaving daisies into the bottoms of her braids. Her mother hand-feeding fledgling seabirds she found washed from their nests. Her mother telling her that she'd been named for the goddess of the sea and sky. Of rainbows. Her mother telling her stories about Aphrodite and Persephone and Medusa.

How all these goddesses had been wronged somehow. How their stories were a howl of fury, drowned out by the heaving sea. Moments, secret and shameful.

Moments when Iris aches for her witch-mother.

* * *

That night, Darcy paces around outside. He swears and stomps and kicks things. In the not-dark, he sounds like Theo. Luda is woken, more than once, as she lies on the mattress by the Rayburn downstairs. Violet snores above her in the loft.

Luda opens her mouth to call out to him, but she's not sure what she'd say. 'Don't,' says Glenda, crossing her arms. 'You'll only make it worse. You *always* make things worse.'

'You shouldn't be here,' Tristan-from-the-in-between tells her again and again.

'Luda.' Joshua's voice, urgent. 'Darcy and Min – they're not okay. Luda?'

'He's right,' Tristan-from-the-in-between says. 'If you ever bothered to think about them, you'd know that. But you don't, do you? Even when it's staring you right in the face.'

'Can you all lay off?' Luda mutters.

'You know what I found out,' Joshua says. 'You *know*, Luda.'

'I don't know! I have no idea what you're talking about.'

'Oh, come on, Luda!' Tristan-from-the-in-between snaps. '*Really?*'

'You need to stop running from them,' Joshua continues. 'We both did it back in Narra. You can't see them properly when you're running.'

'I'm not running.'

Tristan-from-the-in-between snorts.

'Please,' says Joshua. 'Please stop, Luda. Stop so you can see them.'

'They need you,' Tristan-from-the-in-between says, unusually gentle.

* * *

Min curls up on the bed in the caravan, her ankle aching, and does not sleep. She counts the few, faint summer stars that can be seen through the one remaining window. Darcy at the other end of the caravan. He kicks at the wall periodically. Min drinks so much water from the little sink that she has to lurch outside to piss on the grass. She thinks of broken bones and whales. The whales being cut up. The clear curve of the car from the road to the pole where her father's Holden came to rest. Darcy's helpless fury – the time she had taken from him by not telling him sooner. She hears Luda's voice carrying from the ghost house. 'No, that's a lie. Stop *lying*.'

Min puts her hands over her ears.

* * *

Cassandra sees August in the bleary world before she's properly woken up. The earthy smell of rosemary and heather. Of peaty soil after rain. Her long, dark hair. Cassandra can never make out her face.

This, in itself, is nothing new. Cassandra has often seen August in these half-dreams over the years. It always makes her ache.

This morning, August speaks. 'It's nearly time.'

And Cassandra, her old, thin, fracturing body. 'Thank Christ for that.'

* * *

Theo thinks, often, of the rise and fall of Darcy's voice as Darcy read to him. The call of birds and seals and the scent of the drowsing Rayburn. He falls asleep in his tightly packed bedroom, that smell of rot and salt, and wakes up thinking of Darcy, bent low and urgently over him.

Enough. Enough. Theo carries boxes and bags of shells and fishing wire and cuttlefish bones out into the pouring rain. He takes out his jars of sea glass, all clear and green and amber. He keeps going until his room feels bare. He exhales. Cracks his neck. And then he finishes the job he has been working on for weeks – a tenuous balancing act that has involved sweet-talking lots of new people (harder, he has discovered, when he's not drunk and he's trying to do something more complicated than put his fingers in someone's mouth and buy them a drink). But here – the letter. It is addressed to Darcy.

He runs to Seannay.

Min is the only one in the ghost house.

'I need to speak to Darcy,' he says.

The two of them sit on the couch, drinking hot chocolate laced with whisky, the way they had when they were younger.

'Darcy's avoiding Mum and me.'

'And me,' says Theo, sounding almost cheerful. 'Where *is* your mum?'

'In the gorse. With her small ones.'

He doesn't appear to hear this. He waves the letter at Min.

'What's that?'

Theo turns on the couch to face her, bursting with pride and hope. 'Darcy gave me my past.'

'Oh, that's very poetic, T.' She nudges him with her elbow. 'Thought you didn't believe that you came from that creepy island.'

'I don't know that I did, but having that story … it means something. It changed things.' He shifts.

'So … the letter?'

'It's an acceptance for Darcy to study medicine in London. It's just a formality – he's definitely in. The dean confirmed it.'

'Holy shit. *Theofin*. Are you joking?'

He shakes his head, eyes bright.

'I don't get how this is possible. He fucked up his finals. He didn't get the marks.'

'The dean met him at that conference in London. Darcy told him about me and …' Theo smiles, almost shyly. 'Anyway, the dean – John – he called the kirk to try to get on to me to see how Darcy was, because he hasn't heard anything from him in months. And I called him up and we got talking. Darcy *had* got the marks he needed all the way up until the final exams.' Theo leans forward. 'I managed to get enough references and his school records. And with all the extenuating circumstances around Luda, it was the easiest thing. It just fell into place.'

'Theo. This is …'

'It's his future,' Theo murmurs.

'I'll be here,' Min says, after a moment. 'I'll be here with Mum. I belong here, on the islands. Darcy never has, has he?'

'No. He hasn't.'

'So, Darcy can go,' she says quietly.

Theo nods. He puts the letter down on the table.

'What? You're not going to tell him yourself?'

Theo grimaces. 'I think he'd prefer it this way.' Theo suddenly notices that she's greasy-haired, her eyes red-rimmed.

'Theo, what happened?'

Theo sighs. 'I don't know.'

'Something happened.' She looks exhausted. 'And it must be worse than the awful bombshell I dropped on him, or he wouldn't be here.'

'I really don't know what happened. We hooked up and then he ran.' Theo closes his eyes, tilts his head back. 'What bombshell?'

'He can tell you himself. I can't go over it again.'

Theo sits down next to her and opens his arms. She burrows into them, closes her eyes.

'As if he'd tell me. He won't even look at me. I just ... have I imagined it, Min?'

'Imagined what?'

'This ... everything ... with Darcy. I think I built it up in my head into this big thing that it's not. And maybe it never has been.'

'God, T. Of course you haven't imagined it. He loves you!' She sits up. 'Are you seriously asking me whether you've imagined that?'

He nods miserably.

'He loves you so bloody much, T. It scares him.' She hesitates.

He tightens his arms around her. Rocks her a little. 'He doesn't want me.'

Min sighs into his shoulder. 'God, Theofin. Of *course* he does! I've never seen him look at anyone the way he looks at you. And I've never heard him talk about anyone the way he talks about you, either. It's like a whole new voice that he's saved up especially for talking about Theofin Muir.' She squeezes his hands. 'I knew he liked you the moment I saw you with him. He couldn't stop looking at you. He still can't. Don't you *notice* how he looks at you?'

'He doesn't want me, Min.'

'He does! You're good for him. You're *good*. But he's just ... he's so stuck inside himself. He's *scared*. He's scared he won't be enough for you. He's scared he'll never be able to be what you need him to be.'

Theo breathes out.

Min leans back so she can see his face. She taps his cheek. 'Can you promise me something?'

He arches an eyebrow. 'What?'

'That even if he moves away, even if he can never be what you want, you will stay his friend? It'd destroy him, I think, not having you in his life anymore.'

'Aye.' Theo's voice is barely a whisper. He swallows. 'Aye. I'll stay his friend.'

'Good.'

'You're serious, though? That he … that I haven't imagined it all?'

'He's besotted with you. He just can't get out of his own way.'

They sit for a moment, arms wrapped around each other, and then Theo bursts out laughing. 'Then, no.'

Min cranes her neck to see his face. 'No, what?'

'I don't want to just be his friend, Min. I *won't* just be his friend. I'm *tired* of just being his friend. I'm tired of us bloody tiptoeing around each other and never saying what we need to. I'm tired of letting him push me away. I'm going to fucking fight for him, Min.'

Chapter Thirty-four

AUGUST (THEIR THIRD YEAR)

Darcy comes into the caravan late, swearing and muttering and smelling of old books.

'Darcy?' Min says. For a moment she thinks that he has not heard her. She thinks that he is ignoring her. Then she feels the caravan shift again as he sits on the edge of the bed.

He looks down at his hands. 'It's okay, you know. I don't ... it's okay.'

'It's not,' she whispers.

'Min, listen to me.' He turns fully to face her and she looks away. 'You did nothing wrong and I'm sorry if I made you feel like you did. I'm angry at the universe, okay? I'm angry at the climate changing and the farm failing and whatever sent Mum to the dam that day I was crying there. I'm mad at ... but I'm not mad at you.'

Min sniffs. 'I'm still sorry.'

'You don't need to be.'

She sleeps, after that. Dreaming of voices she can't properly make out, dreaming of the caravan sinking into the sea. Early in the morning, Darcy heads to the house and Min tries to doze, but the caravan is buffeted so violently that Min is frightened the whole thing is about to be swept into the water.

She pulls on warm clothes and moves from the caravan to the ghost house.

'The wind,' Min says, her voice small.

Violet is showering, will be heading to her farm soon to make sure everything's secured there. Darcy drinks coffee at the table. Luda sits on the couch, her knees drawn up under her chin like a child. For once, she is not distracted by her laptop or her archival papers; she is not distracted by ghosts or clams or wondering about witch marks. She is not distracted by her collection of stones and wires and water and gorse. She is not distracted by Tristan. For once, she looks at Darcy and Min properly. She looks and looks. And they both grow uncomfortable, neither of them accustomed to her scrutiny. Not like this. Not the scrutiny of things beyond light and composition and the texture of their skin.

'I've fucked up a lot, haven't I?' she says.

Min and Darcy both look at her. Darcy clears his throat.

'We're okay, Mum,' Min says. 'We're all okay.'

Darcy shoots Min a look and she discreetly waves her middle finger at him.

'Did you find your letter?' she asks him.

He frowns. 'What?'

'On the table.' Min points. 'Square white thing with your name on it.'

Darcy picks it up, spots the university logo, and drops it again. He looks up at Min, his eyes narrowed, as though anticipating a prank.

She kicks at the chair opposite her with her good foot. 'Don't give me that look. I had nothing to do with it.'

'You're both hurting a lot more than I realised,' Luda says. 'It's my fault, isn't it? Tristan says a lot of it's my fault.'

'Open it,' Min says. She and Darcy have reached an unspoken agreement to ignore Luda until she snaps out of this strangely verbose mood. 'Please?'

'I'm proud of you both, you know,' Luda continues. 'You've both grown up a bit … odd … but it's a dazzling sort of odd. Oh, Tristan! Stop it! That is *not* too rude!'

Darcy looks at Min, his eyes wide. 'What is it?'

'Theo,' she says simply. 'It's Theo.'

Darcy looks back down at the letter. 'What do you mean it's Theo?'

'Open it.'

'I have apologised!' Luda hisses towards the empty couch. 'Do you mind? I'm trying to connect with my children!'

Darcy lifts the letter, hands shaking. He looks up at Min, back down again. She heaves herself up (her ankle only aches now) and stands beside him as he slips the paper from the envelope. She is there when he staggers. She winces as she takes some of his weight.

'Is this a joke?' he asks, unevenly.

'No,' she says. 'I told you. It's Theo. He sorted it.'

'How ...' And then Darcy begins to shake. *Study hard, get the fuck out of here.* 'Is it real?' he whispers.

She rests her head on his shoulder, feeling hollow. Feeling like he should have had this moment so long ago. That she had somehow robbed him of it. 'It's real, Darcy.' She reaches up and kisses his cheek, startling him. 'You're brilliant.'

'Should I have got you grief counselling? Joshua thinks I should have got you grief counselling. Glenda says it's a crock. I think I turned into Glenda a bit.' Luda looks forlorn. 'Tristan says the counselling might have been good, but what I really needed to do was talk to you. I thought you didn't want me to talk to you – not about all that stuff. I thought I was doing the right thing, keeping us all focused on the future.'

'You did fine, Mum,' says Min wearily.

'I don't even remember why I went to the dam that day,' Luda says. 'Isn't that silly?'

A sudden gust of wind makes the windows groan and clatter.

Darcy closes his eyes, letter clenched in his hand. When he opens them again, his expression is resolute. 'There's a storm coming,' he says, tucking the letter into his pocket.

'I know,' Luda snaps. 'That's why Violet's going to her farm.'

'You should go with her.'

'No. I'm not going back there.'

'Well, they're talking about the storm on the news. It's a big one. We should probably go and stay in town.'

Luda shakes her head. 'No.'

'Mum ...' says Darcy. He makes himself look at her the way she had looked at him. 'If the wind comes from the wrong direction, the whole roof could get peeled off like a tin of tuna. Remember when we first came here and had to stay at Cassandra's because these windows had been blown out?'

'You don't need to talk to me like I'm a child,' she says. 'I'm staying.'

Darcy runs his hands through his hair and glances down at his watch. 'I've got to get to work. I'll come back after my shift. The storm's not meant to hit until later. We'll go into town then.'

Luda says nothing. What she thinks is, *No.*

Darcy leaves and Min sits for a little while longer, staring at Luda, who is still sitting on the couch with her knees tucked up. Min breathes out slowly, feeling on the cusp of something greater than tears. The world roars. 'I'm going out, okay?' she says.

'Your ankle.'

'I need to stop in and see Cassandra. I'll be fine.'

Luda nods.

As Min opens the door to a blast of air that feels almost solid, she hears Luda speak. 'Of course not,' Luda says, her voice so thin.

* * *

Cassandra is reading. She is aware, as she reads, that Iris will be preparing the kirk for an emergency. She can picture Iris opening the side door to put some rubbish out into the recycling bin. Iris startling: the taste of all that wind. Iris closing her eyes and breathing in. In Cassandra's imaginings, she is childlike. She is small and terrified and powerful.

Cassandra senses her beautiful August and comes back to herself. For a moment, she is certain that the wind is a conjured thing. That this storm belongs to *them.*

Fanciful.

It has been so long.

Cassandra blinks as Min lets herself lopsidedly into the front room. 'You're off your crutches.'

'Yeah. I'm fine.' Min looks hollowed out. She sits down next to Cassandra and rests her head against the back of the couch.

Cassandra raises an eyebrow and sets aside her e-reader.

They sit quietly. Cassandra studies Min and then smiles. 'Oh, I'm so glad.'

Min nods. 'Darcy thinks there's going to be an awful storm.'

'Aye, that's what they're saying.' Cassandra considers the view from the window. 'You can all stay here, if you'd like. You might get cut off if you stay on the wee island.'

'Thanks,' says Min. 'We've just got to convince Mum to come across.'

'You will.' She pauses. 'You want to go diving now, though, don't you? After so long out of the water?'

Min smiles, but there's something tearful about her. 'Yes.' She does not move.

Cassandra studies her. The flickers between them are impressions of shadows. Of nothing.

'I feel like …' Min swallows. 'I feel like you're going somewhere. I feel like you're going somewhere without me.'

'I'm very old, Wilhelmina.' Her voice is gentle.

'It feels like something more than that.'

Cassandra touches Min's pale face. 'It's all going to be okay. I promise.'

'Cass …'

'Off you go. Before the bad weather hits.'

Min breathes deeply. 'Cassandra?'

'Hmm?'

Min hugs her tightly, feeling the impossible pound of Cassandra's heart, her breath, the too-small shape of her body.

* * *

Father Lee and a nurse called Janet stand in the kirk and talk about involuntary psychiatric holds. They have both been busy organising supplies, so the kirk could be a refuge for the community – as it has always been – in the wild weather. Iris listens from near the pews, panicked. The feeling of something inexorably leaving her control. She is not sure how to make things right.

'She doesn't need one,' says Janet to Father Lee, impatient. She drops the first-aid equipment that she's brought over from the medical centre. 'Honestly, Father, you've got to let this go. Now I need to leave. I have to get back to the mainland before the weather turns.'

* * *

Min walks down to the docks, her hood pulled down low over her face against the wind.

When Ewan sees her without her crutches, he rolls his eyes. 'Lord have mercy,' he mutters. 'Alright. I'll take you out. We'll have to make it quick. And no diving, okay?'

The tide is already swelling. There will be no taking the boat out for the next few days. Still, Min is glad to be back on the water. She sits in the cabin, and when Ewan stops the boat to collect his creels, she finds herself blinking very fast. The howling wind, the call of the sea. It's almost enough to overwhelm her. Min stands up suddenly. 'Ewan! The whales!'

Min forces the door of the cabin open.

'Managan! Don't you *dare*!'

She strips down to her underwear and she dives. She dives until the world becomes dark and the weight of the water seems to slow her heart. Still, she swims down. Further and further.

She thinks, *I could stay here.*

She thinks, *I've found them.*

They shouldn't be in the harbour. Perhaps the storm moving in from the sea has confused them. Perhaps they've been washed here without really knowing why.

Perhaps something – someone – has called them here.

The whales move slowly, unalarmed by her presence. She reaches out a hand and touches the skin of one. Feels no answering warmth. She should have known better than to expect it. She knows that she could stay down here with them. That she could hold her breath, on and on and on.

The surface seems a very long way up. It is this moment that she has always tasted in the water – in every single dive. She thinks of them all. She thinks of Narra. Of dead men pounding the dusty roads. She thinks of Joshua. Birds into the sky.

Blood thrum. The dark. Salt and skin. She knows that she could stay.

Above her, impressions close to the surface of the water. Of love. Of love. Of *love*.

And then she starts to kick.

Chapter Thirty-five

AUGUST (THEIR THIRD YEAR)

One story about Theo that Carter never uncovered … On the night before Theo was found, Iris had drunk too much sweet wine and stumbled to the stony beach that was near her home.

A full moon.

She bent at the shoreline. As always, she could not even wade into the water. She thought of her empty house and empty car near the kirk and how wide and still everything seemed in this place that she had wandered for so long. She and Cassandra, tracing each other's footsteps. Perhaps they had trapped themselves here. Perhaps it was their penance. Perhaps it was whatever glimmered in their blood; witches could not cross water. Iris was her mother's daughter. Even the ocean had gentled, still lapping but more quietly.

She missed her mother.

She blinked seven tears into the water, leaning above it (she could still do that), and then wept into her hands because she had not been able to shake the old stories from herself. They had burrowed in and lodged there and they were as much as part of her as her bones and blood and skin. Told over the fire inside during the long nights of winter and in the simmer dim of summer, their shutters pulled tight against the light that never really left the sky.

Sometimes August had grown irritated if Iris asked too many

questions or seemed flippant; as though the stories were finite and also hers. August was holding them up to be admired, like a shard of blue sea glass held up against sun. Iris had never been one of them.

Iris waited a little, but not for long. She wondered if her mother had ever been this drunk and sad. Had ever stumbled onto this lip of beach and cried her tears into the ocean.

She shook her head, dizzy with wine. She stood. She was clumsy with fatigue by the time she reached her empty house. Shivering and unsteady. She pulled her wet pants off, her wet shoes and wet socks. And then she collapsed under the sour-smelling blankets on her bed and dreamt of seals.

In the morning, the world spun and Iris's head ached. She was ashamed of herself. And then she remembered her tears, felt a shimmer on the island as though something was altered. She hurried to the shoreline, but found it unremarkable. Water lapping lazily, the colour of steel against the summer sky.

But still.

She paced, like something wild and caged. Something had changed. The island was so quiet. And then she spotted Ewan making his way across to the tidal island, boyish and playful and unmindful. She rushed across to the causeway. She could not cross it. Once, she had been able to. But the sea had shifted and the land with it. Now, the causeway was too much like sea. Slick and unknowable and barred to her. God, how she wanted to cross it. She continued her pacing there, on the edge of Big Island. Her prison.

And then there was Ewan, wide-eyed and less boyish. He carried something small and shimmery. He faltered as he neared her, and Iris wondered dimly how she looked to him right now – if she appeared fearsome and ferocious. Someone not at all like him or anyone else.

The moment that he stepped from the causeway, Iris snatched the small child from Ewan's arms and gazed at him, struck suddenly still with wonder.

Oh, his little butterfly clavicles and giddy way of walking. His salty biscuit smell, like that of a much younger child. For a time, she forgot everything.

She felt his hand in hers. It was a revelation.

* * *

After his shift at the brewery, Darcy stops by the Muir house – not to see Theo; he knows that Theo will be out, preparing Marcia's farm for the storm. Instead, he has dropped in to return the piece of blood-coloured sea glass that Theo had given to him. It seems cruel to keep it, when Theo has given him so much and Darcy has been unable to give him anything at all.

Darcy knocks, lets himself in. Iris is sorting supplies at the kitchen table and her head snaps up.

'Darcy,' she says. 'You shouldn't be out in this weather, lad.'

Darcy shrugs. He still has time. 'Need a hand?'

Iris gives Darcy food packages to sort. As they work, Iris tells Darcy about crying seven tears into the ocean. She tells Darcy about waiting for Theo on Big Island.

'You really believe that you brought him here?' Darcy asks.

'I do. Aye, I do,' Iris says. There is a long pause. 'I always thought I'd brought him here for myself, but now I think that I was actually bringing him here for you.'

* * *

August had always taken such pride in knowing the depths of a place; in knowing the secrets and stories of Seannay. August knew where the darlings had been buried in the gorse. She lingered, often, on the edge of the bay, holding Iris's hand. But that was before. Iris has not been able to leave Big Island for so, so long.

'Something's going to happen here,' August would say, as they stood together, so many years ago, on Seannay. And then something *would* happen – a wrecked boat, washed up. A still-living whale. A raucous gang of lads from the town, too full of ale and howling at the moon.

Everyone knows that the moon belongs to women.

Each time these things happened, Iris would look to her mother and August would shake her head. 'No. Something *else*.'

The night Iris got raging drunk and ended up on the beach – the night before the foundling washed up on Seannay – Iris had dreamt of her mother. Had dreamt that she and her mother had been standing together in the gorse, hair tangled by cold wind, made bright with drizzling rain. 'He's here,' August said, over and over. Until Iris was yelling at her, until Iris was clawing at her so that August's skin gave way like the casing of Neptune's necklace and ocean water bled out of her onto the rocks.

Iris had woken, stared up at the moon. She had turned resolutely over, pillow pressed against her ears. She recited the rosary, imagined herself at the Last Supper (a frequent, guilty pleasure of hers) and how much the Lord would have appreciated her baking. But still, when she fell back into drunken dreams that night, she was watching the prone form of a pale-skinned, web-fingered boy, lying among rocks and seaweed in the ebbing tide.

* * *

Darcy is not at the brewery and so Theo runs home to fetch his bike – or maybe to commandeer Iris's car – but he stops when he spots Darcy coming out of Iris's house.

'What are you doing here?' he asks.

Darcy shrugs, won't meet his eyes. 'Just dropping something off.'

Cassandra had thought that Darcy's particular kind of beauty would desert him before adulthood. Theo stares at him, tense in the wind, and thinks that he has never seen anything so exquisite. For a moment, Theo does not move. He does not breathe. He does not blink.

Darcy's raised voice. 'I opened the letter.'

Theo nods.

'Thank you.' Another gust of wind that seems to shake Darcy. 'I need to get Mum.'

'Wait!' Theo strides across the cobbles. He moves closer and closer and then rests his forehead against Darcy's shoulder and closes his eyes.

'I shouldn't have bitten you. I'm sorry.'

Darcy's voice is guarded. 'Theo …'

'I don't care,' says Theo.

'You don't care about what?'

'I don't care if we never …' Theo laughs, touches Darcy's cheek. 'I don't *care*.'

Darcy frowns and opens his mouth to speak but Theo touches his finger to Darcy's lips and stares at him. 'I don't care,' he says again. 'You're not broken, Darcy. And even if you are, it doesn't matter. I don't *care*. There's nothing that will stop me loving you. Nothing you do or don't do. I just love you, okay? Fuck. I just love you.' And he draws Darcy closer. He kisses him with every moment of longing and uncertainty he has in him.

Darcy tenses. Theo is sure that he's going to pull back, but this time it will not be enough to wound Theo into walking away. They are reading in the loft. They are in the hotel room in London, Darcy's head bent to Theo's damaged, burning hands. He is tangled in Darcy's empty bed – in Darcy's sheets – the night he found the seal pup. Darcy is naked, on the island. Emerging from the sea. Their skin is on display in the kirk. Theo is holding Darcy to him, weeping, on the floor of his bedroom. Darcy is leaning urgently over him, pulling away in wordless terror.

Everything goes very still, even as the world feels like it's shattering around them. Theo can feel Darcy's pulse. He can taste Darcy's breath – Darcy sighing and kissing him back. The lights flicker. Theo feels as though he's flying.

* * *

On the day the foundling child washed up on the island, it rained and cleared and then rained again. There were meals eaten and boats cast off. There were guns fired and Rayburn stoked. There were arguments had and books read and shits taken and whales spotted. As the foundling child who would one day be Theo was cast up onto the shore, another child far from the ocean sat up in his dream-damp bed. This side of the world was dark. It smelt of dry earth and eucalypt. And the child was sure, even as he looked around his bedroom, that he could taste salt; that he was being rocked by tides; that there was nothing above him but open sky. It took him a long time to go back to sleep, and when he did, he dreamt of water.

Of the world being unequivocally, massively and wonderfully altered.

Chapter Thirty-six

AUGUST (THEIR THIRD YEAR)

The wind picks up so suddenly and so loudly that Luda is frightened. She wanders around the ghost house, peering through the windows. 'Where are the children?' she asks.

There is only air.

Tristan's absence is different, sharp-edged. Not one of them responds and she curses them, swears at them, then she shrugs into her jacket and steps out into the wet, roaring world. Her children. All that matters is her *children*.

* * *

On Ewan's boat, rain begins to dash against the glass of the cabin. It begins to rock alarmingly in the growing swell. Min looks up, pale and unsteady but *here*. Impressions of rain on land, of carrying hands. She turns to Ewan, her friend. She tugs on his sleeve. From beyond her, the knowing. 'We need to get to the kirk,' she says, and he begins to move before she's finished speaking.

* * *

Luda yells for her children in the rain. She yells for Tristan-of-the-in-between and Joshua and her mother, who has never visited her here. She even yells for Glenda. People peer out at her, people she does not know. The fronts of their houses are carved with apotropaic markings. Daisy wheels and hexafoils. The shape of the scarred whale, over and over again. Through sheets of rain. Through roaring wind. Luda yells and yells until her throat burns and her voice tangles up with the wind.

* * *

It is Iris who sees Luda screaming in the pouring, flooded street. Iris is standing in the mouth of the kirk. She feels safe in the kirk. Although Iris should feel safe wherever she is. She tells herself that storm damage is really only for people who don't go to mass each Sunday. But she knows the feeling of the howling wind, the way it can be called.

'Darcy!' Luda calls wildly. '*Min!*'

Iris hesitates, on the cusp of something immense. Wreaths of gorse and gentle songs. The island, the darlings there.

'Sit it out with me,' Iris says, holding out a hand to Luda. 'We'll find your bairns, Luda. I promise.'

She feels a rough hand on her own back, then. Father Lee. 'Stand back, Iris. I'll take care of her.'

Luda rears away from him.

He grabs at her arm. 'She needs to go somewhere safe.'

'I'll keep her safe,' Iris snaps. 'We're fine.'

He picks up his phone, dials a number, his large fingers still digging into Luda's slender wrist.

'Marcus! Let *go.*'

'She's out,' Father Lee says into the phone, his voice thick with excitement. 'Luda's out. We need to do something – she could hurt someone. She could get killed. She can't go wandering around in the storm like this.'

Iris thinks, oddly, of the whales caught up on the sand. She thinks of her mother's athame. Her mother's gentle hands, braiding her hair. The way her mother gazed at Cassandra. Her mother's endless *wonder*.

Iris looks at Father Lee, feels her skin tingle the way her mother's had. 'Come with me,' she says to Luda, her voice fierce. 'Quickly. Before he –'

'My *children*!' Luda yells back, pulling away from Iris, from Father Lee. She is taller than Iris and heavier, and Iris dares not struggle with her on the slippery road.

Father Lee begins to speak. It's not safe. Luda's brain is wrong. Dangerous. They're afraid for her, of course they are – of what will happen if she will not go inside during the storm surge. Of what will happen if they force her. It's not safe for any of them. She needs to be properly *contained*.

Iris feels the momentum of this thing that she has been so instrumental in building become suddenly larger than she is. She tries to pull it back because she has let it *go*. Her rage. Her longing.

She has chosen something else for herself.

But everyone else in the kirk turns to Father Lee. They listen and nod with serious purpose. It is a comfort for them, to focus on Luda and her madness. Her *hysteria*. It is a comfort to agree with Father Lee. Luda can be dealt with in a way that the flooding streets and flying roofs cannot.

'Haaken's Hole,' Father Lee says. His voice trembles. He's *enjoying* this. 'It's the only place where she will be safe until the storm passes.'

'No,' says Iris, but he does not listen. Nobody in the kirk listens.

* * *

Luda feels the hands. Brutal male hands. Trying to push her into the cold darkness of Haaken's Hole. But she fights and claws and tears. She is vicious and she is strong.

The men wrap her up in an old woollen blanket, so that she cannot hurt them. Cannot fight. She is roughly shoved into the dark. She is given a torch and a plastic bottle of juice. 'Just until the storm's passed,' the quiet, scared voices tell her. 'Shhh,' says Father Lee.

'No!' yells Iris, her voice very loud, but not loud enough. 'Let her go! Let her *out of there*!'

'You're safe,' Father Lee calls in to Luda, but his hands are the roughest of all. His torch skitters across the inside of the walls. Countless marks in the stone, layered on top of each other into a constellation of nameless terror and hope.

Luda thinks that this is what she's been dreaming of. Not the car. Not the cold water.

This. *This*.

The ghosts from the tidal island have followed her here. All of them. The space is filled with them – their murmuring voices, their rough hands. Except for Tristan-of-the-in-between. He is not here. And the women – the witches – they are not here either. There is only the woman with long dark hair who looks like Iris. Who Luda has sometimes seen gazing toward Cassandra's house, perched up high on its hill. 'Just wait,' the woman says now. The hands. Luda has never seen her up this close. And then she disappears. Luda shivers. She tries to breathe.

* * *

The causeway to Seannay is washed away. The small bay where Theo was found, where the three whales died, is chewed away by the frothing, storm-flared waves. The caravan is blown onto its side. The ghost house itself begins to lose its roof, slate tile by slate tile. Witch markings laid open to a howling sky.

Earth gives way to churning salt water.

Theo and Darcy, hunting for Luda, shelter in the ruins of the long-fallen houses that had once kept the ghost house company. The wind whistles like something living and a lone cormorant flies in place, buffeted and screaming.

* * *

Cassandra's head hurts. The wind is tidal, when it's like this. Waves of it crashing over the rooftops and streets. The drag of it back out to the sea over and over.

They have come for her, as she knew they would. The women who have long visited her, silently, in the space between sleeping and waking.

The four of them. *Her* four, who had pushed her and Iris out through the window of the ghost house so that they would be spared. Oh, how she has wept and raged for them. How they had given her this: the sum of their love and power, all woven together into countless years. Bringing her to this moment. Bringing both her and Iris to this moment.

August. Her beautiful, bright August. Long dark hair. The same clever, loving eyes as Iris. The same impatience.

She is not impatient now.

Tristan, barely there; being pulled back to beige walls, scabbed arms, bright pain. Every part of him an ache; a yearning. He is the only one who speaks and his voice is barely audible above the clawing of the storm. 'Help her.'

The spirits of the women buoy Cassandra from her seat, like a tide; like the deep. For a moment, she is swimming.

She will let them carry her, like rushing water. She will let them carry her down the hill and along the road to the thick doors of the kirk. They will leave her then – or maybe they won't. Perhaps they will charge in with her. She hopes so. Their wrath turning the stale air inside the kirk into something writhing.

Cassandra can feel Min's fierceness. She can feel Iris – her distress, her fury. She and Min and Iris, and all those women who travel with them.

Luda, counting witch marks in the dark.

But not for long. Cassandra knows that they will succeed in this. She is sure of it.

She can feel the certainty of it in her breath, her skin, her muscles. The rhythm of blood and old, old bones. She will do this final thing, with Iris, with Min. With all of them. Her last night, before she finally joins them. She focuses: the dungeon. Yes. The kirk. She steps out into the roar. Is carried. Breathes in and tastes the sea. Min, moving more quickly now. Iris, as steady and ferocious as a building storm.

She is *sure*.

* * *

I love you, Luda thinks, in a pretty way, all spangled brightly with things that have no name.

She is in the in-between, has been there for so long, brought here by spells murmured on a hillside while her daughter dived into the sea.

But not like this. She wants Tristan, but he is no longer in the in-between. Instead, she thinks of salt and air. It's cast orange, like fire.

Like home.

She sings songs about milk and honey and her son looks up from the place in the ruins where he holds a luminous hand in his and does not let go. And her daughter rushes over slippery cobbles, with Iris and Cassandra – with the countless others who blur and merge and carry. Min. Closer and closer, dripping cold seawater as she moves.

Violet, standing in a dusty room on her empty farm, imagining shadows into a particular shape. She does not hear the storm.

And the luminous boy, who thinks wild thoughts, has been set free. Lips to lips. His flesh hands. He thinks, *I remember. What I remember is the sea.* The thud of blood salt in veins. A flesh hand in his. Skirting the skin of the ocean.

Her children's skin is what she has dreamt of, played out to voices that are hers and not.

She thinks of her children. She thinks, *I am home.*

She thinks of skin skin skin.

And she thinks, *Please.* A constellation of hexafoils carved into stone. Milk and honey. *Please.* Her children. Darcy. Min. The thrum of their hearts. *Please.*

I see you.

Acknowledgements

I am indebted to the Australia Council for the Arts for funding research for this book. I am also indebted to Varuna, The National Writers' House, for facilitating a fellowship at the Tyrone Guthrie Centre at Annaghmakerrig where (while focusing on another project) I was still able to dip into this one. My time at Annaghmakerrig was a life-changing one. I'm extremely grateful for all the wise eyes that have been on this manuscript. Firstly, my PhD supervisors, Emily Potter and Indigo Perry, for your guidance, and to Deakin for the gift of time in the form of a postgraduate research scholarship. Fran Flett Hollinrake from St Magnus Cathedral for answering all my questions, Ashleigh Angus for your eagle-eyed reading, Sheena Graham-George for your generosity and the inspiring work you undertook at St Magnus, and the wonderful humans at Orkney Library and Archive for making everything possible. My agent Pippa Masson and the rest of the team at Curtis Brown Australia – I'm incredibly fortunate to be one of your authors. Alex Craig and the rest of the team at Ultimo Press – it's been a joy and privilege working with you. Huge thank you to Gordon Wise from Curtis Brown for championing *Salt and Skin* and finding it such a brilliant UK home with Hannah MacDonald and the rest of the team at September Publishing. My witchy story and I truly couldn't be in better hands. Thank you also to Anna Morrison for the truly breathtaking UK cover. Thank you to my writing queens: Katelin, Carolyn, Charlotte, Kylie L, Kylie O and Lisa. Ellen, for our silly book club. Jessie, for

359

only ever being an email away. Nicky, Maddy, Kate, Ree, Sandra, Mel and Micah for putting up with me at my most ridiculous. Maggie, for your early reading and love. Kirstin for all your babysitting and enthusiasm while I was working on edits. Worth, who knows just when to yell at me to go outside and do something else. My mama for reading this manuscript just about as many times as I have – you've been my champion for thirty-two years and I'm so lucky. Thank you to Ben (no more wibbly wobblies!). Lastly, thank you to my miraculous, shining Hen – who lit up my life while I wrote this book. This story started out as delirious 2am scribblings when you were a newborn and it's a surreal thing to now be watching it fly.